For Pat & Heaini...

THE LAST LAUGH IS FREE

Gordon Noice

LIVE
LOVE
LAUGH!

1

OCT 2024
WAIALUA

THE LAST LAUGH IS FREE

TABLE OF CONTENTS

CLARK'S DEDICATION

First of all, to Joyce Czesnakowicz, for endless instruction to this computer illiterate, encouragement and loving support that kept me going to the keyboard and, in lean times, eating.

To John Kwiatkowski, for having enough confidence in me to give me his confusing computer, true friendship and taking the time to drive out to my cabin in the country with care packages from the big city.

To my furry roommates, Bandit, the Husky and Kelly, the Golden Retriever, for filling the empty days with companionship, unconditional love and taking me for long walks in the woods.

Thanks, guys.

And finally, reserved for a couple of professional literary snobs, smugly snickering behind thinly walled closets, two private words.

-Clark Inger

CLARK'S NOTES

"Write about what you know." That old literary cliché, like all clichés, is basically true and so is this book. Most of the events described in the story did occur and somehow I managed to survive them without any lasting physical damage, but the emotional wounds remained, open sores that would not heal. Doing three years of hard time in Florida's maximum-security prison and chain gangs of the early fifties had left their marks.

Collaborating on this project resurrected those torturous times, many half forgotten and shoved into some dark corner of my memory banks for over four decades. Reviewing these painful memories was a purging of the mind and at last closed the old wounds, leaving only fading scar tissue and The Last Laugh Is Free.

Finally, although some of the characters appearing, and disappearing, throughout this book are fictitious, the story is told as it was lived and spoken by caged men desperately clinging to existence and speaking raw, jailhouse language. Some readers may regard certain characters and speech as offensive, but that's just the way it was.

-C.I.

PROLOGUE: THE PACKAGE

I found the package on my front porch at dawn. It was wrapped in plain brown paper, sealed with Scotch tape, and addressed with black crayon. Just two words were neatly printed: *Clark Inger.*

By whatever mysterious midnight delivery, this package had found me, and when I opened it, all my questions were answered.

I stared down at a dark-brown leather-bound book, elaborately adorned with shining gold leaf. It was a first edition of Herman Melville's classic, *Moby Dick.* Tucked between its pages was an award certificate for a Pulitzer Prize in journalism and a brief hand-written note:

❄❄❄❄❄

Hi, kid,

Forgive the salutation. I know you're not "the kid" anymore, but that's how I will always remember you. I've managed to keep up with you over the years—as best I could, anyway, with somewhat limited resources. I've seen some of your work in the art magazines I receive in the library. You've become quite the painter. You have made me very proud of you.

You're the last of "the Untouchables," and for reasons only you now know, you made my life in this terrible other-world existence a far better one. Thank you for being my friend, and more importantly, thank you for the joy of

6

knowing you are successful. Enclosed are my only earthly remains, which I submit to your keeping.

I love you and I always have. My final reward is that I never saw you again.

—Sam

As I closed the pages of Sam's cherished book, I recalled a line from the epilogue. Through the salty taste of my tearing memories, I whispered, "And I only am escaped alone to tell thee."

CHAPTER 1
CHARLEY TOWN

March 1949

The early-morning sun rising over Lake Michigan flashed through a blur of trees streaking past the screened windows of the police van traveling south on Lake Shore Drive toward downtown Chicago. My hands were cuffed behind me, forcing me to sit sideways as I watched the trees and my future rapidly disappear behind me. I had just turned sixteen.

I was booked into the Cook County Juvenile Detention Center, issued detention whites, and after three hours of processing, shoved into the crowded fifth-floor dayroom. I looked around for a bathroom. It was not hard to find; my nose led the way.

I pushed the button on the wall to flush the seatless toilet inside the doorless stall. As I stood to pull up my pants, a short, stocky black boy approached me, flashing a broad gold-toothed grin. For no apparent reason, he balled up his fist and socked me in the mouth, sending me sprawling to the filthy concrete floor. As I tried to get up, my pants twisted around my ankles, sending me right back to the floor on my side. He kicked me in the stomach, rolling me over onto my back. The boy stared down at me with deadly blank eyes. Then he spat in my face, laughed, and walked away whistling as if nothing had happened.

Well, it had happened. I pushed myself up from the floor, pulled up my pants, and staggered over to a sink. I examined my face in the stainless-steel mirror and blotted the blood off my split lip with a wad of wet toilet paper. Then I went back into the dayroom, walked up behind the black boy, and hit him with every ounce of strength in my skinny one-hundred-fifty pound body. The boy fell instantly, grabbing his jaw on the way down. Then he sprang to his feet just as quickly and beat me senseless.

That was my introduction to Leroy Washington Tanner, Jr.

Leroy's father had been the Illinois Golden Gloves Welterweight Champion at eighteen and had continued on into a professional boxing career. Within three years, he was a top-ten contender for the middleweight crown. His promoter accepted a match with the second-ranked contender, a skilled boxer with a club-fighter mentality named Bobby "Sailor" White. The bout was booked as the main event at Chicago Stadium, and it was a natural. Tanner, the city's brown South Side ghetto comer, versus White, the nation's white hope.

By the middle of the first round, it was obvious that the senior Tanner was hopelessly outmatched. When the bell rang ending the third round, he was walking on his heels, his face a swelling, pulpy mess.

As White headed back to his corner, his bloody gloves raised in victory, a sledgehammer right to the back of his neck smashed him down to the canvas like a slaughtered cow. A dozen more blows rained down on the helpless fighter before Tanner could be pulled off the unconscious man. White sustained serious brain damage and would never fight again, his promising career ending in a terminal blur.

Tanner's boxing career ended as well. He was banned from the sport for life. However, his violent nature thrived in the South Chicago ghetto as a collector for a major numbers bookmaker. He delighted in beating the bookie's unfortunate debtors half to death, and he ruled his son

Leroy with the same brutish iron hand throughout the boy's childhood.

As the sun rose on Leroy's seventeenth birthday, his father burst into their apartment in a drunken rage, screaming, "Happy birthday, you sawed-offed little motherfucker!" For his son's celebratory present, he dragged him out of bed and slapped him across the face.

That was the last time the bitter, vicious man ever struck anyone. Leroy left his father in the same fuzzy place as "Sailor" White. So that was why he was here.

⊞⊞⊞⊞⊞

Leroy was the meanest, toughest inmate in the center and the absolute ruler of the fifth floor. We both knew he could whip me whenever he might have the urge, but he didn't want to get a fat lip in the process and chance losing any respect. Plenty of other kids were around for him to pick on who would not fight back, so I was simply not worth it for him.

I was the only boy who had shown the courage to challenge him, and I had earned Leroy's respect. We began talking over the next few weeks and actually came to like one another. We became something of a fifth-floor novelty. Leroy and Clark: two boys, one white and the other black, actually friends.

My first painful encounter with Leroy and our subsequent friendship taught me the single most valuable lesson of my new life. Surviving in a cage of predatory animals was totally dependent on one critical factor: Respect.

In spite of being well north of the Mason-Dixon Line that separated the former Union North from the still-segregated former Confederate South, Chicago was known as the most racist city in America. And this place was, like most of the city, continually on the verge of a race war. But thanks to my having gained his respect, Leroy saved me from veritable destruction on the predominantly black fifth floor.

The juvenile justice system was backed up like bad plumbing, so it was three months before I went to court, charged with armed robbery, assault and battery, and resisting arrest. My public defender assured me that since this was my first offense, if I agreed to plead guilty to a lesser charge of simple assault, probation would be automatic. I stood before the bench, anxious for the judge to release me into the custody of my mother so I could get out of here and go home. That did not happen.

"Lawrence Clark Inger, I hereby sentence you to be taken from here and removed to the State Juvenile Reform Facility at St. Charles, Illinois, for a minimum of one year to a maximum continuing until your twenty-first birthday. Bailiff, remand the prisoner into custody."

A tidal wave of shock swept over me. I felt like I was going to throw up. Frozen in fear, I found it impossible to move or speak. My life was over.

The bailiff grabbed my arms and handcuffed me. As he hauled me from the courtroom, I frantically searched for my parents. I didn't see my father, but I located my mother from the sound of her uncontrollable sobbing in the rear of the courtroom. I couldn't even wave good-bye.

❊❊❊❊❊

Leroy Tanner and I sat next to each other in the Cook County prison bus during the thirty-mile trip west from Chicago to St. Charles.

"Hope we get to stay together in this place," Leroy said.

"Me too," I replied. "You're a great bodyguard. But hey—if there's mostly white guys, maybe I can return the favor."

"You?" Leroy laughed. "Shit, anybody can whip your dumb honky ass."

I shrugged off the remark. "I hear this place is a shithole. Not as bad as Joliet though."

"Fuck Joliet," said Leroy. "My brother's in there, and if he's makin' it there, we'll make it here. Charley Town ain't like the state pen; it's a kids' joint."

"Wonder what it looks like," I said.

"We'll know soon enough, honky."

"Fuck you, nigger."

"Fuck you, you honky-ass white motherfucker—and yo mama too."

"The best part of you ran down a whorehouse wall," I countered.

"Fucked yo mammy in a bin o' flour, and she shit patty cakes for half an hour."

"Let's not start playin' the dozens game, Leroy. People'll think we don't like each other."

"That's true. We got to stick together, right?"

"Damn right."

As the bus passed through the main gate into the reform school compound, a numbing cold swept over me. *How did I get to this point?*

⛓⛓⛓⛓⛓

My early childhood had been uneventful and reasonably comfortable. I grew up in a lower middle-class neighborhood on the northern city limits of Chicago, in a three-story brick building virtually identical to all the other buildings for miles around. Our modest second-floor apartment had one unusual feature though: a view. The living room windows overlooked a cemetery across the street, and you could actually see greenery. The building also

12

fronted Sheridan Road in the center of the S-turn that left the northern city limits on one curve and entered suburban Evanston on the other. I would sit at the living room window for hours—always alone—watching the traffic pass through the turns and gazing at the trees.

My father traveled almost constantly, selling household furnaces fired by a new coal-based briquette fuel called coke. When I was six and old enough to walk to and from school on my own, my mother got a job with a commercial carpet company on the South Side. She would leave early in the morning to take the elevated train for the long ride across town and be gone from dawn to dark. Our family life consisted primarily of "Hello," "Good-bye," and "What did you learn in school today?" I was a loner.

What I learned in school was very little, both scholastically and socially. The classrooms were crowded and geared to the pace of the slowest students. Recess was mainly a matter of the weak kids trying to protect themselves from the strong. The greatest value of my early education was to become very good at holding onto my lunch money.

By the time I hit the eighth grade at age fourteen, my teacher decided that I was antisocial. I had what she termed "Poor home training," whatever that meant. Her final insult to me came the day before graduation. If I was antisocial before that, she assured it then.

The class sat fidgeting as the old woman babbled on about roads to the future and what they were paved with. When the bell finally rang, ending the last day of confinement in grade school, the class leapt to its collective feet in a rush for the door.

"Wait!" she screamed at the top of her voice. "Everyone be seated!"

The fear of disobeying and not graduating was a strong group motivation to do as we were told.

"Clark Inger, come up here!" she yelled, pointing to

13

her desk.

"What did I do now?" I asked.

"What you did, you hoodlum, was steal the class collection of funds for their graduation gift to me. You stole my gift money!"

I glared at her. "You're full of shit, lady."

"You can't talk to me that way, you little thug!" she shrieked.

"Fuck you, lady," I said. "I'm outta here."

It was downhill from there.

I had not stolen anything, but if I was going to be accused of it, I reasoned, and worse, everyone was gonna believe it, why not just do it?

Good question. Bad answer.

⛓⛓⛓⛓⛓

Our apartment on Sheridan Road was three blocks north of Howard Street, where it ended at the shore of Lake Michigan. From that point to the elevated station, about a mile west, was a strip of liquor stores and nightclubs that stayed open twenty-four hours a day. The Club Detour and The Silhouette were the largest and best-known, with most of the remainder changing names as often owners.

Howard Street was the first elevated train stop inside the Chicago city limits and the first "wet" town for many miles coming from the Fort Sheridan Army Base and the Great Lakes Naval Training Station. During the war years in the early forties, thousands of soldiers and sailors would get off the North Shore train at the Howard Street El Station and head down the steel stairs and through the barred turnstiles with their pockets full of money to spend on booze, crooked dice games called 21, and whores. That was the genesis of the notorious Howard Street Strip.

The side streets were worse: dark, dangerous, and

sometimes deadly. I had walked those streets almost daily for ten years, going to the Gale School, meeting my friends, or just hanging out. It was my neighborhood and I knew every street and alley. The narrow ones, three or four feet wide, could also be navigated from above, by leaping from rooftop to rooftop of the three-story apartment buildings lining the block.

Arny Harris, Whitey Levits, Moe Kwatkowski, and I were the only real family any of us knew and we were inseparable. The four of us were the ringleaders of the forty-four-member Rogers Park Dude Gang—known as "the Dudes"—inheriting leadership by rising up from the ranks as the older boys went on to greater things. The Howard Strip side streets became our turf, and after dark, we owned them.

The neighborhood prostitutes turned their tricks in alleys, darkened doorways, or wherever they could, with the Dudes as their protectors, watching over them for a gratuity of fifteen percent. When the hooking business was slow, we would roll drunken servicemen, emptying their pockets and taking anything of value.

The Dudes were a democratic bunch by organization and more than fair in our distribution of funds. Each member kept ninety percent of his individual rip-offs and contributed the remaining ten percent into what we termed the "Corporate Kitty." This money was hidden throughout various members' basements for future emergencies and expenses, such as bail money, purchase of weapons, and new members' black nylon club jackets with *DUDES* embroidered on the back in bright red and gold.

Weekends were the busiest times for prostitution, and we would break into pairs to watch over the ladies while they took care of business.

Late one Saturday night, Arny and I were guarding Glenda as she plied her trade in a doorway. Her army john dropped his pants but then suddenly changed his mind.

15

Glenda had a few choice words for the soldier, and he knocked her to the ground with a blow to the jaw. Before the G.I. had his olive-drab pants up, he was on the concrete doorstep with Arny on top of him. Glenda was kicking at the soldier, but he ignored her. With the strength of a bull, he caught Arny with a right fist to the face as Arny staggered backward into the wall. Then the john rolled over and rose to his feet to confront me.

What he faced was a familiar sight: an army Colt .45 automatic—pointed straight at his head. That stopped him cold. As I was ordering him to empty his pockets, Arny yelled a warning at me and bolted through the apartment doorway. He continued up the three flights of stairs to the roof and escaped across the rooftops.

My back was to the street, and I never saw them. A searing pain exploded at the back of my head. My vision turned to pure bright white and then silent solid black. The black slowly faded to blurred shades of gray, and the next thing I was aware of was the double image of steel bars in the Rogers Park Police Department's holding tank.

So that was how I'd come to be sitting in a cage on wheels, traveling through the main gate of a miniature penitentiary.

⛓⛓⛓⛓⛓

"Hey, man," Leroy said, peering out the barred window, "check it out! It don't look all that fuckin' bad."

It did not look bad at all. With the exception of a twelve-foot-high chain-link fence, you might think this was the well-groomed campus of a private school. The bus drove down a wide white gravel drive that wound through an immaculate lawn bordered by red flowers. We passed a parking area in front of what appeared to be an administration building and continued down a smaller drive between two rows of widely spaced two-story red-brick buildings that looked like large North Shore homes with security windows.

The crowded bus parked at the rear of a single-story building at the end of the road, and the half-dozen of us boys sitting up front were told to gather our paper bags of personal belongings and get off. The remainder of the passengers would continue south to the State Penitentiary at Joliet.

A man in civilian clothing directed us into the building, where we were processed into the Illinois Youth Center, St. Charles. We were each issued a pair of blue denim pants, a blue work shirt, underwear, and socks. The state shoes and belts were optional, and we were told that we could keep our own if we cared to. When the paperwork was completed, we were told the rules and regulations of our new home and assigned to one of the red-brick buildings we had passed on the way in, called cottages. Fortunately, Leroy and I were both assigned as the newest residents of Cottage D.

We were escorted from the admissions building by one of the senior members of the Cottage D family, a twenty-year-old who had difficulty pronouncing his own name, which was Jera...something. I was amazed that this very dimly witted boy was our sole guide.

During the short walk to the cottage, I noticed some other surprising things. All the staff we had seen so far had been dressed in street clothing, and there was not a uniformed guard in sight. The grounds were beautiful, and I was beginning to believe I was going to a better place than my own home and neighborhood. Leroy was certain of it.

"My man, this is gonna be a fuckin' country club," he said with a wide grin.

I had to grin as well. "No shit, man! This place looks great."

17

"Not really," stammered our escort. "It really ain't...so great here...and whatever ya do...don't fuck with the Y's. They're the real b-bo-bosses in D."

Leroy raised an eyebrow. "Wise? Like they smart or somethin'?"

"N...no, like the le-letter in the alphab-b-b—"

"Fuck the Y's. Sounds like they be in a swimming pool."

"Well, it sure as shit looks good here anyway," I said to our stuttering escort, "whatever your name is."

"Yeah, man. What the fuck is your name anyway?" Leroy asked.

"It's Jera—"

"Never mind trying to say it again," I cut in. "If you can't say your own name, I probably can't either, so I'll just call you 'Jera,' okay?"

"Okay. You're...pretty smart." He smiled. "Everybody else...does too. Here we are."

We walked around to the rear of the cottage and down half a flight of stairs. We entered through the basement door into a large room with a few wooden benches and a row of narrow steel lockers.

"Okay, new guys. Seventeen...and thirty-three are...yours. Take your...p-p-pick."

"Thirty-three's my lucky number," I said. "That's when I was born. That okay with you, Leroy?"

"Sure," he agreed. "Seventeen's how old I am. Works out great."

"There's slippers...in there," Jera told us. "Take off your shoes and...p-put 'em on. Shoes ain't...allowed upstairs. They...fuck up the floors. You don't ever, ever wanna...f-f-fuck up the floors. And they lock this place up...at night. Can't run with s-s-slippers."

We took off our shoes, put them in the lockers, and following Jera, flip-flopped, up the staircase into what they

18

called the living room. When I saw the floor, I understood what Jera had meant. It must have been the most perfect expanse of fine-oak tongue-and-groove flooring in the world.

"Beautiful, isn't it," I said.

It was not a question. It was a statement.

I did not see her at once. She was backlit, standing in an arched opening between the living room and what appeared to be a dining room. She actually blotted out the sunlight radiating through the windows behind her. When my eyes adjusted to her shadowy bulk, I knew that Jera's warning that "It really ain't so great here" was going to prove true.

She was enormous. A fifty-year-old mountain of a woman, standing at six feet and well over two hundred and fifty pounds with a shock of unruly gray hair hanging over two mean slits for eyes.

"I'm Miz Wilson. I'm your housemother. And for the next week or so, that floor is yours until somebody screws up bad enough to take your place on floor duty. You start that in the morning. 'Til then, this retard here'll take you upstairs and show you to your bunks. By the time he's through figuring out how to do that, the rest of the boys will be finished with their work details and be here for dinner. So will Mister Wilson, who if you haven't guessed, is your housefather. At dinner, he'll introduce you two to the whole happy family. Now, get up to the dorm, make up your bunks, and sit on 'em until you hear different."

"What the fu—"

"Shut up, Leroy!" I snapped. "What he means is 'Yes, Ma'am.'"

"You're the smart one, I see," she said. Then she cut her eyes directly at Leroy. "And what was it again that you

19

was about to say...boy?"

"What I meant was..."

"*Leroy...*" The tone in my voice did it.

"What I meant was...Yes, Ma'am."

Our new mother seemed pleased. "Good," she said. "That's very, very good. For a minute there, I thought we were off to a shaky start. Now you two boys go and do as you were told!"

⛓⛓⛓⛓⛓

I felt like I was in the monkey house at the Lincoln Park Zoo. Thirty-eight pairs of teenage eyes were riveted on Leroy and me as we stood at the foot of the dining room table, opposite from our houseparents at the other end. Mister Wilson seemed in pain as he slowly raised his thin five-foot frame from his seat at the head of the table. Even sitting, his wife looked taller than he was. As he planted his palms on the edge of the table to steady himself as he stood as erectly as possible, trying to appear taller than he was, I almost felt sorry for the man. I wondered if he, too, addressed the monolithic Miz Wilson as "Ma'am."

Wilson addressed the room. "Boys, our family has once again reached its full complement of forty young men. Our two newest members stand before you for your inspection."

Leroy and I must have looked the strange pair. With two Scandinavian parents, I was tall for my age at six-foot-one. I was a slender hundred and fifty pounds with a fair complexion, blue eyes, and reddish-blond hair. Leroy, in opposition, was pure southeastern African Zulu, his skin blue-black. He was rather short at five-foot-nine, but a solid hundred and eighty pounds of muscle.

"Introduce your sorry selves!" Wilson ordered.

"I'm Clark Inger," I said simply.

"I'm Leroy Tanner—the new kid on the block."

The room broke into laughter, not having the slightest idea that Leroy meant exactly what he had just said. He was already staking out his turf, and if he had anything to do with it, he would indeed be the new kid on the block. And the boss.

Leroy was quite pleased with the response. His coal-black face cracked open wide, revealing his most distinctive feature: what he called "The Golden Smile." His upper two front teeth were sparkling eighteen-karat gold.

"Okay, Salt and Pepper," Wilson said, smiling, "sit down."

Leroy's wit had not escaped the attention of two older white boys sitting near the head of the table. They stared at Leroy, their eyes deadly. The Y's looked like bad news for my black friend.

"Mother, please say the grace," Wilson mumbled softly.

⛓⛓⛓⛓⛓

At six o'clock every weekday morning, Wilson rang a large dinner bell and the dormitory came alive with forty boys shuffling, slipper-footed and sleepy-eyed, to the community baths at the north end of the large room. We had fifteen minutes to relieve ourselves, wash up, and be ready for breakfast. By seven, the work details were marching across the grounds to their various duties.

Each cottage in St. Charles was virtually its own entity, with individual responsibilities to the institution as a whole. Cottage A was kitchen and food services, B was grounds maintenance, C was construction, and so on. With infinite institutional wisdom, Leroy and I—both from the inner city of Chicago—had been assigned to Cottage D, generally referred to as the Farm House. Agriculture.

Leaving behind Jera, the resident houseboy, and Leroy and me, who were assigned the dreaded floor detail, the thirty-seven other boys went to the basement, changed from slippers to work shoes, and filed out the door for work duty in what was called The Garden.

Jera gave Leroy and I each a pile of worn-out towels that had been torn in halves and a milky white bar of paraffin the size of a large soap bar. Then he instructed us in the fine art of floor-keeping. When he stuttered to a conclusion, he left us to clean up the dining room and kitchen.

"Fuck it, man," Leroy said. "I'd still rather be in here than out there pickin' whatever the fuck they pickin."

We wrapped towels around our knees and, on all fours, rubbed the paraffin over about a square foot of the oak flooring until it was properly covered with a filmy coat of wax. Next came the hard part. Using half a towel, we laboriously polished that square foot of oak until it shone as brightly as all the other square feet of floor around it.

It was a long day, interrupted only by the return of the other boys for lunch and then again when they filed back into the cottage late that afternoon. When our workday finally ended, Leroy and I could not stand up straight. We could barely stand at all.

"I take it all back, man," Leroy sighed. " I want to go pick whatever the fuck they was pickin'."

It was four days before we were relieved from floor duty by three whining fourteen-year-olds who actually walked on the floor wearing shoes. That was a very serious breach of regulations, and Leroy and I could not have been happier.

"What are you little bastards snivelin' about?" Leroy said through his golden smile. "You're real fuckin' lucky the fat lady didn't kick the shit outta ya."

"Yeah, fuck heads," I said, laughing, and then added with a straight face, "Shut up, or I'll do it myself just to get

22

the kinks outta my back. Let's go eat, Leroy."

⛓⛓⛓⛓⛓

I settled into the daily routine of St. Charles and was content to keep my mouth shut, do as I was told, and pull easy time. Working in The Garden bent your back somewhat with picking, hoeing, and the other tasks that went along with working the soil—but compared to floor duty, it was nothing. I enjoyed the outdoors, and we had a distinct advantage unique to the Farm House: Bad weather. When we could not work outside, there was not much to do, so our detail would sit in the equipment shed for hours, cleaning our tools or just shootin' the shit.

Charley Town was as minimum security as a correctional institution could be, and Wilson often went out for long periods during the day, leaving us unattended. When this happened, someone would invariably break out a hidden deck of cards, lookouts would be posted, and some of us would play highly prohibited poker games, gambling for almost anything.

It was during one of these equipment-shed sessions that it finally happened. Joey Klein and Robby Matthews had fallen heavily into debt playing five-card stud, losing several dollars worth of canteen candy bars and their Sunday desserts for weeks. Tight friends, Joey and Robby were known as the Y's for a couple reasons: One was that both of their first names ended with the letter "Y." The other was that when they ganged up on another boy—beating him into submission as an example, to maintain control of cottage leadership—they would always yell their battle cry, "Y-not!"

For a change, the Y's were losing more than candy bars. They were losing control. I looked on with some amusement until things started to get tense and then headed into dangerous. The Y's were becoming more and more angry as their losses mounted; it seemed like a very good idea to break the tension before it erupted into a fight.

I had known something like this would happen since Leroy and I were introduced to the cottage on our very first day, months ago. I had done my best to delay it, but time was running out.

"Leroy," I said, patting him gently on the shoulder, "maybe it's time for you quit while you're ahead."

"Leroy ain't quittin' nothin'," Joey sneered.

"You got that right, motherfucker," Robby agreed loudly, glaring at Leroy. "Play on, asshole, and if I see ya cheatin' any more, we're gonna beat the livin' dog shit outta your nigger ass, right the fuck where you're sittin'. Oughta do it anyway. Ya got a real shitty attitude."

"Yeah!" Joey laughed. "Don't fuck with us, nigger."

Leroy smiled calmly, laid his cards down, and slowly stood.

"I think you're right, Clark," he said. "It's time."

Then Leroy turned his back and, just as slowly, began walking away. I could not believe it. I had finally gotten through to Leroy about his violent temper and destroying anything in the way of his need to rule. There was nothing inside the fences of Charley Town that was worth ruling—and certainly not worth losing years of future freedom over. But the Y's did not think that way. Ruling by fear and brute force was what it was all about for them. Suddenly, I wondered what Leroy had really meant when he said "It's time." Time for what?

Leroy was halfway to the shed door, his back still turned to the Y's. Robby was the first to reach him, his right fist slicing through the air toward the back of Leroy's neck. The blow never got there. Leroy whirled with the grace of a ballet dancer and kicked Robby in the groin like he was punting a football. The impact lifted the husky boy two feet in the air before he dropped to the floor.

Joey was right behind Robby, going for Leroy, when I hit him on the side of the head hard enough to slow him down. Before I could punch him a second time, Leroy ran into him at full speed. Leroy smashed the top of his head into Joey's face, splitting it open from nose to jaw like an overripe red melon. The badly bleeding boy fell soundlessly to his knees and Leroy kicked him in the side of the chest—breaking three ribs and puncturing his left lung, we later found out. Leroy turned his attention back to Robby, who lay in a pool of vomit, curled up into a ball of agony, gasping for breath.

Leroy bent over the groaning boy. "Hey, motherfucker, can you still hear?!" he yelled into his ear.

Robby seemed to nod.

"That's good. Now hear this, puke-face, and hear it real fuckin' good, 'cause I ain't gonna say it again. Cottage D now belongs to me."

Then Leroy grabbed two fists full of hair and smashed Robby's face into the concrete floor. It was over.

Leroy stood and puffed out his chest like a victorious rooster in a cockfight.

"Thanks for watchin' my back," he said to me, flashing his golden smile. Then, "I'm learnin' Clark," he proudly said. "They got me from behind. I was just protectin' myself."

And that was the finding of the Institution's Disciplinary Review Board. Leroy was, however, found guilty of playing cards and spent the next three days on floor duty. My name was never mentioned. The two Y's left through the front gate of Charley Town in an ambulance and were never heard from again.

Leroy was the undisputed lord of Cottage D.

If Leroy was learning, so was I. His streetwise South Chicago survival training made him a master of "Just protectin' myself." It worked, and I was thankful to be his

25

friend. The other boys shared their occasional packages of candy and other assorted goodies from home with us, as if paying homage to the Lord of D. We had all the comforts available to us, and under the circumstances we led a pretty good life. I came to the conclusion that Leroy's way was the right way. It paid off.

The Wilsons had had their problems with the Y's and found Leroy and me the far better alternative. We just took our payoffs, kept our noses clean, and did not cause any real trouble. We were allowed to do easy time.

⛓⛓⛓⛓⛓

The three months I'd spent in the Cook County Juvenile Detention Center awaiting trial had seemed like a year. My incarceration at St. Charles started just as slowly. But as the weeks and months went by and I became comfortable in the system, time picked up its pace.

After a year and a half, time suddenly slowed dramatically.

"You're looking pretty sharp there, Leroy. Neat threads."

"Thanks. My bro got 'em for me."

"How long's he been out?"

"Three, four months. He's doin' great. Seems to got plenty of money."

"I'm gonna miss you, man. Wish I was goin' with you."

"I'll miss you too, honky. But you'll be out soon enough. Three more months ain't so fuckin' bad. Shit, you're a real short-timer now."

"No, you the short-timer," I said. "Minutes is better."

We stood at the basement door because Leroy was wearing shoes. Some of the other boys who had said good-bye were standing around, so any display of affection was completely out of the question. We shook hands.

"See ya, Leroy," I said. "Good luck on the mean streets, nigger."

"You too, ya white-assed motherfucker. I'll be seein' ya, no shit."

With that tender farewell, the blue-black boy with the smile of gold walked out the door and out of Charley Town.

Leroy had been my only friend for over a year and a half. After his release, there was no one I really wanted to have anything to do with. Sure, I liked two or three other boys well enough—but not well enough to share anything with them. My remaining time dragged by and was entirely uneventful.

Once again, I was alone.

About a year ago, my mother had written to tell me that she and my father had divorced. I had no idea where my dad was now and didn't really care to know. My mother had continued on the best she could and sent a few dollars to me whenever she was able. Those dollars had become fewer and fewer as she struggled to find a steady job, mainly piecework for Southside sweatshops. She wrote me saying how guilty she felt about letting me run wild and now being unable to support me in any way. In one of the few letters I had ever written, I told her not to blame herself and that I would be okay. I also told her to go after an opportunity she was being given to turn her life around. At the invitation of a childhood friend, my mom moved to Orlando, a small town in central Florida.

A week before my release, my mother sent me a hard-earned bus ticket to Orlando and some clothing that would fit me now. She enclosed a note saying this would be a great chance for us both to make a new start in a new place.

It had been a long time since I had felt hope, and the prospect of some positive changes excited me.

The food in Charley Town was not great—it was bland and tasteless—but it was nutritious and our regulated life there was a healthy one. I would be leaving in excellent physical condition and fifteen pounds heavier at a hundred sixty-five. My greatest delight was that for the past few months I had not gotten a single pimple. Working five and a half days a week in The Garden had left me with a golden tan, and I thought I looked pretty good. I was ready for Florida and reuniting with the one person who ever really cared for me.

The afternoon of my last day in Charley Town, I was excused from work detail and spent the remainder of the day unsuccessfully trying to pay attention to the mindless, poorly scripted state dialogues directed at me in droning monotones from counselors who were as bored as I was with their self-serving rhetoric. Finally, the release documents and other mounds of bureaucratic paperwork were completed and so was my final day of confinement. Only the evening and a sleepless night remained.

At first light, the Wilsons handed me a cardboard box filled with the too-small clothing I had arrived with and the overnight bag my mother had sent me. They wished me well and gave me permission to skip breakfast so I could go alone to the basement to dress for freedom. I packed the small bag with my old clothes, tucked my new shirt into a stiff pair of unwashed Levi's, put on a fresh navy surplus pea coat, and left through the basement door. I did not have anyone I wanted to say good-bye to.

I waved over my shoulder to no one in particular as I walked down the winding path past the administration building. Then I took my final steps through the main gate,

28

passing out of Charley Town into the free world.

CHAPTER 2
BOYS WILL BE BOYS

December 1951

It was a pure joy taking in the surrounding countryside without seeing it through a chain-link fence. I walked down the quarter-mile drive to the highway, where a bus was due in half an hour to take me into downtown Chicago where I would board another bus to Florida.

I had just taken my first step to cross the highway to the bus stop when a black car screeched to a stop in front of me. I jumped back, thinking I had better get used to this new, free-world environment and start looking both ways before crossing streets. The car was blocking my way, and the driver, a burly black man, did not appear to have any intention of moving. I started to walk around the front of the obstruction and then thought better of it—anyone who drove that insanely might very well run me down; best to go around the rear. As I passed from the car's huge chromed grill down toward its large finned taillights, I noticed how long the thing was: a new Cadillac limousine.

The right rear window slowly hummed down and up popped a grinning blue-black face with an eighteen-karat-gold smile.

"Hey, you honky motherfucker, get your dumb white ass in here!"

"Leroy, you son of a bitch! What the fuck are—"

"You're leavin' Charley Town in style—that's what the fuck. Do ya wanna to hang around here for another coupla years or ya wanna leave that shit bucket behind ya?

Let's go."

Leroy opened the door and slid across the seat, making room for me as I climbed into the limousine and sank into soft, plush leather.

Somehow the driver maneuvered the long car into a U-turn on the two-lane highway and we headed east toward Chicago.

"We going into town?"

"Yep."

"Where?"

"It's a surprise."

"Where'd you get this car? Did you rent it?"

"Nope, we own it."

"We?"

"Yeah, me and my big brother. He's drivin'. Meet Leroy Lincoln Tanner. Call 'im Roy. Bro, this is my best friend I was tellin' ya about, Clark Inger."

The tough-looking driver glanced over his broad right shoulder and I was staring at a bigger Leroy. When he smiled hello, I almost thought he *was* Leroy—sans the gold teeth.

"Hi, Roy. It's good to meet ya," I said.

"Same here. My little bro's told me lots of good things about ya. Says you're a stand-up guy. Tough little fucker too."

"Not as tough as he is; that's for sure."

"That may be true," Roy said, grinning back at me in the rearview mirror. "Sometimes I think he's meaner than our old man was. Told 'im that last time I had to whip his ass." He laughed.

Leroy just nodded with a knowing little smile, and I knew then that his older brother must be one very, very bad customer. He looked it, too.

"Hey, you guys," I piped up, "I got a bus to catch. That where you're takin' me?" I was getting a bit concerned about the time.

"Told ya, it's a surprise," Leroy replied.

"But..."

"Don't worry about it," Roy said, glancing at me in the rearview mirror. "Everything be taken care of. Okay?"

I was not about to take issue with anybody who could whip Leroy, not now or ever, so I just sat back in my seat and stopped asking; there would always be another bus. If I didn't know I was with friends, I would have felt like I was back in custody. In a way I was: the custody of two Chicago South Side street toughs who had survived the ghetto wars unmarked. That in itself was remarkable. I was quite sure that "Everything be taken care of."

The long black Cadillac was now cruising south on Lake Shore Drive toward downtown, Roy weaving smoothly through the heavy traffic with the skill of a veteran big-city cab driver. We turned off the sweeping curve at Oak Street Beach and into the entry drive of the finest hotel in the city, The Drake. The doorman opened the limo's rear doors, and Leroy and I stepped out. Roy's window slid down, revealing a toothy, evil leer on his face.

"Leroy, give me a holler when you guys are ready to split, and I'll send a driver to come and get you."

"Thanks, bro."

"Yeah, thanks, Roy," I added.

"A pleasure, boys. See ya in a couple of days." Roy muffled his laughter by raising his window as he waved and drove off.

"Leroy, what's going on here?" I demanded.

"I told ya before—it's a surprise. Now shut the hell up and come on."

I followed Leroy across the sumptuous lobby, directly to the elevator bank and up to the top floor. We walked down the hallway to the east end, where he unlocked a door whose brass plaque proclaimed that it was the

Wedding Suite. We entered into another world. A world I would soon discover, I would not want to leave.

The large room was the most lavish place I had ever seen, filled with exquisite furniture and original fine art glowing from the late-morning sunlight streaming through a wall of windows overlooking Lake Michigan.

"Surprise!" Leroy said. "Ya surprised?"

"Damn right, I'm surprised. This place is great. It's like a fuckin' palace. How can you afford all this shit?"

"Tell ya that in a minute. But first off, I want ya to know that as far as I'm concerned, you're my adopted bro, and if ya thought ya left Charley Town in style, there's more to come. I'm makin' sure ya leave this city in style too. They'll bring ya anything ya want to eat right up to the room too. Here's the menu; get whatever ya want. All I gotta do is call down to room service and it'll be here in a few minutes. Food, booze, beer, whatever. Pretty cool, huh?"

I thought it was very cool indeed. In short order, I was devouring a sixteen-ounce prime filet mignon, a huge baked potato with everything imaginable piled on top of it, and a salad with large chunks of Roquefort cheese in a chive and cream dressing, washing it all down with an imported beer I had never heard of. It was the best meal I had ever had in my life. And if I thought that was great, dessert was even better. I loved bananas and had ordered what was a mystery to me, something called Bananas Foster. It was so wonderful, I almost wanted to rub it in my hair. When I finished, I was in half-drunken ecstasy, and any thought of leaving heaven right here on earth to go to a smelly bus station was totally out of the question.

But then I thought about my mother waiting in some grubby bus terminal for a son who never showed up and I felt a pang of guilt.

"I'm worried about my mom," I said. "I'd better call her."

Leroy was just polishing off the remains of a prime rib and mumbled a response between mouthfuls.

"Like my big bro said, man, it's all been taken care of."

Once he'd finished and opened us a couple more beers, he went on to explain. Roy had enlisted the services of an articulate young white woman he knew who was attending Northwestern University; she was majoring in drama and working her way through school by turning tricks as a call girl in upscale downtown hotels. This woman had telephoned my mother claiming to be an administrator at St. Charles and told her that there had been an unfortunate delay in receiving my release papers from the state capitol in Springfield. She was very sorry but there was absolutely nothing she or anyone could do for a day or two at the most, and that I would call her before my departure. She then assured my mother that the bus ticket could be used at any time. My mother bought the story.

"There's two bedrooms here," Leroy said, looking at me slyly. "Yours is on that side. Why don't ya take your beer and go check that mother out, my man?"

"There's more?!" I looked around in amazement. "I thought this room was it. Shit, it can't get any better than this."

"Might be. Go see."

The room was magnificent and so was she. Tall, blonde, and a body to die for.

"You must be Clark," she purred, smiling warmly and closing the door. "I spoke briefly with your mother and she seemed very nice on the phone. She was a bit worried about you at first, but I made that go away. I'm very good at making things go away. I'm even better at making things come. Mmmm...you're very young. I'm going to enjoy this. So are you—and for as long and as often as you like."

When I awoke, the light of day was turning to dusk and I was alone in satin sheets of the king-size bed. I was glad she had left; there was nothing more to say to her and certainly nothing more I could do. I put on the heavy terry-cloth robe with the embroidered Drake Hotel logo that was lying at the foot of the bed and went into the living room, yawning and rubbing the sleep from my eyes.

Leroy was sitting on one of the couches in an identical robe with his bare feet on the coffee table, one hand holding a beer, the other on the thigh of a beautiful young woman who bore a striking resemblance to Lena Horne. She was fully clothed, and as I entered the room, she stood and without a word, quickly left the suite, closing the door softly behind her.

"Well, honky," Leroy said, laughing, "did ya get your ashes hauled?"

"Feels like I got everything hauled," I told him. "Where's the beer?"

"Behind the bar in the fridge, dumbass. Get me one too, will ya?"

"You bet. The least I could do, my main man. This sure as shit beats floor detail."

"Beats most of the shit in the whole free world, too."

"Beats anything I ever had," I said, returning with the bottles of beer. "The girl, I mean."

"Thanks. Now that we've both fucked our brains out and before we get too fucked up drinkin' this good German shit, there's somethin' I'd like to talk to you about." Leroy's voice took on a serious edge.

"Shoot."

He laughed. "That might be part of it."

"Shooting?"

"Not if ya don't have to pull the trigger."

35

"I'm not about to go back to the slammer," I said. "Shit, Leroy, I just got out."

"That ain't likely."

"Just what in the hell are you gettin' at?"

"What I'm gettin' at is this: Now, hear me out, and if ya wanna do it, ya can leave this city in two days with your pockets and that bag of yours over there crammed full of more money than you've ever seen in one pile in your whole fuckin' life."

I gazed at him silently.

"These kinda hotels and broads and whatever else ya want will be yours to your honky heart's content," he went on. "I'd do it my own self, but I can't. I need help and Roy ain't allowed. He's too good at doin' what he's doin' and our bosses won't let 'im take the chance. But it's *my* chance to prove to 'em what I'm worth.

"I been off the streets too long now to know anybody I can trust at my back, so that's why I'm talkin' to you. This deal is up to me. I'm freelancin' it, and if it goes down good, I'll be a fuckin' hero. If you want to back me up, it'll be kinda like a goin' away present from me to you. And from you to me."

My intuition said no, but my pockets were telling me yes.

"It won't hurt to talk," I decided. "Go ahead."

"Okay, then," he said. "Here's the deal: I'll tell ya why, what's what, and how it got there. But don't butt in 'til I'm done. I'll fill ya in from the very beginning."

⛓⛓⛓⛓⛓

Roy had served his time and been released from the state penitentiary just three weeks after Leroy entered reform school for turning their father's brains to jelly, forcing Pop into early retirement. The elder Tanner's position had

36

not yet been permanently filled, so when Roy was freed, he was the logical replacement. His credentials were perfect: He had assisted his father for almost two years, virtually running their part of the business, and running it quite well—doubling revenues annually. Most importantly, he was trusted. So the job was his for the taking and he did.

Henry "Knees" Johnson was the boss of the South Side numbers game, ruthlessly ruling his territory for a decade using fear and an eight-pound short-handled sledgehammer. He was talented at what he did, but over the years, he had become overconfident and a bit careless. That was all Roy needed. It took him nearly a year, but he ultimately managed to gain access to Johnson's financial records. He confirmed what he had suspected, and so—as any ambitious mid-level corporate executive would do—he went over his bosses' heads for the good of the company. And himself.

Roy's executive meeting with the Ciceros was held in the back seat of a black Ford sedan in a grimy alley with two white men. Roy stated his case precisely and concisely, presenting evidence that proved beyond any doubt that Johnson was, and had been for some time, skimming significant money off the top of his operation and stuffing it into his own pockets.

The Cicero family was basically a diversified corporation. They were a powerful one, at that, with estimated annual revenues exceeding those of any company in the state. But unlike other big businesses, which were continually mired in time-consuming bureaucracy and petty infighting, Cicero family decisions could be made and executed immediately. Because of Roy's service and loyalty to the family, he was granted Johnson's territory on the spot. There was only one condition.

The following evening, Henry "Knees" Johnson left his favorite neighborhood tavern shortly after eleven p.m. to walk the four blocks to his home. He made it two before he was shot in the face with twin blasts from a double-barreled twelve-gauge sawed-off shotgun. The weapon was found at his feet, totally clean of fingerprints, its serial numbers etched away by acid. The crime remains unsolved.

Roy took over and the turf was his to rule. He maintained the responsibilities of directing both bookies and collectors until the return of Leroy, at which time he appointed the younger Tanner as the Director of Accounts Receivable. So with the blessing of the Ciceros, the brothers Tanner were doing well for themselves.

The Ciceros ultimately controlled everything illegal on the South and West Sides along with many legal enterprises, including trucking, construction, liquor distribution, and vending machines. They were also a major force in Cook County politics. The Tanners were a minor but very profitable cog in the well-oiled gears of the Cicero family empire.

The Italians despised the blacks, deeming them subhuman with only three redeeming traits that contributed to mob profit: Huge amounts of money were siphoned out of the ghettos from drugs, prostitution, and gambling. There was no love lost the other direction either, so most blacks refused to deal with the Italians under any circumstances. That is where a few select blacks like the Tanner brothers had real value to the Ciceros. Roy was now the CEO of a major profit center for his very silent Mafia partners.

Occasionally a problem would come up facing the Cicero family that required discretion. If solving the problem themselves might even remotely implicate them, they covered their non-involvement bases by contracting an outside source. The hired help were always people no one would ever expect to be involved with the family.

Here is where Leroy came in. A black street kid still in his teens, not long out of reform school—hardly a candidate for the highly professional Ciceros, given their well-known hatred of blacks. He was perfect for the job. So with Roy's recommendation, he'd been contracted to fulfill a family service.

⊟⊟⊟⊟⊟⊟

Ever since the Capone versus O'Bannon wars of the Prohibition era, the Italian and Irish underworlds had periodically fought for control of the North Side. An unnatural but predictable evolution had followed its inevitable course. Now it was Cicero versus Doolan, and it was about to begin again. But the Ciceros did not want a shooting war on their hands. They decided to finesse it.

Their first move would be to hit the Irish hard financially while appearing uninvolved. Meanwhile, they would lead their foe to believe that through some serious breach of the Irish's own security, they were vulnerable to petty street thugs. This would accomplish two goals: The first was that the Doolans would turn their attention inward, toward their perceived vulnerability, and begin second-guessing the loyalty of their own people. The second was that in doing so, they would open a *real* crack in their security, allowing a flanking attack from another direction. Leroy's task would be the opening move in a high-stakes chess game, with the Irish forced to into the match with a major piece already taken. Check, and then mate. The Ciceros were quite pleased with themselves.

The Doolans had divided the North Side into three areas: Near, Mid, and Far North, each with a centralized cash collection point that was a restaurant. All day and into the evening hours, Celtic corporate men would flock to the restaurants for business lunches or dinners, each carrying a thick leather briefcase. At sometime during the course of the meal, a busboy or food server would stop at the table with a

39

four-sided metal service cart and switch a cash-filled briefcase for an identical one filled with newspaper. The money would be wheeled into the manager's office, stuffed into a canvas duffel bag, and stored in a closet safe until closing. At that time, it would be transferred by an accountant with two armed guards to a car with an armed driver waiting curbside.

The procedure was simple and efficient, but the Italians considered it sheer complacency and typical Irish arrogance. Each restaurant was vulnerable to some degree, and Mid-North to a large degree. The Killarney Irish Pub & Grill would be the first target.

Leroy was to enlist the help of a second party and tell him only that this was an armed robbery involving a large sum of money; that would be incentive enough. Leroy was taking a real risk by not only telling all, but by recruiting *me,* a white boy, as the second party. The Italians would no doubt assume his accomplice would be black. But I was the only person he felt comfortable with, and he was convinced that after our success, all would be well with the Ciceros.

I was amazed at Leroy's acceptance of Roy's relationship with the Italians and even more surprised that he was willing to take money from his own community and pour most of it into the coffers of people who hated him simply because of his skin color. But to Leroy, that was just a part of ghetto life. Survival.

When Leroy finished telling me the details of the job, his innate sense for survival was the main reason I agreed to back him up. That, and the money...a great deal of money...helped erode my fear of returning to jail. And it was just this once.

The chess game was about to commence. This promised to be high adventure.

Two nights later at ten-thirty, Leroy and I boarded the Evanston Express elevated train at the LaSalle Street station, rounded the loop that circled downtown, and went north to Fullerton Street. We left the El station walking west and traveled past Wrigley Field for four blocks to the parking lot at the rear of a large commercial bakery. We walked down a long row of parked panel delivery trucks and slipped on our tight-fitting black cotton gloves as we approached the last truck in the line. It would be the final truck to load for early-morning deliveries and the last to be missed.

The truck was unlocked so we did not need the Slim Jim to open it. Before I had even settled behind the wheel, Leroy had hot-wired the ignition to start the engine. I drove slowly, turning out of the lot west onto Fullerton. I turned north onto Clark Street and after a few blocks turned onto a dark side street and parked.

Leroy and I went to the rear of the truck and buttoned up black jumpsuits over our clothing and donned black navy watch caps that we would later roll down to cover our faces except for eyeholes cut out of the cloth. We checked our identical German Mausers—broom-handled machine pistols—and jacked rounds into the chambers and engaged the safeties. I put the truck into gear and we continued north down darkened side streets to Montrose Avenue, where we turned right and continued on for two more blocks.

I backed the truck into an alley thirty yards from The Killarney Irish Pub & Grill on the other side of the street— just far enough to be in total darkness but still have a clear view of the front entrance of the joint. Leroy disconnected the hot wires and stopped the engine while I cut the lights.

I handed Leroy my Mauser, took off my watch cap, and unbuttoned the top of my jumpsuit. I took my arms out of the sleeves, rolled the top down to my belt, and tied the arms around my waist to look as though I were wearing pants. I got out of the truck, walked on our side of the street twenty yards past the pub to a dark-blue Oldsmobile Rocket 88 coupe parked at the curb. We had stolen it that morning and parked it in one of the several spaces made available by people leaving for work.

I unlocked the driver-side door, got in, and shoved the key into the ignition. Next, cracked open the passenger-side door so it was slightly ajar and turned the steering wheel hard to the left, pointing the wheels toward the street to assure a quick getaway from the curb. I got out of the car and, leaving the driver's door unlatched, retraced my steps to the alley. Making certain that I had not been seen, I climbed back into the truck and untied the jumpsuit sleeves so I was dressed as before. Leroy returned my pistol and we both clicked off the safeties.

There was nothing to do now but wait. Wait, and swallow the fear rising in my throat in the form of bitter, acid bile.

❋❋❋❋❋

It was just past midnight when I saw the glare of headlights on the pavement of the nearly empty street. A red-and-white DeSoto four-door sedan pulled into the loading zone at the pub's front doors. The driver turned off the lights but left the engine running, then reached behind the front passenger seat to open the rear curbside door.

A light somewhere in the back of the restaurant went off, and in a moment I made out several dark forms approaching the front of the room. One of the front doors opened, and a tall, heavyset man stepped out, nodded to the driver in the DeSoto, and moved to his left, looking up and down Montrose Avenue. A second large man came through the door exactly as the first, only he stepped to the right. Following closely behind them was a third, squat little man carrying a duffel bag in both arms.

I depressed the clutch pedal, put the truck into first gear and pulled the watch cap down over my face. There was no fear in me now. Adrenaline was pumping into my system like a river bursting through a dam. I felt like I could snap axe handles with my bare hands.

Leroy pulled his cap down as he reached across my lap and rewired the ignition to start the engine. The three men started moving across the wide sidewalk to the car parked at the curb.

"You ready?"

"Ready as I'll ever be," I replied, trying to hide the quiver in my voice.

"Let's go bowling!"

I pressed the accelerator flat to the floor, and the delivery truck burned rubber out of the dark alley, fishtailing left as I turned right. I pointed the hood ornament straight at the three terrified men standing wide-eyed and motionless on the broad sidewalk. The four-thousand-pound missile slammed into all three.

The impact hurled the left-side guard into the air and sent him crashing through the plate-glass window of the pub. The short man and his duffel bag were thrown onto our hood, ripping off the ornament and smashing into the windshield. I ducked to avoid the hail of shattering glass. The guard on the right had finally moved, but only enough to avoid a dead-center hit. The blow from our right front fender crashed into his right side, catapulting him twenty feet down the sidewalk.

I had a white-knuckle grip on the wheel as I pushed the brake pedal into the floorboard and the truck careened to a stop, spinning into the side of the DeSoto at the curb. Leroy leapt to the concrete, his Mauser machine pistol in

43

hand, as the DeSoto driver fired a .38 revolver through his windshield at the flying black man. Leroy dove to the sidewalk, rolling. He rose to his knees and emptied his machine pistol into the car. The man jerked inside like a puppet on a spastic string as the slugs ripped into him.

The right-side guard had managed to pull himself up to one knee and with great effort was slowly raising his Colt .45 at Leroy. Leroy stood, turned, aimed, and pulled the trigger. Nothing happened. The fallen man got off a round, hitting Leroy in the thigh and dropping him to the concrete. The Colt was now pointed directly at Leroy's head. I grabbed my machine pistol and emptied it into the kneeling man, throwing him backward with his head exploding in flying red chunks.

The whole thing lasted only a few seconds, but I could already see lights turning on behind apartment windows. If there were any sounds, I could not hear them. The roar of the gunfire at close quarters was deafening, leaving only a screaming, high-pitched ringing in my ears.

Leroy staggered to his feet and hollered something as he limped toward the Oldsmobile.

"What?" I yelled. "I can't hear a damn thing. Just get to the fuckin' car. I'll get the money."

I dropped my empty weapon, pushed the squat man off the hood of the truck, and grabbed the duffel bag. It wouldn't budge; his hand was frozen in a death grip. I picked up my pistol and hammered his fingers with the butt, breaking them. Then I ripped the bag from his hands.

Sliding on ejected shell casings, I sprinted across the street to the Oldsmobile. Leroy was still crawling into the car as quickly as he could. I jerked open the driver's door, threw the duffel bag and myself into the front seat, and pulled the rest of Leroy into the car by his left arm.

"Drag your fuckin' leg in here, man," I said. "Let's get the fuck outta here."

"It's in. haul ass!" Leroy yelled, slamming the door.

⊟⊟⊟⊟⊟

I tore away from the curb, narrowly avoiding a car that had stopped in the middle of the street. Almost losing control, I gunned it to the next corner and turned right, tires squealing, taking it in a four-wheel drift. I raced to the next street, turned left, and then slowed. I turned right and continued driving south, away from Montrose Avenue, at a normal rate of speed.

Leroy wheezed through clenched teeth. "Man, ya saved my ass back there big time. That .45 looked like a cannon pointed at me. I knew I was a dead man."

"There wasn't anything else to do."

"Yeah, well maybe. But there's somethin' else ya can do, too. You're smarter than me 'bout some stuff. Since you're so good at savin' ass, tell me what to do to save my fuckin' leg."

I glanced at him. "Take your pants off, if you can. If you can't, rip 'em off."

"Maybe you should take that mask off your face too," he said.

"Shit, I forgot. I'm starting to shake, Leroy."

"Me too," he said. "That was some pretty scary shit back there. I can't take the pants off. Can't move the leg either; hurts too much. I'm rippin'. And while I'm rippin', keep headin' south and find a phone. It's just startin' to sink in. We killed those fuckers, didn't we?"

"Shit. Goddamn. Yeah, three for sure."

"Hey!" Leroy pointed. "There's a pay phone over there. Call my bro and tell 'im about the leg and that we're comin' in."

I parked the Olds next to the phone booth, and as I was getting some change out of my pocket, I asked for Roy's

45

number.

This was the first look I got at Leroy's leg. Blood was everywhere and lots of it. I ripped one sleeve from my shirt and tore it in half.

"Okay, let me do this as best I can," I said. "Try not to yell."

"Do my best, honky."

"Shut up and grit your golden teeth."

Fortunately the bullet had gone through his thigh cleanly and missed smashing any bones. I wasn't sure that what I was doing was exactly right, but I didn't want Leroy to know that, so I took command for a change. I twisted one torn half of the sleeve into a rounded point and pushed it into the hole in the back of his leg. I did the same in the front with the other half. I ripped off my other sleeve and wrapped it tightly around both makeshift dressings, then I removed my belt and made a tourniquet above the wounds. The bleeding seemed to stop.

"You're a gutsy little nigger," I told Leroy. "You didn't hardly make a sound. 'Course, that may be because I still can't hear perfect. Now, what's Roy's number again? I forgot. My nerves are going to shit. Never mind the number, just yell it out the fuckin' window, okay?"

"Yeah, okay. I'm not feelin' so hot either. Go call."

My hands were shaking so badly that I dialed two wrong numbers before I got the right one.

"Roy!" I yelled into the phone. "Your brother's—"

"Clark?"

"Yeah, it's me! Leroy's been—"

"Clark!" Roy yelled back. "Shut the fuck up and quit yelling," he continued in a normal tone. "Calm down, lower your voice, and tell me what's wrong, okay?"

"Okay."

"That's better. Now, what's the problem?"

"Leroy's alive but he's been shot. So have my nerves.

He needs a doctor and I need to know what to do."

"Where was he shot?"

"The leg. His thigh."

"Do you know how to apply a tourniquet?" Roy asked calmly.

"Yeah, I've already done that."

"Good. Make him lie down and put his leg up as high as you can. Are you on the North Side?"

"Yes. Near Montrose and Ravenswood."

"Okay. Now listen carefully, Clark. You listenin'? And do exactly as I say: Whatever happens, stay cool. Do not speed and keep Leroy's head down; they'll be looking for two men. Go south to the first busy street, turn east, and blend in with traffic and go with the flow. When you get to Sheridan Road, hang a right and get to the Planetarium in Lincoln Park. Go to the far north end of the parking lot, and I'll meet you there in the limo."

The line went dead. I hung up and went back to the car. I tossed the duffel bag onto the rear seat, making room for Leroy to curl up and lie down out of sight. I helped him get his leg up on the seat.

"Oh, man," Leroy moaned. "I'm beginnin' to feel a little woozy; cold too. I think I'm fadin'. I hate to admit it, but I'm gettin' scared."

"Not as scared as those Irishmen must have been."

Leroy managed a faint smile. "That's true," he said. "Could be worse."

"So could your leg," I told him. "You're gonna be okay. Just hang on; we'll be there in a few minutes. If it makes you feel any better, I'm scared shitless too."

"Good. I'm not alone then."

"You never were."

❍❍❍❍❍

Before the Oldsmobile came to a complete stop, all four doors of the limousine flew open with Roy and three other black men jumping out and running over to us. As I got out, two of the men opened Leroy's door and carried him to the rear of the limo, gently maneuvering him onto the back seat. They shut the doors, pulled down the blackout shades, and turned on the dome light. One man dropped the twin jump seats while the other opened a black doctor's bag. They both sat facing the rear seat and went to work on Leroy's leg. The third man got in the Olds, tossed the duffel bag to the ground, and drove away. Roy picked up the bag, put it the trunk, and motioned me to get into the limo's front passenger seat as he took the wheel.

It was not until we were out of the parking lot and headed south on Lake Shore Drive that a word was spoken. The blacked-out privacy widow separating the front from the rear rolled halfway down and Roy spoke over his shoulder to the men in the back. "How's he doin'?"

"Pretty good, considering," the man with the bag at his feet replied. "The slug went through clean, just tore away some meat. I shot 'im full of sodium pentathol so he won't feel nothin' 'til he wakes up. When that happens, I'll fix that, too, with a good hit of morphine; he'll feel great."

"Hey, white bread," the second guy said to me. "You know, you done a—"

"Shut the fuck up, motherfucker," Roy almost screamed and then hissed in a whisper: "You show this boy some goddamned respect. His name is none of your fuckin' business, but if you're a smart nigger, you'll call him *Mister* White. Now, what was you gonna say?"

"Uh...sorry...Mister White. What I was gonna say was, my partner back here says ya most likely saved his life, stoppin' the bleeding and gettin' here as quick as ya did."

Roy turned to me as the privacy window closed. "Thank you," he said and then asked, "How ya feelin'?"

"Better, I think."

"What happened?"

I told him everything. Then I threw up on the floorboard.

Roy smiled softly and patted my shoulder. "I promise ya, you're gonna feel better. I remember the first time I wasted a guy and made my bones. I felt just like you do. Keep that to yourself, though—I don't want to blow my badass rep."

I almost smiled. "That ain't likely," I told him. "So what do we do now?"

"Don't worry about it," he said. "Everything will be taken care of."

"Thanks." I sighed. "I'm not gonna worry about it, then. Last time you said that, everything worked out fine." I felt my eyes drooping. "When you guys take care of Leroy, can we go someplace where I can lie down? I feel like warmed-over shit."

"We're almost there...bro."

⊟⊟⊟⊟⊟

I awoke in near blackness. The dull luminescent green hands of the clock next to the bed glowed. It was a little after six p.m. I swung my legs off the bed and stood, realizing I was still fully dressed.

A vertical crack of dim light emanated from somewhere and I walked toward it, wondering where I was. The light was shining between heavy drapes and when I opened them, the lights of the city reflected from low-hanging clouds told me the exact answer. I was right back where this whole thing began: the bridal suite of the Drake Hotel.

Since it was evening, I knew I'd slept for nearly seventeen hours. I was still only half-awake when my memory banks slowly began functioning by degrees. It all started coming back to me:

At about one in the morning, Roy had parked the limo at the service entrance of the hotel's underground parking facility. We were met by two uniformed black bellboys, who carefully placed the unconscious Leroy into a large laundry cart and covered him with rumpled sheets. The man who'd called me "white bread" drove off in the limo.

One of the bellboys went through the service entrance doors as point man while the other pushed the laundry cart to the freight elevator and held it for us. Roy, carrying the duffel bag; the man with the black medical bag; and I followed the second bellboy into the elevator and up to the suite. That was it. Easy in and, I hoped, easy out.

Leroy was wheeled into the bedroom he had occupied previously and the two bellboys lifted him carefully from the cart onto the bed. They spoke briefly with Roy, who gave them each an envelope, and then left the suite, pushing the cart along with them.

The man with the black bag pulled a chair up to the bed, opened his bag, and motioned for Roy and me to leave as he changed the bloody dressings. We closed the door behind us.

"Is that guy a doctor?" I asked.

"No," Roy said," but he's attended to more gunshot wounds than the Cook County Hospital's emergency room— and perhaps with considerably greater expertise."

"You gonna stay here?" I asked him.

"Yes. Would you care for a drink or a beer? Or if you prefer, that little black bag in the other room holds enough assorted drugs to send you to whatever place you might desire."

"A beer'll do," I said, collapsing on the couch.

Roy made himself a double Scotch and water and

retrieved a beer for me. He sat down beside me on the couch.

"Are you feeling any better now?" Roy asked.

"Not really," I admitted. "I'm exhausted and I'm not real happy about killing people. But..." I went on, "I'm not too tired or stupid not to snap to the fact that you're sure as shit talkin' a lot different all of a sudden."

Roy lifted his lip in a half-smile. "Sharp little smartass, honky motherfucker, ain't ya, boy?"

"I'm not too sure anymore."

"You're smart enough," Roy said. "You just have some rough edges."

"I'm beginnin' to think you're two people."

"I am."

That's the last thing I remembered. I passed out.

❂❂❂❂❂

I stood at the window, watching gray waves roll in off the black lake and brushing glass shards off my jumpsuit as I collected my scattered thoughts. The bedroom door slowly cracked open and Roy's smiling black face peeked in.

"Good evening, Clark. I trust you're well rested. Between you and Leroy, I haven't had much company today."

"How's he doin'?"

"Sleeping. He may limp for a while, but he'll be fine."

"I'm glad to hear that."

"Are you hungry?"

"Starved."

"Excellent. I am as well and I hate eating alone. Why don't you take a shower? Just leave your clothes on the bed and I'll send them down to be cleaned—though I doubt you'll need that jumpsuit any longer, so I'll just trash it.

51

There's a robe at the foot of the bed. I'll order dinner for us while you're cleaning up, assuming you trust that I'll order something enjoyable."

"If there's anybody I trust right now, Roy, it's you. Gimme a few minutes, okay?"

"Sure, take your time. I'll either be in the living room or the other bedroom, checking on Leroy."

"What did you mean about being two people?"

"We'll discuss that after dinner."

⊡⊡⊡⊡⊡

"Roy, what was that orange fish with the soft black seeds on it that we had before the chicken...whatever?"

"Smoked Nova Scotia salmon with capers. And the Chicken-Whatever was Chicken Kiev; Kiev is a city in Russia. Was it good?"

"It was terrific. Better than steak even."

"With your share from that duffel bag over there, you'll be able to eat Chicken-Whatever for a long, long time."

"I don't give a fat rat's ass about the money."

Roy looked at me thoughtfully. "Your share is over eighty thousand dollars. You earned it."

"It ain't worth killin' people over," I told him. "Fuck the money. Give it to Leroy."

Roy stared at me pensively; I could tell he was sizing me up in a different way.

"You saved my brother's life," he said, "so I'm in your debt. I always will be. That's one of the reasons I'm going to share some things with you that I've never even brought up with Leroy. He wouldn't understand and I wouldn't expect him to at this point in his life. Do you want to hear this?"

"Sure." I shrugged. "Go ahead on. I respect you and

what you think, but I still say it ain't worth killin' at least three people, even to get eighty grand. Not to me it ain't, even if they're crooks and scumbags. It seemed like a great idea at the time, but now I think it was a rotten idea and I feel even worse."

Roy did not respond for a few moments. He stared into his Scotch and water, his brow furrowed in some deep and secret thought, looking for words in the glass. He appeared to be in pain.

"Did Leroy ever tell you that when I was working for my father and collecting debts at night, I was a student by day and graduated from the University of Chicago with a degree in English Literature?"

"No, he didn't."

"Did he ever mention that I have a near genius IQ?"

"No."

"Good. I didn't think he had, so those were rhetorical questions. He would never betray my confidence to anyone, even you."

I nodded but remained silent.

"The reason I'm mentioning this to you now," he went on, "is that before I go on, I want you to realize that I'm a reasonably intelligent man."

"Can we talk honest here and you won't get mad?" I asked.

"Yes."

"How come you did time, then?"

"That's a logical question," Roy said through a pleased grin. "I did time because I was careless. I was caught in an alley slapping around a welsher, by an off-duty cop coming out of a bar to take a leak. He threw down on me and I did a little over a year for simple assault. It won't happen again."

"Slappin' around deadbeats, or doin' time?"

That one broke Roy up.

"Doing time," Roy replied. "Or maybe both. Punching out deadbeats is Leroy's job now."

"I believe you're smart, Roy," I said, bringing us back to his original subject. "No doubt about that, really. So why don't you use your education to get ahead instead of breakin' heads and the law?"

"Another good question and a very good one at that," he said. "As a matter of fact, that's what this conversation is *really* all about: Choices."

"Choices?"

"Yes—like the one you just asked about. When I graduated, I did everything I knew how to find an honest job—a job of any kind—and never got past the first interview. I even tried to teach, and that was just as bad. I was rejected everywhere I went."

Roy couldn't hide the lingering bitterness of failure as he continued. "You're a Chicago kid and you know exactly why. I'm colored...a nigger trying to crack the white man's world. Well, that won't cut it in this town. I finally gave it up. And I admit it still hurts. I'm angry at the world and so maybe what I'm doing is very wrong by most standards, but those aren't *my* standards—not anymore. So here I am, making a great deal of money tax-free, using the speech patterns of a semi-literate thug so my own people won't look down on me or perceive me to think I'm better than they are. And I can never, ever show anything close to sensitivity. It's considered a sign of weakness and I would lose respect. If that ever happens, I'm a dead man. So that is not going to happen. Ever."

Roy paused to finish his drink and then went on.

"Now here's what I'm getting at," he said, standing up. "I really didn't have a choice from the beginning. But you do. You are basically a smart kid, and I gather from your refusal to take the money that you possess an innate sense of ethics. So, get out of Chicago. Leave it and all this other garbage behind you. Get out of town and as far away as you can from last night's Cicero-Doolan thing. All four of those guys are dead. That's four murders and a death sentence hanging over you, just waiting to happen—if not by the state, there are always the Doolans to worry about. Those Irish are just as bad as the Italians, and they have very long memories. But if you're out of sight, you're out of mind. Go to Florida, get off the streets, get a job and an education. Knowledge is a far more powerful weapon than a gun. You are now at a crossroads in your life, so save it. Save it right fucking now. Make the right choice!"

⛓⛓⛓⛓⛓

As the Greyhound bus crossed the state line, droning its way south through the moon-shadowed night, its headlights flashed across the face of a large orange-and-green roadside sign: *Welcome To Florida, The Sunshine State.* I replayed my final day in Chicago and the life I was leaving behind...

The new Gruen Curvex watch I was strapping to my wrist told me my last day in Chicago was coming to an end. I stood at the wedding suite's window, buckling the watch's alligator band and looking down on Michigan Avenue being transformed into a tunnel of red-and-green blinking miniature Christmas trees. The holiday was three weeks away, but the floor of the suite was already scattered with torn holiday giftwrapping.

As promised, Roy had gathered up all my clothing the night before and instructed the hotel valet to have everything cleaned and pressed by morning. In the process, he had noted all the sizes. At eleven this morning, I was unwrapping a dozen assorted red-and-green packages that had been packed into a saddle-leather Hartman suitcase, delivered to the suite by courier from Chicago's most

55

exclusive department store, Marshall Fields. The card read: *For Clark, my brother who chose the right road. Travel well, Roy.*

A few days ago, Leroy had been right about one thing: I would be leaving town in style. I was dressed in a dark-brown Scottish tweed sports coat, tan slacks, a white silk shirt, and brown Italian loafers with a matching belt, all topped off by a belted camel-hair overcoat. My old clothes were packed in my new suitcase and I was ready to start my new life in Florida.

"Thanks for your advice, Roy," I told him, "and thanks for the outfit too."

"It's the very least I could do. Hell, you're the reason my little brother is still alive—and besides that, you just gave him over eighty-thousand dollars in tax-free cash. And you think *I'm* extravagant."

"You know how I feel about that money. He's welcome to it. I just hope he don't blow it on a bunch of broads and booze."

"He won't," Roy assured me. "I'm putting his share, along with yours, into an escrow fund, where he won't be able to touch it until he graduates from somewhere with a degree in something. If that isn't incentive enough, I don't know what is. And speaking of money, here's a going-away present. It's only a little over a thousand dollars, but that's all I have on me."

"I don't want any damn blood mon—"

"It's not blood money," he said. "It's mine, and it's from me to you. Sorry there isn't more, but I wouldn't take any from the duffel bag out of respect for your wishes."

I nodded to him. "Thanks."

"You are quite welcome. You're the only white brother I have, and I care about you. If you ever need anything, anything at all, call me on my private number. Remember that!"

56

"I will."

Roy extended his hand for a shake but then pulled me into a brotherly embrace. With a firm pat on the shoulder, he released me. "I'll explain everything to Leroy when he's awake and his brain is functioning without the morphine. I'll tell him good-bye for you. I'd take you to the bus myself, but you know I can't leave my brother right now. The limo is waiting for you downstairs. The driver won't speak to you; I ordered him not to and to just do exactly as he was told."

I nodded and turned to go. Then I had a final thought: "Tell Leroy I'll graduate high school before he does. That ought to help kick his competitive ass in the right direction."

Roy laughed. "I think you're right! Now get the hell out of town and go kick the straight world in the ass."

CHAPTER 3
CHOICE AND EFFECT

December 1951

The tip of the orange sun was breaking through a pink-and-purple-cloud-streaked sky when the bus pulled into its parking bay in the downtown Orlando depot. Thirty hours ago, I had left Chicago in a freezing December blizzard, battling stinging sleet blowing in off Lake Michigan. I stepped from the bus into another world.

A warm, heavy humidity welcomed me to the Sunshine State like a sticky slap in the face. I picked up my bag from the luggage cart and walked into the depot, where I was accosted by the garbled announcements of arriving and departing buses that rudely interrupted the merry static of piped in Christmas Muzak.

We saw each other at the same time.

My mother pushed her way through the faded-green plastic-wreathed front doors of the depot with wide-open arms of welcome and a broad smile that was even wider. I dropped my bag to the floor and we hugged as only a mother and son can.

"Hiya, Mom," I said into her shoulder.

"Hello, Son," she replied, teary-eyed.

She pushed me away with her hands on my forearms to get a good look at me. "My, look how you've grown up. You're almost handsome for an Inger. And, oh my, quite well dressed, too."

"Yeah." I looked down. "Been saving my canteen money and living the good life. I notice you've held together

58

pretty good yourself," I told her. "You don't look a day over thirty."

"I'm not!" she said with mock indignation. "Well, forty maybe. Come on, let's go home, and perhaps we can start making that 'good life' you've been leading a better one."

I lifted the suitcase at my feet and slung my overcoat over my shoulder. As we strode out hand-in-hand into the rapidly warming humidity of the early orange morning, I was reminded of what a fine-looking woman my mother was. What I had said was nearly true: She really didn't look much over thirty. She was tall at five-feet-nine with a slender Nordic bearing that belied her fifty years. She seldom applied makeup other than lipstick to her clean, straight features, and her only vanity was dying her graying shoulder-length hair to its original light-brown color. I had a terrific mother that I respected and even liked. I loved her dearly.

"Son, the city bus stop is a couple of blocks down the street and it's only a short ride home, if you don't mind riding a bus again."

"How short?"

"A mile or so. If you would rather walk, that's fine with me. I sit most of the day and could use the exercise."

"It's after seven o'clock," I realized. "Do you have time to do that and still get to work?"

"It's a special day, so I took it off."

I smiled. "Well, in that case, seems like I've been sitting half my life on a bus. Let's walk it."

"Good." A serious expression fell over her face as she added, "That will give us some privacy along the way. There is something I need to tell you, just between you and me, before we get home."

We walked in silence through the small downtown area. I knew my mother would speak when she knew precisely what she wanted to say, so I kept quiet, letting her think about whatever she was thinking about.

We walked north along Orange Avenue between the two tallest buildings in the small downtown area, both department stores not more than six stories high and directly across the street from each other. Their display windows were decorated with identical smaller-than-life shabby Santa Claus dummies sitting in gift-laden sleighs fronted by eight tilting miniature reindeer. When I read the stores' names, I wondered if they were related. One was Dickson & Ives and the other Ivey's.

From that point on, it was two-story storefronts for a few blocks and that was that for thriving downtown Orlando. I fervently hoped I was not walking through this architectural time warp in Tiny Town, U.S.A., and down a one-way dead-end street.

We turned right for a block to Magnolia Avenue and then turned north again before my mother finally spoke.

"I'm sorry I couldn't come visit you. I have to work six days a week and haven't taken a vacation until today. I simply couldn't take the time off or loss of income to make the trip. I hope you understand and please don't think for a moment that I abandoned you in any way. I never did."

I stopped walking. I dropped my suitcase and faced her. "I know that," said, squeezing her shoulders. "Besides your being my only mom, you've always been my best friend."

She looked at me, tearful once again. "Thank you. You will never know how much that means to me."

"What's bothering you?" I asked.

"My goodness, you certainly have learned how to come directly to the point in your old age, haven't you?"

"What is it?"

"I'll just come right to the point as well then," she said. "I've remarried."

Thoughts of my practically non-existent father mixed

60

with a sense of hope for new beginnings. "I'm going to be living with a stepfather?" I said. "I hope he likes me."

"I do too."

The house was a half-block east of Magnolia Avenue on Pasadena Place, a narrow street lined on both sides by modest pastel homes, many with the obligatory flamingo in wrought iron on the front-door screen or frozen in bright-pink plastic on the lawn. The structure was a typical forties Florida single-story, cement-block three-bedroom, one-bath home with aluminum awnings shading the windows, and a single carport. My new home was painted a putrid pastel pink, but thankfully, it lacked a plastic pet flamingo stuck helplessly into the front-yard grass.

My mother showed me to my small bedroom where I put my suitcase on the single bed, hung my overcoat and jacket in a cramped closet filled with my old clothes—all a size or two too small for me now—and went into the living room. My mother made a fresh pot of coffee, and we sat on a floral-print rattan sofa, eating sweet rolls with steaming mugs of black coffee from a book-cluttered, glass-topped cocktail table.

We talked through the morning. I told her I figured leaving her lifelong hometown of Chicago and moving twelve hundred miles south must have been frightening for her. She smiled and explained that the only difficult part was leaving me. Her marriage was over, she'd disliked her job, and the daily grind of two hours on public transportation was just too much. Plus, she had always hated the miserable weather and the havoc it wrought on her arthritic knees.

Meanwhile, my mom's dearest childhood friend, Betsy Rollins, had moved to Orlando a few years previously and had repeatedly told my mom how much she would love the place and the pleasant, small-town lifestyle that went with it. Betsy invited my mother to come stay with her for as long as it took to get situated and settle into a home of her own.

Two weeks later, my mom was in Orlando.

Two weeks after that, my mom obtained employment sewing commercial fabrics and vinyl into seat covers for a kind, elderly couple, the Crumps, who owned and operated Crump's Custom Covers. She was installing a set of vinyl covers into a prewar Ford two-door sedan when she met her new husband-to-be, Jim Nolen.

It was a whirlwind romance. Within the month, my mother left the hospitality of Betsy and her husband, arm-in-arm with Nolen to the old Ford sedan with the shiny new plastic seats, and they drove two hundred miles north to Valdosta, Georgia, just over the state line. They were married at midnight in the shabby living room of a drunken, speech-slurred justice of the peace, with his sleepy-eyed wife leaning against the wall in a worn flannel nightgown, standing—half-standing, that is—witness for the tender ten-minute ceremony. Eight hours later, Nolen pulled the Ford up to the side of Crump's Custom Covers, just in time for my mother to be at work on time. The honeymoon was over.

"Mom, can I ask you a question?"

"It's 'May I.'"

I tilted my head. "May I"?

"Yes, 'May I.' It's 'May I ask you a question?'"

"Okay, then. May I ask you a question?"

"Of course you may."

"Why did you rush into it like that?"

She sighed. "I was lonely."

"I know the feeling."

❈❈❈❈❈

When Jim Nolen walked his trim, six-foot-four-inch frame through the front door, his false smile and cold eyes made it hate at first sight. He stood there with an empty leather mailbag slung over the left shoulder of his sweat-stained post office uniform, with a thinly disguised snarl on his handsome face.

"Hello, Myrle," he said to my mom, looking straight through me. Then, "You must be my wife's son."

"Yeah, that's right," I said, standing to shake hands. "Glad to meet you."

"Uh-huh, me too," he replied through clenched teeth.

Not making a move to take my outstretched hand, Nolen dropped the mailbag to the floor and headed down the hall, speaking over his retreating shoulder.

"I'll be back in a few, Myrle. I'm gonna go clean up."

When he disappeared, I said, "I don't think he likes me, Mom."

"It takes a while to get to know him."

"It didn't take *you* too long."

"Don't get smart with me—not now, please," she said. "I know he doesn't come off too well at first sometimes, and unfortunately, this appears to be one of those times. You two will be fine. As I said, it just may take a little while."

I thought it might take a very long while.

⛓⛓⛓⛓⛓

I managed to get a night job at Ivey's department store, so I could pay my way at home and have a little spending money. I was hired on a trial basis as an assistant window trimmer, creating watercolor show card signs with brief descriptions and prices to display at the base of the merchandise. I did well and was taken on as a full-time employee.

At the comparatively advanced age of nearing my nineteenth birthday, I enrolled in Boone High School, where I elected to attend classes for the first half of the day and take a Fine and Applied Art course at the Orlando Vocational School for the second. I had always been slow to make friends, and as far as high school was concerned, I was content to remain detached from the younger students and concentrate on making better-than-passing grades.

It was in art class that I excelled. The students were an eclectic group, ranging in age from sixteen to sixty, and I got along well with all of them. I always had good hand skills and had been able to draw before I could scrawl my own name. But I now became aware of a real and untapped talent. My teacher was Mister Robinson, a brilliant and patient instructor, blessed with the gift to teach. And teach he did.

My first try at watercolors came two months into the course, on a class field trip to paint the fountain in the center of Lake Eola near downtown Orlando. Robinson was so impressed with my painting that he entered it in an art contest sponsored by the *Orlando Sentinel Star*. Two weeks later, he posted the results on the class bulletin board; the lead story on local events page of Friday's paper featured photos of the three winning entries. My painting had been awarded second place. After class, I walked to work knowing what I wanted to do for the rest of my life. I was going to be an artist.

It had been a long day by the time I finally finished at the store. I got home later than usual with a dozen copies of the morning's paper tucked under my arm.

"I am so proud of you, Clark!" my mother said through a bright, beaming smile. She pointed to the opened paper on the sofa. "You've accomplished a great deal in a very short time," she continued. "I'd always hoped you would become an artist and now look at you: a prize-winning one!"

I smiled back at her. "Thanks. I am beginning to feel pretty good about myself."

"I'm glad somebody feels good about 'cha," Nolen interrupted in a raspy, wheezing voice. "I sure as shit don't."

He was leaning against the jam of the kitchen doorway, drinking a bit unsteadily from a nearly empty pint bottle of Wild Turkey. I did not want another petty confrontation with Nolen; we'd had several over the past few months and when he was drinking, he could be particularly abusive. I did not need to hear any more of this right now and neither did my mother. To maintain peace in the household, a strategic retreat was in order.

"Well, it's been a long day," I said. "I'm going to bed. Goodnight, all."

"Night's ass—I was talkin' to you, boy!" Nolen yelled.

"Take it easy, Jim," my mother pleaded. "He didn't do anything."

"That's his fuckin' trouble, Myrle: he don't do shit around here except piss me off. I never wanted this little bastard in the house in the first goddamned place."

"Jim!" my mother snapped. "You're drunk; let it go. Just shut—"

"Don't tell me to shut up, you fuckin' bitch."

The arcing blow was like a streak of lighting slashing across my mother's face, knocking her bleeding and senseless to the floor.

Nolen's eyes were red from the alcohol, and a thin line of spittle ran down his chin as he trembled in an uncontrollable rage. He looked like a mad phoenix rising from hell as he turned to face me.

Everything around me stopped and then began again in very slow motion. A familiar, freezing cold filled my lungs, turning my body to ice and my mind to a single screaming thought.

"Let's go bowling!"

"Wh—"

The heavy crystal statue of the Virgin Mother

smashed into Nolen's face like a cannonball, shattering both in a hazy red explosion. Nolen landed on his back halfway into the kitchen, clutching his broken face with one hand and feebly attempting to rise using the other, by propping himself up to one knee.

"I'll kill ya," he gurgled through a torn mouth full of blood and broken teeth. "You're gonna die, you little motherfucker."

"Get up, Nolen," I said stoically.

He tried. He was struggling to both knees when my foot thudded into his groin, knocking him backward, headfirst into the sink counter, cracking solid oak with the top of his skull.

"Get up, Nolen."

Now he could not even try to get up; nothing seemed to work. He flopped around like a dying fish in a widening pool of blood.

"Can't get up, big man? Too bad; that was your last chance to ever stand again for as long as you're gonna live, Nolen. Watch this."

Nolen's glazed eyes stared up at me in horror as I lifted a cast-iron skillet off the stove with both hands and smashed his kneecaps into mush.

This phoenix would not be rising again to strike my mother.

❈❈❈❈❈

I was held incommunicado in the Orange County Jail for seventy-two hours, during a preliminary investigation of my case by Orlando detectives and the district attorney's office, pending the charges against me. My first contact with the outside world was on the fourth day. I sat looking through a heavy steel visiting booth screen into the swollen, very black and tearful eyes of my mother.

"How are you doing, Mom?"

"Mentally, I'm a wreck," she said. "Physically, I'll be fine; he just broke my nose."

"I know this isn't the time for jokes," I said, "but you look like a raccoon."

"You're right; this isn't the time for humor." She stared at me. "My God, Clark, you damned near killed him."

"I'm sorry, Mom, but when he hit you, I guess I went a little crazy."

"That's what your lawyer is going to say."

"What do you mean?"

"When Jim got to the emergency room, he was in critical condition with a fractured skull and severe brain hemorrhaging. The doctors managed to pull him through that, but his face is a plastic surgeon's nightmare and he'll be in a wheelchair for the rest of his life. Against my begging and threats of divorce, which I would do in any case, he's pressing charges. The district attorney is filing for attempted murder."

"Attempted murder?" I said. "If I wanted to kill him, I would have."

"I know that. But you are *not* a murderer."

"Not now, I'm not," I said.

"What did you mean by that remark—'Not now'?"

"Nothing. I'm just scared and not thinking straight. I'm in deep trouble, ain't I?"

"Aren't I," she said, still being the corrective mother. "And yes, you are. Now before you get too upset, let me go on—it may not be as bad as you think. I've retained a very good lawyer for you. Betsy and her husband never liked Jim. The people I work for, the Crumps, can't stand him either. They chipped in several hundred dollars each and with that added to my savings, we have a defense attorney who knows what he's doing. He has already reviewed the case and will be here this afternoon to tell you what's going on and why."

"Thanks, Mom. Thanks for everything."

"What else could I do? You're my only child and I love you more than anything in the world. Try not to worry too much. I've got to go to work now, but I'll see you tomorrow. Bye for now." She blew a kiss through the screen.

"Good-bye, Mom. I love you, too."

Good-bye to you too, Nolen, I thought, watching my mother walk away. *You'll never be able to walk away from anything, even on your knees. I should have smashed your fuckin' elbows too, so when you're sitting in that wheelchair you're going to married to for the rest of your miserable life, you couldn't even roll that hideous face of yours around in circles. Bye-bye, half-man.*

⛓⛓⛓⛓⛓

"Hello, Clark. I'm your attorney, should you go along with your mother's decision to retain me. My name is David Rothstein. I don't believe in standing on formalities with clients, so just call me, Dave, okay?"

"Hi, Dave. Are you Jewish?"

Rothstein smiled. "I'll bet you guessed that from my name," he said. "Yes, I'm a Jew."

"Good," I said. "My mother always told me that if I ever got into trouble, to get a good Jewish lawyer. How's your win-loss record?"

"That's a good question," he said, "and one I don't get asked as often as I should. I win a hell of a lot more than I lose, and I'm a damned good country lawyer. My fees will bear that out, although I'm taking your case quid pro quo."

"What does quid...whatever mean?"

"It's Latin, and it means something in exchange for something. My something is getting little more than costs in return for the something of kicking the prosecutor's butt in litigation. Besides not liking the man," he went on, "I'm accepting you as a client because I don't believe you to be guilty of attempted murder, but I know the prosecuting attorney will do anything to further his political ambitions, including throwing you in jail on an inflated charge. If I have anything to do with it, and I will, that's not going to happen."

"You're hired."

"Excellent. Now, let's get down to business. Do you want me to sugarcoat it, or do you want it straight?"

"Straight. It'll come to that anyway, and besides, straight is faster."

"You're a smart boy," Rothstein said, obviously pleased with my response. "Here's where we're at: I had two meetings with the prosecutor and, frankly, didn't get anywhere, so I went over his head. The D.A. is a close friend of mine, and a reasonable man when he's not on the golf course. We discussed your case and agreed to cut a deal that would ultimately be the same as the outcome of a trial and save the taxpayers a great deal of money. He spoke with the prosecutor, telling him that he could never get a conviction for attempted murder and that he should save the D.A.'s office the embarrassment of looking like jerks in court and most importantly, in the media. The prosecutor agreed with his boss, as I knew he would, and accepted the deal."

He looked at me.

"What's the deal?" I finally asked.

"Cop a plea to aggravated assault and the D.A. will drop the attempted murder charge. You'll get—"

"I'm going to prison?" I interrupted. "You mean to tell me I'm going to fuckin' prison?"

"Yes."

"What's such a great fuckin' deal about that?" I asked. "Isn't there anything else we can do?"

"Sure there is, young man. You could choose to go

69

to trial and very possibly get twenty years."

"I thought you said they'd never make the attempted murder thing stick. Didn't you say that?"

"I said that to the D.A.," he told me, "but to be honest with you, I'm not at all sure I could win at trial, and here's why. First of all, even though your record as a juvenile can't be brought up in court, it sure as hell can be referred to, and your history is one of violence. Secondly, your attack on Nolen could, at best, be construed to have been in self-defense and protecting your mother from further harm, but the kneecaps would bury you. That was indefensible. When the man got to the hospital, he was near death and the doctors say he's pretty damned lucky that he'll be a deformed, hopeless cripple for the rest of his life."

I nodded noncommittally.

"To make matters worse," he went on, "during questioning, you showed absolutely no signs of remorse. To tell you the truth, I think they'd win. You had better take the deal before the D.A.'s office comes to its senses and changes its mind. Also, if you elect for trial, you'll sit in county for months before that process even begins and all that county jail time will *not* accrue to your sentence. That alone will cost you several more months of lost freedom."

"How much time are we talkin' about?"

"Five years."

My guts churned. "Five—!"

"But if you keep your nose clean and don't beat the shit out of anybody else," he continued, "you'll be out in three and a half. That's the best I can do, and I assure you, it's the best deal you will ever get. What's your answer?"

"I'll take it."

CHAPTER 4
CAMP COUNSELORS

June 1952

I served the first two weeks of my five-year sentence in the Florida State Maximum Security Prison at Raiford, in what was called the "New Cock Block." All new inmates were herded into one of four overcrowded sixteen-man cells, two for whites and two for blacks. We were totally isolated from the general population, confined to the block during the fourteen-day process of admission and orientation into the system.

At the end of the second week, prison administration evaluations of the new inmates had been considered and judgments made. It had been determined exactly where and how each man could best serve the state and be rehabilitated. About half of the men would remain where we were and do relatively easy time. The others, mostly black, would not be so fortunate.

My graduation class lined up in a nervous row as, one by one, names were called. Assignments were given and inmates were ordered to divide into three groups: two white going to cellblocks A or B, and one black destined for the segregated C Block. The barred "New Cock Block" door slid open and the three groups of men marched into the main yard, going to their respective cellblocks and work details.

Seventeen names had still not been called, thirteen blacks and four whites. A terrified black boy stood next to me as the steel door clanged shut in front of us.

"Maybe we're goin' to that first-timer kid joint," I said. "You know, the one upstate in Marianna."

"I wish," he replied in a trembling voice, "but that ain't what's happenin' here, man. That place is for juvies. We're in for some hard fuckin' time, white bread. They're shippin' both our dead asses outta here to one of those motherfuckin' chain-gang road camps."

$$\rightleftharpoons\rightleftharpoons\rightleftharpoons\rightleftharpoons\rightleftharpoons$$

The prison van parked just inside the closing gate of Florida State Correctional Facility 33. The driver unlocked the rear door as the guard seated next to me in the back unlocked my wrist and ankle shackles and ordered me to get out.

The guard followed behind me as we were met by another guard leaning on a thick walking stick in the center of the rutted dirt road. This one was not wearing the familiar blue uniform of Raiford but was dressed for the heat in light-tan belted slacks, a white short-sleeved shirt, brown boots, and a leather-banded white-straw western hat. Unlike the other guards I had seen, he was not fat. He stood a couple of inches taller than me and looked tougher than his leather boots.

It was not until the van disappeared down the road toward the highway in a trail of dust that he spoke.

"I'm Boss Huggins. You 55109? Inger, Clark?"

"Yes, sir. I—"

The butt of the heavy walking stick smashed into my solar plexus, dropping me to my knees. I looked up from the dirt, gasping for breath.

"That's 'Yes, sir, BOSS,' asshole! Don't ever forget that, ya hear?"

I tried to answer but could not speak.

"Can you hear me, butt-fuck?"

I nodded.

"Good. Now get your sorry ass on your feet or I'll crack your fuckin' skull wide open. Now!"

"Yes, sir...Boss," I wheezed. "Gettin' up as fast as I can."

"Just remember this, boy. Your fuckin' soul might belong to Jesus, but your sorry ass belongs to me."

"Yes, sir, Boss. I believe you, Boss."

"You're learnin' fast for a dumbshit new cock. Now, march your ass in front of me to that small building on the left with the 'Office' sign on it. I'm bookin' you into this shithole."

I opened the screen door and entered a single small room with four walls also made of screen. It was not much of an office, just two filing cabinets and four metal desks painted a drab olive-green. Only one person inhabited the room, an older man of about fifty, seated at the desk nearest the door. He was a convict, and I could tell from the four-digit number (mine was five digits) stenciled over the left pocket of his faded-blue work shirt that he was an old-timer.

"Sit!" Boss Huggins snapped at me like I'd been a bad dog. "Old Dixon here'll take care of the paperwork and he'll tell ya what ya need to know. Orientation takes about five minutes and it's real simple. If it isn't and you're still a little confused, let me know and I'll straighten you out."

Boss Huggins turned on his boot heels and left the office, the screen door slamming behind him.

The old man stood from behind his desk and offered me his hand. "I'm William Dixon; call me Dix. It's okay. You can stand now and shake hands—although from what I saw in the road, you may prefer to stay sitting."

"I'm Clark Inger. And I appreciate your not taking offense for not getting up." I reached for his hand from my chair. "I'm tryin' not to puke."

"None taken."

73

"Can I ask you a question?" I asked.

"I'm sure it will be the first of many. Go ahead."

"I noticed when ya stood up that insteada blue pants with a white stripe, yours are white with a blue stripe. How come?"

"I'm a trustee," he explained. "Seems like it ought to be the other way around though; white would be easier to see if you're a runner—something I strongly advise against unless you have a death wish. Can't outrun a walking boss's twelve-gauge and the tower guards got scoped .30-.30s. They like using them too."

"I don't think I'm gonna to be going anywhere for a while," I said.

"That's for damn sure," he agreed. "Let me get this paperwork out of the way and then I'll show you your new home. The place is nearly empty right now since everybody is out until dusk on work details, so we'll have plenty of time for me to get you settled in. Look around if you want, but whatever you do, don't leave this room without me."

Dix began pecking away on an antique Royal typewriter as I slowly pushed myself to my feet. The pain in my gut was subsiding as I surveyed the grounds through the screens.

The office was the building nearest the gate, with the entrance facing the road while the other three sides afforded a complete view of Road Camp 33. The compound was not large, only about a hundred square yards, and was surrounded by a twenty-foot chain-link fence topped with three strands of electrified barbed wire, cantilevered inward at a forty-five-degree angle. At the corners stood thirty-foot-tall guard towers with roof-mounted searchlights, each apparently unmanned at the moment. In the center was a hard-packed-dirt exercise yard with a basketball backboard and a few concrete picnic tables.

The yard was surrounded by four wooden buildings,

including the office, covered by galvanized tin roofs. Each of the other three had a sign over its door: "Barracks," "Mess Hall," and "Trustee Cottage." Scattered around were several outbuildings and a large parking shed. Just outside the main gate were two residences also with signs, one reading "Captain Scruggs" and the other "Boss Huggins." From what I could see, everything looked clean but far from shining. This place was a scrubbed-up run-down dump.

Well, Clark my boy, I thought, *you may as well grow to love it. You're out of choices now.*

When the clickety-clack of the old typewriter stopped, Dix slid a file folder into an inbox on another desk and walked to the door. He held it open for me.

"Come on, Clark. Let's take the tour."

We walked the perimeter of the grounds, Dix pointing out the obvious while chanting a mandatory litany of prescribed chain-gang rules for survival.

"There," he finished. "Now that you've heard what I had to tell you, we can talk like one con to another. Any questions?"

"Yeah. What's up with those two one-holer shithouses over by themselves just outside the fence?"

"Those are definitely not outhouses," Dix replied with a thin smile. "Those are the boxes." He paused. "Come to think of it, though, you're not too far off. They are kind of like shithouses."

"What's a box?"

"Somewhere you don't want to go. If you screw up, they will throw you in there and you will sit or squat in your own shit with a bowl of beans, a slice of bread, and a cup of water once a day until Captain Scruggs decides you got your mind right."

"What's getting your mind right?"

"You seem to be a pretty bright kid. You figure it out."

"I just did."

"Thought you would, and keep this in mind: Since I've been here, those damned things have killed several people."

"How long have you been here?" I asked.

"Four years longer than the previous record-holder: fifteen years, going on a hundred. About five years is the average, not counting time served or dying. This place will break most men down like a shotgun until they simply can't cut the work anymore. When that happens, they're shipped back to Raiford to fatten up. Don't worry though, you're young and strong, and according to your file, you won't do more than three, three and a half years. Stay out of trouble, don't piss off any of the bosses, and you'll make it here just fine."

I shook my head. "Shit, sometimes I wonder how the hell I got into this mess."

"You know damned well how," he said. "You almost killed that Nolen guy."

"How'd you know about that?" I asked.

He raised his palms. "Your records. It's all in your file. I know almost everything about everybody in this joint, including the staff. Don't worry about that either—I keep my mouth shut, mind my own business, and eat well. I am going to let one thing about you slip through the cracks though, and by lights out, most of the guys are going to know why you're doing time."

"That's really none of their fuckin' business, Dix."

"No, it isn't, but it's in your best interests that they know."

"Why?"

"Because there's a hierarchy of respect from the cons in the joint. Murderers are generally at the top, unless they raped and killed an innocent woman or at worst a child, which puts them at the bottom. You came very close to murder by protecting your mother, so in a weird, convoluted way that's good. You will automatically get some respect. Don't lose it."

"I'll try not to," I agreed. "But why are you tellin' me all this stuff?"

The old man frowned before replying. "To tell you the truth, selfish reasons, really. You're the youngest guy in here now, just a kid, and if you don't have respect, these guys will eat you alive and not even bother to spit out what's left of you. Every once in a while, I like to do something good for somebody. Makes me feel good about myself for a change. And you had better keep your mouth shut about this conversation or you will have a very powerful enemy in here, and that's me. Besides Captain Scruggs, I practically run this joint and I can't show favoritism. I must remain neutral or I'm a dead man. I'm taking my ass in my hands by telling you this. Do you understand?"

"Yes, I do. And if you thought for a minute that I'd say anything, you wouldn't have said a word to me other than what you were supposed to."

"I see we're both good judges of character," Dix said, grinning.

Our tour of the compound ended when we entered the barracks. We stood in a narrow rectangular room with walls of screen, the same as the office. A row of fifteen double-deck bunks with a pair steel lockers between them ran against each long wall. The open area in the center was crowded with half a dozen wooden picnic tables lined up end to end, with nothing on them except shoeboxes of state-issued rough-cut tobacco and rolling papers.

I followed Dix to the end of one line of bunks to a low plywood wall that separated the main room from an open communal bath. Dix explained that bunks were assigned by seniority, the most desirable being nearest the entrance and the least desirable by the bath. I would be spending my nights atop the last bunk on the right, the closest to the toilets.

Linens and a thin pillow were rolled up in a coarse, gray wool blanket at the foot of a stained, sagging mattress stacked with two changes of clothing. One was for work, Dix explained, and the other was to be worn only in camp.

"You won't have this shithouse bunk for too long," he assured me. "We've got five or six short-timers here and you'll move down the line a couple spots in a month or so."

I slowly turned three-hundred-sixty degrees, sizing up my new living quarters. Home not-so-sweet home.

"We've got a little time left," Dix said. "Let's park it for a while. I'm getting old and I'm tired of standing."

We sat down at one of the tables, and Dix continued with the official introduction to State Correctional Facility 33. The camp was staffed with twenty state employees, nineteen of whom were uniformed and to be addressed as Boss. Only one man dressed in civilian clothes; he was the captain and would be addressed as such.

The inmate population was seventy men, divided into four groups: three work details of twenty men each. Two of the groups worked the road and one the brick plant. The fourth group was made up of ten trustees assigned to various duties.

Five days a week, each work gang with one trustee water boy left the compound at dawn in an open, side-railed truck with a canvas top, towing a shotgun guard trailer behind, and went to that day's work location. They each returned at dusk. Weekends were spent inside the compound with freedom of movement restricted only to within ten feet of the fence. Sundays, the office was used as a chapel in the morning, and after noon, as the visitation area.

"That's about it," Dix finished. "The work details are coming in now and I've got to go do the headcount. Anything else?"

"Just one more question."

"What's that?"

"No offense, Dix, but it doesn't seem like you're tellin' me all that stuff—stuff maybe you shouldn't have—just to make yourself feel good. That wouldn't be worth the risk of maybe feelin' a hell of a lot worse for it. What's the real reason?"

Dix gazed at me. "You remind me of my son. He died two years ago."

I didn't know what to say, so I said nothing at all. Neither did Dix. There simply was nothing more to be said.

"It's good to meet 'cha, Dix. Thanks, thanks for everything."

"Same here and you're welcome. Good luck, kid."

⛓⛓⛓⛓⛓

The old man went back into his office and then reappeared outside holding a clipboard under his arm. He stood at the door as two trucks rolled to a stop just outside the compound and two loads of sweat-soaked men filed one by one through the open gate with four rifle barrels pointed at them from the now-manned guard towers. A third truck arrived and the men who hopped off the back were more than just sweaty; they were drenched. The last two off the truck were shackled.

I sat at the barracks table, expecting the unexpected as the men shuffled inside. They went to their lockers, removed relatively clean clothes from hooks, and put them on their bunks. Then they threw their dirty work clothing to the bottom of the lockers.

The men walked naked past my table, staring at me as they headed for the showers. Some nodded or raised a hand in half-hearted greeting, but most just gazed at me without expression and moved on.

No one said a word. I felt a distinct twinge of raw fear. This was a tough-looking bunch.

The last two men to enter did not go directly to the showers. They headed straight for me and sat down at a table. Both were slender and hard-looking, with not an ounce of fat between them. One had a pock-marked face and a dirty-blond flattop. They were the two who had been shackled—and still were.

Flattop was the first to speak. "Hey, new cock," he said. "Welcome to Shit City. I'm Johnny Johnson and this here's Bunny O'Hara."

O'Hara was lean and tan with coal-black curly hair and piercing green eyes that said *Don't fuck with me.*

"Clark Inger," I replied, remembering Leroy's philosophy of respect and trying to look as flinty-eyed as possible.

"How ya doin', Inger?" asked Bunny in a lilting Irish accent.

"Better than you, it looks like," I said, pointing at his shackles. "You gotta shower in your pants?" I asked.

"Yeah, arsehole," Bunny replied. "That's why we're sittin' here takin' 'em off."

"Yeah," said the one named Johnny. "It's a fuckin' art form. Try to avoid it."

I watched their human contortion act in amazement. They actually performed it so quickly, I did not catch exactly how it was done.

"Well, gotta get cleaned up for mess," Johnson said.

"Yeah," said O'Hara. "We'd better hurry it up, too. See ya around, smart mouth."

They picked up their pants, went to their lockers, and did the same as the other men had. Then they clanked off toward the showers as the rest were already exiting or at their bunks, putting on their off-duty camp clothes.

Now dressed, a diminutive boy about my age

80

appeared at my side.

"Hi, mind if I sit here?" he asked.

"No, go ahead," I replied.

"I'm your bunkmate," he said. "Name's Chris Bacon. Call me Crisp."

Crisp was a full foot shorter than my six-foot frame and his head, which I could view the top of, sported a light-brown crew cut. The most noticeable thing about him, though, was how extremely thin he was.

I stuck out a hand and we shook.

"Crisp it is," I said. "Seems everybody here's got a nickname; anyone use their real one?"

"Most actually do—except the paper hangers. They get stuck with the name they used to forge their hot checks with."

"Really?"

"Yup. Kind of a reminder, I guess. Like, you used the name, you live with it."

I shrugged. "I suppose that makes sense," I said. "As much as anything does these days, that is."

"I just hope they don't stick you with Clarkie or Laaaarry." Crisp giggled.

"You already know my full name?"

"A lot of guys do, Lawrence Clark Inger. Rumors get around pretty quick in here, even to a new guy like me."

"Call me Clark. What's the rumor?"

"Okay, Clark. The word is you got a bad rap, protecting your mom and all. Shit, anybody'd do the same—except maybe for Crazy Crowder over there sitting on his chair."

Crisp pointed out a hunched-over man still in the bathroom, fully clothed with his pants up, sitting with his legs crossed on the end toilet.

"That's 'his chair'?" I asked, bewildered. "Can someone use it when he's done?"

Crisp raised his eyebrows and shook his head. "Best not to. He don't talk, but he wrote that sign hanging up over his crapper. It says, 'For my ass only, Crowder.' He means it, too."

"Huh. That's one nickname that seems to fit," I said. "He must be a real nutcase. What was that you said about him not protecting his mother?"

"He sawed off his old mom's head with a dull, rusty pocket knife—must've taken 'im hours. And when he was done, he stuck the bloody fuckin' thing on the goddamn mailbox so's the mailman would be sure to know where to leave her social security checks. Funny thing is, they say he cashed two or three of 'em before he got busted."

I shook my head. "Good police work will catch you every time. Goddamn! He should be locked up in the nuthouse in Chattahoochee."

"He was," Crisp told me, "but they're crowded to the bars. I guess they figured he's not as bad as some of the guys in 33, so they shipped his crazy ass over here."

"Nice neighborhood. Thanks, Crisp. I feel much more at ease now."

"Nice neighborhood," Crisp said, laughing. "That's a good one."

We were interrupted by a trustee standing at the entrance to the mess hall and clanging away loudly on a large iron triangle.

"Come on," said Crisp. "It's chow time. Follow me and do what everybody else does, okay?"

We headed for the door. "Okay, lead on," I said. "Say, how come you're so damned skinny?"

"Mosquitoes got me a few months back," he said. "Malaria 'bout killed me."

ೞೞೞೞೞ

The mess hall was just that, a mess. Rows of wobbly wooden picnic tables with attached benches filled the cramped room, along with a food-service counter manned by four trustees. There was no kitchen, only a long work counter with overhead storage cabinets and two deep laundry sinks; one to wash, the other to rinse.

The food was trucked in twice a day, Crisp told me, in stainless-steel thermal containers from a centralized kitchen in a black camp a few miles across the Chattahoochee River. It went to this camp and two others within a fifty-mile radius. The morning delivery was for breakfast as well as lunch containers that were loaded into the camp's trucks, headed to their various work details. The evening delivery was for dinner. No food was ever left over.

Following Crisp along the food line, I did as the others did with their metal food weapons. I put a soupspoon in my shirt pocket and held a tin cup in one hand and a twelve-inch plate in the other. I was given two slices of Wonder Bread and then collected ladled portions of black-eyed peas with small greasy chunks of fatback, collard greens with small greasy chunks of fatback, and a cup of tepid black chicory coffee with a thin film of grease floating on the surface. The term greasy spoon took on a whole new meaning.

We found seats and sat down under the growing *dink-dinkity-dink* sound of metal spoons striking and scraping over metal plates. Talking was allowed but held to a minimum as hungry men shoveled spoons full of slop into their mouths like a pack of starving wolves.

"Bone Appateet, or however the fuck you say it," said a man across the table. His craggy face was etched with lines, I assumed from years of exposure to the intense Florida sun. "Pass the salt, will ya, Crispy Bacon?" He stuck out a hand that was more weathered than his face.

"Here ya go, James."

In spite of his leathery appearance, the man seemed likable enough.

"You must be James," I said.

"Yep, that's me. James James."

"I'm Clark Inger and I don't have a nickname. I'm not going to have one either. What's yours?"

"James," he said. As he smiled, the lines in his face deepened.

"The first man I've met here with a sense of humor," I said. "May I call you James, James?"

"Please do," he said between mouthfuls. "And I'll just call you by your new nickname, Clark."

"That'll work," I said.

This exchange seemed to please Crisp to no end. "Glad to see you two getting along," he said. "James is my friend. You can be, too, Clark, if you want."

"Friendship is earned, Crisp," I said, "but I'll give it a shot. Can somebody pass the pepper?"

"No," replied James.

"No?"

"It's impossible. There isn't any, thanks to Bunny O'Hara."

I looked around to make sure he wasn't in earshot.

"I met him earlier," I told James. "Seems like a surly asshole, too. What did he do?"

"Well, since you get off on nicknames so much, you might find this a bit funny. I don't know his real first name, and I don't care to, but he got 'Bunny' because he's a runner. Done it twice, too. First time, the dogs got him a few miles from here in the swamp. Second time, he made it as far as Atlanta before the Georgia cops ran him down in a stolen car."

"Where does the pepper part come in?"

"Simple. The time he made it to Georgia, he used pepper to throw off the dogs. They couldn't smell each other's shit for a week. Now there's no fuckin' pepper in the whole damn prison system."

I raised my eyebrows. "That was pretty smart though, I gotta admit."

"Not really," James said, licking his spoon. "He started off here with only ten years on a plea bargain for murder two. They added a year with two weeks in the box for the first escape and, for the second, along with grand theft auto, he got four more, including thirty days in the box that damn near killed him. Now he's doin' a fifteen-year stretch and all hard time. Not real smart, if you ask me."

"You're right," I agreed. "You can outrun the cops and a lot of other shit too, but ya can't outrun the system." I said this while thinking to myself that it was not entirely true. I had. Other than two trusted friends in Chicago, the murders of four men were my private, personal history. And it would stay that way.

"Well, boys, I've done all the damage I can do here," James said.

"Me too," Crisp said, putting his cup and spoon on his plate. "Let's turn in this stuff and hit the yard."

I followed the frail boy as we passed our metallic dining tools over the end of the food counter to one of the trustees, under the watchful eyes of a guard who was making certain that everyone returned each plate, cup, and particularly spoon. A spoon, Crisp had explained, was one of the most coveted pieces of contraband an inmate could possess. With the handle filed to a sharp point, it made a very serviceable weapon. And even if not used as a shank, it was a valuable item for prison barter and trade. I watched my greasy miniature goldmine being dumped into the washing sink and left the mess hall with Crisp and James.

We sat at one of the concrete tables in the yard. As we talked and watched a three-on-three pickup game of basketball, a fourth man joined our group.

"Good evening, gentlemen."

James broke into a big smile. "Hey, Dix, my man. Have a seat."

"Thank you. I believe I will."

Old Dix seemed to be quite the popular figure around here.

"Hi ya, Dix," Crisp said, also smiling as he moved over to make room for him on the bench. "Good to see ya."

"Same here, boy," Dix replied and then turned to me. "I figured you to be a good judge of character. You chose two pretty good guys to talk to first time outta the—forgive the term—first time outta the box. How you doing so far?"

"Fine," I told him. "How else could I possibly be doing after dining on such a truly delectable feast?"

Dix laughed. "You'll like it well enough tomorrow."

"I doubt it," I said.

"I know it," he countered. "Tomorrow, you will work your narrow ass off and then you will stagger in here when the day is done, starving what's left of your narrow ass off, and you will love that shit."

"Where's he workin'?" asked Crisp.

"Gang B, Boss Busby."

"Shit, Dix," James said, "it'll be his first day. Couldn't you do any better than that?"

Dix shrugged. "I don't pick them; I just write them down."

"I know," said James. "Sorry."

"That's okay, James. Seems like you've taken to the boy. That's good, since you're workin' the same gang. Watch over him when you can. He's just a kid, and—"

"Hold up a minute, you guys," I interrupted. "You're all talkin' about me like I'm a piece of meat."

"You are," Dix said through a thin smile. "You will be tomorrow, anyway. Don't take that too bad, though; we

86

all are. It's only a matter of degrees, right?"

"That's about right." James sighed. "It could be worse, Clark. You just landed somewhere in the middle."

"I think that's true enough," Crisp agreed. "I'm in Gang A, and the work's the same. It's just that you guys got Busby for a boss. That about right, Dix?"

"I don't make no judgments on walking bosses, son," Dix replied carefully. "I know one thing that *is* right, though. Dealing with Busby is a hell of a lot better than having to deal with the brick plant."

"Oh man," Crisp howled, "that's the fuckin' truth."

James closed the conversation for the evening. "Don't worry about all this bullshit," he told me. "You'll find out for yourself soon enough when we truck it out of here in the morning."

CHAPTER 5
WALTZING WITH YO-YOS

July 1952

A strong hand gripped my arm, jerked me out of line, and pulled me to one side. I was looking up at a fat red face and two of my own, reflected in mirror-lens Ray-Ban Aviator sunglasses.

"Inger, I'm Boss Busby."

"Yes, Boss."

"Don't fuckin' interrupt me when I'm talkin' to you, boy!" he sneered.

When I did not respond, he nodded and then continued, "As I was sayin', I'm Boss Busby. Do your work, do it right, and do as I say. Remember the 'do's.' *Do* all that, and you'll do just fine. *Don't* do all that and you'll sure as shit wish ya had."

I thought it best to remain silent.

"Well, goddammit, did you fuckin' hear me, boy?"

Now I was certain it would be best to respond.

"Yes, Boss. I heard you loud and clear, Boss."

"Get back in fuckin' line!"

At the moment, the 'do's' were at the top of my mind, and I fell into place at the rear of the line as quickly as possible. The twenty-man gang moved along in single file, past the open door of a tool shed. Each took a sling blade sickle handed to him by the gang's trustee water boy as they walked by. I brought up the rear, and as I was given my tool for the day, the trustee motioned for me to stop.

"James asked me to give ya a good smooth handle,"

he whispered quickly and then waved me on toward the waiting truck.

A hand reached out for mine and pulled me up onto the flatbed, under the canvas top.

"Thanks for the lift," I said, sitting down opposite my helping hand, at the end of one of the two benches that ran the length of the flatbed's wooden side rails. A balding man with wire-rimmed glasses gave me a thin-lipped smile. Although muscular, this guy looked like he belonged in an accountant's office.

"I'd say 'It's a pleasure,'" he said, "but nothing here is a pleasure. My name's Harry Conlin. I'm the row leader."

"Well, Harry," I said, "it's almost a pleasure to meet 'cha."

"Same here, Inger. Clark, isn't it?"

"Yeah. Clark's my *nickname*, too," I answered with a smile.

"Harry's mine—though some call me Doc or Doc Harry. Doesn't matter much to me one way or the other. Well, here we go, off to find new job opportunities."

The water boy slammed shut the cab's passenger door, and with Busby behind the wheel, the truck rumbled forward, hauling a two-wheeled trailer carrying a shotgun boss named Waters. We exited the camp's main gate, bouncing off the dirt washboard onto the smooth blacktop, and headed for the highway, traveling east into the first dim light of day.

"Scootch over a little and give a long-timer a seat." It was James.

"Of course," I said. "Have a seat. And thanks for the smooth handle."

"You're going to need it for a few days," he said. "Doc, where are we going today?"

"Three Rivers State Park."

"Near the lake?"

"Yep. Right on the beautiful shores of Lake Seminole."

"Shit!" said James. "Mosquito city."

"Shouldn't be too bad," said Harry. "Looks like the wind'll be coming in off the water for a change. Even better, we'll be whackin' down weeds, not brush."

"That's the first good thing I've heard today," said James. "Probably the last, too. Take that back—it'll be half an hour before we get there and another half coming back. You're lucky, Clark, you'll have a short first day."

"Yeah, I feel blessed," I snorted.

"By the time the day's over, you'll feel like shit," said James. "Harry, since we're sitting here bullshitting, you gonna fill the kid in on how to act?"

"That's why I'm sitting here," Harry replied. "It's part of my job."

"What do I need to know?" I asked.

"Not much," said Harry. "It's pretty simple, really. I told you before that I was the row leader; now, I'll tell you what that means. When we hop off the truck, I'll be the lead guy on the left of a staggered line, with each man two steps back of the man on his left. That's so nobody gets hit from either side when we start swing our yo-yos. Now, I'll be—"

"Sorry to interrupt, but what's a yo-yo?"

"It's what you're holding in your hand," said James.

"This sling blade?"

"That used to be a sling blade," he said. "Now it's a yo-yo."

"Why?"

"Boy, you sure are full of questions," said Harry, smiling at me again as he replied. "It's a yo-yo because all day long, the fuckin' thing goes up and down, up and down like a yo-yo, okay?"

"Okay, now it's a yo-yo."

James was beginning to giggle. "A truly wonderful

tool," he observed. "And I notice that yours has an unusually fine handle."

"Yes, my good man," I said. "It was made lovingly by old-world master woodworkers over two centuries ago."

"Knock off the bullshit, boys," Harry snapped. "I don't give a damn if the fuckin' thing was made out of zebrawood by Amazon women with big tits in the rainforests of Brazil. Do you want to know what's happening, or do you want to jump off this truck and not have a clue about what to do?"

"Sorry," I said, contrite. "I'll shut up."

"Good. Now, where the hell was I?"

James ceased his giggling. "You were saying 'up and down, up and down,'" he reminded him.

"Thanks. I don't know what I'd do without your help."

"Sorry, Doc," he said. "I'll shut up."

"Jesus Christ, now you two are talking like the fuckin' Bobbsey Twins."

James and I looked at each other conspiratorially, but we resisted saying "Sorry" in unison.

So far this was a fun day, but I knew very well that it was time to pay attention and keep my mouth shut. I recited what I knew so far. "You were talking about the men lining up in a staggered line with each man two steps behind the man on his left so he wouldn't be hit by a flying yo-yo."

"At least you pay attention," said Harry, nodding. "That's exactly right. As the row leader, I'll be in front on the left, setting the pace. Everyone will follow me, swinging at my pace, leaving a wide trail of cut weeds behind. When we get to the end of a row, I'll move the line left or right, make a new row, and we'll do the same thing, going in the direction that we came from. James will show you how to handle the yo-yo with maximum efficiency and minimum effort. Got that so far?"

"Yeah, I've got it. Anything else?"

"Yes. James, do you want to tell him what to expect and how to act?"

"Sure," James said, his voice serious now. "This is important stuff; it could save your life. First and foremost, if you hear anyone shout 'Hit it!' fall to the ground as fast and as flat as you can. It means that a con is running and that a crossfire of double-aught buckshot will be flying just inches over your head. These boss assholes don't fool around with runners. They aim low, for the legs. After the first few rounds, if the man is still moving in any direction other than back to them, they'll blow his fuckin' brains out."

I could not believe what I was hearing. "Holy shit!" I said. "They don't holler 'Freeze' or 'halt' or anything, they just shoot your ass?"

"You got it, kid. The only thing they holler is 'Hit it!' and that's at the same time they're clicking off their safeties to fire."

"Goddamn!"

"God probably does. There are a couple of things you may have to do today: one is piss and the other is take a shit. If you have to shit, let the boss know by yelling out to him 'Diggin' a hole, Boss.' If Busby nods at you, take a few steps back, dig a hole with your yo-yo, shit in it, and cover it up. To piss, yell 'Pullin' it out, Boss,' and again, if he nods, turn around and do it. And the last thing is this: Sometime before lunch, you're going to run out of gas; you won't be able to keep up with the pace. But the main thing is, go just as long and as hard as you possibly can until you drop. And you will drop. But don't worry about it; that's expected by everyone, even the bosses. In a weird way, it's like you're on stage with a—pardon the pun—captive audience of critics watching you perform. Show 'em what you got."

"James?"

"Yeah?"

"I'm not gonna to drop."

The truck lurched to the side of the hard-packed sandy road we were on, a few yards from where it led into a public boat ramp on the south shore of Lake Seminole. Busby got out of the cab, looked over the expanse of tall weeds, and walked about twenty yards from the truck. He cradled his gun and nodded to Waters, approving their respective positions for a field of crossfire, and then ordered us off the flatbed.

While Harry was lining up the men just as he'd described, Busby called James over. He spoke to him briefly and then waved him back to the gang. James took me aside for a crash course in weed-whacking.

The yo-yo is held with one hand. Grasping its thirty-inch shovel-like handle, you swing its horizontal, fourteen-inch double-sided blade in a downward arc, sweeping it close to the ground to cut the growth in its path. James showed me the correct way to swing the tool one-handed on the downstroke, then to stop it with the other palm on the upstroke, and then to push it back for the returning backswing. When my arm tired, I should change hands and reverse the process.

"Simple enough."

"For some of these idiots, it has to be," said James. "I wanted to be next to you, but that fuckin' ass-kissin' water boy, Chester Dillon, saw us getting chummy on the way out here, so Busby just told me he doesn't want me anywhere near you. Same for Doc Harry. So, here we go; you're on your own now. Hang in there."

This yo-yo thing was not so simple. I had trouble swinging the blade parallel to the ground, and my sweaty palms kept slipping up on the handle, making the blade slam into the earth with a jarring, arm-stinging shock. After about half an hour, I was getting better at handling the yo-yo, but the muscles in my upper body were beginning to burn. By the mid-morning break, my arms were on fire.

I vaguely remember James giving me a pep talk and cups of cool water. I vividly recall going back to work and the pain starting all over again.

After an hour, my arms cramped up and felt heavier by the minute. Going on an hour and a half, I was numb from the waist up except for my brain, which was bubbling like molten lead. I had to make it until the lunch break. I forced my mind to push the pain away, forget it, and keep on swinging. Quitting was unthinkable. I was not going to drop.

⊟⊟⊟⊟⊟

It was refreshingly cool lying in the darkening shade of the huge old live oak. A stiff breeze blew in across Lake Seminole, gathering strength and dropping the temperature rapidly. Billowing black clouds moved in with a chilling wind and the first drops of rain began to fall. I was suddenly very cold, and now my resting place was gently rocking from side to side, rolling sleep away. I did not appreciate this in the least! I just wanted to go back to sleep, but the rocking persisted. Reluctantly, I forced my eyelids open. From out of the dark, a bespectacled face hovering over me slowly came into focus.

"Is that you, Harry?"

"Yes, it's me."

"Where am I?"

Harry seemed to find the question quite amusing. Through a big grin, he managed to respond: "That was original."

"What?"

"The 'Where am I.' You sounded like bad guy in a movie who's just taken on John Wayne."

"Never mind, Harry. I know where I am now. What

happened? How'd I get here, stretched out on the floor of the truck?"

"We carried you."

"I dropped?"

"You dropped."

"Damn! How long did I last?"

"Longer than most. You almost made it to lunch break, over four hours. You've been out of it for about an hour. Right now, we're driving through a thunderstorm. Going home early."

"I don't really remember the morning break either. Did we take one?"

"Yes. Yours was longer; you passed out."

"James was right," I said over the acid taste of rising bile. "I feel like warmed-over shit."

"I know damned well you feel like shit. You had a pretty heavy-duty heatstroke. I had to have the water boy use up all our ice on your stubborn 'I won't drop' ass."

"How'd you know to do that?"

"I've had a checkered past. I was a doctor."

"Yeah?" I said. "What kind?"

"I specialized in heatstrokes."

"Lucky for me," I mumbled. "Well, I gave it my best shot."

"That you did. Evidently, you even impressed Busby. He actually let us ice you down." Harry looked up and waved his arm in a semicircle to include the other eighteen men in the truck. "You guys didn't mind if Inger here used up all the ice and half our water, did you?" he asked.

The response was a jumbled chorus of laughing answers.

"Shit, no."

"Nice try."

"Tomorrow, let's carry the kid a little."

"Okay by me. He's got guts."

I started to get up but was gently pushed back.

"Stay where you are," James ordered. "Save your strength for tomorrow. You're going to be very sore in the morning. By the way, that guy up front is right. You're a gutsy little bastard."

As bad as I felt, the remainder of the trip back to camp was a joy ride. I had been accepted.

⛓⛓⛓⛓⛓

Crisp was close to yelling to be heard over the loud metallic clatter of a torrential downpour furiously pounding the barrack's tin roof.

"Sorry to wake ya!" he hollered. "But it's chow time and ya gotta eat."

"What time is it?" I asked, wiping the sleep from my eyes.

"It's time for dinner. Ya better hit the deck."

"I need to shower."

"Too late for that now. You slept through it. Everybody's done."

"Okay, screw it." I offered a weak smile. "I didn't put in a full day of sweat anyway,"

I rolled off my top bunk and sat with Crisp on his bottom one to lace up my high-top work shoes.

"I guess I've only been sleeping for about an hour or so, and I'm already stiff. Tough day."

"That's what I heard," said Crisp. "Heard ya done pretty damn good too."

"Coulda been better."

"Coulda been worse—coulda been a sunny day. We're the last ones outta here. Let's go and get us some of those good groceries before they're all gone."

"Don't they give out ponchos or something?" I asked

over a booming clap of thunder.

"Ya gotta be kidding."

"Okay, then, I'll take my shower now," I said, going for the door. "Let's hit it!"

"Better hit it slow, Clark," Crisp snapped quickly. "Ya don't want to get shot for running. Don't ever fuckin' run here, man."

We left the barracks, breaking through the sheet of water cascading over the eaves, and walked rapidly through the stinging rain across the flooded, muddy yard to the mess hall.

Tonight, it was navy beans and greens with small greasy chunks of fat back. The grub did not seem nearly as greasy as before and the residue on my plate was sopped up with slices of Wonder Bread. Dix had been right yesterday: Tonight this slop wasn't half bad, and my stomach was rumbling contentedly. I was feeling much better, in fact. Aside from the stiffness in my upper body and my blistered palms, I felt almost normal.

James fell in line behind us as we turned in our dinnerware and left the mess hall. The rain had stopped and the clouds were breaking up, showing patches of clear sky. We slogged through the quagmire of mud left by the storm over to one of the concrete tables in the yard. The benches were wet, but so were we, so we sat enjoying the built-in air conditioning of our soaked clothing as the late-afternoon sun appeared and the temperature began climbing.

Crisp punched James playfully on the arm. "Nice short day, huh?" he asked.

"Yes, and lucky for Clark," James replied. "How are your hands?" he asked me.

"Blistered," I answered, showing him.

"Not too bad. I'll tell you what to do to relieve 'em once they break and become raw meat."

"What?"

"You might not believe this, but it's an old chain-gang trick, and it works." He paused. "Piss on 'em."

"You're shittin' me."

"No, he ain't," Crisp said, waving his palms at me. "It's really true."

"You'll have pretty calluses on your hands soon enough," promised James.

"Worked for me," said Crisp. "Look at mine!"

"I'd rather have 'em on my butt," I said, laughing.

Crisp looked strangely at me.

"Not your hands on my butt! Calluses on my— fuck it, never mind."

Crisp and James fell off the bench laughing.

⛓⛓⛓⛓⛓

The second morning out with the gang began the same as the first. But once our yo-yos started swinging, I noticed a subtle difference. The two men on either side of me, whom I had yet to meet, were slashing into the edges of my space, making my workload a little lighter.

"Just keep the pace with your swing, kid," said the tall man to my front left, who was built like a linebacker. "We'll take up some slack for you along the way."

"You don't even know me," I said. "Why bother?"

The Mexican built like a fireplug to my right answered simply, "Why not?"

"Well, thanks," I responded. "After yesterday, I'm smart enough to know I can use all the help I can get."

"No thanks needed," said the linebacker.

"Well, thanks anyway," I said. "I owe ya."

"That's true," said the voice on the right.

"What's the catch?" I asked them. "What do I owe you guys?"

"Just one thing; no big deal," replied Linebacker.

"Yeah, it really ain't much, kid," said the Mexican. "Just keep that fuckin' yo-yo goin' and look like you're doin' your share, because this carryin' shit ain't allowed. Okay?"

"You got it," I said. "The yo-yo's swingin'. I still owe ya, though."

"You don't owe a damn thing, I'm tellin' ya," said Linebacker. "All we got in this shithole is each other, and the good guys got to stick together."

"That's it," the Mexican agreed. "Someday, I might need you to pick up my slack and by then you'll know what we're talkin' about. You'll do it, too. Seeing you fall out yesterday proved that. You're a fighter. You're one of the good guys. It's just flat in you. I been on the road long enough to figure that out just by watchin' people. Now let's all shut the hell up and put our energy into waltzing through this fuckin' day...together."

❄❄❄❄❄

Crisp and I were at a distinct disadvantage listening to Harry and James, sitting at what was becoming our group's usual after-dinner table in the yard. They were deeply involved in a serious discussion about the various talents of what sounded like a never-ending procession of the most beautiful women to have ever graced this planet. As we listened to them wax on about their sexual gymnastics and tumbling in and out of their beds, neither of us had any real experiences to add to the conversation. I thought about mentioning the prostitute Roy had sent over to the Chicago hotel but decided against it. I would privately remember her in my bunk tonight, after lights out.

"Those were the good old days," Harry said with a big grin.

"Good old nights, you mean," James corrected.

Harry tilted his head side to side. "Nights too, but a

99

lot of good old days."

"You mean office hours?" asked James. "Gynecology was your life, right, Doc?"

Crisp finally had something to say. "What's gyne...whatever?" he asked, looking at the two men rather dimly.

"Gynecology," Harry answered. "I was a gynecologist."

Crisp remained confused. He had no idea what Harry was talking about.

"It's a doctor," James informed him. "A pussy doctor."

"Oh," Crisp said, brightening considerably and looking at Harry with newfound respect. "That's neat," he added.

"Some were," Harry replied wryly. "Most weren't."

"A pussy doctor, huh?" I said. "Now I know what you meant when you told me that you specialized in heatstrokes. Sounds like you stayed in heat."

James doubled over in laughter and Crisp rolled off the bench holding his sides. Harry could barely contain himself, but he tried very hard to appear the detached, humorless physician of old, getting ready to deliver a punch line.

Then, suddenly, he was totally without humor. "The heat died when I walked through that fucking gate over there."

We all fell silent.

"But you didn't die," I finally said. "None of us did."

"That's true," Harry observed somberly. "Not even in this puke bucket." Slowly he broke into a wide smile. "You know, the wonderful thing about masturbation is that you never have to look your very best."

"That's for damn sure," Crisp said, taking Harry's comment seriously. "Not in here, anyways."

"You jerk-offs talking about jerking off?" Dix addressed the group. Not needing to be invited, he sat down.

"Subject for the day, unless you have something better to lay on us, old man," James replied.

"As a matter of fact, I do," Dix said. "Harry, Gang B is going to have two new men in the morning. One yo-yo, one shotgun."

There was no levity at the table now. Both Harry and James became so instantly rigid that I sensed this conversation had turned deadly serious.

"Let me guess," said Harry. "Huggins is riding shotgun?"

"Yes sir, that's half of it."

"Who's the other half?" Crisp asked.

"Shut up," James snapped. "Let these two talk."

My bunkmate was now as tense as the others, but for the wrong reason. James had hurt his feelings.

"Relax, Crisp," Harry soothed the pouting boy. "That was the next logical question." He turned back to Dix. "Who's the other half?" he asked.

"Johnny Johnson. From the brick plant to you."

Harry nodded. "So my second guess is—and you know damned well I'm right—Scruggs has decided, as he would say, that 'the boy's mind just ain't quite right. Lord knows I've tried.'" Harry frowned and shook his head. "And to tell the truth, he has. Johnson is as tough as he is mean. He just won't break—am I right?"

Dix looked at Harry sternly. "You know damned well that I don't have opinions, just a little information. That's all you're getting from me, okay?"

Harry held up his hands. "Okay. How did he fuck up this time?"

"He and that asshole Bunny O'Hara got into it on the truck coming in from the brick plant. They got tangled in their chains, and in the struggle, Johnson managed to loop one over O'Hara's neck. You know how popular Bunny is—every con on the truck was screaming for his blood and nobody made move one to break it up. The only thing that saved his ass was Deets' hearing the racket of the chains banging around on the metal truck bed. You can figure out the rest."

"O'Hara's in the box?"

"For a week."

"He got the better deal."

⛓⛓⛓⛓⛓

Johnson shuffled along in his shackles at the rear of the line as we boarded the truck. The last to embark, he sat across from James and me in the back, with his chin resting on his hands atop the end of his yo-yo's handle and his eyes cast downward. Other than Dix, Johnson had been the first inmate to speak to me in the camp, and at the time, he had seemed like a decent sort of fellow. He now had the look of a cornered rabid dog poised to attack.

After what happened with Bunny, Harry and James had both ordered me to stay as far away from Johnson as possible. When we'd lined up this morning and I saw his contemptuous stare locked on Huggins riding shotgun in the trailer, I knew why. This guy was bad news indeed.

I spotted the two men who had flanked me the previous day sitting up front talking with Harry. Harry caught my eye and motioned me forward.

"James, hold onto my favorite yo-yo for me, will you?" I explained that I was going up to talk to the guys who'd bailed me out yesterday.

James looked down the row and nodded. "That's Novak and Cabrera," he said, waving at them. "Take your time; they're a couple of the good guys."

The pair waved back at James and slid apart to make

102

room for me between them, facing Harry.

"Glad to meet 'cha," said the linebacker, after I got settled and formally introduced myself. "I'm Theo Novak."

"The pleasure's mine," I told him. "Hi, Theo."

I turned toward the Mexican.

"Cabrera, Pablo Cabrera," he said. "And don't ever call me Mex."

I smiled. From the looks of Cabrera, I was going to call him whatever he wanted me to call him. Physically, he was a lighter-complexioned twin to Leroy Tanner, gold teeth included, with a lyrical Mexican accent.

"Will Pablo work?" I asked.

"Yes," he said, and then chuckled. "I worked some for *you* yesterday."

I laughed. From this point on, I would also consider these two, good guys—very good guys.

I turned back toward Novak. Unlike Pablo, his build was similar to mine—with two exceptions: he appeared to be ten inches taller and made of solid granite.

"Hey, Harry," I asked. "How come, besides a couple of trustees, there's no fat guys in 33?"

Harry smiled, and without answering me, addressed the very good guys. "It won't take you boys long to understand that this kid is the camp's question man."

"Not a bad question, though," Novak said.

"Yeah, you used to be a doctor," Cabrera said. "*Por qué?*"

I nodded at my two new friends. "See there, *Doctor* Harry, I ask good questions!" I said. "So, why is it?"

Harry remained silent, as if searching for an answer simple enough for three dimwits to understand.

"Have you guys ever seen any of those photographs of prisoners in the Nazi concentration camps?"

"Yeah."

"Sure."

"Yep."

"Did any of you ever see a fat guy?"

"Nada."

"Nope."

"Never."

"There's your answer," said Harry. "Big work, little food. Except in our case, we're pretty well fed—nutritionally, at any rate." The three of us nodded as Harry warmed to his topic. "This is beside the point, but—overeating aside—the medical experts claim that fatness can be the result of genetics, glands, and a long list of other bullshit. Let's see them try explaining that to the guys in here. In my opinion, fat people in the free world should just sew their mouths shut. Speaking of mouths shut, this conversation is over. It's time to line 'em up."

The truck stopped, the shotguns took their positions, and the yo-yos started swinging. Another day, another day fewer.

⛓⛓⛓⛓⛓

"Roll 'em up!"

Busby called the mid-morning break. The gang dropped their yo-yos where they stood and walked over to where the water boy Dillan had set up his station, under a shady stand of water oaks on a large, slightly raised patch of ground, known in Florida as a hammock. The dehydrated work gang took dented tin cups from an orange crate and lined up for Dillon to ladle cool water into them. The men who smoked dipped into a shoebox filled with state tobacco, filled their folded cigarette papers, and then expertly began to "roll 'em up."

I gulped down my third cup of water and, as I'd been instructed by James, stopped at three and returned the cup to its crate. I walked back to my previous spot in the shady

104

hammock with James, Novak, and Cabrera.

"How're the hands doin'?" Novak asked me.

"Better than yesterday," I replied, showing him my raw palms.

"Don't look so hot to me," Cabrera said. "What do you think, James?"

"Let me see those things, Clark," James demanded.

When he was satisfied with his inspection, James looked around, making certain the bosses would not see him. Then he reached into his shirt pocket and removed a thin packet of something wrapped in toilet paper. He slid it across the ground to Novak, who passed it on to me. I rose slightly and sat on it.

"What is this?" I asked.

"Contraband. Dix stole it from the office first-aid kit last night and palmed it to me this morning when we checked out at headcount."

"What the hell is it?"

"One-inch-wide waterproof Band-Aids. Need I say more?"

I looked him in the eyes and nodded my understanding.

James had taken a risk in doing this, and I was not going to put him or myself in jeopardy by chancing discovery—by anyone; this was nobody's business but our own.

I needed a moment of privacy to pull off my illegal Band-Aid caper. I could think of only one way to move away from the men around us, turn my back, and not be seen by them or the guards.

I stood and yelled over to Busby: "Diggin' a hole, Boss!"

He nodded.

I walked a few yards away, dug a hole, dropped my pants, and squatted. I covered my broken blisters with the

105

Band-Aids and then buried the empty wrappers in the hole. I returned to our group with my fists balled to prevent exposure.

When the break ended and the work began, I felt like a new man. To the surprise of my sidemen Novak and Cabrera, I managed to do most of my share and still keep pace with them. It was nearing lunch break and with another hour's rest, I felt confident of finishing the day's work on my feet. Thanks to my friends, I was not going to be dropping this day.

Wrong.

❄❄❄❄❄

"HIT IT!"

I catapulted my body forward in a flat dive, crashing headfirst through tall weeds, and smashed my face to the ground. The split-second-later roar of shotgun blasts drove my face even deeper into the dirt.

But most terrifying was what followed: An absolute absence of sound. The void seemed to hang over me forever.

Huggins' voice broke the silence with a single word: "Clear," he said, speaking calmly over the *chick-chack* of another round jacking into the chamber of his still-smoking twelve-gauge. He had no need to yell again.

"Get your fuckin' asses up!" Busby practically screamed. "Everybody on the truck, right fuckin' now!"

I pushed up to my shaking knees, hoping my legs would hold me erect as I stood and unsteadily turned for the truck. That's when I saw Johnson.

He was lying on his right hip and his left shoulder, twisted in gore. Two loads of double-aught buckshot had nearly torn him in half, spilling his white guts over the ground in a widening pool of dirty blood. His eyes were riveted on Huggins, spewing raw hate. Then he gurgled, twitched once, and the hate faded to peace.

Somebody grabbed my arm, violently jerking me and my frozen feet in the direction of the truck. Cabrera was as strong as he looked.

"*Vamanos, chico.* Get your draggin' ass in gear."

"You got it, Pablo," I told him. "I'm with ya, but you're tearin' my arm off."

Evidently I was not the only shocked slow-mover in the group. Cabrera and I were climbing aboard the truck before most of the men in the gang arrived. Harry herded the stragglers along like a sheepdog and was the last to swing up onto the flatbed.

Huggins was leaning on the trailer, loading shells into the tube of his shotgun with his mirrored Ray-Bans facing us, reflecting nothing but a blank glow. Then, taking control, he calmly started barking orders.

"Busby, go up front and radio the captain. Tell 'im exactly where we are and that it's time to call in the troops. No hurry on the ambulance. Dillon, go fetch those roach buckets and feed this fuckin' gang where they're sittin'. Do it now!"

Once Busby was radioing from the cab and the water boy was fifty yards away gathering up food containers, Huggins walked to the rear edge of the flatbed and leveled his weapon. He was grinning.

"Any of you assholes see anything besides a fuckin' runner?"

No one said a word.

"Good. Very fuckin' good. For once, no answer is the smart answer."

The troops, as Huggins had called them, rolled in within minutes and we sat on the truck for over an hour, surrounded by four Jackson County sheriffs, two highway patrolmen, and two unmarked cars. It was a crowded lot of flashing red lights.

Lunch was a disaster. The ambulance must have taken the "no hurry" advice to heart, so Johnson's body still lay there, oozing under a cloud of buzzing flies. His shackles had been removed.

We rode back to the camp in silence, with Huggins' twin mirrors trailing behind, shielding the eyes of a cold-blooded killer holding a twelve-gauge and the power to wantonly blow men in half. I wondered if I was any better than he was.

⛓⛓⛓⛓⛓

"Fuck it, life goes on."
"Not for Johnson, it don't."
"Remember Wallace?"
"Another guy runnin' his ass off in chains."
"Yeah, right. Aimed for his legs."
"And blew off his fuckin' *cabeza*."

And so the after-dinner conversations went in the camp that evening—caged men at the mercy of sadistic, subhuman pigs, discussing their own possible fates and convincing themselves that it would always be someone else's. It was mental masturbation for survival, geared to the ridiculous. We were all vulnerable, every single one of us.

I had always thought of myself as bulletproof; but that afternoon, watching Johnson's guts spill out, I realized my own mortality. It was a frightening concept and one I decided not to accept.

Fuck it, I told myself. *Life goes on. At least, mine will.*

My final initiation into life on the road was complete. I, too, was now a master of denial.

⛓⛓⛓⛓⛓

"You look tired, Clark. How are they treating you here?"

"Fine, Mom. I just didn't sleep very well last night—I was excited about seeing you today. You look terrific."

"Well, you don't. I think I'll talk to that Major...what's his name? Scruggs?"

I thought fast. "Ummm...that wouldn't be such a great idea, Mom. Don't get me wrong, now—I'm sure he'd listen to you; but I don't want to get any special treatment here. The other guys might resent it and I really want to get along with them. You know; it's kind of a guy thing. I don't want to be any different from the rest of the inmates. I'm fine. Forget about talking to Captain Scruggs, will you, please?"

"Oh, you men and your machismo. All right. If you insist, I won't make things any easier for you. I will not speak with Mister Scruggs. Although, in spite of his horrible grammar, he seems very nice."

I could not believe she'd just said that, but I smiled my way through it. I smiled my way through the rest of our two-hour visitation and when she finally left, I was glad to see her go. Deceiving myself was one thing, but lying to my mother was intolerable.

⛓⛓⛓⛓⛓

The weeks dragged on and so did I.

But not when it came to work. That was my only release and I attacked it with a vengeance. The tools of the camp turned into weapons in a competition for the survival of the human spirit in an inhumane arena. Being able to work the man next to me into the ground was a great source of pride, and now, if challenged, I could do it with the best of them.

If a good guy in the gang began to weaken, I would position myself next to him and carry part of his load. It had been done for me and I would do it for him. Novak and Cabrera had saved me from extinction and I would never forget that. The good guys in the gang worked together; we had to. Hard time was the alternative.

CHAPTER 6
THE GRUBBIN' HOE BOOGIE

For the past three weeks, we'd worked along the shoulders of Highway 69, swinging our yo-yos, whacking down weeds between Dellwood and Two Egg. Now that working vacation was over.

Today, instead of yo-yos, we had each been issued a mattock. This tool had a heavy steel-headed, hoe-like blade set at a right angle on the end of an axe handle. The idea was to swing it in a downward arc with enough force to dig the blade into the earth and then pull it back up, turning hard ground into hard clods. This backbreaking device was lovingly referred to in chain-gang parlance as a grubbin' hoe.

In spite of the hated grubbin' hoe held in each man's hands, the bouncing flatbed was a happy place to be sitting this October's early autumn morning. The next best thing to being rained out was cooler weather, and the temperature had dropped dramatically during the night, dipping into the low fifties. At headcount, Dix had issued coarse flannel-lined denim jackets to the gang, and we were delighted to get them.

Dawn was coming later now, and traveling through the welcome chilly darkness, I missed watching the waking free world pass by.

"Hey, Harry," I said. "I can't see a damn thing out there. Where are we going today?"

"The river."

"Shit, the Apalachicola," James lamented. "We're in for good weather and hard clay to screw it up. I hate workin' that damn—"

"You hate workin' that damn anytheeng, *cabrón,*" Cabrera interrupted.

"Fuck you, Pablo," James countered. "The only thing you like workin' on is your dick."

Novak laughed. "Nah, that used to be true," he said, "but it ain't no more. He's wore it down to a nub and now he can't even find the little bitty 'theeng.' Right, Pablo?"

"It's beeg enough to find your smart mouth, Theo," Pablo whispered through a dangerously thin smile.

I had been around Cabrera long enough by now to know his hot buttons. Putting down his Latino manhood was not a wise move. A little jailhouse tact was definitely in order here.

"Who's the new guy up there taking Smith's place?" I asked, quickly changing the subject.

"Name's Grundy" was Harry's reply. "Ed, I think. They shipped him in last night from Camp 17 over in Live Oak."

"Sounds like a demotion to me," I said. "Why'd he end up here?"

"I don't know yet, but we'll find out tonight. Dix knows everything."

The truck slowed and then squealed to a stop at the edge of the river. Harry was first off the flatbed, and as the gang hopped off after him, he called Novak and Cabrera aside.

"As usual, I want you two to work beside this new guy today. You know the drill."

"Ya got it," Novak said. Then he looked over at me with an impish grin and said, "You know what, Clark? If it's okay with our row leader here, maybe you'd like to take my place for a while. I'm gettin' to be a short-timer now, and you're the only guy I know dumb enough to put up with Pablo once I'm outta here. It's time ya did somethin' worthwhile anyway. What d'ya say, Doc Harry. Good idea?"

Harry thought it over before making a decision. Finally he nodded. "That's fine with me, but it's up to you, kid. What d'ya say?"

"Sure, I'll work with the new guy," I agreed. "I'm just not too sure about Pablo," I joked.

"All right then," said Harry. "That's settled. Theo, you work with me for a—"

"Conlin!" Busby started yelling. "What the fuck's goin' on over there? Get these motherfuckers to work or I will."

"Okay, Boss," Harry hollered back. "Linin' 'em up now."

When working with hoes, we stood side by side, each man responsible for six blade-widths in front of him, a path three feet wide. We dug from left to right, keeping our swinging blades from crashing into the next man's. Backbreaking labor was encouraged, but the state had no tolerance for breaking tools.

When Harry had the line set the way he wanted, he yelled over to Busby again. "Ready to grub, Boss."

"It's about goddamn time, Conlin. Let's get it goin', you sorry buncha bastards. From now on, I don't want to be seein' nothin' but fuckin' assholes and elbows."

Busby, you moron, I thought, as the line of men started forward, *you don't know the difference between your elbow and your asshole.*

⬖⬖⬖⬖⬖

Harry and Dix were perhaps the only men in the camp, including the staff, possessed of anything beyond a high school education. They were the leaders of the camp's limited intelligentsia. The four of us—Harry, James, Dix, and fortunately, myself—sat at our usual table in the yard along

113

with our adopted mascot, Crisp.

The topic under discussion this evening was, by chain-gang standards, deeply philosophical in its search for the subject's meaning in our lives.

"Why was Grundy transferred here, Dix?" I asked.

"Well," Dix told me, "you may find this quite amusing." He looked around the group. "So will the rest of you. He is here, believe this or not, for his own protection."

This revelation prompted some chuckling around the table. But strangely enough, Crisp was the only one who found this incredible irony funny to the point of hysteria.

"Yeah, sure, Dix," he gasped, wiping away tears of laughter streaming down his downy cheeks. "That's a good one. So was Johnson, right?"

That brought the house down. If nothing else, the slow, good-natured boy was a constant source of comic relief.

"You're not joking, though, are you, Dix?" James asked seriously.

"No, I'm not. Two hard-asses in 17 came close to slitting his throat in the shower. I heard that if not them, it would be someone else, sooner rather than later. He seems to be a very unpopular character. How did he do today, Doc Harry?"

"I really don't know," Harry replied. "It hasn't been discussed. What about it, Clark? You worked next to Grundy. What was your impression of him?"

"The same as Pablo's," I told him. "We talked about it on the way in." I straightened. "He's one of the bad guys, and before you ask, I'll tell you why: Cabrera says the work in 17 is the same as here in 33. The guy's been on the road for a while and knows how to swing a hoe, that's for sure, but he said he couldn't keep up and do his share of the row. He kept whining to both of us that he wasn't up to it yet and would we carry him for a while. You know Pablo. He's a good guy and wanted to help. I'm new at this shit, so I went along with him. At least until a few minutes before we knocked it off for the day."

"What happened then?"

"Nothing happened; just something I noticed. The son of a bitch had barely worked up a sweat. He's a loafer. In my opinion, that makes him a bad guy."

James nodded. "Sounds like you're right."

"Did you say anything to him?" Dix asked me.

"Not yet!"

"Well, don't," Harry said quickly. "That would not be smart. Want to know what I'd do?"

"Hell, yes, Harry," I said. "Like I said before, I'm new at all this shit."

Harry nodded. "Okay, how does this sound, then? You and Cabrera work beside this jerk-off again, only don't pick up his anything. Fuck him; he can keep up or fall behind. If he drops back, let Busby handle it, and you can bet your sweet ass he will. Right then and there."

"Harry knows what he's talking about, kid," Dix said. "It's good advice."

James agreed and then added, "I'll tell Pablo the same thing, and I'll work next to Clark tomorrow, just in case."

"Good idea," said Harry. "Do it." And then breaking into a fatherly smile, he turned to the silent Crisp. "You've been awfully quiet over there, Crispy Bacon. What's your considered opinion?"

"Oh...that's a real neat idea," Crisp replied, and then brightening, asked, "Hey, do you guys know why they're called grubbin' hoes?"

We all said no. "Why are they called grubbin' hoes?" we asked.

"The coloreds started callin' 'em that," Crisp explained. "It means a greedy workin' whore."

115

Our nightly roundtable adjourned in roaring laughter.

⬡⬡⬡⬡⬡

The day began bright, clear, and cool. We were taking our positions in the line when Pablo tapped Grundy on the shoulder.

"Good morning, Grundy."

"What d'ya want, taco-bender?"

Amazingly, Pablo remained placid.

"I just want to be helpful here," he said. "Can I see your hands, *por favor?*"

"Let's get this straight, right goddamn now," Grundy snarled. "I don't need no help from any of ya, 'specially you, ya fuckin' pepperbelly. I ain't showin' ya shit, spick."

I was moving around Grundy before he finished his last sentence. I grabbed Pablo and pushed him away before he could attack. James now held him back as well, trying to do the impossible: calm Pablo down.

Busby and Waters, the shotgun, were watching all this, grinning in anticipation of a good fight. They loved it and seldom interrupted, unless weapons were involved or the fight was a cover for something else.

"You fuckers gonna get it on or we gonna go to work?" Busby shouted.

"Just horsin' around with the new guy, Boss," I yelled back.

Grundy just stood there sneering with his thumbs hooked in his belt. "Told ya I don't need no fuckin' help, asshole," he said to me. "Butt out or I'll waste you and that fuckin' beaner."

I tilted my head. "Well, since you put it to me that way, let me put it to you this way."

It appeared that I simply dropped my hoe, but the

steel head slammed down on his foot, doubling Grundy over, so he was gasping through the pain. I drove one knee into his groin and smashed my right fist into the back of his neck as he fell face-first to the ground. I kicked him in the stomach, flipping him to his back.

"Here you go, Pablo," I said, holding up two limp hands. "Have a good look."

Pablo came over. "Just as I thought," he said. "He's got more calluses than I do."

Pablo's inspection was interrupted by Busby's screaming.

"Inger! Let go of 'im. That's it!"

"Yes, sir, Boss. That's it."

"You and James—drag his ass over to Waters," Busby yelled.

"We're draggin', Boss," James said.

We did as we were ordered.

"Leave him lay right there," Busby commanded. "James, get back in the line. Inger, get your ass over here!"

"I'm comin', Boss."

"Inger," he said, scowling, "you are truly a big disappointment."

A disappointment? What the... "Boss, can I—"

"No! None of your fuckin' questions. You are no goddamned fun at all. That sure as hell wasn't much of a fight. Next time pick on somebody bigger'n you. Now haul your disappointing ass back over there and get to work."

"Yes, Boss," I said, with a sigh of great relief.

As I turned to leave, Busby gruffly added, "And if I was you, Inger, I'd wipe that shit-eatin' grin off your sorry face, unless ya want to meet up with the box."

I complied immediately.

I returned to my place between two rather grim-looking friends. Harry motioned for the right side of the line to move in a space, filling Grundy's empty spot, then he

117

looked down the line and caught my eye. He dropped his gaze and unhappily swayed his head from side to side before waving us forward.

At the same moment, Busby screamed:

"HOLD IT!"

The hoes froze mid-stroke and Dillon, the water boy, dove to the ground, thinking he'd heard the dreaded cry, "Hit it!"

Any tension in the gang this morning evaporated into gales of laughter.

Busby was not amused.

"Goddammit, you stinking, rotten, dirty, motherfuckin', sons-of-bitchin' bastards. You...you damn...damn..."

Now, no one was amused.

Busby seemed to have absolutely no idea why he had shouted out the order "Hold it." His dull mind was frantically searching for something to scream, but no words came out of his gaping jaw.

Then Busby began to twitch around like a man being electrocuted. Spittle drooled down his chin and veins popped out on his forehead like mole trails. His fat face looked like a huge blood clot about to pop. This lethally-armed psychopath was going to explode.

No one uttered a sound. No one. A long, frightening silence hung in the air for what seemed like an eternity.

Then it happened.

Pablo desperately tried to contain himself by snickering through his nose, but when a snort emerged, he fell into a contagious laughter that spread uncontrollably through the gang like a deadly virus.

Busby had completely lost control of himself and the men. He stood there like a big red-faced rock, dangerously teetering on the edge of a precipice. The single most alarming thing about his inaction was the growing fear of what this dangerous psychopath might do when he did make his move to restore command.

The deafening roar of Waters' twelve-gauge firing into the air tipped Busby over the edge. Down he went. And when he hit the dirt, the twitching stopped.

Waters instantly took control of a very bad situation. He reacted calmly and began snapping out orders in a surprisingly normal tone of voice.

"Anybody moves, I shoot 'em! Conlin, see what you can do for Boss Busby. Dillon, you know how to work the radio; get on it. Call the camp, talk to whoever answers, and tell 'em to get an ambulance out here—right now. The rest of you, relax and sit down where you're standing."

Harry was kneeling next to Busby, who was trying to lift one hand to his shirt pocket. His mouth was moving slightly, so Harry leaned close and put his ear to Busby's lips. Then he held the fallen man's hand tightly as he reached over with his other hand and held his fingers on Busby's neck for a full minute, feeling for a pulse.

Harry shook his head and stood, looking at Waters.

"He's dead, Boss."

"Heart?"

"I think so, Boss. It's hard to tell without a medical kit. And, Boss, if it makes you feel any better, he didn't suffer. I never got a pulse; he died a few seconds after hitting the ground."

"Thanks, Conlin. Get the roach buckets. We're done for the day."

When Harry reached the food containers, I noticed him dig his toe into the dirt and drop something into the depression. As he picked up the food, he dragged one foot to cover the shallow hole and then turned on his heel to bring the gang's early lunch.

The object Harry had buried was what I had seen Busby reaching for in his shirt pocket: a small dark-brown pill bottle.

Lunch was served within a few yards of Busby's whitening corpse; for the second time in a month, I lunched with a murdered man. This time I cleaned my plate.

The camp was strangely quiet that workday afternoon. The other gangs would not return for several hours and the bunch from Gang B welcomed the day's break. The men were doing what we usually did on weekends: relaxing and enjoying the cool, sunny day.

Other than our mascot, Crisp, who was still out with Gang A, the roundtable group was gathered in our usual spot, joined by Cabrera and Novak, talking over the events of the morning.

"I never thought I'd see the day when Busby would give us an afternoon off," Pablo said, laughing.

"And the motherfucker couldn't have picked a better way to do it either," Theo cheerfully added.

"Well," I said, "I oughta get a little credit for getting things started."

"You shouldn't have done it," Harry said.

"You mean gettin' Busby started," I asked, "or Grundy?"

"Fuck Busby. I'm talking about Grundy."

"Well, I did do it. Screw Grundy. And I wish you'd stop shaking your head like that every time you look at me. Get over it."

"I'll get over it," he said, "but it isn't over."

"You mean it isn't over with Grundy?" I asked. "Or for you?"

Harry looked at me intently. "I just said I'd get over it. Just what the hell do you mean by *that* crack?"

Harry's eyes gave him away. He knew exactly what I

120

meant.

"Nothing," I answered carefully. "At least I didn't kill the man."

"Grundy really pushed it," James interjected in my defense. "Clark just did what Pablo was about to, except that I was holding him back. Right, Pablo?"

"*Es verdad,*" Pablo agreed. "Only I *would* have keelled heem. He was begging for it. That *pinche cabrón* has got one bad mouth."

"That's not all he's got, boys," Dix said. "Remember I told you he almost got his throat cut? I just heard why it was 'almost.' He kicked the shit out of those two guys—took their shanks away from them and stuck both of them. And they weren't what you'd call easy money, either. The captain in 17 told Scruggs to watch him. In the war, he was a commando; he got medals for killing a dozen Germans behind enemy lines with his bare hands. He's homicidal and bad to the bone. Harry's right, Clark: watch your back."

Still looking at Harry, I warned, "Don't say 'I told you so.'"

Harry was staring straight through me, his eyes narrow, probing slits. He nodded again, only this time slowly, up and down, up and down.

"I've always thought you were one of the good guys, kid, so I won't say anything at all. You'd do the same for me, wouldn't you?" he asked meaningfully.

"You can count on it." It was my turn to nod.

ⴲⴲⴲⴲⴲ

We rolled along through the morning darkness, checking out our new shotgun who trailed behind in the glow of the taillights. Scruggs had promoted Waters to walkin' boss, and everyone agreed that we could have done a lot worse.

121

We started the day where we'd left off yesterday. Harry stood next to James, about to line us up, when he stopped. He nodded to Pablo and me and flashed his eyes to my right. I stood between Cabrera and a grinning Grundy.

"Clark," Pablo uttered softly, "change places with me."

"Chickenshit?" Grundy whispered to me.

"I like it here, Pablo."

Harry waited a few seconds before reluctantly signaling the line to start moving. I wished to God he would stop shaking his head at me.

When a man is working with a grubbin' hoe, it is next to impossible to complete a sentence without gasping during the downswing. Grundy was the first to speak, and working the hoe did not seem to bother him in the least.

"Inger, ain't it?"

"That's right."

"You know I can't let this go."

"Wish you would."

"Can't. Gotta get 'cha outta the way, so's I can go butt-fuck your ugly, two-bit whorin' mama."

"You're pushin' it, Grundy," I said, fighting to keep my breathing even. "Let's just fuckin' drop it."

"Only thing I'm droppin' is you, cocksucker. How 'bout at roll-'em-up break? And without that fuckin' hoe in your hands."

"You got it, asshole."

"There's a good little girl," he sneered. "I want everybody to see this. Then later on tonight, after lights out in the barracks, I wanna have everybody in this fuckin' camp watch you eat my cock."

"Fuck you, Grungy."

The deal was done. Grundy had gotten what he wanted so there was no need for any more of his jailhouse taunting. We worked on silently, side by side and stroke for

122

stroke, neither of us breaking a sweat.

Waters might call the break any minute now and I knew very well that this trained assassin was perfectly capable of killing me and still not break a sweat. In the joint, respect is survival—but in this case, my surviving Grundy was the name of the game. I had no choice.

Our hoes kept swinging in unison, digging deeply into hard red clay.

Swing, thunk, pull. Swing, thunk, pull. Swing, THUNK!

Grundy shrieked in horrible agony, clutching at his right hand and falling on his splintered hoe handle. Blood spurted into the air in great pulsating streams from where his right thumb used to be. He rolled over and over, his eyes glazed in shock as he hysterically screamed for help.

"Gonna have everybody watch me eat you, huh? Watch this, Grungy."

I picked up his severed twitching thumb and shoved the gory thing into his gaping mouth.

"Eat this, cocksucker."

<hr />

Dix was checking in the crew, counting heads at the gate. When he got to me, he stopped.

"Clark, go to the office. The captain wants to see you. I'll be along in a minute."

"Dix, what's he—"

"Just get your ass over there. I'll see you when I'm finished here."

"Okay. Cool down, will ya?"

"Oh, I'm cool. Go."

I went.

The office was empty, so I sat next to Dix's desk, hoping he'd return before Scruggs got here. I knew that if given the opportunity, Dix would at least prepare me for what was coming.

The screen door flew open and before the spring hinge had started pulling it shut, Dix was talking and he was talking fast.

"Scruggs left his house and he's on the way now. When he gets here, I'm gone, so listen up. It's pretty bad, but I think it could be a lot worse. Here's what I know: Scruggs can't take any more heat from Tallahassee over camp fatalities, and Grundy was a killing just waiting to happen. What might save you from some really deep shit is the fact that Grundy's on his way back to Raiford and I saw Scruggs laughing for the first time in a couple of years. Today he's a very damned happy captain. That's it. Here he comes. Stand up!"

Dix put his head down and was pecking away on the old Royal as Scruggs came striding through the door.

"Dixon, leave us alone."

"Yes, Captain. I'm leaving," he said. Dix was out the door as quickly as he had entered.

"Inger," Scruggs began, "it seems ya just ain't real accurate with a grubbin' hoe. Ya do Grundy on purpose?"

"No, Captain," I said solemnly. "It slipped."

The faintest hint of a smile tugged at the corners of Scruggs' thin lips, but it was replaced instantly by a cold, unwavering stare. He walked to the corner desk and sat down behind it, now staring at me from across the room without expression. Several very long seconds passed before he spoke.

"Inger, step over here."

"I'm steppin', Captain."

When I was standing before him, he leaned back in his chair and put his feet up on the desk.

"I think you're lyin' to me, boy," he said. "But lucky for you, today I'm in a real good mood and I ain't gonna press it."

I sighed internally but didn't respond.

"So, now, just for the hell of it, let's you and me play like you was tellin' the truth. *If* ya was tellin' the truth," he went on, "ya ain't got no fuckin' business with a grubbin' hoe in your slippery hands. Makes ya a danger to everybody 'round ya. Ain't that right, boy?"

"Guess so, Captain."

"You guess? I guess ya just don't listen real fuckin' good, boy. I think yer mind is not only not right; it's weak. I'll ask ya one more goddamn time, Inger. Ya got any business with a hoe in your hands?"

"No, Captain," I replied quickly, before my throat completely constricted with a cold, growing fear. I was going to the box.

"Now your weak little mind is gettin' it, boy," he said. "No more grubbin' hoes for you, no siree. No more yo-yos, no more shovels, no more nothin' like that. From now on, you ain't gonna have to deal with none of that kinda dangerous tool shit no more. Startin' tomorrow, you're gonna start lovin' bricks."

Shit. The brick plant.

"Now get your sorry thumb-hackin' ass outta my face."

⛓⛓⛓⛓⛓

Harry's head-shaking was becoming a real irritation. The man had lost any right to pass judgment on me, so now I resented it.

We left the mess hall together and as we walked toward our table, I saw him cutting sideways glances at me, resigned disappointment on his sad face, his head once again moving from side to side. I considered asking him if he was coming down with some sort of nervous disorder, but I

125

decided against it. This was not the time for humor.

"Harry, I need to talk to you," I said seriously, "and it's not about the Grundy thing. It's personal. Can we talk somewhere in private?"

Harry was no fool. He sensed immediately my change in tone. His shaking head reluctantly changed directions and nodded up and down in the affirmative.

"Sure," he said. "Let's go over by that corner tower. Nobody likes sitting under a damned Winchester; it's a good place to not be bothered."

Careful not to step over the white line into the ten-foot killing zone between us and the fence, we sat down cross-legged, facing each other.

"What's bothering you, kid?"

I sighed. "I don't know for sure. Well, yeah I do. I just don't know what's goin' on in my head anymore," I told him honestly. "I've never felt like this before in my life. I'm tired, Harry—very fuckin' tired of fightin' everything. I feel like I'm about to give up."

Harry looked at me sternly. "You're a smart kid, Inger, and you know damned well by now that you can't do that, not in here." He paused. "Well, not in your head, at any rate. If you let them kill the mind, you let them kill you."

"Johnson didn't give up," I countered. "He never stopped fightin' back, and look at what happened to him. He's as dead as you can get."

"True," said Harry, "but that's 'cause he was fighting the wrong fight."

"What the hell do you mean the wrong fight?" I cried. "It's all a damn fight! A fight for survival. Well, I'm sick of it, all of it."

"Aren't we all?" Harry said. "But that doesn't mean you have to quit. Now, I'm gonna explain something and, please, don't just hear me. *Listen* to me for a minute, will you?"

126

"That's why I'm talkin' to you now, Harry," I said. "I respect your opinions. I'm smart enough to know I need some help here, and I'll listen. Go ahead—I won't even interrupt you."

He laughed. "That'll be refreshing."

His smile faded and he went on, speaking slowly and deliberately. "When I said Johnson was fighting the wrong fight, that's exactly what I meant. And I'm not talking about something like your hacking off Grundy's thumb. Forget about that; what's done is done. That's all beside the point now anyway. Johnson was fighting the system—not a person— and he was never going to win, ever, because he went about it the wrong way. He was openly defiant, begging to be broken, and that's what he got—simple as that."

Harry removed his glasses and took a moment to polish the lenses with his shirttail. Then he went on.

"Now, I'm not for one minute suggesting that you quit fighting, as I said before. Do that and you're dead. The war can be won, but the only single way to defeat the bastards is to go along with them, go with the flow. These imbeciles live to break the human spirit and win the war for your mind. Make them think what they love to believe, that you 'got your mind right.' Give a little, get a lot. Outwardly, you seem to lose the battle, while inwardly, you ultimately win the war. Does that make sense to you?"

I nodded. "It makes a lot of sense," I replied. "But if...wait a minute. If you really believe what you just said about not fighting the system, going with the flow and all that, weren't you fighting that same system the other day when I stood there and watched you let Busby die? Hell, Harry, you killed the son of a bitch."

Harry did not answer and I assumed he wasn't about to. His only reaction was to sit there frowning at the ground for a full minute. Then he let out a long sigh and looked up at me with a solemn expression that could not mask the glint in his eyes.

"I believe what I said and I know it's true," he told me, with a hint of a smile. "But for every rule, there exists the occasional exception. What happened with Busby was one of those rare exceptions."

I stared at him. "What was the exception?"

"This time I could get away with it."

Now Harry was grinning sheepishly, like a guilty child caught doing something evil to a bug.

"You were a doctor, Harry," I argued. "I thought you were supposed to save lives, not take them. What happened to your hypocritical oath?"

"Ha!" Harry doubled over in hysterical laughter as I sat there dumbfounded. "That's a great question," he finally managed to reply. "That is absolutely the greatest, most ironic question ever!"

"What's so damned funny, Harry?" I demanded. "Did I say something stupid?"

"No, Clark," Harry assured me, gathering himself together. "You didn't say anything stupid, just ignorant." He put his glasses back on. "You just hit a nerve with an accidental truth."

"What do you mean, Harry," I asked.

"When I was in practice," he explained, "I took a few unborn lives, performing what I determined were necessary, but illegal, abortions. When they threw my ass in jail for it, losing my freedom for ten years was bad enough; but when the American Medical Association revoked my license for life, my Hippocratic oath, as it's actually called, went down the toilet, along with everything else. With few exceptions, the only life I give a shit about now is my own. So, fuck Busby. Chalk one up for the cons for a change. He was lucky he lived at all. I was just a little bit late in aborting that sadistic, inbred idiot."

I was listening intently to Harry, as asked, and what

I'd just heard shocked me into understanding a new, hard reality. The Busbys of our caged corner of the world may not have succeeded in "getting Harry's mind right"; however, they had seriously twisted it, bending it down to their own level of justified inhumanity.

What I feared growing in myself I now saw manifested in Harry. He had come to be the same as the brutal bosses he despised. In fact, he was worse. He had once known better. And now it was Harry who was the real loser; he had no idea that he had been defeated in his own bitter war.

There was nothing more for me to ask of Harry now, and if there were, I would not. From this point on, I would answer my own questions. The word "Hippocratic" was in the dictionary.

"I want to thank you for being so honest and for trusting me," I said gratefully. "And most of all, for the good advice. I'll follow it."

"I'm happy to hear that," he said. "I hope you've learned something from it."

"I've learned more today than you'll ever know."

CHAPTER 7
THE BEST OF THE WORST

October 1952

South Georgia red clay washes down the Flint and Chattahoochee Rivers, which merge at the Florida State Line, forming Lake Seminole, and then flows into North Florida down the Apalachicola, turning the riverbanks into the mud source for the dark-red bricks used to construct virtually every major state building in Florida.

This raw material, along with coal, was trucked in by outside contractors and dumped at the brick plant, creating two never-ending piles, one red and the other black.

The plant was a twenty-four-hour-a-day operation. A four-trustee night crew was assigned two basic duties: one using the red mud and the other, the black coal.

The crew attacked the red pile by tossing shovelfuls into wheelbarrows and dumping them into a mixer. The proper amount of water was added and thick mud churned out, delivering a long rectangular stream onto a conveyor belt, where it was cut by wires into raw bricks, twice the size of the final product.

The belt ended at a narrow-gauge track, lined with old mining-car chassis mounted with double-decked steel racks. The raw bricks were stacked onto the racks, spaced like a house of mud cards. When the racks filled, the cars were pushed by hand down the track and then switched into the entrance of one of four dryers.

The dryers were long, narrow brick tunnels in a single low structure with a five-foot ceiling, just high enough to clear the mud stacked on the top rack of the cars. When the tunnels were each filled with a line of eight cars, the entrances and exits were covered with thick asbestos curtains, sealing the dryers from the outside.

The black pile was reduced by shoveling coal into a large hopper wheelbarrow mounted on dual-spoke wheels and unloading it into fireboxes: four for the dryers and a group of smaller ones that heated four large kilns. The bricks spent their first forty-eight hours curing in the dryers and then graduated to the kilns for firing.

The trustees stoked the fireboxes throughout the night while large fans blew their heat into the kilns and through the sealed tunnels to the dryers. By morning, the dryers had done their job, shrinking the mud blocks by a third into brittle, unfired bricks, all neatly stacked on the rows of cars, waiting in searing-hot total darkness for the brick gang's day to begin.

⊟⊟⊟⊟⊟

"Clark, remember what I told you. See you after mess tonight."

"Okay, Dix, see ya later."

I checked out at the gate for the morning work detail's headcount and fell in at the end of the line, behind the chained Bunny O'Hara, who shot me a mischievous wink with his green eyes. I followed the shuffling man, chains clanking, thinking how strange it felt to be going to work without a yo-yo or grubbin' hoe in my hand, when I heard my name called.

"Inger, step over here."

"Steppin', Boss."

"I'm Boss Deets. Shotgun's Boss Pogue." I looked over to see Pogue—six feet, seven inches of chiseled stone with a white-blond flattop, standing ramrod straight. "I hear

131

you're a good worker," Deets went on. "You're gonna show me that, ain't ya, Inger?"

"Yes, Boss."

"Get on the truck."

"Gettin' on, Boss."

O'Hara and I were the last to climb aboard and sat across from each other at the rear of the flatbed. Pogue lifted the staked tailgate, dropped the pins in place, and took his seat on the two-wheeled shotgun trailer, cradling his twelve-gauge in the general direction of O'Hara, who seemed to smile directly into the black hole of the muzzle.

What Dix had reminded me at checkout would not be forgotten. Seeing O'Hara smile contemptuously down the barrel of a twelve-gauge was proof enough for me that Dix was correct in his assessment: This guy was crazy dangerous. However, if I didn't know how nuts he was, I would say his melodious Northern Irish accent was almost seductive.

"Top o' the mornin' to ya, O'Hara," I said.

The sardonic smile shifted to me, softening with mild amusement.

"That's the worst Irish I've ever heard, Inger," he said, running his fingers through his black hair. "But since you gave it such a bad shot, and I dearly love bad shots, call me Bunny."

"All right. Bunny it is," I said, laughing genuinely at the "bad shot" pun.

"Then I'll drop the Inger," he replied. "Clark, ain't it?"

"Yes."

"Allow me to formally introduce you to the rest of this elite group. Hey, boys!" he yelled forward. "Meet the newest member of the brick gang. Clark's the name."

I was acknowledged by everyone on the truck with a wave, smile, or simple nod of welcome. Perhaps this gang was not going to be as bad as I'd thought.

"Hi, guys," I responded, rising slightly with a shallow bow. "Wish I could say I'm happy to be here."

The man sitting next to me jerked me violently back to my seat. He was not laughing as he pointed behind me. Pogue's shotgun was pointing directly into my eyes.

"I wouldn't stand up all that quick 'round here if I was you," said O'Hara, chuckling.

"Goddamn. That was pretty stupid of me."

The man who'd pulled me down said, "Don't worry about it; nobody on this truck is real smart or they wouldn't be here." He had a Puerto Rican accent and a teardrop tattooed at the outer corner of his left eye. "My name's Jose Garcia. The 'Jose' don't seem to work for these assholes, so call me what they do: Josie." He smiled, revealing perfectly straight white teeth, with the exception of one front tooth that was capped in gold with a diamond set in the middle.

"Thanks for sittin' me down, Josie."

"My pleasure. I coulda been shot, too."

I nodded my acknowledgment. Man, I had to be careful here.

"You saw my buddy Johnson cut down, didn't you?" Bunny broke up my thoughts.

"Yeah," I told him. "Well, no, I didn't really see it. It was all over by the time I pulled my face out of the dirt. But when I looked up he was still alive." I paused. "I watched him die."

"He say anything before he went?" asked Bunny.

"Not a word," I told him. "I don't think he could. But if looks could kill, Huggins would have died on the spot."

Bunny looked down at his hands. "Funny thing is, Johnson knew it was coming—we all did when he was reassigned to your gang—but he never bitched about it. He was one tough hard-ass, that Johnson. He never quit fighting. Never did, never would."

133

I nodded. "Yeah, I think you're right," I said, hoping that made him feel a little better about his friend's death. "It was written all over his face, even at the end."

Bunny pierced me with an intense green-eyed stare. "Just watch what you're doing here," Bunny warned. "Don't let that happen to you. Pogue hasn't blown anybody away in a couple years, so he's way behind on his quota." Bunny rattled his chains to substantiate the point. "There isn't one con on this gang who's ever going to make trustee, that's for damn sure. We're all fuck-ups, like Josie said. If we weren't, we wouldn't be pullin' this shite detail."

"There's one good thing about it, though," Josie interjected. "Makes for a shorter work day sittin' on the truck, comin' and goin' for an hour or so."

"True enough," Bunny agreed with a smile. "Hell, we got twenty more minutes to sit around bullshittin'."

And so we did, with others joining in the conversation. We joked all the way to the plant like a bunch of suits gathered around the office water cooler discussing the office's newest secretary.

When O'Hara had introduced me to the brick gang, sarcastically referring to them as an elite group, he'd spoken the truth. This light-hearted flatbed was not the road gang's grim truck by any means—the grubbin' hoes and yo-yos were left behind for the boys. The tool for these empty-handed men to survive was laughter.

Road Camp 33 was the most dreaded white camp in the state for a couple of reasons. One was its incredibly high inmate mortality rate; the other was the infamous brick plant. No inmate in the whole of the Florida State Prison System was subjected to more brutal working conditions than those of the plant, not even the blacks who generally got the worst of it, working in snake-infested malarial swamps or the sweltering cane fields of South Florida.

The brick plant was the worst of the worst, and this

134

group of men truly were elite, simply because they survived it with a smile and kept on going. And in doing that, the brick gang became a uniquely proud and closed prison society, limited to twenty special men. These convicts had the reputation of being a very tough bunch and they looked it.

The truck slowed and turned down an inclined dirt road, which leveled off right before we passed through the gate into the plant.

The compound looked about the same size as the camp: one hundred or so square yards, secluded by dense forest and surrounded by a sixteen-foot-high chain-link fence topped with triple strands of electrified wire. A single gun tower stood twenty feet high atop a ten-foot man-made hill in the center, commanding a clear, three-hundred-sixty-degree field of fire. Security was simple and had proven to be quite effective. No one had ever escaped from this well-hidden compound.

Deets stopped the truck at the foot of the hill and took the shotgun from Pogue. As he pulled the pins on the tailgate, Pogue climbed up the tower ladder with a scoped Winchester slung over his shoulder.

Once again, another day, another day fewer was about to begin.

⛓⛓⛓⛓⛓

Although these men had greeted me pleasantly enough, earning their acceptance, I knew, would be an entirely different matter. I would have to work for that harder than I had ever worked for anything before. But after four months on the road gang, I was ready for it. This time, with this gang, I was not going to drop.

Not today. Not ever. No way.

My first day at the plant began with a remarkable

difference from the field. The walkin' boss was not yelling. Deets stood silently on the hill, watching the gang file one by one past the trustee water boy who dug into a cardboard box and handed each man a new pair of thick rough-cut leather work gloves.

"Here ya go, Inger—one size fits all," he said cheerfully as I followed Josie past him. "When ya need water, don't worry about it. Just holler." He was considerably older than the other water trustees and leaned to the right at an awkward angle, limping as he walked.

"Thanks, I will. What's the name I should holler?"

"Lift," he replied with a happy smile.

"Lift what?"

"It ain't 'What'; it's Hanks. Lift Hanks. Lift's my nickname."

"Oh. How'd you come by that?"

"Got a short leg and a lift in my shoe," he explained. He looked around furtively. "Best go on now."

Josie tugged my arm. "He's right," he said. "Let's move it. Come on."

"Comin', Boss," I said jokingly.

As I walked on, I noticed that O'Hara had dropped out of line and remained standing next to Lift and three other trustees.

"Where's Bunny going, Josie?"

"He ain't goin' nowhere," said Josie. "He just ain't goin' with us."

"Why's that?"

"Because we're goin' to the dryers now and it's too hot in there for his chains; they'd burn his feet off at the ankles. Those two trustees next to Lift are stokers—they keep the fireboxes goin' during the day. The other guy is maintenance. Between the three of 'em, they draw straws to see who's unlucky enough to take O'Hara's place in the dryer."

136

As Josie answered, he removed his shirt as we walked.

I could not believe what I was seeing. "What are you doing?" I asked. "I didn't think you could take your shirt off no matter where you were working on the road!"

"You're not workin' a road crew now, kid. This is the fuckin' brick gang. And while you're taking off that shirt, get your belt off too. If ya don't, when you bend, that buckle'll blister your stomach."

"Damn, Josie, just how hot is it in there?"

"That depends on the weather," a new voice replied at my side. The man next to me was not cut from typical Jewish cloth. This guy was two hundred pounds, built like a tank, and spoke with an Israeli accent. "I'm Abe Weinstein. And to answer your question, it's very hot right now—somewhere around three hundred degrees. When the thermometers go down to one-sixty, we go in. Welcome to the hottest game in town."

I offered my hand to shake. "Thanks for the welcome, Abe. I'm Clark."

"I know who you are," Weinstein said. "And I sure won't be giving *you* the finger—or my thumb either." He jerked his hands behind his back.

"What—is this whole gang a bunch of stand-up comics?" I asked.

"A perceptive observation for a gentile," he replied, laughing. Then his tone turned serious. "But this is not so funny," he said. "The dryers are what kill you here. You'll see what I mean when you go in, and you'll be damn well certain what I meant when you come out. The kilns afterward really aren't any worse than the road crew's day when you get used to them—except that by the time you get there, you'll already feel like you've worked half a day just from coming out of the dryer. You end the day the same way," he continued, "back in the dryer. Only then it's worse:

137

The mud is wet and the cars are heavier."

Abe bent over and rolled his pant legs up an inch.

"Are you done now scarin' the boy, Abie, my Jewish rose?" asked Josie.

"Yes, my yellow rose of Rico. Please, carry on."

"Thank you, Abe," Josie said mock-formally. "Thank you very much. And now for our next act. Clark, you and me'll work with Abe and that guy over there by himself, Crazy Crowder."

I nodded my recognition. He was the inmate Crisp had pointed out sitting on his own private toilet bowl my first day at 33.

"And don't worry about Crowder cutting off your head like he did his mother's," Josie assured me. "He's harmless if you don't piss 'im off or sit on his toilet. He don't even talk. Right, Abe?"

"Right," Weinstein replied with a chuckle. "Doesn't give you any mouthy bullshit at all, do you Crowder?"

Crazy Crowder shook his head no and stepped over to me, offering his hand. I shook it and, thankfully, he grinned in return.

The four of us gathered around the dryer entrances, laying our shirts and belts on the ground with the rest of the gang. A few of the men removed their wedding rings, the only jewelry allowed in prison, and pocketed them.

Lift limped along the dryers' entrances, tying back the thick asbestos curtains at the ends of the tunnels, allowing the first blasts of scorched air to escape as he read the thermometers.

"Okay now, we got a few minutes before we go in," Josie said, "so here's how this works: Four men to a dryer, two on each side of the cars. Stay on the planks along the sides of the track and don't step off; there's a two-foot drop down to the hot air vents under the rails.

"We push the cars out one at a time, the front one

first. You and me will go to the right. Go in behind me, because it's easier to push from the back. There's only about a foot and a half clearance between the cars and the walls, and only inches from the top rack of mud to the ceiling, so stay stooped over and don't ever straighten up or scrape the wall. You do that, and you're covered with a ton of soot that ain't comin' off all day long.

"Now, here's the most important part. Whatever you do, don't let any bare skin touch the steel racks. The night trustees fry bacon and eggs on 'em."

As Josie finished talking, I noticed Lift looking to the hill and waving up to the walkin' boss.

"It's one-sixty, boys. Roll 'em on out," Deets ordered, barely raising his voice.

The brick gang obeyed his command instantly. Along with the others, I slipped on my heavy-duty leather work gloves and then followed Josie, Abe, and Crowder into the searing heat belching from the entrance of dryer number four.

"Breathe through your nose for as long as ya can," Josie instructed. "It's easier on the lungs and ya won't get dry mouth so fast. Follow me to the front. Front car first."

I followed him along the narrow planked walkway down the tunnel, passing the row of eight cars to the front of the line. Stinging salty sweat was already pouring into my eyes, making the dim light blur into a cloudy heat-shimmering haze. I was certain I did not have a hair left in my nostrils and before I got out of here, my lungs would be seared for life.

"This is a hell of a way to start the day," I wheezed.

"Yeah, no shit. But the faster we're outta here, the better. Now listen good, *amigo*. When we start to push the car, for Christ's sake, don't jiggle the damn thing. If ya do, bricks'll fall off and block the tracks, and then we'll be in here forever pickin' 'em up. Just do as I do and start off

139

slow, okay?"

"Okay," I agreed. "I don't want to be in here any longer than you do—fact is, I don't want to be in here at all."

The men guiding me through this sweltering hell chuckled. Even Crazy Crowder joined in, snickering through his nose.

"One...two...three..." Abe said. Then: "Go."

The heavy car began rolling slowly forward and we smoothly pushed it out the exit into the light of day. I immediately filled my lungs with what seemed like ice-cold air.

"Clark," Josie said, "let her roll down the track and then start to pull back gently...now."

The car stopped with a slight jerk. One brick fell and splintered when it hit the ground.

"Well, will ya lookie there—only one brick," Abe said, gulping in air and pointing to the other three tracks, two with cars already parked. "And better yet, we're ahead of number three. We'll cool off for a minute and then do it again."

And we did. Again and again until forty-five minutes later, we parked the last car with bricks intact, still a car ahead of number three.

"I'll be damned, with a new guy too," Josie said.

Crowder nodded.

"Very cool." Abe smiled.

"Cool, my ass," I gasped, bending over, my hands grabbing weak knees to steady myself.

"Take deep breaths, new guy," Josie said. "And let's hit that water bucket while it's still cool."

We joined the men out of the dryer before us who were gathered around Lift at the water bucket. Each of us poured a couple cups of what felt like freezing water over our steaming heads and sat down with our tin cups full, waiting for the last car to roll out of number three.

140

It was at this point that I discovered my new best friend: Water.

I knew I was dehydrated, and my fuzzy head was telling me to stretch out and go to sleep. I felt just as I had when I'd dropped my yo-yo and my unconscious body to the ground my first day on the road crew. But that was four months of hard work ago, and now I was as hard as most of these men. I shook it off, got up, and walked a bit unsteadily to get another cup of water.

No one asked how I felt. That would have been a breach of prison etiquette and shown me disrespect. I was standing and that was enough. I sat back down, sipping my water and feeling rather proud of myself.

I seemed to be the only one of the group still out of breath, as the conversation around me went on as casually as it had on the truck coming in this morning.

"Those guys in three musta dumped it."

"Shit happens."

"Pick 'em up, put 'em back, and roll 'em out."

"Tough shit. Longer they're in there, longer I sit here."

"Suits me."

"Think I'll roll up another one while they're fartin' around in there."

Bunny O'Hara clanked down from the hill and joined the group, seating himself between Josie and Crowder.

"How's your new dryer podner here doin'?" He asked Abe, nodding toward me.

"We're sittin' here waitin' on three, aren't we?" Abe replied.

"Looks like it. Sure seems like it oughta be the other way around."

Josie spoke up with an edge to his voice. "May seem that way to you, O'Hara, but it seems to me this same

141

bunch'll hit number four for a while and keep waitin' on you to get out of those chains that manage to keep ya from the real work. Don't be lookin' for us to be last out either."

"No offense, Josie," Bunny said, raising his hands in mock surrender. "Just askin'." Bunny glanced at me. "We'll see how he does pitchin'. What team's he on?"

"Don't know yet," said Josie. "Will in a minute though," he hissed as he stood and raised his gaze toward Deets standing on the hill. "Boss—" Josie raised his voice just enough to be heard. "Got a question, please."

"What is it, Garcia?"

"Can I catch for the new kid?"

"Inger?" Deets laughed. "What the hell ya wanna do that for?"

"We're gettin' along, Boss."

Deets shrugged. "That wasn't my plan, Garcia; he was goin' to B Team. But if you want to stay in the kiln longer than usual, I'll change it just to see you sweat for a change. And understand this: since you asked, from now on, that's the way it'll stay. Just don't let me catch you two takin' long showers together."

Josie smiled. "Thanks, Boss."

"My pleasure, Garcia. And while you're settin' up some kind of shithouse competition with your best buddy, O'Hara, there and Inger, I don't want to hear any more crap comin' out of any of ya. And O'Hara, you'd damn well better do your best to show Inger how to pitch. If ya don't, your ass is goin' back in the dryer, chains and all. Crowder, you just got promoted from pitcher to conveyor. Ya hear me, Crowder?"

Crowder had heard him alright. His head jerked once in a singular display of barely contained anger. He looked at Josie in disbelief and then at O'Hara with nothing short of pure hatred.

O'Hara returned the glare with a blank, unwavering

142

stare. Then he slowly smiled, snorted, and rose to his feet. He clanked away to the water bucket just as he had come.

Obviously Bunny was not all the friendly, outgoing Bunny I had first thought. He was not only dangerous; he was a crafty manipulator. Josie's hot button had been pushed without his even knowing it. There was some very bad blood here.

Josie was the first to speak. "Sorry, Crowder. I know you love to pitch to me, but I just got pissed off. I'm sorry."

Crowder's lowered head nodded again, this time with sad resignation.

Abe patted Crowder on the arm. "Well, boys," he said, "this ought to be interesting. And by the way, Clark, the only guy Bunny ever got along with at all was Johnson and, as you probably heard, those two best buddies damn near killed each other. So, do the same as the rest of us and watch your ass around this guy; he lives on stirring up shit."

I shook my head. "I thought that damn dryer was a bad enough way to start the day, but this takes it. Is the guy a total psycho?"

I felt a light tap on my shoulder, and I turned to see Crazy Crowder wearing a big grin and vigorously nodding yes!

⛓⛓⛓⛓

Now about ten minutes since we had finished in the dryer, the last car rolled slowly out of number three pushed by four staggering sweat-soaked men covered with pitch-black soot. The car was a total mess. Broken, dried mud bricks littered the top rack and the bottom was not much better. One inmate fell to the ground, but only for a moment; he was immediately brought to his feet by the other three and dragged along with them to Lift and his water bucket.

Deets finally raised his voice. "Lift, go get the hose and wet those men down. Right now!"

"On my way, Boss."

"Anderson," Deets demanded, "what's the problem in there?"

"Track broke, Boss," Anderson rasped softly.

"What? Speak up."

"Track broke. We derailed, Boss."

Anderson looked thoughtful. "Okay, you men stay where you are and take a break. B—you'll go with half a team for a while. You guys figure it out. Let's go, boys."

The gang stood as a man and went to work.

The four tracks leading out of the dryers fed into a single track running perpendicular to them that fronted a row of four kilns at the rear of the plant. The cars would be steered left or right and rolled to the front of the kiln being filled to fire.

Each domed brick kiln was twenty feet in diameter and just as high in the center. As one was being filled, a second was firing, a third cooling, and the final being emptied. The cycle of a single kiln, I was told, was two days. The stages were staggered to keep a steady flow of bricks moving out of the plant.

Filling the empty kiln was an eight-man crew. Two pushed cars to the kiln and two unloaded the cars, two bricks at a time, onto sectioned steel-roller conveyors. The bricks were then rolled into the kiln where two men pitched the bricks, two in a stack, to two setters who caught them at the apex of their arc and set them in place with air space between each, building pie-shaped sections that grew to the top of the dome.

Emptying a fired kiln also used an eight-man crew. Two at the top of the kiln placed the now-much-lighter finished bricks four at a time onto a conveyor elevated on stanchions. Once full, the conveyor was lowered and rolled down to two men on the floor who gently tossed the bricks out of the kiln's low entrance in stacks of four. The two men outside pitched the stacked bricks up to two setters, who loaded them onto a thirty-foot flatbed trailer to be hauled to a state construction site.

I'd gotten the full rundown of the brick plant operation from Jose and Abe.

The day crew of the brick gang, as I knew, was a compliment of twenty men. Two teams, A and B, were each composed of eight men, who began and ended each day spending about forty-five minutes in the dryers. The rest of the day we worked the kilns, A and B alternating between filling and emptying them.

The other four men were trustees: two stokers, a water boy, and a maintenance man, whose duties were to keep the plant's machinery oiled and running, but primarily to keep foliage yo-yoed to the ground around the perimeter both in- and outside the fence.

The four-man night crew was virtually invisible and seldom seen by anyone in the gang. They were proven trustees with little time left to serve; they lived unguarded in a shack in the woods just outside the compound. When one was released, he was always replaced with a short-timer from a different camp. Even the all-knowing Dix had no idea who they were.

Abe Weinstein was the leader of the A team with Josie second in command. They were the team's setters, the only duty in the plant with real and serious responsibility. Occasionally, the stacked bricks being fired in a kiln collapsed during shrinking and that was forgivable. But if a collapse occurred when the men were working, someone could be seriously injured or even crushed to death. And if a load of bricks shifted while being hauled on an eighteen-wheeler's flatbed, several things could go terribly wrong, all of them bad. Those things used to happen in the past, but not anymore. Deets would not allow it.

In spite of the brick plant's well-earned reputation as a brutal workplace, Deets was known to be a fair and decent boss. He was one of the very few guards in the state whom inmates held in respect. This was primarily for one simple reason: He took care of his men. Besides being humane, it was the smart thing for him to do, because in a convoluted way, his job was dependent on our productivity. This symbiotic relationship between master and slave was unique within the prison system, hidden away deep in the woods of North Florida.

Deets was also a valued cog in the prison system's bureaucracy. He had taken over an antiquated, broken-down operation that had existed only as a tool of fear and pain to break the spirit of misfits, malcontents, and the most dangerous inmates. Over the years, Deets had changed the plant's priorities, transforming it from a place of punishment into a smoothly running profit center. He had seen to it that the brick plant was and would continue to be the system's greatest cash cow.

⛓⛓⛓⛓⛓

O'Hara's chains rattled up beside me. "Welcome to the A team. I didn't mean to piss ya off a little while ago—just kiddin' around. But we will be competitors, you and me, pitchin' against each other to see who empties his half of the car first and sits down while the other catches up. Everything here is a competition to sit on your ass first and longest, waitin' on the other guy. Nothing personal, okay?"

"Okay," I replied, smiling. What I thought was *Yeah, right. Up yours.*

"One more thing," he said. "Crowder was pretty damn good. On his best day, he'd give me a run for my money. I'll teach ya right. I love the competition."

146

I donned another fake smile. "That's really swell of you, O'Hara. I'll try to live up to it."

"Call me, Bunny, okay?"

I lost the smile. "Something tells me we're not going to be on a first-name basis anytime soon...O'Hara."

"Well then, that just suits the shit out of me...Inger. Let's go."

Our eight-man team emptied our water cups and returned them to Lift, and then six of us started down the slight incline from the dryers to the kilns. The other two, Ed Jones, a tall, impossibly thin man naturally nicknamed Bones, and his totally opposite partner, Eric Schmidt, a short, powerfully built chunk of rock aptly known as Bull, headed for the dryer tracks to roll the first car down to the waiting kiln.

"Great names in this place, Josie," I remarked, laughing. "Bones Jones and Bull Schmidt. Bull looks like he could push that car one-handed."

"That's no Bull Schmidt," Josie chuckled, playing on the pun. "He could if he wanted to. Makes it easy for Bones. Oh yeah, that guy walkin' next to you is Willie Jacobs. He'll work the conveyor with Crowder. We just call 'im Willie."

"Hi, Willie."

"Uh-huh."

Josie gave Willie a friendly slap on the back and went on to tell me, "Willy here talks about as much as Crowder. I'm sure they'll be swappin' jokes all day. Am I right, Willie?"

"He's a good listener," Willie answered with a shy grin.

We gathered around the low, arched entrance to Kiln C and watched Bull slow the first car rolling down from the dryer as Bones jumped ahead and threw the switch to the kiln track. The first load of the day was on its way.

Abe ducked his head and, stooping, waved Josie,

O'Hara, and me to follow him into the dim, brick rotunda. The only light in the kiln was a thin, hazy shaft of sunlight coming through a small vent hole in the center of the dome, like a searchlight trying to cut though a dusty brick red fog.

"It's your lucky first day, my new pitchin' partner," Josie said to me as he and Abe carefully climbed to the top of about four feet of set, unfired dried mud bricks.

"Why's that?" I asked.

"Because it's a lot easier pitchin' to me this low. The higher, the harder."

"Hey, Inger, you think you're tough enough you're gonna be doin' this bare-handed?" O'Hara asked through a smug smirk.

Shit. I had left my gloves behind at the water bucket.

"Abe?"

"Don't sweat it. That's one thing we got plenty of. That and water. You're going to wear them out, going through that leather in a couple of hours. When you see a hole, get some more. Go get a pair from Willie outside."

As if on cue, a new pair of gloves flew through the entrance and plopped down in front of me.

"Thanks, Willie," I hollered.

I got no response. Willie might not talk much, but it appeared he was even a better listener than Crowder.

The only sound that did come from outside was the steel wheels of the heavily laden car squealing to a stop on the narrow-gauge track, echoing into the nearly empty kiln. The first pair of dried, red mud bricks, lying side by side, rattled down the steel rollers and came to a gentle halt at a rubber bumper at the end of the conveyor. Two by two, more quickly followed, stacking up behind the first pair.

I slipped on my gloves and looked over at O'Hara. "Now what?"

"Watch me," he said. "Put your hands on either side of the bricks and push 'em together. Then flip 'em over flat,

148

one on top of the other, and cup your hands under 'em, like this."

As soon as O'Hara had removed the bricks, the conveyor moved forward. I grabbed the next two as he had.

"Now, I pitch 'em over to Abe," he said. "Like this."

The two bricks floated through the air as one for about six feet and then hung motionless before settling between Abe's outstretched gloves, one hand palm up and the other down, holding the stack together. Abe separated the two bricks, one in each hand, and leaving about an inch of air space between them, gently crisscrossed them on top of the pie-shaped pile he was building next to him.

"Your turn," O'Hara said as he picked up the next two bricks. The line of them now disappeared out the entrance. "And don't pitch 'em too hard," he warned. "Ya don't want to knock Josie up there on his ass. He might fall off and hurt me."

"Might be worth it," Josie responded through a thin smile. "But he's right, Clark—easy at first. Go ahead."

I imitated O'Hara's pitching technique. It all began well enough, but about halfway up, the bricks separated, one smacking into Josie's left hand and the other flying past his right shoulder.

"I said easy, damn it!"

"Sorry, Josie."

"That's okay; forget it. One out of two ain't bad. Calm down. Try to relax and just let 'em kind of lift off your hands with the upswing."

O'Hara pitched his next two to Abe and as I took mine, his instruction continued. "Think of it this way: Imagine you're holding a basketball between your legs trying to sink one of those underhanded free throws. Play like Josie's hands are the basket. Ya wanna make it just clear the front of the rim and swish it in. Turn it into a game."

I took my stance at the free-throw line.

149

Josie cheered me on. "Okay, kid, nothin' but net."

This time it was better. Josie caught one in each hand.

"Try it again," he told me. "Just a little slower."

The next free throw almost made it. The bricks hung in the air where they were supposed to with only a small space between them. Josie caught them easily, but they slammed together causing one of the brittle, mud bricks to shatter to the floor.

"All right, my man," Josie encouraged, "this is it. Game's on the line now. Let 'er fly."

Now Abe was chiming in. "Yep, game's tied up. This is the last chance to win it all."

I was at the line for the final shot when coach O'Hara called me aside. "Ya gonna win this one, Inger," he whispered, "or ya gonna be the fuckin' loser I think ya are?"

"O'Hara," I said out loud, "if you want to rattle something, wrap your fuckin' chains around your dick and go play with yourself."

The next shot was perfect. The crowd went wild.

⛓⛓⛓

An hour later, the fun of the game was long gone. And so were my arms. They had that old familiar feeling of hot, molten lead. Josie was standing a few feet higher now and the bricks I was pitching were barely reaching his ankles.

"Abe?" Josie ventured.

"Okay," Abe answered, examining the position of the thin shaft of light glowing through the dome's vent. "I see by the old sundial hole it's about time for the morning break anyway. Climb on down, Josie. Clark, you sit. Bunny, pick up the pace and we'll cover for him."

Oddly enough, this seemed to please O'Hara to no end. His face was positively glowing with delight.

"We'll cover for 'im, all right. You ready to get covered up, Abe?"

"Give it a shot," Abe told him. "I'm waiting on you."

"Let the real games begin then," Bunny proclaimed. "Coverin' ya up."

"Still waiting on you, Bunny," Abe said.

O'Hara bent down to address the pair outside. "Boys, load this mother up and keep 'em comin'."

Then in one swift, spinning motion, O'Hara swept his right hand across the conveyor and the bricks began to fly, each creating a graceful arc before settling gently into Abe's waiting hands. As Abe set each pair of bricks, two more were reaching their apex with another pair already in the air behind them. The conveyor's rollers were spinning at amazing speed with the space between the incoming bricks growing larger by the second. If this started as a game, it was quickly becoming a war.

Suddenly, Deets declared a truce.

"Break! Roll 'em up."

We filed out of the kiln, squinting away the blinding sun, and gathered with the others around Lift who was handing out tin cups from a dolly loaded with four buckets of cold water. He unloaded two buckets and continued on toward the B team, two kilns down the track.

"You had me going there, Bunny," Abe said to the panting man.

"Yeah, I was goin' too," Bunny gasped. "Wasn't goin' for a draw though."

He pulling off his worn leather gloves, tossed them into an empty cardboard box, and got a fresh pair from a full one next to it.

"I need some of that water, Abe."

"Me too," Abe told him. "After you."

I sat down next to Josie, "Goddamn, that was something in there," I said between gulps. "I'll be honest

151

with you, if O'Hara thinks I'm ever going to be any competition for him, he's nuts."

"He's a little nuts, that's for sure," Josie agreed. "Damn good pitcher though."

"Shit, I'll never keep with him."

"Don't let 'im psych ya out," Josie said sternly. "He started that shit just to fuck with your head. Looks like he succeeded, too."

"No, he didn't," I said. "I'm just being realistic."

"No, you're not," Josie argued. "If Crowder can do it, so can you."

"I'll try."

"You'll *do* it. Bunny'll make sure of it himself."

"Why? If he's fuckin' with my head that doesn't make sense."

Josie looked at me like I was an idiot.

"It makes sense to Bunny. Makes sense to me, too. He does this shit all the time, just for kicks. First he shakes ya up, then he'll piss ya off to the point that you'll do anything to kick his ass at anything. He's Irish—loves a good fight; it's as simple as that."

"He loves being a total asshole," I muttered. "That's what he loves."

"There ya go," Josie said. "Nobody'll argue with ya about that one!"

"That's it!" Deets called down from the hill. "Back to work. Crowder, you pitch for a while. Inger, you work outside with Jacobs 'til lunch."

Emptying the cars onto the conveyor was easy duty, and after the usual lunch of beans, bread, and water, I was ordered back into the kiln. Two hours later, at the mid-afternoon break, Deets knew I would be fading and true to his reputation, mercifully ordered me back outside with Willie. As the workday wound down, I was actually feeling pretty good.

Then we hit the dryer again.

On the way back to camp, I sat in the truck with my head between my knees, trying very hard not to throw up on my shoes.

Despite ending my first day's hard labor with the brick gang, baking like a potato in the dryer's awful heat, I had to feel good about one thing. Thanks to Deets' good management, when the gang unloaded back at camp, I hopped off that flatbed truck and landed standing tall. I walked through Dix's headcount with a smug grin on my face.

"I see you're still among the living," said Dix.

"Damn right, I am," I said proudly.

I passed through headcount and, along with the rest of our grubby gang, headed directly for the barracks. I walked down the aisle, stripping off my filthy, sweat-soaked clothes as I went; dropped them on the floor at the foot of my locker; and hit the showers.

I stood under the showerhead until the hot water ran out. The cooler it got, the better it felt. I would have stayed there until the pipes dried up, but time was running out; it was almost time for mess call. As I toweled off, I passed Crazy Crowder sitting on his personal toilet, already dressed in fresh camp clothes. I went to my locker and pulled on my pants, tucked in my shirt, and grabbed my shoes. But as I sat down on the bottom bunk to lace them up, I realized something was terribly wrong.

Crispy's bottom bunk was stripped bare.

CHAPTER 8
FROM BRICK TO BLOCK

October 1952

Dix was the last to join our solemn roundtable the evening of Crisp's disappearance. Rumors were flying through the camp concerning our friend, but we discarded them, waiting for Dix and the truth.

"Most of what you guys have heard from the road crew is probably true," Dix told us. "Crisp stepped into a nest of pygmy rattlesnakes and after a couple of hours of redneck first aid, he lapsed into a coma, before good old Captain Scruggs finally got around to getting an ambulance over there to take him to the state hospital in Chattahoochee."

"The fuckin' nuthouse?"

"No, James, the hospital part of it."

"How's he doing?" Harry asked.

"He's not." Dix frowned. "Crisp was dead on arrival."

⛓⛓⛓⛓⛓

I thought I had come to the hardened point of being able to finish off a meal in the face of death, but not this morning. Dix patted me on the shoulder as I passed through headcount to the brick gang's truck with an empty stomach and an empty heart.

O'Hara gave me his hand and pulled me up onto the flatbed with a surprisingly warm smile. Then, in a very soft voice, he said, "I'm sorry about Bacon. I know how tough it is havin' those bastards kill a friend."

"Thanks, O'Hara."

"It's Bunny, okay?"

"Okay. Thanks...Bunny."

"Clark?"

"Yeah?"

"If ya ain't up to this pitchin' shit today, don't sweat it; I'll carry ya some. My game's over for a while."

"Ah, fuck it, Bunny. Let's play it on out."

Bunny's somber face broke into a wide grin. He leaned closer. "Atta boy!" he whispered. "I like your style, kid."

∈∋∈∋∈∋

It came without warning shortly after the last car had rolled out of the dryer. I was gulping down my fourth cup of cool water on an empty stomach when suddenly the cup exploded in my face. Blinded by the hot, stinking acid of my own vomit, my fuzzing brain managed to rebel against the stinging pain in my eyes. "That rips it" came the unthinkable demand. "You're done. Drop!"

"Fuck you! I'm not droppin'. I'm not—"

Bunny knew that I was talking to myself when he interrupted. "No, you sure as hell ain't—not as long as I'm on this fuckin' team. You guys with me?"

They were. And from that moment on, so was I.

Life is strange, I thought later. Something as disgusting as one guy puking in a tin cup can finally bring eight men together as a real team.

∈∋∈∋∈∋

Abe, Josie, Bunny, and I sat on the thirty-foot flatbed parked in front of Kiln D, waiting to load it. The other half of our team was setting up the final conveyor section on stanchions inside the kiln, where they would begin emptying it. The holiday for the men who'd been outside was over. Now they would be inside, in over a hundred degrees, emptying the still-cooling kiln from the dome down.

Bull and Bones would start at the top, pitching down to Crowder and Willie halfway up, who would load the conveyor that would roll the bricks out toward the trailer. Bunny and I had the relatively easy duty of pitching the finished bricks, four in a stack, to Abe and Josie about eight feet up, who would set them on the flatbed.

"First week of December and it's still in the high seventies," complained Josie, frowning up at the sky. "Where in the fuck is winter?"

Abe shook his head. "I think this is Florida," he replied. "This is still Florida, isn't it, Clark?"

"Yeah, the fuckin' Sunshine State," I said. "Right, Sunshine?" I asked Bunny.

"Beats me, and I don't wanna think about that," he said. "I'm havin' way too much fun right now just sittin' here danglin'."

"Dangling?" I asked.

"That's right: danglin'. Danglin' my legs off the edge of this flatbed without havin' 'em pulled out of my hips by twenty pounds of chains."

Abe nodded. "After thirty days in the box and however many months in shackles, that's gotta feel really good."

"I can believe that without knowin' about it," Josie agreed. "And I don't ever want to know about it either."

"My mom told me something when I was a little kid that I never thought about much," I remarked to the group. "Now, I think about it a lot."

"You're still a kid," Bunny countered. "But what did she say?"

156

"She said..." I paused. "'It is a wise person that learns from others' mistakes.'" Her wisdom was really hitting home, like a punch to the gut. "It's true. I shoulda listened to her a long time ago. I guess you won't be running again after all the shit *you've* been through, will ya, Bunny?"

The first bricks came rattling down the conveyor as Bunny hopped off the flatbed smiling.

"Not today," he replied. Then he quickly asked, "Think ya can keep up with me, kid?"

"I can out here."

"Yeah, you can now," he agreed. "Fuck it—there's no reason to be bustin' our butts anymore. There's really nothin' left to prove between us, is there?"

I smiled crookedly.

"Maybe just one thing," I said.

"What's that?"

"O'Hara, you gonna prove to me that you're the loser I think you are?"

Bunny's face lit into a wide smile. "Now, that sounds familiar," he said.

Watching us from the trailer, Abe and Josie shook their heads in unison. "Oh, shit," they said to each other.

"Coverin' ya up, Abe."

"Coverin' ya up, Josie."

Deets told us our flatbed was loaded in record time. The laughing A Team took a record break waiting for the next trailer to arrive.

⛓⛓⛓⛓⛓

It began on a workday that was not a workday.

The brick gang jumped off the truck to find the plant totally shut down. Deets walked up the hill and motioned for the gang to gather around him at its base.

"Boys, I know y'all have already figured out that

157

you're not gonna be doin' any work today. Now I'm gonna tell ya why."

Deets squatted down to pick a crabgrass stem to chew on. "Today, the only work you're gonna be doin' is workin' up a hunger for lunch. Miz Deets is drivin' in here about noontime with a trunk full of fried chicken, potato salad, and homemade cornbread with real butter."

Our crew looked around at each other.

"And I don't give a damn who ya tell about it later," Deets went on, "'cause I make this place run and nobody's gonna screw with me over it—fuck 'em. You're my gang, and for one day I'm gonna feed y'all right with a good meal the day before Christmas."

It was no joke! With that, a twenty-man cheer went up that must have been heard a mile away.

When the noise finally subsided, Deets added with a fatherly smile, "Those thermos ice chests over by the dryers are full of enough Cokes to float all of your boats for the rest of the day. And for you boys that smoke, that cardboard box next to 'em is full of tailor-made Chesterfields. Weinstein, you're in charge of this portable radio, as long as you don't play any of that classical crap. Enjoy yourselves and merry day before Christmas."

⛓⛓⛓⛓⛓

It was dark when the truck passed out through the gate of the plant, bouncing along the dirt road through a black, moonless Christmas Eve. The flatbed was loaded with the stuffed stomachs of a very contented brick gang. All except one.

"What's wrong, Bunny?" I asked. "You look like this is the worst day of your life."

"Nothin's wrong," he said. "But I'm a wee uptight right now."

"Why?"

Bunny glanced around and then leaned toward me. "I'll tell ya if ya won't butt in. I've only a couple a minutes and I don't have time to fuck around answering a bunch of your bleedin' questions, okay?"

I nodded. "Okay. What is it?"

"This is the last time we're gonna be talkin' on this gang's truck," he told me. "And when we're done, I'm jumpin' and I'm runnin'. You're a good kid, so listen to me: It's all I got to leave ya."

I nodded mutely.

"Everybody's chained to some damn thing," Bunny told me. "If it wasn't this sorry gang of convicts, it'd just be somethin' else. Somethin' like your nasty, fat-arsed old lady swillin' down rot-gut gin and yellin' at ya about not goin' to a job ya hate goin' to and lots of other shit. Or somethin' like the Man—and then the rest of the whole damn free world—lookin' down its snotty courtroom nose at ya just because ya finally got sick and damn tired of gettin' yelled at, so you hacked off your old lady's screamin' head with a Boy Scout hatchet. Well, fuck 'em all, and good for me. I ain't chained to that old bitch no more and even after bein' locked up in this shithole, it was worth it. I was free from her fat, yellin' arse forever.

"Look for the weak link, lad," Bunny said fervently. "That's the only damn thing that can ever really set ya free. And if ya find it, no matter what, bust that son of a bitch wide open and toss off your damn shackles. Find that weak link and ya ain't chained to nothin' more than the wind."

Bunny slapped me on the shoulder as he stood.

"See ya in hell, kid. I'm outta here!"

Bunny walked to the front of the flatbed and stooped under the flapping canvas top just as Deets pulled up to the stop sign before entering the highway. In an instant, the canvas was slashed open with a razor blade and Bunny was

159

gone.

Bunny landed with a *thunk* on top of the cab and jumped from the passenger side, where he fell out of sight of Pogue's trailing shotgun and Lift's presence in the passenger seat shielded him from Deet's line of fire. Bunny landed in weeds at the roadside and rolled past the stop sign into deep brush; but when he rose to run, he fell headlong into a drainage ditch. His left ankle had been snapped in half by his fall.

Pogue leapt from the trailer and flicked off his gun's safety before his feet touched the ground. He landed and fired point-blank into Bunny's back. A geyser of bloody ditch water still hung in the air as he jacked another round into the receiver. But he never had a chance to pull the trigger for the second time—and he never knew what hit him.

I dove off the end of the flatbed so my chest crashed into Pogue's head, knocking him sprawling to the ground with me on top of him. I ripped the shotgun from his hands and smashed the butt into the back of his neck, driving his comatose face into the dirt.

"That's it, you motherfucker! Enough! Enough!"

"Drop it!" I vaguely heard Deets screaming behind me. "Drop the fuckin' gun, Inger!"

I dropped it.

"Kick it away! Right fuckin' now!"

I kicked it away. And then I slowly turned to face Deets. "Why didn't you shoot me?" I managed to ask through gasps for breath.

"It's Christmas Eve."

"Merry Christmas," I said.

"Inger, shut the fuck up and sit the fuck down. Anybody moves on that truck, you're dead meat. Lift, call the state troopers; number's on the dash. Tell 'em what happened and to send an ambulance for Pogue. And don't call Scruggs; I don't need to be lookin' at any more dead

160

men tonight. We'll take care of our own here and let the cops take care of Inger somewhere else."

Deets was true to form. He took care of his men.

My second holiday meal was served to me on a sectioned metal tray in the isolation cell of the Jackson County Jail at noon on Christmas day. I sat on the single steel bunk finishing off the last of the sliced ham with all the traditional trimmings, knowing that this could very well be the last decent meal of a condemned man. Tomorrow, it would be state business as usual, and Scruggs would haul me back to 33, throw me in the box, and let me sit there in my own waste rotting to death. If I was lucky, it would be less than a month or so before he simply had Huggins blow me away.

On this Christmas day, I was not celebrating the birth of Jesus Christ. I was remembering slaughtered men and doing my best to get ready to join them.

A deputy sheriff acting as temporary holiday turnkey opened my cell door. "Inger, it's time for ya to make that one phone call we owe ya that ya put off from last night to today. You ready?"

"Yes," I told him. "Thanks."

"You bet. Come on out and hang a left. Walk in front of me down the hall to the guard station and use the phone on the desk. If it's long distance, call collect."

I did as I was told; I sat down at the desk and picked up the phone. "Operator, I'd like to place a long distance call and reverse the charges to Hollycourt 5109 in Chicago, Illinois. The party I'm calling is a Mister Leroy Lincoln Tanner."

A very large man stood at my cell door with a very large grin on his face.

"Inger, I'm Sheriff Wade Simmons," he announced. "And I don't have the slightest idea how the hell you did it, but you did. That asshole Scruggs from over at the camp just came by to pick you up and then left in a raging fit. He was damn near foaming at the mouth."

I was speechless.

"Did you hear what I just said?" the sheriff asked, laughing out loud.

"Yeah. I mean, yes sir, I did," I replied, a smile beginning to form. "What's so funny?" I asked the laughing man. "What happened?"

"I'll tell ya, son. What's so funny is everybody around here hates that asshole Scruggs. It was a pure delight to see him come stormin' in here demanding his prisoner and basically being told to go fuck himself."

"You told him that?"

Simmons chuckled. "Wish I had of, but no not me. An attorney did."

"Sheriff, I don't have a lawyer."

"Maybe not, but this guy walked in behind Scruggs and saved your young ass, big time. And he's an assistant state's attorney, at that. Came over here from Tallahassee with a state hold on ya. So we're holding ya."

"Can I talk to him?"

"Afraid not. He left right after Scruggs. But on his way out, he did ask me to tell you a couple things."

"Damn, Sheriff," I said. "I'm not believin' all this. What did he say?"

"Well, son, seems like we'll be holding you here through the holidays, and then, first thing after New Year's, you're on your way back to Raiford. He also said to tell ya 'Hello' from the family and some guy named Roy."

162

CHAPTER 9
PAYBACK IS HEAVEN

January 1953

A new year and a new life began at heaven's gates. They rose twenty sparkling feet high, topped with triple strands of shining barbed wire, reaching for a sunny, clear blue sky. The gates slowly slid open, welcoming me into the bright-white paradise of the Florida State Maximum Security Prison at Raiford, affectionately known as "The Rock." This was the most joyful day of my life.

The guard behind the admissions counter completed his paperwork, stuffed it into my thick file, and looked up at me with a quizzical expression on his fat face.

"What are you smiling at, Inger? Something funny about this?"

"Just glad to be here, Boss," I replied.

"It ain't 'Boss' no more, Inger; a plain old 'sir' will do. You ain't on the road no more."

I smiled. "That's why I'm happy to be here...sir."

He tried to maintain his guard-like composure but could not suppress a chuckle as he pointed to an ancient, white-haired black trustee standing by the door at the rear of the office.

"Go with that boy over there," he told me. "He'll get ya your new clothes and linens and take ya to your cellblock. And try not to look too happy, okay? It might piss somebody off."

"That won't happen, sir," I promised. "The last thing in the world I want to do now is piss somebody off."

The elderly black man silently led the way through a second gate into the main prison complex. As we walked across a small fenced concrete yard to the laundry, he finally spoke.

"Just come in off the road? Camp 33?"

"Yeah," I told him. "The brick plant."

"Look better than mos' comin' from 33," he observed with a laugh.

"You think that's funny, old man?" I asked.

"Nope, sonny; sure don't. Just trying to be friendly, dat's all."

"Sorry," I replied sincerely. "I didn't mean to be rude."

"Dat's okay," he said. "The brick plant, huh? Bad as they say?"

"You get used to it."

"I hear it's worse than the coloreds get. Dat da truth?"

"I heard that too, but I wouldn't know for sure," I reasoned. "I'm not colored."

"Got a tan, though," the old man observed, grinning. "You make it through that nigger duty," he added, "den, far as I'm concerned, you an honorary nigga'."

"Well, thanks a lot, old-timer," I said, thinking about Roy Tanner. "Fact is," I told him, "I've been an honorary nigger for a long time."

"I wouldn't mention dat to whitey if I was you, sonny."

"Don't worry about that," I said. "We'll keep it between us. By the way, how'd you know I came in from 33?"

"I work in da warden's office."

"Oh. Well, that explains that then," I said, following my guide into the laundry.

I was issued fresh new clothes by a trustee standing

164

behind a low counter, along with linens, a blanket, a brand new mattress, and a pillow.

"Change your clothes here," the trustee instructed. "And when you're done, kick dose stinkin' road-trash rags over in dat corner. This is your lucky day, Inger; you gots all new stuff."

I smiled. "You have no idea just how true that is."

After doing as instructed, I rolled up my new items in the mattress, situated it under my arms, and headed for the door where the old man was waiting. We walked the length of the small, narrow yard between the one-story building we'd just left that housed the laundry and mess hall, and a three-story building that was Cellblock B. It was not until we had passed through another gate into the main yard, turned left, and passed the entrance to Block B, that my escort spoke again.

"Didn't mean to be rude by not talkin'," he explained, "but it's best not to look like old friends, you and me. Not that we is or nuthin', but the guards make up their own minds about shit like that. Anyway, the name's Leroy."

"Leroy!" I exclaimed. "Well, I'll be damned. That's a great name. Glad to meet ya, Leroy. Mine's Clark."

"I know."

"I'm sure you do," I said. "Trustees seem to know just about everything that goes on in the joint. Guess they have to, since they practically run the whole fuckin' prison system. I'm a little surprised to see a colored leading a white guy around, though."

"Well, white guy, I been here a bunch of years, and now I'm kinda the warden's Uncle Tom," he said frankly. "Don' like kissin' white ass so much, but it's easy time for an old nigger like me. No offense about the 'white ass' remark."

"None taken, Uncle."

"Kep' your sense of humor, I see," he said. "That's good; makes things easier sometimes. Speakin' of easier, looks like you gonna be doin' a little easy time yourself for a change."

"Shit, Leroy, just being off the fuckin' road seems like easy time to me," I said. "But what do you mean by that?"

"I'll tell ya what I mean, but when I's done, I's gonna forget about it—ain't none of my bidness or nobody else's for that matter. You gots some friends in high places," he told me. "High enough to call in a marker here and there. See them new clothes and what have ya? Well that ain't usual and that ain't all of it, either. You be goin' to the best cellblock here; it's the furthest from the yard, at the edge of the compound, and yo' cell is on the third tier, facin' nuthin' but trees, the highway, and da free world. Besides all that good shit, ya gots the best ventilation in whole the damn joint."

Before I could respond, Leroy said, "Well, here's A Block. This's as far as I go; dem guards inside will take it from here. One more thing: tell Sam that Warden Rosco is spectin' dat nex' chapter by the end of the week, ya hear?"

"Who's Sam?" I asked.

"The best damn friend I gots in this place. And you was damn sure right about one thing, sonny: This really is your lucky day. You Sam's new cellmate."

I looked around. This was the Drake Hotel compared to where I'd just come from, but the reality of more time behind bars was starting to sink in.

"You know, Leroy, it seems like my whole fuckin' life has been nothing but a series of security doors opening in front of me and slamming behind me, and that I'm always going in the wrong direction. This last time, when I was sent to the road, another old guy told me a bunch of stuff he didn't need to, and I wondered why. Well, I asked him why and he told me. So now, I'm asking you: What the fuck is your story? Why?"

166

At my question, Leroy's face transformed. "Ain't no need to get fuckin' smart-mouthed with me, you little motherfucker," he snapped. "I don't give a big rat's ass 'bout choo or what the fuck happens to you, now or ever. What I do care 'bout is Sam. I wanted you to know you got a sweet fuckin' deal going here and if you fuck up and cause him any fuckin' trouble whatsoever, I'll kill your fuckin' honky ass. Or if'n I can't do it, I'll find somebody who will. You'll have a shiv stuck in your gut, slitting you from ass to appetite. I don't give a shit if you are a goddamn fuckin' Untouchable. Now, get out of my fuckin' face, you skinny little motherfuckin' cocksucker."

The old black man began trembling in a barely controlled rage.

"Nice talkin' to you, Leroy," I said.

Leroy turned on his heel and rapidly walked away. As he disappeared around the corner of B Block, I thought, *There goes my "honorary nigger" status.*

Two guards were stationed at the Tier One entry gate into Block A. One was as thin as a bamboo stalk, his uniform belying lean strength. The other was a whale stuffed into a captain's uniform. His plastic nametag read "Pitts" and he was bent over as far as he could, slapping his thighs in laughter. An old schoolyard rhyme popped into my head that stayed with me whenever I saw them together:

> *Fatty and Skinny went to bed.*
> *Fatty made a fart and Skinny was dead.*
> *Fatty called the doctor. The doctor said,*
> *"Anymore farts like that, we'll all be dead!"*

"You're off to a great start, Inger," the whale wheezed, grinning through his blowhole. "Ya just pissed off the warden's favorite psycho."

True to form, Fatty ripped an obnoxious fart.

167

"Sir?" I said. "He's a psychopath?"

"Yep." He nodded. "Twelve years on death row'll do that to ya. Good thing you're not a nigger over there in C Block or ya might not live 'til morning. And it's Captain Pitts to you, Inger."

"Maybe I can help keep our new guest alive to see the light of day," said the first guard. "Think that's possible, Captain Pitts?"

"It's possible, Mister Walcott—*just* possible. Do what ya can. Well, let's see here..." He looked at his clipboard. "*55109, Inger, Clark, cell A-340.*" He looked up at me. "You lucked up there, Inger. That's one of the best rooms in the house."

"Inger," Walcott instructed, "walk ahead of me over to those stairs and up to Tier Three. When you get to the top, go down the right-hand corridor to the end."

The guard followed, with me still carrying my belongings, up the stairs and down the hallway. The long hall was lined on one side by open security windows. On the other side, I counted forty white-painted eight-by-twelve two-man cells, open and unoccupied. I noticed that all had some sort of personal touch and a few actually looked almost homey.

The guard behind me stopped. "Here we are, Inger. Block A, Tier 3, Cell 40. A-340 for short."

I faced him. Walcott seemed like a good guy and I wanted to start off right with him. "Sir, thanks for the tour."

"Go on in," he said, motioning toward the cell. "I hope you get on well here," he told me. "And you'd better bust your ass to keep it that way, because we'll be seeing a lot of each other. This is my tier and you can forget the 'Sir' crap. You will address me as Mister Walcott."

"Yes, Mister Walcott," I said, tossing my rolled-up mattress onto the bare top bunk.

"Work details are almost over," he informed me, "so

168

the men will come filing in here in about thirty minutes. Dinner mess is from six to seven and that's optional; nobody has to eat if they don't want to. Lockdown and lights out are at nine. Wake-up is at five, breakfast six, work begins at seven, and it ends at four with an hour for lunch at eleven. Tomorrow is Saturday, so you'll have the weekend to learn your way around here. Your work detail will be assigned to you Monday morning at seven." Walcott paused. "You've got a very good deal going here," he admonished me, "but don't think for a minute that as far as the administration is concerned, you're what some cons call Untouchable. That's bullshit. Every con in this joint is 'touchable'; you just have a great opportunity to do some very easy time. Treat the prison personnel with respect and most will treat you the same," he went on. "If they don't, keep your mouth shut, take your lumps, and let it go. If you don't, you'll end up in deep shit, and you can kiss easy time good-bye. One last thing, and remember this well: that captain in Road Camp 33 would dearly love to have you back, and as far as I'm concerned, if you in any way screw with Sam, that's where you're going. End of speech. Keep your shit together, and I'll be seeing you around."

"I'll remember what you said, Mister Walcott," I promised.

"Good. You had better."

As the guard turned to leave, I asked, "Mister Walcott, what do they mean by Untouchable?"

Already headed down the corridor, he replied over his retreating shoulder, "Ask Sam."

Left alone, I finally had time to take this all in. *Who the hell is this Sam guy?* I wondered. That psychopathic nutcase, Leroy, seemed ready to die for him. Even Walcott, a guard, was protective of him. And these were just the first two people in Raiford I had talked to at any length. Well, I would meet this man soon enough, in thirty minutes or so.

And this "Untouchable" thing had me more than curious. Its connotation was obvious, but how did one get it and what exactly did it entail? Obviously Roy was at the root of all this, and I wondered how he had managed so many amazing feats on my behalf.

When I'd tossed the mattress on the bunk, the pillow had slipped behind it to the floor and out of sight. Searching for it was the first time I really looked around the cell. After retrieving it, I put the pillow on my bunk and crawled up top to lie down and wait for Sam whatever-his-name-was.

Gazing around, I realized that perhaps I did have something to thank Sam for. My new home was a combination library and very comfortable den. I really hoped this guy would like me and that my good fortune would continue. Sometimes, things change faster than expected.

⛓⛓⛓⛓⛓

I was back in the road camp, sitting in the office, and there was old Dix behind his desk, typing away, booking me in for my death sentence. One thing was very different, though: The old man's typing skills had picked up considerably. His fingers were flying over the keys of a new and very well-oiled IBM Electromatic Model 04 typewriter. *Slow down, old man,* I thought, *I'm not in that big a hurry to meet up with a load of double-aught buckshot.*

My eyes snapped open and I was suddenly very wide awake.

The nightmare evaporated, leaving only the sound of the typewriter coming from the small oak desk against the wall opposite the bunk bed, in A-340. A green-glass-shaded library desk lamp backlit the figure hunched over the keys, typing at great speed. He suddenly stopped typing and

170

swiveled his matching oak desk chair around to face me.

He was a good-looking man, almost handsome, who appeared to be in his mid-thirties. His hair was dark brown, with just a hint of gray in his well-trimmed sideburns. High cheekbones framed a subtle Roman nose with just the slightest olive tint in his skin tone. Classic Italian, except for the eyes, which were light amber.

In fact, they were the kindest eyes I had ever seen. I instantly felt completely at ease with him.

"I hope I didn't wake you with my writing," he said in a rather deep voice with an accent I couldn't quite place. "I'm finishing a couple pages of copy, and I've only half an hour before lights out."

"I'm glad I woke up when I did," I assured him. "I was in the middle of a bad dream that was only getting worse. Oh, the warden's crazy black trustee said to tell you that Warden Rosco is expecting the next chapter by the end of the week."

"Yes, I know," he said. "That's precisely what I'm working on: *The Warden Papers.* That is not my title—I'm not fond of it—but Rosco insists. I'm his ghostwriter."

"J. Thompson Rosco," I said. His name appeared on every prison document I'd ever seen. "Wonder what the J stands for."

"No one knows," he replied. "'Jelly' would be appropriate. At some time in his life, he got his names turned around—much like his concept that a convict should write his book on criminology."

"Well, don't let me disturb you," I told him. "I've had a long day and I can go back to sleep."

"It would appear that you could use it," he told me. "You slept through dinner until now like a dead man."

"If that dream went on any longer, I would have been," I said. I stretched my hand down to him from my bunk. "I'm Clark Inger."

171

He gripped my hand firmly and a hint of a smile crossed his face before disappearing back into his eyes.

"I'm Sam. Sam Miller. Get some sleep, kid. We'll talk in the morning."

My very lucky day—this is a good guy, I thought. Then I immediately fell into a deep and, this time, dreamless sleep.

❃❃❃❃❃

I was jerked from unconsciousness into a straight-up sitting position by a very loud, shrill noise drowning out the sound of two hundred forty cell doors simultaneously grinding open in the block.

"Gets your attention, doesn't it?" asked Sam, who was already up and dressed, sitting at the desk reading what I guessed was the copy he had written last night.

"Damned right it does," I said. "What kinda asshole plays a bugle first thing in the morning, for Christ's sake?"

"It's the public address system," he explained. "They play a recording of 'Reveille' every morning, except Sundays, for the wake-up call. On God's day, it's a *heavy*—pun intended—dose of Kate Smith, belting out something like 'For a Closer Walk With Thee.'"

I stretched. "Oh, well. It beats the shit outta the road, where some moronic redneck guard thinks it's still funny—after God knows how many years he's been doing it—to walk down the aisle hollering 'Drop your cocks and grab your socks!' I guess I can get used to the bugle." I grimaced. "But Kate Smith, I'm not too sure about."

"Ah, a discerning critic of music I see," said Sam. "And an accurate critique, as well. Kate Smith is a *giant*—pun number two—pain in the neck."

I tilted my head. "What the hell does 'discerning' mean?"

"It means insightful or perceptive," Sam replied. "Generally speaking and in this case, simply being correct in your judgment."

"Guess you're an educated man," I said. "Do ya— No...it's just that..."

"What's on your mind, kid?"

"No offense," I said. "You're older than me, and..." I trailed off.

Sam waited and then, smiling, replied, "None taken."

"Right. My mom always said it's better to learn from people who are smarter than me."

"Wise woman."

"Do ya— I mean, do *you* mind if I ask you stuff like that sometimes? Like the meaning of words and stuff?"

"Not at all," said Sam. "I'm glad you asked. Most people are afraid to show ignorance—that they don't know something." Looking quite pleased, Sam added, "Your decision just now to use the word 'you' instead of 'ya' is a wise choice already."

"Thank you." I smiled, feeling wiser already.

"You're welcome. Let's go get some breakfast."

Sam headed down the corridor at a leisurely pace, and I followed. We wound down the block's three flights of stairs to the first-tier exit and ambled across the small yard toward the mess hall at what seemed to be the speed of a lazy snail.

"Sam," I said tentatively, "I haven't eaten anything in almost twenty-four hours and I'm really hungry. At this rate won't all th—"

"No, all the food won't be gone," he said. "Not to worry; this isn't a camp with fewer than a hundred men to feed. There are several hundred men moving through that mess hall right now, with a lot more coming in behind us. No hurry, kid."

We stepped to the rear of a long line of men moving

along a cafeteria-style serving counter. At the head of the counter, we each took a compartmentalized metal tray, a soupspoon, and a cup. The smell of hot food was overwhelming now, and I was starving. As we moved down the row of steam tables, I ladled my tray to the point of overflowing with mounds of powdered scrambled eggs, grits with sausage gravy, and cornbread, all topped off with a cup of steaming-hot black chicory coffee, with no grease floating on top. As I followed Sam with my heavily laden tray to a vacant metal table, I felt better than I had in a long time. Finally, a real prison meal.

We did not speak until I had finished eating. Conversation would have been useless, since my mouth was continually crammed full of food. I stuffed myself to the threshold of pain before finally pushing away my nearly finished tray with a deep, resounding burp.

"Feel better now?" Sam asked.

"My stomach's a little uncomfortable, but it's a lot better than the alternative," I replied.

"Put that tray on your lap and out of sight," he demanded.

"Why shou—"

"Do as I say and do it now!"

I did it.

"Okay, okay," I said. "What's the matter?"

"Just out of idle curiosity," he asked, "did you happen to notice that large sign over the steam tables?"

"What sign?"

"That answers my question," he said. Then he repeated: "The sign over the steam tables."

I looked, and there it was. Huge red letters painted on a four-by-eight-foot white plywood sign hanging from the ceiling clearly read, for all but me to see: *TAKE WHAT YOU WANT. EAT WHAT YOU TAKE!*

"Oh, shit!" I said. "What'll I do? Dump it on the

floor?"

"No, that's too sloppy," Sam admonished. "What you should do is pay attention to your surroundings at all times. That message is a serious one; they don't tolerate waste here."

"It's a little late for that piece of wisdom, isn't it?" I snapped.

"No, it is not!" Sam said sternly. "It's never too late to learn."

"I'd like to learn how to get rid of this fuckin' leftover food," I said.

Sam reached into both front pockets of his pants and removed several sheets of folded newspaper, which he handed to me under the table.

"Divide the leftovers into two packages. We'll each stuff one into our pocket, go back to our cell, and flush the contents down the toilet."

I did as he instructed. As I slipped him his half of the crime, I could not help laughing.

"You knew this was going to happen, didn't you?" I asked.

"Perhaps you're just fortunate that I'm a bit odd and keep my pants stuffed with yesterday's news," he answered, straight-faced.

I grinned. "You anticipated me, right?"

"Kid, you can ask all the questions you want, but please skip the really stupid ones. They're rhetorical and an insult to your own intelligence. Let's get out of here."

We showed our empty trays, spoons, and cups to the guard, placed them on the rubber conveyor belt to the kitchen, and were checked out. Then we walked, hands in pockets, to our cell and flushed the incriminating evidence down the seatless steel toilet.

"Sam?"

"Yes."

"Can I— May I ask you something?"

"What did I say just a few minutes ago? That's another one of those rather annoying rhetorical questions, isn't it?"

"Yeah, I guess," I said, "but that's what it's about."

"Oh?" he said. "What is it?"

"Rhetorical question. What is that?"

Sam contemplated me. "It's a question that requires no explanation. One you already know the answer to, such as, Did I anticipate your eyes being bigger than your stomach?"

I nodded. "Okay. I got one more for you, Sam, then I'm done for the day."

"Finished. It's you'll be 'finished' for the day."

"Done. Finished. Same thing," I said.

"Not really, kid. Used in that sentence, 'finished' is the correct word. 'Done' indicates a distressing lack of vocabulary. Do you want to go through life speaking English or babbling redneck?"

"English works for me," I said. "I appreciate the correction. But by the way, Sam, that was a rhetorical question."

For the first time, I saw the man actually smile.

"Well, I'll be," he said. "You got me there, kid. I believe you may show some promise, after all. Now, then, what was your final question on this, your first day of English 101?"

I spread my hands wide. "I'm standing here in the best cell, in the best block, talking to what seems to be a nice guy who likes to teach proper English and doesn't show any signs of being into butt-fucking. This was planned. Why you and A-340? What all can you tell me about this 'Untouchable' business?"

The instant the question popped out of my mouth, I regretted it. Sam's eyes narrowed to dark slits under a deep

176

frown before he silently turned his back to me and faced the wall.

In the short time I had spent with Sam, two things about him had become evident. The first was that he was withdrawn, cloaking any emotion behind a wall of non-expression. The second was that there was a crack in the wall: his eyes. That was my current concern; I could not read his eyes. As a familiar chill of fear crept up on me, I had no idea what to do. So I did not do anything at all.

It was a very long minute before Sam turned to face me with those pale amber eyes. The chill had warmed; he was not angry.

"Kid, that certainly is one final question." He spoke to me for first time without a patronizing tone. "I hope that's it for the day, because it's going to take a good part of the rest of it to find answers for you."

"Since you don't have the answers and I'm involved in the questions," I said, "maybe between the two of us, we can deduce the conclusions."

"It also seems I've grossly underestimated you," said Sam. "I don't care to discuss this matter here. The main yard is the only place for any real privacy, and if I'm perceived to be 'in conference,' we won't be disturbed. Let's go. I've got my own bit of territory out there, and we can sit and chat until we arrive at some conclusions. And between the two of us, they'll be the correct ones."

We sat in the dirt, our backs against the shaded north wall of A Block, shielded from the already-hot mid-morning Florida sun. The main yard was filled with men playing checkers, softball, and a pickup game of basketball. A few lifted weights, but most just walked the yard or milled around aimlessly in groups of two or three, no one coming within ten yards of Sam's territory in the dirt.

And so our "conference" began.

"Okay, where do we start?" I asked, attempting to

establish myself as an equal but not believing it to be true for a minute. I was smart enough to realize that this man was way beyond me—for now.

"We'll begin at the beginning," he said. "The beginning of your serving time is the logical starting point. In order to save time and a lot of needless conversation, I'll tell you what I know about you up until now. If I'm incorrect about something or going off in the wrong direction, feel free to interrupt and correct me."

I nodded.

"You were here in Raiford for the mandatory two weeks of brainwashing," he continued, "and then shipped out to Camp 33, captained by a sadistic redneck moron named Scruggs, who has the remarkable record of more deaths per capita than any white boss in the system. You were assigned to a road gang, where you screwed up by chopping off a gentleman's thumb. As a reward, you were assigned to work in the notorious brick plant, which you managed to survive for a few months before screwing up in major fashion. A runner, aptly named Bunny, jumps the truck and is cut in half by a load of double-aught buck, before you—rather heroically, I must admit—jump the guard, take his shotgun away from him, and beat him with his own gun. At this point in your checkered career of service to the state, it's a mystery to me why the walking boss didn't blow your brains out then and there. Surviving that miracle, Scruggs would have cheerfully thrown you in the hole and let you starve to death, but for some reason, the cops got to you first and held onto you for a week or so. Then, by an even greater miracle, you were ushered out of town before Scruggs could retrieve you and finish you off. How are we so far?"

"So far, so good."

"That's it, then," he said, "except for one more thing. With a record like that, there's no way you should have lived

178

through 33, let alone have been transferred back to Raiford. So I have a question for you, kid: Do you have any idea why you're still among the living, talking to me now?"

I took a moment to add it all up. "I do," I said. "And it's a couple of reasons. Regarding the runner, all that shit hit the fan on Christmas Eve, and I swear to God, that's why I'm still alive. Believe it or not, my boss's spirit of Christmas saved my ass. Simple as that."

Sam nodded as a slight smile crossed his face. "I believe you," he said. Then he frowned and added, "But not the part that it's as simple as that. You mentioned two reasons. What's the other one?"

"A present from a Ghost of Christmas Past."

"Cute," he said. "But come on, kid. What happened?"

I hesitated. If I told all, I'd be betraying Leroy's confidence. And I'd promised myself that no one would ever know about the murders I'd committed. But to hold back might leave gaps in my story, putting me at odds with Sam's trust. I saw only one choice.

I told Sam everything.

First about Deets' saving me from Scruggs by demanding the sheriff take me into custody for my own protection. I then informed him of the assistant state's attorney's putting a hold on me and my subsequent call to Roy. I explained my relationship with both Tanner brothers, including why they were indebted to me. And because I knew Roy could not possibly have accomplished all this without the help of some very heavy hitters, I told Sam about the reasons behind the Doolan robbery and the Tanners' longtime business involvements with the Cicero family.

When I had finished, Sam stared silently across the yard at nothing. It was then that I realized why he had turned his back to me in the cell. When he threw his quick mind racing into deep thought, he blocked out all distractions, focusing only on what was essential. It was a trait I would learn to respect and even mimic in the future.

Sam's thought process had lasted a long minute back in the cell, but this time it took mere seconds. When those amber eyes clicked back into reality, I knew that our mutual questions were about to be answered.

"Kid, we've known each other less than twenty-four hours, so it's truly premature for us to be having this conversation at all. But," he said, looking directly at me, "I believe in both divine appointments and in evolution, even at this rate of speed. I also believe we would have come to this point eventually, so we may as well do it now. I'm going to trust that you will keep what I am going to share with you in the strictest confidence. If I didn't think you would, our discussion would terminate right now. But that is not going to be the case."

I nodded simply, not wanting to interrupt his flow.

"First of all, let me clear this up for you," he said. "Up until now, besides me, only one other man in this institution of higher learning has been given the label of Untouchable, and that other guy is on death row—the term by no means indicates any kind of immunity from the system. What it does mean, however, is that you are under an unwritten code of protection from the general prison population, enforced by a very powerful and feared outside organization. It is a simple fact that if any inmate harasses you in any way, he's as good as a walking dead man."

A light came on. "So, *that's* what being an Untouch—"

"Please don't interrupt me," he barked. "Now, as I was about to say, the first time I heard your name was from a well-known Miami defense attorney. He came up here early last week under the pretense of being my lawyer, needing to discuss legal matters. An attorney cannot be denied access to speak with his client in complete privacy.

180

"This attorney asked if I would consider being a guardian of sorts over an incoming young inmate. You, to be precise. He went on to say that I was under no obligation, but should I choose to do so, it would be considered a service to this outside organization and they would be indebted to me for this favor. This is beside the point," he added, "but they already are in debt to me. My being an Untouchable is part of the repayment of that debt. These people always honor a service, so in my best interests, I agreed. That's why you are my cellmate."

My brain was putting all the pieces in place as I traced a line in the dirt with my finger.

"But the real question remains unanswered," Sam went on. "How did the Florida State Prison System get its arm twisted to the point of yanking your good-as-dead young self out of the clutches of Scruggs in 33 and transferring you back to the safety of Raiford as a protected Untouchable? What do you think?"

My response was immediate. "Sam, I think that was a test question and an easy one, now. When I called Roy Tanner and told him that my life was on the line, he contacted the Cicero family and the two cut some kind of deal involving, as you say, a service. That has been my assumption all along."

Sam nodded.

"However," I went on, "since the Chicago mob can't have a lot of pull in this state—at least not with the prison authorities—they contacted somebody who does. My guess is—and I bet I'm right—that the Chicago Italians, the Ciceros, call the Miami Italians, the Spataros, aren't they? So the Spataros twist the state's arm and contact a prison Italian. That's you, right? With all these Italians callin' each other, these so-called services must have been flyin' around like a flock of crazed Italian birds of prey. And that's why I'm here with you. How am I doin' so far?"

181

"You're *doing* well," Sam replied, a pleased smile cracking his stone face. "Makes perfect sense to me."

"I think that's about as far as it goes, don't you?" I asked.

"As far as it needs to go, anyway," he agreed.

"But you know what's funny?" I asked.

"What?"

"You and I are sitting here in the dirt, in the middle of a maximum security prison, and we're the only ones out of the whole bunch of players involved who aren't in debt to anyone."

That slight smile appeared again, but Sam's eyes were laughing loudly.

"To paraphrase Humphrey Bogart at the end of *Casablanca*," he said, "'You know, kid, this could be the beginning of a beautiful friendship.' Let's walk for a while."

We stood, leaving our butt-prints in the dirt, and emerged into the bright, warm morning sunshine.

"Sam?"

"Oh, God," he said. "Another question?"

"That's a curious question," I replied.

"And that's redundant," he said.

"What's redundant?"

"It means—"

"I know what the hell it means, Sam," I interrupted. "What I don't know is, what did I say that was redundant?"

"'Curious question' is what you said, kid."

"And...?"

"Of course it's curious; it's a question," he replied, lapsing back into English 101. "So what is *your* question?"

"Forget about it," I demurred. "Not worth asking, really. I don't have a question."

"What in the hell are you talking about?"

"Nothing," I said, looking away.

"What is it?" Sam asked. "What's on your mind,

kid?"

"Nothing."
"Kid, don't do that to me."
"Sure you won't mind?"
"Yes, I'm sure! What is it?"
"Why are you here?"

CHAPTER 10
ADDIO, MARCO; HELLO, SAM

August 1920

Marco Mastrangli's birth was a long and painful one for his mother. Over twenty hours of strenuous labor drained all the strength from the frail woman, such that it took great effort for her just to open her eyes to see the crying infant her husband, Vincenzo, held proudly for her to see. A faint smile crossed the exhausted woman's gaunt face as her eyes glazed under slowly closing lids. The moment Marco came into this world, his mother left for another.

Vincenzo's initial joy of having a newborn son was crushed by the overwhelming grief of losing his beloved wife. He believed his son to be the sole cause of her death and could not stand the sight of this matricidal infant. The man's devastation was so complete, he could scarcely function as a human being, let alone a father. He did not know what to do with himself or the child. He did the only thing he could do.

Vincenzo Mastrangli's nameless son left his father's home in a basket, cradled in the arms of his paternal grandmother, Sophia. In Roman Catholic tradition, she named the boy after Saint Marco.

Together, Sophia and Marco traveled by mule cart to the village of Carini, thirty kilometers west of Vincenzo's home in Palermo, Sicily. There he stayed, raised in a home filled with motherly love and incredible wisdom. He grew to be a nice-looking boy with a quick mind and an unquenchable thirst for knowledge. His tutor was an elderly British woman, the widow of an Italian count, who also gave

Marco English lessons.

Things Marco's grandmother did not know—which was not much—he soon discovered for himself. Sophia's greatest delight in Marco's education was when, at the age of ten, he confided to her why he thought the *Mafioso* would ultimately rule Palermo. She knew that would certainly come to pass and prayed that Marco would live beyond that bloody day. She was certain she would not.

And she did not. Two years later, when Marco was twelve, the old woman died peacefully in her sleep.

Over the years, Vincenzo Mastrangli had softened his attitude toward his son. In fact, he had begun to feel guilty. He knew Marco had no one else to turn to, so, once again, he did the only thing he could do.

He returned to Palermo with the boy, where he tried, with great success, to be the father he had never been. He warmly welcomed Marco into his home and his life. They became equal partners in everything. Mastrangli Seafood Supply became Mastrangli and Son Seafood Supply.

Six days a week, weather permitting, father and son cast off their small outboard-powered wooden boat and fished the blue waters of the Tyrrhenian Sea. The senior Mastrangli was a legend on the Palermo docks, considered almost mystical by the other fishermen. He was a master weather forecaster, always knowing when to sail and when to return to port. His knowledge of which beds to fish and when was unrivaled. If *The Sophia* had not been one of the fastest vessels in the fleet, half the fishing boats sailing out of Palermo would have followed her. *The Sophia* was not always the first to cast off, but she was usually the first to return to the docks, supplying her day's catch to the finest restaurants in the city.

Marco loved the sea. Life was good.

The only unpleasantness in the boy's life was

Palermo. He hated the city. He thanked God he did not have to work in town or go to school there. To Marco, the only thing in the whole city worth his time was the public library, which allowed him to continue his education. He loved reading and learning almost as much as his life at sea. He often thought, with some amusement, that if he ever stopped learning, his grandmother would return from the dead and give him a fat lip.

As Marco grew, so did his disdain for Palermo. He considered the city a poor, dirty, noisy place. The thing that disturbed him most was the thinly disguised fear that permeated the air itself. Palermo seemed to be in a constant state of anarchy, with the women dressed totally in black, continually mourning the death of loved ones. No one ever complained; they just mourned.

Finding Palermo increasingly depressing, Marco found the sea increasingly cleansing. Six days a week, his life was great. He often wished to he could spend Sundays on the water with his father, breathing the clean, fresh salt air of the sea.

⛓⛓⛓

Vincenzo planned to make this particular Sunday morning one that would bring his son great joy. It was Marco's eighteenth birthday, and by God, this was one Sunday Vincenzo was not going to witness the boy falling into his weekly Palermo Sulk.

Marco was still rubbing the sleep out of his eyes when he approached the kitchen table for their traditional Sunday morning breakfast. This was always the highlight of Marco's day. His father was a wonderful cook, and Sunday breakfasts were something Vincenzo took great pride and joy in preparing. And Marco in eating.

It was not until Marco pulled his chair up to the table

that he looked at his plate. There was no food on it. Instead, he found a package wrapped in plain brown paper. On it, carefully printed in black crayon, was just one word: *Marco*.

Vincenzo Mastrangli's only child opened the gift, and what he found left him speechless. He could not even smile, so numbed was he with shock and happiness.

The gift was the most wonderful thing in the world: A book. And what a book it was. A hand-bound volume encased in dark-brown leather, elaborately decorated in shining gold leaf. It must have weighed two kilograms. Printed on the parchment flyleaf, in English, were the words "First Printing." This marvelous book was a first edition of Herman Melville's classic, *Moby Dick*.

For the first time in the six years since his grandmother's death, Marco cried. As he wiped away his tears of delight, he looked up at his father, whose his eyes were now filled with love.

It was at that moment that Vincenzo Mastrangli's head slammed facedown into his breakfast. He died instantly from a massive brain hemorrhage.

Marco's eighteenth birthday was the worst day of his young life. He managed to hold himself together throughout the day's traditional Sicilian rituals of death. The priests, the last rites, and the mourners were morbidly black. The whole city was black. Everything was black.

The next day was not any better. Monday was devoted to the morose formalities of death. The coroner, the death certificate, the lawyers, the last will and testament, the bank, more priests and mourners, all dressed in black. Even the sky was black.

Tuesday was brighter. The morning broke sunny and clear as Marco boarded *The Sophia* and cast off, sailing out of the harbor with her course set for the open sea. Trailing in her wake was the fishing fleet of Palermo.

When Marco came directly over his father's favorite

fishing beds, he cut the engine and stopped dead in the water. The other fishing boats slowly surrounded *The Sophia,* forming a giant circle on the calm water. Once all the engines shut down, the only sound was that of the sea, softly lapping at the circle of wooden hulls.

Marco approached the port side of the bow, dragging a heavy canvas sail bag. He gently slid the weighted bag over the side and watched his father's body sink slowly out of sight into the depths of the place they both loved so much.

Marco returned to the stern, started the engine, and headed back to port alone. The other fishermen waved him fare-thee-well and began their business of the day. Marco's day was just beginning as well, but it was not going to be fishing. He had other matters to attend to.

By the end of the week, Marco's business was completed. He had sold his grandmother's house in Carini, his father's home on the outskirts of Palermo, and *The Sophia.* The eighteen-year-old fisherman from Sicily was financially secure.

Early Saturday morning, Marco walked up the gangplank of a rusting British tramp steamer sailing for America. He handed his one-way passage ticket to the purser and was directed to his cabin. He unpacked his single suitcase, stowed his gear, and made ready for a long voyage.

When Marco felt the first soft vibrations of the diesel engines, he knew they were ready to cast off. He went up to the bridge deck and watched the port of Palermo slide by for the last time. When the ship cleared the harbor breakwaters and passed the final bobbing buoy, she picked up speed and headed for open sea. Marco walked back to his cabin, closed the door, and never looked back. His journey to the new world had begun.

And a new world it would be indeed.

Marco got out of Italy just in time. Although the depression of Europe only lightly impacted the fishing industry, the European economy was still shaky, and the ruthless Benito Mussolini was conscripting young men for his fascist war machine. Few of those boys would survive the next six years.

Back on the ship, the image in the cabin mirror reflected the figure of a young man looking older than his eighteen years. Like most Italian boys, Marco had matured early. Physically, at just under six feet and a trim one hundred seventy pounds, he appeared to be in his early twenties. Aside from striking amber eyes, Marco bore classically Roman features, with straight dark-brown hair and a light olive complexion. Like most young Italian men, he only owned one suit but it was a good one, well tailored out of soft tan wool and silk. He would never wear black again.

Marco spent most of his time cloistered in his cabin, reading the classic gifted to him by his father. He practiced his second language diligently. Marco had always been quite the mimic. Although his rolling Italian tongue occasionally got in the way of perfect pronunciation, he'd found it easy to imitate his tutor's ("countess," she'd insisted) accent. With the intermittent intrusion of his Italian inflection, his English sounded vaguely Irish or Scottish.

Marco was aware that the text he was reading contained outdated modes of speech, some of which gave him difficulty, but he plowed on, sometimes reading aloud in his lilting accent. Even though he couldn't understand all he read, his love for language increased with each day on board. He was determined to be truthful, literate, and skillful in his use of words.

Sixteen days later, Marco closed the book, picked up his suitcase, left the cabin, and walked to the portside top deck. When he saw the Statue of Liberty emerge through the morning fog, he knew he was home.

Marco's introduction to America was the same as the countless thousands who had come before him. He walked down the gangplank to disembark and set his first foot on American soil on an island in New York harbor. It was Ellis Island, the major port of entry for Europeans crossing the Atlantic Ocean to the eastern coast of the United States.

The immigration center was a foreboding red-brick structure of immense proportions, filled with the garbled hum of voices from many different nations. When Marco entered the gloomy building, a man in an official-looking uniform pinned a large yellow tag to his lapel, which read in large black letters: *W.O.P.*

Throughout the process of customs and immigration, Marco was addressed only as "Wop." Though he had learned to speak English quite well, he had no idea what this term meant. He knew one thing, however: it was derogatory. He could tell from the way people said it as they looked at him with thinly veiled disgust.

Marco looked through the crowd and spotted an Englishman he had met aboard ship. He asked the man if he would be kind enough to translate the meaning for him.

"It means 'With Out Papers,'" the Englishman told him. "It also means—I regret to inform you—that none of these colonialist copper blokes think very highly of you or any of your Italian mates. I wouldn't worry about that a great deal though, young man. It's nothing personal. These bloody coppers don't think too awful well of anyone who is not exactly the same as they are. From the appearance of these red-faced louts, that means Irish. Damn shame, too, because my family here tells me that once you get past these bureaucratic arses, the Americans actually seem to be a decent lot." With that the man turned to leave. "Good luck to you, my boy," he said. "Cheerio."

The process went on and on, one long line after

another, each ending with what seemed to be an unscalable mountain of paperwork. Early the following morning, Marco handed his last handful of papers to a gruff official sitting on a stool behind a high counter. The man directed Marco to sign yet another series of documents. Marco was given a pen and ordered to sign his name—if he could, he was told sarcastically—on each dotted line preceded by an "X." Marco did, and after much stamping and sorting, a copy of each document was given to him. His immigration was complete.

When Marco finally walked into the city of New York, he was no longer Marco Mastrangli. He had signed at all the "X's" as Sam Miller.

ᄇᄇᄇᄇᄇ

Sam Miller felt free. He was free of the past and free of his Italian heritage that from a first impression was a hindrance in America. Sam was aware of prejudices; he saw how the people of Palermo treated outsiders. Even other Italians from the north were looked at with a healthy dose of scrutiny and suspicion.

When Sam signed his new alias to the paperwork at Ellis Island, he was simply avoiding what he thought would be minor ostracism. He had no idea how many doors of opportunity had just become available to him. The first door would open shortly.

On the final ferry ride to the metropolis, Sam was amazed and slightly intimidated by the vastness, both horizontal and vertical, of New York City. He had never seen buildings so tall, some of which disappeared into the lifting fog. From a distance, Sam could hear the big-city cacophony, and it grew as the boat approached the docks.

The anticipation and excitement of his new life had Sam gripping the ferry railing, impatient to the point of wanting to jump in the harbor and swim the final feet of the journey. The boat was finally tied up and Sam was the first passenger to disembark. He jogged the length of the dock and stopped where the wooden planks met the pavement.

Sam turned, looking eastward across the harbor and out to sea, as if to catch a last glimpse of the Port of Palermo he had left over two weeks ago. Sam chuckled at the absurdity then suddenly felt very alone. A moment of doubt and longing for what was familiar hit him, but it passed just as quickly. *"Addio, mia Italia,"* Sam whispered and then turned and took his first step on the ground of his new home.

⛓⛓⛓⛓⛓

Sam didn't get far. He was met by dozens of men all shouting questions at him at once.

"You speak English?"

"Looking for a place to stay?"

"Hey, you wanna girl?"

"What kinda work you do?"

These were the infamous wharf hustlers. Their job was to gain someone's confidence and then quickly relieve the unsuspecting patsy of whatever money or valuables they had brought along. More than a few had spent their first, and sometimes last, day in America as a victim of these leeches, who preyed on the vulnerability of new immigrants. Sam had seen this sort in his own homeport and had the situation in control.

"Thank you so much," Sam replied in his oddly accented English, "but my family is coming to meet me. Must be on my way."

Sam didn't like the lie, but he needed a quick excuse. As he shouldered his way through the throng, he was jostled by a large, ruddy-faced man wearing a shabby pea coat and a black woolen cap. At precisely the same time, a

192

boy who was a miniature version of the big man—coat, cap, and all—grabbed at Sam's suitcase and started to run. Sam's grip on the bag tightened instinctively and he tugged back violently. The boy lost his grip and found himself running sideways in midair before crashing to the ground face-first.

"What'd you do to my boy, you guinea bastard?" the big man shouted, hurling a bear-pawed fist at Sam.

Sam ducked and swung his suitcase at the man's feet. With the combined force of Sam's move and the launch of his own punch, the man fell to the pavement—hard. As the father-son criminal team lay on the ground shaking off their mostly-pride-inflicted wounds, the rest of the crowed howled with laughter and cleared a path for Sam and his belongings. Sam looked down and noticed the yellow "W.O.P." label still affixed to his jacket. He tore it off, crumbled the paper into a small ball, and threw it into the first litter-can he saw.

As he continued walking, Sam was absorbed in thoughts of finding work and a place to stay. Sensing a presence, Sam turned and found a man dressed in a tailored suit and fedora hat following him. The man had a suspicious air and a deadeye stare.

"I don't want trouble," Sam said as he faced off with the slim, olive-skinned man.

"Not here to give you any," the man replied. He appeared to be confused by Sam's speech. "You paisan?" he asked. "Siciliano?"

"I suppose you could say I was," said Sam. "What do you want?"

"I saw the way you handled those Irish dipshits back there," the man said. "My boss needs a guy who knows how to take care of himself. Pays pretty good and the benefits are even better."

Sam focused in on the idea—closing his mind off from his surroundings but remaining wary of potential danger.

"What does it involve?" Sam asked.

"Why don't you let him tell you?" the man asked. "C'mon, it's right nearby."

Sam hesitated.

"Look, I ain't gonna hurt ya or nothin', alright?" he promised. "Just hear what he's gotta say, an' if you don't like it, no problem."

The man's friendly smile with perfect white teeth disarmed Sam at once. Sam knew he was out of danger, for now.

"Okay," he agreed. "I thank you for taking interest on my behalf."

"Like I said, no problem. Hey, you part limey or somethin'?"

Sam chuckled. "No, my tutor was a Lady of the Manor, though."

"Name's Tony Nucci," the man told him with an exaggerated bow. "Allow me to welcome you to our fair city."

"That's quite gracious of you," said Sam. "Sam Miller, I'm pleased to make—"

"Hey, what the fuck gives with that talk?" interrupted Tony. "I gotta tell ya, it's too fuckin' funny to hear that fuckin' voice come out of a fuckin' dago!"

Sam listened to Tony's accent and managed to mimic a very passable "What da fuck is wid all the fuckin' fucks?"

Tony laughed, and as he did, his long, lean body seemed to coil and uncoil vertically. Sam thought he looked like a car's shock absorber in motion.

This was no chance meeting, Sam would learn. Tony was an underling in the hierarchy of La Cosa Nostra and his boss was a made man. They mainly handled the numbers games, in addition to the occasional loan sharking. Both businesses had their share of shirkers, so every now and then a little "reminder" had to be put out. The memo usually consisted of dark men in darker suits with the darkest ideas about how to collect unpaid debts. Tony's job was to recruit what he termed "famiglia fresca": single-male Italian immigrants, fresh off the boat, who had the ability to pull out a can of whoop-ass and use it with extreme prejudice. This responsibility was awarded to Tony, thanks to his charming yet unintimidating good looks and the fact that he was brother-in-law to his boss.

VROOOM!!!

The number of cars, taxis, trucks, and buses was staggering. Sam and Tony had walked through the Battery and now entered South Manhattan. As Sam looked up Wall Street, and then *up* at Wall Street, his gasp was audible. Even more magnificent at close range, the buildings soared into the sky. The chattering and shouts of the fishmongers on the docks of Palermo had been the highlight of Sam's auditory experience of humanity; here, the chaotic mixture of metropolitan sounds had a stirring harmony all its own. The symphony of this city intrigued and excited Sam. As he listened to the man-made canyons echo the orchestra of voices and vehicles, he knew he wanted to be part of it.

Sam lowered his eyes to street level and they landed on a newsstand. So many papers and magazines! Sam was excited at the wealth of reading material. It would aid him in becoming familiar with the language of his new land, which would lead Sam to his calling.

Tony hailed a taxi and they took the short drive to Greenwich Village. En route, Sam's fascination with the surroundings kept him distracted.

"You hear what I said?" Tony asked, not masking his frustration.

"I'm sorry. What was it?"

"I said, you like osso buco?" Tony re-inquired.

"Yes, of course."

"Well, where we're goin', they gotta osso buco to forget about," Tony announced, smiling and rubbing his tight stomach.

"Why would you be excited about something you'd rather forget?" Sam was genuinely confused.

"No," Tony said. "When I say 'forget about it,' I mean it's to die for."

"Why on earth would anyone die— Ahh, I get it. It's sarcasm."

Tony wrinkled his brow. "Yeah, sure."

Sam's intellect obviously took Tony off-guard. And, Sam figured, he'd probably never come across an Italian with an Irish-sounding accent. Tony shrugged it off.

"But you gotta remember," Tony cautioned, "*sometimes* when I say 'forget about it,' I mean, forget about it."

"I believe I understand."

Sam was enjoying the mental challenge of following Tony's dialect. He had no familiarity with the slang of the city, so he absorbed Tony's vernacular. As this went on, Sam realized how he could use his love for words and phrases.

He also realized the situation he was currently in. He had no intention of going to work for the Mafia. Though Palermo was a small town, the Mafioso dealings in America were common knowledge. What was uncommon knowledge was La Cosa Nostra's magnanimous side. Many people were known to have received good "recommendations" on their behalf for legitimate work. This was one of the myriad methods the Mafia used to cleanse its conscience.

They arrived at Maria's, a small one-window storefront squeezed by two larger buildings on either side. Inside, the restaurant was lit in a soft, buttery light. It reminded Sam of sunset, and he noticed how easily the patrons melted into the shadows. Sam didn't sense danger, but the atmosphere had a lurking feel to it.

A beefy man in a perfectly tailored navy-blue silk suit sat at the last booth, beyond which lay the kitchen entrance and bathrooms off the hallway. A door at the end of the hall was barred. At the booth just before it, two men burst out laughing, one with a gravelly guffaw. As Sam and Tony approached them, the more boisterous of the two, the gravel-laugher, looked up.

"Hiya, Tony. How ya doin?"

"Yeah, how ya doin'?" Tony replied. "Boss, how ya doin'?"

"How ya doin' Ton?" The man who spoke was examining Sam as he addressed Tony. His deep olive skin absorbed the dim light, causing his head to appear like a bronze bust with black hair. Sam couldn't tell how tall he was, but he could see the man was fit and around mid-forties.

"Boss, I met this guy havin' a dance with a couple wharf rats," said Tony. "Sam Miller, this is Vincenzo Carlotti and Sal Ribisi."

"How ya doin', Sam?" Carlotti reached across the table and shook Sam's hand.

Sal put out a big mitt with a gold-wrapped three-carat ruby on the pinky finger. "How ya doin'?" he repeated.

Sam wasted no time. "How ya doin'?"

Tony started his Slinky impersonation again, chuckling rhythmically. As it subsided, he continued. "Boss, guy just come in from Ellis. Thought maybe you could put him to work."

"Where you from, Sam?" Vinny inquired.

"Palermo, sir. I grew up in Carini."

"Where'd you learn to talk English that way?"

"My tutor"—it came out *tyu-tah*—"was English. She did inform me that you Americans spoke a bit differently."

It was Vinny's turn to laugh. "Yeah, you could say that. So what kinda work you do?"

197

"I spent some time fishing with my father."

"Hard work," Vinny said. "Makes you tough then breaks your back."

Sam took pride in his father and the ache of loss still throbbed. "He did quite well, though," Sam said. "The other fishermen thought angels rode on his bow."

"The Greeks got most of the fishing business here," Vinny told him. "At least till it gets to the docks."

Tony and Sal smiled at that one.

"You wanna put some of that muscle to work?" Vinny probed.

Sam saw his chance. "Actually, sir, it would be a great deal of help if you might refer me to a newspaper in need of a writer."

❈❈❈❈❈

Sam managed to find a clean but cheap furnished fifth-floor flat on the southern edge of Little Italy bordering Chinatown. He was fascinated with the pockets of ethnicity; to him, New York City was a microcosm of the entire world.

After two restful nights and some Italian and Chinese meals under his belt (the latter being his new favorite), Sam took his first subway ride toward Broadway.

Named for the newspaper's former location, Times Square was humming as Sam made his way to 229 West 43rd Street, the new home of *The New York Times,* where his afternoon interview was scheduled. His appointment had been personally made by Vinny the day before, whose cousin's sister-in-law worked as a secretary for the junior editor. Being "connected" can consist of many layers.

At eighteen stories, the year-old Annex building was a runt in comparison to the skyscrapers that adorned the Manhattan skyline. Sam made his way inside, where he was directed to Randall Williams' office on the fourteenth floor.

On the way to the elevator, Sam could smell the ink and bleached paper of the evening edition being printed.

When the door opened on fourteen, Sam looked across the foyer and knew he was finished. In an instant, the woman looking at him stole his breath and heart.

Walking toward her desk, Sam managed to mouth the words, "Mister Williams, please."

"Good thing you're not on radio with that voice" was her quick reply. "Mister Williams, you say?"

Her voice was smoky syrup and Sam knew he wanted to hear it forever. Blue-black hair framed an impossibly perfect alabaster face unadorned with makeup. She didn't need any. A Roman goddess incarnate in an electric blue dress.

"Yes, dear. I mean, madam...Forgive me, ma'am. Oh my. Yes. Sam Miller to see Mr. Williams, please."

The receptionist suppressed a giggle. "You're not from around here." She pressed a button on her intercom and informed Mr. Williams that Mr. Miller had arrived. Sam didn't have the chance to respond before she told him, "Mister Williams will see you now. Third glass door on the left."

"Right. I mean left. You said left, right? Yes?"

This time she giggled out loud and it made Sam's heart skip. She nodded and pointed toward the office.

Randall Williams leaned against his doorframe, puffing on a cigarette, as Sam approached. He had a full head of slicked-back white-blond hair and was short at five feet five inches. He was very fit and did not appear to be intimidated by having to look up at Sam.

"Randall Williams," he said. "Call me Randy. Drea tells me you're here about a job."

"Yes, sir. Drea?"

"My secretary, Miss Andrea Trepani. Everyone calls her Drea."

"Lovely." Sam sighed.

"What's that?"

"I said it would be lovely to discuss what's available at your paper."

"C'mon in and let's get to know each other."

⧳⧳⧳⧳⧳

One hour and twenty-five minutes later, Sam walked out of Randy Williams' office as the newest cub reporter for the crime section of *The New York Times*. Williams told Sam he was impressed with Sam's language and writing skills, but explained that when writing for the paper, he would need to dumb it down a bit.

"Write your copy like you're talking to a fourth grader," Randy advised, "and you'll do great."

Sam passed Drea's empty desk and took a moment to glance around.

"She's gone for the day." Randy chuckled as he retreated into his office. "See you bright and early."

HURRICANE CLAIMS OVER 700 NEW ENGLAND LIVES

WAR TAXES RESOURCES AND HEARTS OF AMERICANS

FIVE HUNDRED DIE IN BOSTON NIGHTCLUB FIRE

These were a few of the stories Sam would write about during his tenure at *The Times*. It wasn't all bad news, though. The U.S. economy was now recovering. The World's Fair captured the imaginations of the forty-four million who attended. Sam became a hockey fan and

200

watched his New York Rangers win the Stanley Cup.

After the attack on Pearl Harbor, Sam volunteered for service with the navy, who kept him in the reserves and pulling double-duty as a writer for the *Bureau of Naval Personnel Magazine*. The Times Square celebration of V-J Day and the end of World War II was a sign of America's prosperous days ahead.

Following four years of courtship, Sam received Drea's father's blessing to marry his one and only daughter. After the newlyweds spent two years living under the Trepani family's roof, Sam and Drea moved to a small apartment on St. Mark's in artsy Greenwich Village.

One evening, after redrafting some last-minute copy for the morning edition, Sam wandered by the Café Society on his walk home. Being a jazz-lover, he recognized John Coltrane's stylistic saxophone pouring its soulful notes onto Sheridan Square. He was tempted to stop in, but he wanted to get home to Drea.

As Sam ambled down the next block, he heard a woman's frantic scream in the shadows of a narrow alley. Instinct overrode his fear of the unknown as he ran headlong into the darkness. As his eyes adjusted, he saw a woman fall to the pavement as her assailant brutally punched her in the face. She no longer made a sound as the man reached into his trousers, about to make this violent episode even worse. Sam dove at him from six feet away, knocking the rapist against the brick wall with a textbook hockey-style body check into a row of steel trashcans.

Two men bore down on the scene, drawing pistols from shoulder holsters.

"Fuckin' move again and I will drill one between your eyes!" shouted the first, pointing his snub-nose .38 at Sam's head. "Police! On your knees and put your hands where I can see 'em!"

Sam also saw his partner aiming at him. As his vision

adjusted, he looked confused. "Sam Miller? What in the..."

Sam knew Detective Thom Forrestall and First Detective Parker Campbell well from his crime-reporting days. They immediately shifted their pistols to the man on the ground as he regained consciousness.

Sam was breathing heavily. "I heard this woman and ran down to see what was the matter. This man was giving her quite a beating and I'm certain he was about to– Oh, dear God."

Sam recognized the woman. It was Carla, the wife of Vinny Carlotti, the man who had helped Sam get a job at the paper all those years ago. He had met Carla when she and Vinny attended Sam's wedding.

The next realization was even stranger. Sam felt his gut churn when he recognized the big ruddy-faced man getting handcuffed by Detective Campbell as the same wharf hustler Sam had fought with on his first day arriving to New York. He was also obviously acquainted with the two detectives.

"Peter Burkey, you piece of shit," Campbell said. "You picked the wrong neighborhood. Thom, get a squad car down here to take this fuck-stick uptown. Then we can take Sam and this lady's statements."

Forrestall headed out of the alley to find a pay phone as Campbell smacked Peter Burkey on the head. Hard. Burkey winced and looked over his shoulder at Sam, glaring with seething rage, as if to say "This isn't over."

"Sam Miller, oh my God!" It was the first thing Carla had said since Sam's arrival in the alley. "Please, we can't tell Vinny about this. If he knew I was in a nightclub without him, he'd blow a fuse."

"Carla, listen to me," Sam told her calmly. "You found yourself in our neighborhood and were on your way to say hello to your favorite cousin, Drea. I was on my way home and happened along just in time. Got it?"

"Thanks, Sam" was Carla's grateful reply. "You know Vinny's gonna want to repay you somehow."

"Think nothing of it," said Sam. "Glad I was here to help."

After the detectives took their statements, Sam walked Carla back to his apartment.

Drea had been wondering why Sam was so late. After seeing Carla's swollen eye and hearing the whole story, she took a deep breath.

"Carla," she said, "I'm glad you're okay and you might as well hear something that will lift you up. Guess who's going to have a baby?"

The two women squealed with glee as the exciting reality hit Sam: he would soon be a father!

⛓⛓⛓⛓⛓

The paper had a field day with the sensationalism surrounding the attempted rape trial of Peter Burkey. The cast of characters was a dream: a career criminal with a mile-long rap sheet, an alleged mob lieutenant's wife, and one of their own reporters as the local hero. The story was followed by newswires around the country.

When Sam testified at trial, he did his best to avoid eye contact with Peter Burkey. But he could feel the cold stare of the psychopath boring into him throughout his testimony. That same pit in his stomach as when he recognized Burkey in the alley was a warning Sam couldn't shake.

After four days of hearing the evidence, the jury reached a decision in less than forty-five minutes. With a credible eyewitness and two police officers' testimonies, the guilty verdict was handed down: Peter Burkey would spend ten years in Sing Sing Prison with no chance for early release.

Upon hearing the verdict and sentencing, Sam felt an inexplicably strong sense of relief wash over him. He would never see that lunatic again.

⛓⛓⛓⛓⛓

Waiting was the hardest part. Sam was standing outside the delivery room at Mount Sinai Hospital. One of the nurses instructed him to remain in the waiting room, but Sam was having none of that. He wanted to be there the instant his child came into the world. Just for laughs, he'd bought both a blue and a pink teddy bear from the gift shop downstairs and was feeling smug about being so well prepared.

When Sam heard the newborn's wailing announcement of its arrival into this world, he could no longer contain himself. He bolted into the delivery room.

All he could see was the blood that seemed to be everywhere.

"She's hemorrhaging. Give me that clamp and a lot more sponges. And I need suction, dammit!" The doctor turned to see Sam at the doorway. "And get him the hell out of here!"

Everything blurred in Sam's mind as the infant continued to cry and the doctor shouted orders. Sam refused to move and watched helplessly as the life drained out of Drea. He vaguely felt a nurse touch his shoulder and wondered why he was now seated on the floor, leaning against the doorframe.

"I'm so sorry, Mister Miller. We did everything we could to save them both. We managed to keep your daughter alive, but it hurts me to say that your wife is no longer with us."

They were the last heartbreaking words Sam heard before he passed out.

The next two years were a contradiction between time flying and standing still. Young Jessica was growing so quickly.

Sam threw himself into his work, with Drea's parents taking care of little Jess when Sam was at the paper. Sam was tortured by the memories that haunted him at every corner of the city: fun nights at Café Society; the little Chinese restaurant on the corner; summers in Central Park. They all brought back Drea and that dreadful day in hospital.

Sam picked up Jess from the Trepanis' flat and headed back to the apartment he no longer considered home. He absentmindedly pulled the mail from the box and fumbled with it in one hand as he held his precious daughter's hand with the other. When they reached the door, Sam unlocked it, and Jess bolted inside to retrieve her favorite pink teddy bear.

A bittersweet smile crossed Sam's face as he opened the letter from the *Miami Herald* stating they would like him to begin work with them as soon as he could get to Florida.

CHAPTER 11
GO SOUTH, YOUNG MAN

January 1932

Bubba Red MacDonald—his real name—was conceived somewhere in Appalachia, West Virginia. His was an unfortunate pregnancy brought to term by his twelve-year-old mother screaming behind a one-hole outhouse. The young girl, it seemed, was unable to outrun her faster, fourteen-year-old twin brothers. Which of the twins fathered Bubba is unknown.

The family MacDonald did not think anything unusual about this birth and accepted their newest inbred addition, nurturing him with all the Appalachian love they could muster. Appalachian love, from the MacDonald clan point of view, consisted primarily of affectionate slaps upside the head and large wooden bowls heaped with mounds of greasy fried food of undetermined origin. Bubba developed a high tolerance for the slaps and an abiding love for Granny MacDonald's cooking. The next best thing to eating Granny's slop was playing with his food and watching it slide down the side of his bowl in congealing, greasy globs.

As Bubba's love for food grew, so did he—to massive dimensions. He was only five-foot-eight and appeared nearly as wide, at something over two hundred and fifty round pounds. His fat face was framed by a shock of stringy bright-orange hair, which graced a perpetually slack jaw and blank pale-blue eyes half-hidden by heavy, drooping lids. And true to the family MacDonald's genetics, Bubba possessed the intelligence of a gerbil.

Nothing is known of Bubba's formative years. No records of any kind even indicate he existed. He never possessed one single piece of personal identification. It is known, however, that at some point during his nineteenth year in 1952, he evidently grew tired of slaps upside the head and left home, walking down Highway 23, following his nose south in a never-ending quest for greasier food.

Bubba did not have much going for him, but he did have one redeeming trait: He possessed a remarkable, bird-brained primal instinct for heading south. His successful migration to South Florida was a wonder. Bubba had absolutely no idea how he managed his miraculous journey other than saying, with great pride, "I'm pretty good at crossin' streets."

It was in West Miami where Bubba got lucky. He was hired by the Silver Star drive-in restaurant as a dishwasher and given sleeping space in the storeroom, where he served as night watchman as well. This was heaven for the slow-witted young man. His tastes were simple, his needs were few, and he didn't have to worry about a thing. He had a place to live where he could devour the endless supply of food that he lived for.

Saturday nights were the most hectic time for the restaurant, and for Bubba. Every car bay was always filled, and lines of automobiles parked on the street waiting for a space. This was the night when hundreds of teenagers came to the restaurant, to socialize and show off their cars.

Tonight, Bubba was busily washing stacks of dirty dishes while dreaming of how his dual responsibilities would ultimately lead to an executive position. His arms were immersed in dirty, gray dishwater before they were jerked behind his back with a wrenching pain and he was violently thrown to the floor. He was handcuffed and dragged out of the kitchen to the parking lot by two extremely agitated police officers. They threw him into the back seat of their patrol car and, before a crowd had time to gather, the larger of the two hit him on the side of the jaw with all the power he had.

Bubba was blinded by pain so excruciating that whatever light was on in his dim brain went to black. He tried to speak, but the only thing that came out of his mouth was a gush of blood and two molars. The big policeman snapped Bubba's head up by jerking a fistful of orange hair.

"Can you hear me, cocksucker?" he hissed into the bewildered bloody face.

Bubba barely managed a nod.

"You bastard. I'm going to ride back here with you, motherfucker, and *if* you live to get downtown, you're going to wish you hadn't, you sick son of a bitch."

What felt like a sixteen-pound sledgehammer slammed into Bubba's stomach. That was all he remembered of the first time he was ever in a police car. In fact, that was all he would remember for the next two days.

ӠӠӠӠӠ

Sam and Jessica had adjusted well to Miami life.

Moving to the slower-paced Miami had given Sam time to reconnect with his daughter, swimming and laughing in the turquoise waters of South Beach. They spent hours digging up coquinas in the sugar sand at low tide. Jess loved to go fishing and chase crabs on Key Biscayne. Sam bought a nineteen-foot mahogany Lightning, and on weekends, they would sail together through the inlets and waterways surrounding the city's numerous islands, pretending to be pirates one day, explorers the next. Every summer, they would fly to New York for two weeks to visit Jess's grandparents and open her eyes to northeast culture and cuisine.

At four years of age, Jess was already fluent in both

reading and speaking English as well as Sam's native Italian; she was also versed in Spanish, with the help of their housekeeper, Marissa, who taught Jess a word or phrase every day. Aunt Mari, as Jess called her, was a lovely woman from Puerto Rico. Mari and Sam had become a great team at raising the keen young girl, and while Jess would hint at it in not-so-subtle fashion, Sam wasn't ready for romance yet.

It was bittersweet for Sam to watch Jess grow into the perfect likeness of her mother. He was occasionally reminded of his loss when her mannerisms and speech mimicked Drea's. The tragedy that had struck on the day of Jessica's birth was softening in Sam's memory but would never be wholly forgotten. There was no blame: He knew the maternity team had done their best. And though his grief evolved into a quiet emptiness that neither he nor Jess could fill, his love for Jess was boundless.

Solace came in the form of a pastor Sam met while investigating a church embezzlement scheme. The story won Sam a Pulitzer Prize for journalism, a few enemies, and a friend for life. Augustino Castillo was a Cuban immigrant, who, having also lost his wife in childbirth, turned to God for answers. Castillo walked away from his Catholic upbringing and embraced Pentecostalism, seeking a personal relationship with his creator. His ministry began in Havana, but like Sam, the memories were too many and too near. He opted to move and get a fresh start.

The two men became close in their common bond of loss and met regularly for lunch, their conversations ranging from the Bible to every known spiritual practice. At times, this friendly discourse became a spirited debate, with Augie's Latino and Sam's Italian passions stoking the fire of their arguments. Anyone walking by might have thought a fight was brewing, but they were always respectful of each other and never made it personal.

Sam had no desire to join an organized religion, yet

he found comfort and fulfillment in the words of the New Testament. He especially enjoyed reading scripture in Latin and was studying Greek and Hebrew so he could reflect on older forms of the text.

This day, the two had just finished their sandwiches with a scrappy dialogue of Zen Buddhism on the side. Sam had Pan con Bistec (steak slices with fried onions, potato sticks, and melted cheese) and Augie had ordered the Cuban (roast pork, ham, Swiss, pickles, and mustard, pressed in buttered Cuban bread). Both meals were washed down with *batido,* a tropical fruit shake.

Sam walked to the back of the restaurant to a pay phone to let the paper know he would be in Hialeah for the afternoon investigating a story. As he hung up and walked back to the table, he saw Augie slumped over in the booth at an awkward angle.

"Augie. *Augustino!* What's wrong? Look at me. Can you hear me?"

Augie was obviously in pain. "I hear you fine. My arm feels like it's on fire and I think someone dropped a vault on my chest."

"Can you stand? Do you think you can walk?"

"*Sí.* Yes, yes, amigo." The pastor's eyes were squeezed shut in agony and he was gasping for air.

Sam helped his friend to his feet. He was fortunate to have parked near the front door of the restaurant. He laid Augie out in the back seat of his green 1949 Ford "Shoebox" sedan and shouted to the manager to call Miami City Hospital and let them know a heart attack patient was en route.

When they arrived at the emergency room entrance, two doctors and a nurse were waiting with a gurney for the ailing pastor. They stabilized him quickly and had him resting comfortably within a few hours. But it was Sam's fast thinking and driving that most probably saved Pastor

Augustino Castillo's life. Sam was relieved to know he would have future days to break bread with his friend and explore esoteric mysteries.

It was twilight when Sam pulled into his driveway, feeling drained and more than a little hungry. Normally at this time, almost seven-thirty, the lights would be on with Mari preparing something delicious and Jess getting her homework finished before dinner. But the house was dark.

As Sam got out of the car, he sensed heaviness in the air. He glanced upward to see if a thunderstorm was brewing. But aside from some puffy clouds glowing pink on the western horizon, the sky was clear. But something felt wrong. Sam recognized it now as the same sense he had when responding to a tip on a dangerous story.

As Sam neared the front door, he spotted broken glass. His cheeks flushed and adrenaline started to pump as he threw the door open.

Nothing could have prepared Sam for what he saw next.

Blood was everywhere. It was as if someone had sprayed the entire hallway crimson. The metallic stench of it was overwhelming.

Sam called out to Jessica and slipped on the red slickness coagulating on the terrazzo floor. Nausea almost overpowering him, he looked into the living room and saw Mari sprawled on the coffee table, her face unrecognizable.

Sam screamed out more frantically for Jessica.

But when he got to the kitchen, his heart broke for the last time. Jessica's school uniform was slashed to the point of rags, strewn about the floor. He rounded the counter to find her little naked body, just one black patent-leather shoe halfway on, lying facedown, broken and lifeless.

The coroner later stated that Marissa Alvarez had been murdered a few hours before the time Jess would have made it home from school. The cause of death was blunt force trauma to the skull, the steel head of a vacuum cleaner being the probable weapon. He went on to say that the four-foot-one-inch tall body of Jessica Miller had seventy-eight stab wounds and lacerations. Her pelvis was shattered, most likely from impact by a large amount of weight.

Shock and violation assaulted every nerve in Sam's body. In spite of the many crime scenes he had covered, he would never get the intense pain out of his heart or the gruesome images and odor out of his head for the rest of his days.

Sheer will moved Sam as he stumbled to the phone and called Miami Police Department Homicide Division, a number he knew well but never imagined he would be calling from his own home. Sam stopped twice, forced to redial because his hands were shaking so badly. He spoke with a detective, hung up, leaned against the wall, and slid to the floor, still staring at his beloved Jess. All he could do now was wait, cry, and die a thousand deaths with each passing minute.

Much later, as the flood of tears and racking sobs finally began to settle, Sam felt his anguish simmer into silent yet wrathful resolve. He knew that payment would come at an extremely high cost when he discovered the killer's identity.

⛓⛓⛓⛓⛓

Bubba regained consciousness strapped to a hospital bed in the Dade County jail's psychiatric ward, in terrible pain. Confused and disoriented, his first conscious memory came rushing back. The big cop had been right: Bubba wished he were dead.

"Well, well, well, Mister MacDonald. I see that you finally woke up. Are you in much pain?"

Bubba looked up into the mean, squinting eyes of a

middle-aged man, dressed totally in white.

"You a doctor?" Bubba asked.

"Yes. Do I have to ask you everything twice? Are...you...in...pain?"

"Yeah, it hurts a bunch."

"Good." The doctor smiled. "Would you like something for the pain?"

"Uh-huh."

"Well, Mister MacDonald," said the doc, "that's just tough shit. The only thing you're going to get in here is booked for two counts of murder one. Somebody will be here soon to wheel your fat ass downstairs and book you in. I hope you get what's coming to you. And if I ever see you again, I hope it's on a slab."

The doctor glared down at Bubba for a full silent minute and then turned and walked away.

Bubba Red MacDonald was not the brightest crayon in the box, but he was beginning to get the idea that he was in for a very hard time. That's when something began to overcome the pain: Cold fear.

Two guards arrived at Bubba's bedside. He was unstrapped from the bed, hoisted and strapped into a wheelchair, and wheeled to the elevator. They descended to the first floor, where Bubba was rolled into the booking room. After fingerprinting and mug shots, he was officially booked into the Dade County jail, charged with resisting arrest, attempted escape to avoid prosecution, and attempted murder of a police officer.

He was also charged with the murder of Marissa Alvarez and the brutal sexual molestation and murder of an eight-year-old girl named Jessica Miller.

On a good day, Bubba would have had difficulty comprehending what was going on. This was not a good day, and through the haze of pain, he knew only that he wanted to get out of here, go back to the restaurant, eat, and go to sleep.

That did not happen. Instead, he was wheeled into an interrogation room and the chair was parked at a gray-painted steel table with two chairs behind it. The guards left, slamming the door shut and locking it behind them.

Bubba was thankfully alone.

He was wishing to God that he could move his hands and scratch his nose when two men in suits entered the small room. One of them was fit with a poker-faced countenance, and was sporting some sort of fancy tailored suit. The other, who was even larger than Bubba, spilled out of the top of his cheap suit pants as his sweat-stained shirt strained at the buttons. They both seated themselves and stared at him with no expression whatsoever. Then the big man smiled, speaking with a lisp that accentuated his flabby cheeks and chin.

"You're having kind of a bad time here, aren't you, Mister MacDonald?" he said. "May I call you Bubba?"

"Yeah," Bubba responded. "That's my name."

"Don't be a smartass, MacDonald," whispered the well-dressed man.

"I wasn't being a smartass. It's just my name."

"Of course it is, Bubba. We know that," said the big man, still smiling. "We know all about you. We know you're not really a bad guy; you're just in a giant shitpile of trouble, and we want to help you out of this mess you're in."

"Help me?"

"Yes, we really do want to help you. But you have to help us first."

"Help you?" Bubba repeated.

"Yes, you dumb motherfucker," said the fit man. "You fuckin' hard of hearing? And if you don't help us, I'm going to beat the livin' dog shit out of you, right here and now!"

"Hold on there, Stan," cautioned the big man. "Just

214

hold on for a minute. Let's all calm down here. Sorry about that, Bubba, but Stan just gets real pissed off when he thinks somebody's jerking him off." He took a deep breath, held it, and sighed. "Let's just start all over again. Let me introduce myself. I'm Detective Jackson Whiting. Please, just call me Jack. And this is Detective Stanley Kozloff. It might be best to call him Detective Kozloff. He's very pissed."

"He don't like me," Bubba mumbled through swollen lips. "Nobody does no more."

"It's not that he doesn't like you, Bubba," Whiting said. "It's just that he hates it when he thinks somebody's lying to him. It makes him go a little nuts. And when he goes crazy like that, there's no way to control him. You don't want that to happen," he warned. "You really don't, do you?"

"No," Bubba said, looking at the floor. "No, don't want that. Don't want nobody hittin' me no more."

"Well, Bubba," Whiting said, smiling again, "we don't want to hit you. But it's like I said before: You've got to help us out here. You help us and we'll help you. Now, we're going to ask you a few simple questions. All we want is the truth; that's all. Okay?"

"Okay," Bubba said, still looking at the floor.

"That's good, Bubba. Now we're getting somewhere. Just one more thing," Whiting added. "Can you look at us when you answer? Stan likes to look you right in the eye. That way he can tell if you're telling us the truth."

Bubba raised his blank eyes toward the detective. Whiting was the only person who had spoken kindly to him since this horrible experience began, and Bubba trusted him. However, looking over at Kozloff took all the courage he had left in his battered body. The mean detective seemed to have calmed down, but his eyes still blazed in anger. Bubba was very frightened of Kozloff, and the last thing in the world he wanted to do was make him go crazy.

"Bubba, do you know why you're here?" Whiting

asked.

"No, not for sure," said Bubba. "Didn't kill nobody though."

"Well," Whiting told him, "some people think you did. That's why Stan and I want to talk to you. And if you didn't do it, you're out of here. But first, we want ask you about something else. Do you like children, Bubba?"

"Sure do," Bubba said. "Like kids a lot. They're always nice to me."

"Are you always nice to them?"

"Yeah." Bubba nodded. "Can I go now?"

"No, you can't go now." It was Kozloff talking now. "And if you don't stop fuckin' around with us and start telling the truth, you're never going anywhere ever again, asshole. You got that?"

"Yessir, got that." Bubba now nodded up and down rapidly. "Tell the truth."

"Bubba, I want to believe you," Whiting said. " I really do. And so does my partner here. We know you want to get unstrapped from that chair and go home. And we want to make things easier for you, make you comfortable, and we can do that. All you have to do is tell us what we want to hear. Do you think you can tell us what we want to hear?"

"Yes, sir," Bubba replied, trying to think of what they wanted to hear. He desperately wanted to get out of here and go home.

"Okay, Bubba, that's very good." Whiting smiled again and then continued, "We've just got a couple more real simple questions for you, and if you give us the right answers, we'll see if we can get you out of this trouble and out of that chair."

"You said earlier that you liked kids." Kozloff took over again. "Let me ask you this: Do you like little girls the best?"

Bubba thought about this for a moment. What should he say?

"Should I say yes?" he finally asked.

"It would be a good start," Kozloff replied.

"Well, then, yeah, guess so."

"You guess so!" Kozloff shouted. "What the fuck do you mean, you guess so?! Do you or don't you? What the fuck is it, yes or no?"

"Yes."

"Yes, what?"

"Yes...I like girls the best."

Bubba thought he saw the hint of a smile on Kozloff's thin lips. Maybe everything was going to be better. Maybe it would be like Whiting said: Give the right answers, and he could get out of this mess and go home. Now, all he had to do was tell them what they wanted to know.

"You're doing real good, Bubba," Whiting said. "You're making us feel better about this. A few more truthful answers like that and we'll get you out of that chair, okay?"

"Yeah." Bubba smiled. "I'm doin' good, huh?"

"So far, so good," Whiting confirmed. " You're doing better. The more you help us, the more we can help you. It's kind of like a two-way street."

Bubba was beginning to feel hopeful. He was going to think very hard, give some really good answers, and get away from this terrible place.

"You work and live in the same place, the Silver Star drive-in, just off Highway 826 in West Miami, is that right?" asked Whiting.

Bubba exhaled. This was an easy one. "Yes, sir."

"Four days ago, last Friday evening, did you get off work early and hitch a ride with one of the customers, a Mister Meyers, who dropped you off on North Collins Avenue, in Surfside?"

217

"Yes, sir." Bubba began nodding again.

"What did you do there, Bubba?"

Bubba hesitated. "I walked around, then I walked ba—"

"That's a long way to go just to walk around," Kozloff interrupted. "And it's a long walk back to the restaurant. Several miles, in fact. Can you tell me why you would go to all that trouble just to walk around?"

"I like to look at the pretty houses," Bubba replied.

Whiting got up to stretch his legs and began walking around while Kozloff sat on the desk, continuing the interrogation.

"Now, I want you to think very hard about these next few questions," Kozloff said. "If I get the right answers, you'll make me very happy. It's got to be the honest-to-God truth though, and if it isn't, I promise you, you'll be in this shithole forever. You said you like to look at pretty houses. Do you like to look at pretty little girls, too?"

"Uh...I uh...I guess. No, wait...don't guess. Yes."

It was Kozloff's turn to nod. "Okay, good answer. Just a couple of more good answers, and you're out of that chair and we're all out of this shitty little room. You said that you like to look at pretty little girls. Now then, do you like to touch them, you know, under their dresses, stuff like that?"

Bubba did not answer. Even his limited gray matter knew what Kozloff wanted to hear, but he had been pushed around enough. He was not going to admit to hurting anybody. If he liked little girls, it was his own damned business. He knew he might have to endure more pain, strapped to this wheelchair, but he was not about to fry like a crispy chunk of dead meat in the electric chair. This had gone far enough. His brain shifted into its primal survival mode.

"No!" Bubba yelled, his voice rising hysterically to cover the coming lie. "Don't even look at pretty big girls that

218

way!"

The blow came from behind, smashing into the base of Bubba's neck with enough force to send the wheelchair careening into Kozloff. He grabbed Bubba by the ears and would have thrown him halfway across the room if Bubba had not been strapped into the chair.

"Not exactly the answer I wanted to hear!" Kozloff screamed, spitting into Bubba's swollen face. Blind rage was in his eyes as he caught something midair that Whiting tossed over Bubba's shoulder.

"Is this your cap?" Kozloff asked. "It was found one block from the murder scene. Don't even think about saying no, you motherfucker; it's got your goddamned name in it, you child-murdering son of a bitch. And this is what'll really do your fat ass in: We've got an eyewitness swears he saw you walking away from the scene of the murder at the time of the little girl's death. You killed them, didn't you?"

"No, didn't kill no—"

Kozloff hit Bubba in the face with a left hook, followed by a right cross, sending the wheelchair tumbling over, crashing backward to the floor. When Bubba opened his eyes, Whiting's face was inches from his own, red with fury.

"You're going to sign this paper," Whiting ordered. "If you don't, we're going to slowly and very painfully beat you into an unrecognizable, bloody piece of raw, rotting meat. Sign the fucking paper! Now!"

"Fuck you!"

⊡⊡⊡⊡⊡

Whiting looked up at Kozloff, defeated.

Bubba had called their bluff. There was nothing more they could do. If they beat him any more, he might die on them, and as much as they both liked Sam Miller, he was not worth losing their pensions over. So they simply quit. They had done the best they could.

Stepping out of the interrogation room, Kozloff was the first to express his frustration.

"You and I both know he's guilty as hell."

"Yep," Whiting said, nodding slowly. "It's a damn shame the taxpayers will have to pay for the courts to burn the bastard."

⛓⛓⛓⛓⛓

"Well, well, well, Mister MacDonald. I didn't think I would see you again, but here you are, better than ever."

Bubba thought he must have just awakened from the most terror-filled nightmare he had ever had. He was in the same room where he began this pain-filled dream. The same snotty, white-jacketed doctor, the same bed and straps, the same ceiling. Everything was the same, except that he was not in the same awful pain. It must have been a nightmare. If Whiting and Kozloff had been real, he would be hurting more than he was; of that he was certain.

"How are you feeling, Mister MacDonald?" asked the doctor.

"Pretty damn good. Yep, feelin' real good, alrighty."

"That's a big disappointment for me," the doc told him, "but unfortunately, it's my job to fix you up and make you look presentable. Are you in pain?"

"Pain? From what?" asked Bubba.

"Your injuries, you moron."

"Those cops were real, huh? Not a dream?"

"If it was a dream, it was a very bad one indeed." The doc glowered at him. "You ought to see your face. It's a nightmare all by itself. Now, answer the damn question—if you know how: Are you in pain?"

"Fuck you."

220

"Now, now, Mister MacDonald." The doctor's voice was tight, restraining anger. "You've developed a really bad attitude since I last saw you. But I'm going to give you a hypodermic anyway and then we're going to change your dressings. Your face is a mess, but that's what you get for attacking police officers and trying to escape. Here comes the morphine."

The doctor went to work. He was swift and professional in skill if not in manner, and in a few minutes, the bloody dressings had been removed and fresh ones applied. The morphine was taking affect now, and Bubba was feeling better than he could ever remember.

"There, now," the doctor said, admiring his handiwork. "That ought to do you for a couple of days. I'm going to give you another injection as well. We don't want you waking up in your cell, moaning and groaning, disturbing the other prisoners, now, do we? Good night, shithead."

<hr/>

Bubba regained consciousness in a small, dim cell with only one bunk, a metal toilet, and sink. He was vaguely aware of a fuzzy white form bending over his bruised, limp body. He was given another injection and lapsed back into a deep, dreamless sleep.

The evening of the following day, Bubba's stomach woke him. It was growling loudly with a gnawing emptiness. He was hungry. Really hungry.

He drew himself into a sitting position on the mattress, surprised that he was no longer restrained by leather straps. He swung his legs over the side of the steel bunk, planted his feet on the floor, and actually stood up. In spite of his weight, Bubba was quite strong and had amazing recuperative powers. Considering his injuries, the simple act of standing upright was proof of that.

He had been placed in a solitary cell, one of four, dedicated to suicide watch or protective custody. In the hierarchy of jailhouse social structure, the bottom two rungs of the ladder were reserved for cops and child molesters. Bubba was on the bottom rung, and if he had been in the dayroom with other inmates, his chances of seeing the light of the next morning would have been doubtful. Here, he was isolated from harm and under constant surveillance.

The moment Bubba showed signs of movement, a guard appeared at his barred cell door. He was very thin with a hawkish face and dark, intense eyes. He reminded Bubba of Kozloff, and Bubba flinched in fear for his life. The guard laughed.

"Don't worry, MacDonald," he said. "Nobody's going to beat the shit out of you anymore. That's all over with. Matter of fact, I'm here to kind of watch over you. So are the guys on the other two shifts."

"You're not going to hit me?" asked Bubba. "You look like the guy who hit me."

"No, I'm not going to hit you. You must be thinking about Kozloff." The guard grinned. "I've heard that before. Are you hungry? Do you want some breakfast?"

"A lot!"

"A lot of hunger or a lot of food?"

"Both...please."

"Okay, I'll be back in twenty, thirty minutes. You ought to sit down; you don't look too steady on your feet."

Bubba sat down. The guard was right: He was not too steady on his feet. But he was very steady in his vigil for the coming of food.

He was feeling much better. The hot, searing pain he had felt earlier was considerably numbed by the morphine. Now his injuries were a collection of dull, throbbing aches. The single largest pain in his whole body was in his empty

222

stomach. He was starving. To Bubba, the coming of food was like the Second Coming of Christ, and it seemed to take just as long.

"Here ya go, MacDonald."

The guard slid a partitioned metal tray through the space allowed for it under the cell door.

"If that's not enough for you, just holler," he said. "You don't look like you need it, but we're under orders to fatten you up and make you look pretty before you go to trial. Chow down."

"Thank you," Bubba replied, smiling shyly. "Looks good."

"Enjoy," the guard said, walking away.

The tray was heavily laden with large portions. The main course was navy beans mixed with chunks of fatback pork. On the side were greens flavored with bacon grease, and four slices of white bread. This feast was garnished with a large metal cup filled with strong, black coffee and a soupspoon. Bubba lifted the tray, sat down on his bunk, and ate every bite. When he had finished, the tray looked like it had just come out of a dishwasher. Bubba was continuing his profession from the Dade County jail.

Three times a day, the metal trays slid under the barred door, piled high with food disguising heavy doses of morphine. Bubba was happy as a pig at a trough.

He was being very well treated. The guards were always pleasant and he was given everything he needed, within the rules of the jail. An orderly from the hospital ward came every morning to change his dressings and give him a small paper cup containing antibiotics. His wounds were healing quickly, and after a few days, the bandages were no longer needed. He was not allowed to have anything sharp in his cell and his growing beard was beginning to cover his still-swollen jaw. Other than the itching stubble of whiskers, he felt better than he ever had. Bubba thought his new life here

223

was terrific. Everything was absolutely terrific; he did not even have to work for food. This was great.

And the morphine kept coming.

It was almost one month later when a pleasant-looking man in his mid-twenties appeared at Bubba's cell. He looked quite handsome in his beautifully tailored tan Brooks Brothers tropical suit. But Bubba did not like anyone dressed in suits. Lately, every time he'd run into someone in a suit, they had inflicted a lot of pain on him. He was glad for the barred cell door. He wished the man would just go away and not hurt him.

"Hi, Bubba," said Tan Suit. "My name is Bobby. Sounds a lot like Bubba, doesn't it?"

"Yeah," Bubba acknowledged. "Bobby...Bubba. You didn't come here to hit me no more, did ya?"

"Heck no, Bubba! Why in world would anyone want to do that? I just dropped by to check up on you. You know, see how you're doing. See if you're being treated right. I was worried about you."

"You were?" asked Bubba. "Why?"

"Because I care about you. Lots of folks here care about you. Look how good everything has been since that terrible incident that happened when you first got here. We're all very sorry about that. Very sorry. We're trying to make up for it. How're we doing so far?"

"Good, I guess," Bubba replied, still thankful for the steel door separating him from the tan-suited Bobby. "I like it here."

"That's great, Bubba," said Bobby. "I'm happy to hear that. I want you to be happy. Lots of people do."

"They do?"

"Yes, they really, truly do. Look, Bubba, I'd like very

224

much to be your friend, if you'd let me." Bobby gently slid his hand through the bars of the cell door. "Allow me to more fully introduce myself. My whole name is Robert West. I'm a lawyer and I'm not here to hurt you; I'm here to help you. Nobody is ever going to hurt you again—I'll see to that. All that stuff's over with, Bubba. It's in the past—I promise. Now, if you don't want to talk to me, that's all right. If you do, would you please just call me Bobby?"

"Okay...Bobby," Bubba answered haltingly. "Do you promise...you know, about the hittin' stuff?"

"Yes, I promise," West replied, smiling reassuringly. Bubba tentatively shook the attorney's hand as Bobby continued. "Would you like to get out of here for a little while? Go for a ride in my car, maybe?"

Bubba hesitated. "It's almost lunchtime," he said. "Can we wait 'til after?"

West's smile broadened. "Sure we can, Bubba. I'll come back when you're ready. See you later."

"Okay, Bobby. See ya later."

When West left, lunch came sliding under the door. Today it was butter beans with fatback. Bubba finished the meal, leaving the tray spotlessly clean, as always. Then he sat on his bunk with his back against the wall to wait for his new friend, Bobby.

Bubba liked it here; it was safe. But it might be neat to go for a ride in a car. He liked cars.

Bubba did not have to wait more than a few minutes for the return of Robert West.

"Hi, Bubba," West announced. "You ready to go for a ride and get some fresh air?"

"Uh-huh." Bubba nodded. "I washed up and everything."

"Good, let's go then."

The cell door slid open and there stood West, flanked by two uniformed city policemen. Suddenly, Bubba was not so sure he wanted to leave this safe haven.

"No," he said, backing away. "Not now."

"Why not, Bubba?" West asked.

"Those two guys. They're the same kind of guys who beat me up."

"There're not going to beat you up," West reassured him. "What did I promise you?"

"Don't care what you said. You're not big enough to stop 'em."

"That's true." West clasped his hands together. "I'm not. But I have the *power* to stop them," he said. "And I would. If you don't believe me, ask them."

"Not askin' them a damn thing," said Bubba. "I'm not fuckin' goin'. No way."

"I'm very disappointed, Bubba," said West. "I thought you trusted me. But if that's the way you want it, I guess that'll be the way it is—I'm not going to make you do anything you don't want to do." He lowered his eyes to the floor. "I told you that I want to be your friend and that hasn't changed, even if you think I'm a liar."

"Don't think you're a liar," Bubba countered. "Just not goin'. Want to stay here."

"That's too bad, Bubba," West said softly, his eyes still cast downward. "That's really too bad. And after all I've done for you. Who do you think was responsible for the doctors fixing you up, and for this nice quiet cell where the other prisoners can't get at you to kill you? And who do you think ordered the cops to stop beating the crap out of you in the first place?

"And the food?" West went on. "I'm the guy who knows how much you like to eat and demanded that you be fed properly and looked after. And...well...I don't know what else I can do to prove to you that I'm your friend. I'm just honestly so hurt by this."

"Didn't mean to..."

"Come on, guys," West said, raising his sad eyes from the floor. "Let's get out of here. Good luck, Bubba...and good-bye."

"I..."

"Good-bye, Bubba!" West called again, disappearing from sight.

⛓⛓⛓⛓⛓

Bubba did not know what to do. Whatever it was, it was too late now. Bobby was gone.

Bubba needed to think about this, but right now he was too confused. When he faced this kind of dilemma, his limited brainpower was severely taxed and sapped all of his strength. He decided to take a nap and think about it later. He actually slept through the noon meal.

A harsh, rasping, metallic sound woke him. It was the evening food tray sliding under the cell door. As soon as Bubba saw the tray, he knew something was terribly wrong. The only things on it were a peanut butter sandwich and a tin cup of coffee that looked tepid at best. This was serious. He had to get in touch with Bobby!

Bubba flushed the coffee down the toilet and began banging the cup on the bars, yelling for the guard.

"MacDonald," the guard shouted back, "shut the fuck up!"

Bubba knew he was in deep trouble. He also knew that he *had* better shut up. He would think about this tonight. Maybe he could figure out something in time for his next meal. He would do his very best.

⛓⛓⛓⛓⛓

The jail kitchen was on a strict schedule, distributing the meals on time every time. West imagined Bubba poised at his cell door, awaiting the arrival of breakfast. His morning meal was now five minutes late, and after last night, he was probably wondering if he would get any breakfast at all. Hell, the guy was so stupid, he was probably wondering if he would ever eat again.

West's footsteps echoed loudly on the cement corridor. When he reached Bubba's cell, West could tell his charge was disappointed that he was not the deliverer of the beloved food tray. Beyond that, Bubba's expression made it clear that he considered West the guy who was ordering that Bubba be starved to death.

"Good morning, Bubba," West said slowly, trying to sound as contrite as possible. "I'm really sorry about yesterday," he said, "but you really hurt my feelings."

Bubba turned away and sat down on his bunk, blankly staring into the toilet.

Jesus Christ, this giant fat-ass is moping like a child.

West had not expected this kind of non-response. He would have to approach this idiot like a stray dog he was befriending. Gaining Bubba's trust was critical.

West grabbed the cell bars and squatted down to Bubba's eye-level, praying he was not too severely wrinkling his impeccably pressed slacks.

"Bubba?" West whispered.

The only detectable response from the sulking bulk was a long sigh. West found this rather remarkable, as well as a bit frightening. Bubba was actually trying to think.

"Come on now, Bubba," cajoled West. "Please at least look at me. I'm truly sorry that I wasn't very nice yesterday. But no kidding, you really hurt my feelings a whole lot—you really did."

No response.

"Bubba? Did you get breakfast yet?"

That did it. West wondered if there was a certain irony in the way Bubba turned and looked up from the toilet directly to him. The thought prompted West's first sincere act of the day: He could not help smiling at himself.

Bubba finally spoke.

"No breakfast today. Shitty dinner, and people are startin' to yell at me. Hurt my feelings too."

West tried to maintain his sincere smile. "Maybe I can make up for it," he said. "A little bit, anyway. I've got a surprise for you."

When the morning-shift guard appeared at the cell, Bubba's face registered his shock. The breakfast tray held generous portions of ham, scrambled eggs, home-fried potatoes, pancakes with maple syrup, and buttered toast, along with two cups of ice-cold milk.

West stood up. "I've got to be honest with you, Bubba. This isn't going to happen every day," he said, "but after that crummy dinner you got last night, I ordered them to make it up to you. That's the best I can do. I hope you enjoy it. If you ever need to talk to me, just ask one of the guards."

With that, West smiled a big smile, waved a cheerful good-bye, and walked rapidly away, smoothing his wrinkled slacks as he went. He had a meeting to attend and he had no intention of being late.

The elevator light indicated it was three floors below and going up. West took the stairs down, two at a time.

❈❈❈❈❈

By any standards, the breakfast was a good one. By Bubba's limited standards, this was the meal of the year and he happily devoured every wonderful crumb. He knew he should ask to see Bobby and thank him, but right now he was stuffed and wanted to take a nap. He was getting very good at naps; he was sleeping between twelve and fourteen hours every day.

229

West was seated at a small conference table along with two other people: a man and a woman.

The woman was late-middle-aged and very attractive. She had a trim figure and a virtually unlined face, topped by natural dark-blond hair pulled up into a severe bun. One of the top district attorneys in South Florida, she had a well-earned reputation for being an extremely tough lady. The name on her ID badge read "Sondra W. Bloom."

The man was Maxwell Hurst, the lean, gray-haired Dade County chief of detectives, also a tough cookie.

West was one of the brightest and most promising assistant D.A.'s on Bloom's staff. Although by far the junior member of the group, he was, at the moment, the most important. It was his responsibility to obtain a signature from MacDonald confessing to the murders of Jessica Miller and Marissa Alvarez.

West was a charming man when he needed to be, gifted with the ability to sell himself to anyone. A natural-born con artist, getting signed confessions was something he excelled at. MacDonald was West's personal project.

Sondra Bloom leaned back in her chair. After glancing at Hurst, she set her gaze directly on West.

"Why didn't you bring MacDonald to my office yesterday?" she demanded.

West responded quickly and to the point: "Well, Sondra, he simply refused to come. The two cops scared the hell out of him; he thought he was going to be beaten again. Of course, we could have forced him, but that would have been unwise. Whatever confidence he has in me would have been completely blown."

"Good choice, Robert," the D.A. agreed. "You did the right thing."

Hurst nodded his approval.

"Let me ask you this," Bloom continued. "Do you think we could get this moron's name on the dotted line by talking to him in his cell? That's not too intimidating for this guy, is it?"

"Actually, that's precisely my plan," West said calmly. "He feels safe there. And we already know we can't beat it out of him—if Whiting and Kozloff couldn't, nobody can."

West took a moment to mentally summarize his impressions of Bubba before presenting his assessment.

"McDonald's like an animal," West told the group. "As long as I feed him, he'll respond to me and trust me. But if we scare him, he'll just shut down what's left of his mind and retreat into a shell. That'll pretty much be the end of it."

"Robert," Hurst said, "I appreciate all the thought you've put into this, but do you think you can hurry it up? The press is wondering why it's taken over thirty days to indict this guy for murdering the daughter of one of their own. And everyone who knows Sam Miller—including me—wants to see justice done, and right damn now! How long is this going to take?"

"It'll take—"

"My question, too, Robert," Bloom interrupted. "The press is all over our ass downtown about this. And, for once, their questions are valid. I'm running out of excuses. In fact, I am totally out of excuses. How long?"

"Well..." West said, a smile creeping onto his face, "would the end of the day tomorrow be too late?"

The tension in the small conference room lifted immediately. Everyone smiled broadly at the thought of finally getting Bubba Red MacDonald out of their hair and into the electric chair.

"There's just one thing," West said. "Sondra, it's

231

essential that you go with me tomorrow. You can carry the lunch tray."

Sondra's eyebrows shot up. "What the hell are you talking about, Robert?"

"Lunch. Will you go?"

"If you feel it's necessary, of course I'll go," she said. "But what's with the lunch tray, Robert?"

"You'll see tomorrow," West said, laughing out loud now. "You'll be his new best friend. You know, he really likes 'pretty big girls' too."

"Robert, that's enough!" Sondra Bloom glared at him. "I hope you know what the hell you're doing. I'll meet with you tomorrow, as you suggest, at a few minutes before noon in the county jail solitary tier. And Robert,"—she paused—"if you embarrass me, I'll have your nuts cut off.

"This meeting is over. Good afternoon, gentlemen."

⛓⛓⛓⛓⛓

At precisely twelve noon, Bubba was thrown into rapture. Standing at his cell door was a vision: a tall, slender, fine-looking woman holding the noonday food tray, which was heaped with huge portions of gourmet cuisine. It looked almost five-star. The woman was flanked by West and a guard, both of whom held identical trays. A second guard appeared, unlocked the cell door, and slid it wide open.

"We thought you might enjoy a decent meal for a change," the vision said. "May we come in and enjoy it with you, Mister MacDonald?"

Bubba could barely contain himself. "Yeah, sure, you bet!" he choked. "Come on in. I'll sit on the toilet, and you and Bobby can have the bunk, okay?"

"That would be fine," said the woman. "Robert and— I mean, Bobby and I appreciate your hospitality. Don't we, Bobby?"

232

"Absolutely," West responded. "Bubba, I'd like you to meet Sondra Bloom. She's one of the people I told you about who cares about you. Lunch was her idea. Looks like a pretty good one too, doesn't it?"

"Looks real good." Bubba was practically salivating. "Thanks a bunch."

"You're welcome, Mister MacDonald," Sondra said. "But right now, I'd like to eat. How about you?"

The guard gave Bubba his tray, and Bubba sat down on the toilet with it. Bloom and West sat on the bed, their trays also in their laps.

"Bubba," whispered West, once the guard had locked the cell and was out of hearing range, "this really is breaking the rules here, so you can't tell anyone or we'll get into a lot of trouble, but..."

Bubba leaned forward in anticipation.

"Since this is a special occasion," West said, "Sondra smuggled some knives in here. You can't eat a filet mignon with a spoon, can you?"

Bubba shook his head vigorously and reached for the utensil.

West and Bloom seemed to relish their meal as much as Bubba, but not nearly as quickly. They were not close to half-finished when he placed his empty tray on the concrete floor.

Sixteen ounces of prime filet mignon along with equally large portions of potatoes au gratin, asparagus spears with hollandaise sauce, and a magnificent chocolate mousse had disappeared within minutes into Bubba's orange-bearded mouth.

"Great," Bubba said, trying unsuccessfully to suppress a giant burp. "Love to eat good stuff. This was better even than that breakfast you got me, Bobby. Good stuff, thanks a lot. So what do ya want?"

West appeared shocked by the bluntness of Bubba's

question. In fact, he seemed to be struck dumb.

"We want to help you out is what we want," the woman—*Sondra, was it?*—cut in, her demeanor shifting rapidly from the pleasant tone of their lunch together. "And to be perfectly honest about it, we want to help ourselves out as well," she said. "Now pay attention, because I'm only going to say this once, Mister MacDonald: You're in very deep shit. You're charged with the murder of a woman and the rape and brutal murder of a child—the daughter of a very well-liked and respected newspaperman. He's the crime reporter for the *Miami Herald*, so every cop, prosecutor, and judge in the city wants to see you burned to a crisp in the electric chair."

"Sondra," West interrupted, his voice tight, "perhaps we shoul—"

"Shut the fuck up, *Bobby*. You've kissed this guy's ass enough. Now, let me continue, Mister MacDonald. Am I going too fast for your dull wit to understand? Are you with me so far? Are you?"

Bubba knew this was important so he made every effort to remain focused—but it was hard because all the food had made him sleepy again.

"Yes, ma'am," he said. "Deep shit."

"That's exactly right," she said. "Very, very deep shit. And there's only one way—and that's it: *One*—that you can save your own life. If you don't go along with me, you are going to be burned to a black smoking piece of overcooked stinking dead meat! The only way you can avoid that is to plead to a lesser charge. In plain English, if you go to trial for two counts of murder one and are found guilty, which I assure you will be the case, you'll be sent to death row, where you won't get shit to eat for God knows how long. Then they'll strap your ass into the electric chair and you will die a horrible death. How does that grab you?"

Bubba felt a surge of nausea. "It don't."

234

"I didn't think it would. Now, here's the good part: If you do what I suggest, you will be charged with murder in the second degree. You can live out the rest of your life, safe and sound, out of the general prison population, where they would gut you like a fish. You will be given three square meals a day and everything else you need to lead a pretty comfortable life; you won't even have to think about how to survive. That sounds like a pretty good deal to me," she said, "and if I were in your shoes, I'd take it and I'd take it right fucking now! Do you hear me?"

"Yes, ma'am." Bubba nodded feverishly. "Don't want to fry like a burger. What do I gotta do?"

"First, give me back the knife."

Bubba handed her the knife, handle first, and as she returned it to her purse, she drew out several neatly folded sheets of white legal-size paper and a pen. She unfolded the papers and along with the pen, gave them to Bubba.

"Sign each sheet at the bottom," she instructed, "just above your name." She pointed. "Right there on the dotted line where the 'X' is. This your only way out, Mister MacDonald," she repeated, "the only way."

"Yes, ma'am." He looked up at her sincerely. "It's the only way, huh?"

"Yes, unless you want to spend the rest of a very short life with a lot of people much worse than Whiting and Kozloff."

That did it. Bubba signed his confessions to the murders of Jessica Miller and Marissa Alvarez, sitting on a steel toilet looking at two half-eaten gourmet lunch trays.

"I done good, right?" Bubba asked shyly—and then added, "You didn't hardly eat nothin'. Can I have the rest of the food?"

"Get us out of here, Robert," ordered Bloom.

"Guard!" West shouted. "Open it up."

The guard quickly unlocked the cell door and slid it

open. The two attorneys left without a word.

As the door closed behind his guests, Bubba went to the bunk and began spooning down the remains of the two trays of cooling food.

⛓⛓⛓⛓

Going down in the elevator, West still felt minor shock waves from the surprising tactics of Bloom. He had seen her mean streak before, but this time she had been on the edge of losing it; he was amazed that she had not totally blown it. In fact, the strategy had worked.

Bloom still looked angry as they left the building and walked rapidly toward the parking lot. There was a lot of work to be done before trial.

"My car's over there, Sondra," West said. "I'll see you back at your office."

"Hold on a minute, Robert."

He stopped. "What is it?"

"This is what it is, Robert," Bloom said softly. "You're a good man and a fine lawyer, but you're too soft on assholes like MacDonald. I hate to tell you this, Robert, but you're just not tough enough for the job. Don't meet me in my office. Go to your own and clean it out. You're fired."

Sondra Bloom turned her back, walked quickly to her car, and drove off.

West stood frozen in disbelief—but only for a moment. He was a survivor. His quick mind was already working overtime.

West knew his professional life was not going to be threatened—he would not be fired; he would be asked to resign. And he would, leaving the district attorney's office with an impressive résumé. Walking to his car, West began considering private practice and the money that would go along with it.

By the time he had settled behind the wheel, West had devised a plan. He had always wanted to live on the beach, and as he headed to his office, he was already imagining his exciting new lifestyle.

Screw private practice, he thought. *Screw everybody. This will work. I'm going to be fucking rich.*

West left his office for the final time with three things: A cardboard box filled with personal belongings; a fat file folder containing newly copied legal papers, interoffice memos, and notes of meetings; and a smile on his face.

There was just one more thing that he needed to do.

In thirty minutes, West had an appointment at the Dade County Court House in the private chambers of Judge Solomon Coen.

⛓⛓⛓⛓⛓

The small courtroom was filled to overflowing with angry media reporting on the plea hearing of Bubba Red MacDonald, the cold-blooded killer of the young daughter of their very own friend and respected colleague, Sam Miller. They knew what the outcome would be. They all had been around the justice system long enough to know the maximum penalty for second-degree murder, and considering the brutality of his crimes, MacDonald would be sentenced to life in prison with no chance of parole; they could have reported the formalities from their desks. They were really here to show their support and sorrow for Sam Miller. Their only question was, where was the lead prosecutor on the case, Robert West?

Judge Solomon Coen emerged from his chambers and took his seat behind the bench as the bailiff called the court to order. Another bailiff with a handcuffed Bubba Red MacDonald entered the courtroom through the prisoner's waiting-room door, and the accused was seated to await his sentencing.

"Mister MacDonald," said the honorable Solomon Coen, "would you please rise and approach the bench?"

"Yessir."

Bubba pushed back his chair and did as asked.

"Bailiff," the judge said, "please release the defendant from his restraints."

This command got serious attention from the press corps and everyone else in the room. Something very strange was going on here.

"Ladies and gentleman," the judge yelled, banging his gavel over the rising din in the courtroom, "I demand that you keep order in my court."

Coen rose slowly from behind the bench, banging the gavel even louder on the way up. "As much I despise even the thought of having to say this, under the law, I must." The courtroom fell completely silent. "The defendant's confession was obtained under the effect of drugs, coupled with cruel and unusual duress. Mister MacDonald, all charges against you are dismissed. You are free to go."

Bubba did not know what had happened, what to do, or where to go. He stood there like a stone, confused and frightened.

A mass of hysterical and outraged reporters screamed questions at him and calling him foul names at the same time. Bubba was on the edge of panic when he saw a familiar face breaking through the angry crowd, its owner elbowing his way to Bubba's side.

It was Robert West.

"Come on!" West had to yell into Bubba's ear to be heard over the garbled racket of the press corps. "Let's get the hell out of here. Follow me. Damn it, move!"

West grabbed Bubba's arm and began to propel him out of the courtroom with surprising strength.

"Just do what I tell you, and you'll be alright!" West continued yelling. "I'm your attorney now, and I'm the one who got your freedom for you. Do you understand that?"

"Yeah, Bobby," Bubba said. "But what's going on?"

"Just a bunch of crazy reporters. They don't know what's going on either, and they're not going to right now. Don't answer any of their questions. If they get us cornered and you've got to say something, just talk about food, okay?"

"Okay."

With West's help, Bubba maneuvered his ample bulk out of the courtroom and into the hallway, where he was again mobbed by those gathered outside the crowded courtroom. He and West were pressed against the wall by a throng of reporters hollering questions.

The most aggressive was a pretty red-haired newswoman with a badge from a local television station. She was pushed against Bubba by the press of the crowd and the cameraman directly behind her pointing his lens right at Bubba's face.

"Mister MacDonald, Mister MacDonald!" Her voice rose over the mob. "May I have a statement, please?"

Bubba smiled. "Uh-huh, ya got red hair just like me."

She responded with a flirtatious smile. "Yes, I do," she said. "Perhaps we have even more in common. How do you feel about your acquittal?"

"Good, I guess," he said. "Ya got red hair."

Bubba could see the reporter working to come up with a new tactic. "How were you treated in jail, Mister MacDonald?" she asked, her eyes bright.

Bubba shrugged. "The food was okay—at first."

"At first? Then what...did they starve you?"

"Pretty much," Bubba said. "Don't like beans. The fatback was good. Like fatback. Hate beans."

His interviewer did not look amused. "Do you mean

239

to tell me that your only complaint was the beans?"

"No."

The red-haired reporter's eyes narrowed to ice-blue slits. "The judge mentioned you were 'under duress,'" she pressed. "How were you mistreated?"

"Uh...I..." Bubba hesitated before remembering West's instructions to talk only about food. "Treated bad," he said, "'cause of no bender-backs."

"What?" the reporter asked. "What's that?"

"No bender-backs."

"What in the world is a...that?"

"Ya never heard of a—"

"No!" the reporter was losing it. "What is it, Mister MacDonald?"

"Well..." Bubba relaxed a bit, starting to enjoy all the attention. "First, ya take a piece a white bread, okay?"

"Okay..." she replied.

"Then ya smear a bunch a mayo on it and slap down a chunk a bologna on it. And then..." Bubba paused for dramatic effect. "Ya bend 'er back."

In spite of the press corps' hatred for MacDonald, the jammed hallway erupted in laughter. Even the red-haired reporter chuckled.

Bubba, however, did not see the humor in any of this. There was nothing funny about food.

⧉⧉⧉⧉⧉

One other person in the jammed hallway did not see any humor in this either. He was completely isolated, his back against the far wall of the corridor.

Bubba was the only person in the crowd who looked toward the man, and the moment their eyes locked, he wished he hadn't. Since his arrest, Bubba had been looked at with disgust and raw hatred, but nothing like this. The

240

single thing he saw reflected in that flat, cold stare was his own death.

It was Sam Miller.

CHAPTER 12
FLORIDA SUN SETS HARD

May 1951

"That's it! That's it!" West was shouting at the top of his voice. "No more questions and no more comments from my client. I will tell you this much, though: There's going to be hell to pay in the district attorney's office, the police department, and the county jail. By the end of the day, people from every area of law enforcement are going to be fired in disgrace and have criminal charges filed against them. Their careers of cruelty will be over." West raised his hands. "I'll hold a press conference as soon as I find office space—I'll tell you when and where in a day or two. End of comment!"

West had to push the red-haired reporter and her cameraman out of the way to form a break in the crowd. He pulled Bubba off the wall and shoved his way forward as best he could with the large young man in tow. His best was not good enough to make much headway, though, and his momentum stalled.

Bubba tapped West on the shoulder.

"You follow me now, Bobby!" he said, smiling.

Bubba threw his huge frame into the mass of human barriers with the power of a tank. Six men fell to the floor instantly. Bubba cleared a path through the press like Moses parting the Red Sea.

"Which way, Bobby?"

"Hang a right!"

"You got it."

So hang a right they did, straight down the hall and out through the heavy courthouse doors onto the sidewalk.

"Come on!" Bubba yelled over his shoulder. "I'm good at crossing streets."

The pair bolted through traffic and once they reached the other side of the broad avenue, West took over.

"The car's right over there," he said. "It's the white sedan. Let's get the hell out of here fast. You're one strong son of a bitch, Bubba!" he added. "That was like knocking over bowling pins."

"Don't know 'bout those." Bubba grinned. "Good at knockin' down people, though, huh?"

"I'd say so," West said, laughing as he unlocked the car. "Get in. We're out of here, big guy."

West threw the car into gear and took off. He made several random turns to make sure they were not being followed and then headed for West Miami.

"Bubba," West said, speaking rapidly now and without hesitation, "I'm going to give you some money. I know you don't have a cent on you—any money you had when you were arrested is in the police property room in an envelope, along with whatever else you had in your pockets. Don't worry about it; we'll get that stuff later. So here's twenty-some dollars."

Bubba took it without interrupting.

"Now, before we go any further," said West, "there's something I need to know, and this is important." He glanced over at Bubba. "Do you want me to be your lawyer and continue to help you?"

Bubba nodded immediately. "I sure do, Bobby."

"Good, that's what I want too," said West. "But first, you have to retain me as your attorney. Give me a dollar."

Bubba handed him a one-dollar bill.

"Bobby," he asked sincerely, "does that mean I got my own lawyer to get out of deep shit, like rich people got?"

243

West laughed. "Yes, Mister MacDonald," he replied, "just like rich people got. And in a few months, you're going to be one of those people. You have just hired a lawyer who is going to get you more money than you will ever learn how to spend in your lifetime. I'm filing suit against everybody and everything that hurt you. You are going to be a very wealthy man. Are you ready to get started kicking some ass until huge sums of money start rolling in?"

Bubba chuckled. "Wow! You bet, Bobby. I'll buy a drive-in. So, what now?"

"First, we're going to get your stuff from the Silver Star," West answered, "and then you're coming home with me. There's plenty of good food there and you'll be sleeping in a comfortable bed for a change."

West checked his rearview mirror to be sure they weren't being followed.

"Bubba, I need to fill you in on some stuff," West began. "While you were in jail, they gave you drugs every day—tons of the shit. That's why you slept so much."

Bubba nodded thoughtfully but didn't comment.

"Now, remember a few days ago, when a different doctor took some of your blood?" West asked. "Well, that was the state's doctor—my doctor really—and the tests proved that you were so fucked up on pain medication, morphine to be precise, that you couldn't possibly have known what you were doing when you signed that confession. That jailhouse quack doctor went to pieces under interrogation and also admitted that you had been beaten within an inch of your life."

West slowed to a stop at a four-way and turned to look directly at Bubba.

"Now, I want you to stay with me for a while, out of sight in my apartment," said West. "It's very important that you understand that. Out of sight, okay?"

"Yeah, Bobby," said Bubba, frowning as he tried to

match his new roommate's intensity. "Bobby, ya look mad. That why ya doin' all this?"

"Hell, yes, I'm mad," said West. "It's not just the money—I think you got screwed around and I'm pissed off at the people who did that to you. They did it to me, too, and I'm going to nail their collective asses to the wall for what they did to both of us. We're going to hit back hard, and hit 'em where it hurts the most."

"Those detectives too?" Bubba asked. "The ones that hit me?"

"Whiting and Kozloff?" said West. "Yes, them too. They're probably walking the streets right now, wondering how they're going to make a living without beating the shit out of people. But especially Sondra Bloom," West went on. "That's the bitch who got you to sign those papers. She's going to be disbarred. That means she'll never practice law again. She not only knew all this was going on, she's the one who condoned it. I knew too, but I since I came forward to tell them how wrong I thought it was, they gave me immunity. They can't touch me, Bubba, or you either. We're both free and clear. I know all this is a lot for you to absorb all at once, but I'll explain everything to you later. There's the Silver Star."

West turned into the entrance and pulled into an empty car bay.

"Go on in and get your things, Bubba," West instructed. "Don't worry—they know you're coming and everything is packed up and ready to go. It's all stacked on a dolly in the storeroom. Just bring it out here."

When Bubba returned wheeling the dolly, West was standing next to the open trunk. They loaded the boxes into the car, shut the trunk, and left the restaurant, driving away from Bubba's old home, heading east for Miami and his new one.

The second bedroom in West's apartment was given over to Bubba. The only restriction was that he keep the blinds on the single window closed at all times. That was easy enough; the dim light made it easier to see the picture on his very own television set.

Overnight, television became Bubba's second love and obsession. He watched it hour after hour, except when he was in the kitchen that West had stocked with enough food to withstand a siege. He was told that he could have the run of the apartment as long as he followed the house rules, which were only slightly more stringent than his room rules. He was asked not to answer the doorbell for anyone, not to answer the telephone (unless it rang twice and then again right after that), and not to turn on the hi-fi or television set in the living room. He was to pretend he was invisible.

These rules were simple enough, but West had to be certain that Bubba understood them, so they went over them time and time again. West could not run the risk of his houseguest being discovered.

West had made some very powerful enemies in the past few days, including two violent and sadistic unemployed detectives who probably remained heavily armed. A growing list of people would cheerfully kill West and his only client, but West was not paranoid about it. He knew the chances of being murdered were remote. Still, with millions of dollars at stake, he was not taking any chances. He rented a second apartment about a mile away and changed his mail delivery to that address and listed its new telephone number in information. West parked his white sedan in the space in front of the new apartment's entrance and left it there. He was aware that he was not too sophisticated at going into deep cover, but it would do for a few days.

Early the next morning, while Bubba was preparing

246

his breakfast, West reviewed the house rules with him once again. It was not until he was certain his client understood everything perfectly that he felt free to leave the apartment.

"That looks like a fine breakfast you got going there, Bubba," he said. "Just follow the rules like we discussed. I don't know when I'll be back. It may be late, but don't worry about it; I've got a lot of work to do today. Enjoy the television, but remember to keep the volume turned down. I'll see you later."

"Okay, Bobby." Bubba smiled while filling his plate. "See ya."

The gray nondescript rental car pulled out of its parking space, turned onto the street, and headed south for downtown Miami. West had a full day ahead of him and he welcomed it. He was having fun.

Over the next two days, West accomplished a great deal. He leased space in one of the finest art deco buildings in Coconut Grove, a prestigious community near downtown Miami. It had two offices, a reception area, and a small storeroom for files. West purchased furniture for every room and a complete set of legal volumes to fill the new bookshelves; he hired a very good-looking and articulate young woman as his secretary and receptionist. The telephones and other equipment were installed, and his name was put on the door.

The new law firm of West and Associates officially hung out their shingle. That meant the senior—and at the moment, only—partner, Robert West, was in business, with one of Miami's most famous criminals as his client.

It was early evening, the sky hot pink with the glow of a beautiful Florida setting sun, when West finally left his new offices after attending to every detail for the coming day.

Tomorrow the receptionist would be at her desk, looking glorious, and announce to him over the intercom that several members of the press were here to see him. He would emerge from his office with great dignity, impeccably attired in a dark-blue Brooks Brothers suit, black Gucci loafers, a white Egyptian cotton shirt, and a red silk tie. In complete control of the room, he would hold his press conference. And when he concluded, he would be considered one of the greatest crime-busters and champions of the downtrodden masses in the history of the State of Florida.

Robert West was feeling festive. As he drove home to an apartment that would soon be far beneath his status, he decided a celebration was in order. He turned into the parking lot of Wolfie's, a Miami delicatessen famous for having the best Jewish food outside of New York City. At the to-go counter, West ordered large quantities of everything behind the glass, including two cheesecakes. A waiter had to help him to the car with his heavily laden boxes. In regal deli-food splendor, West would feed himself and Bubba Red MacDonald, his precious cash cow.

⌬⌬⌬⌬⌬

The morning of the next day, a few minutes before the scheduled ten o'clock press conference, the various members of the print and electronic media elbowed their way into the offices of West and Associates. The receptionist behind her desk looked as glorious as West had predicted—except for the expression on her pretty face.

"Good morning," one of the reporters said. "Would you please tell Mister West that we're here?"

"He hasn't come in yet," the receptionist replied. "He should be here very shortly."

"He's not here?" The reporter was slightly aghast. "Where is he?

"I don't know where he is." A slight nervousness crept into the receptionist's voice.

248

"What do you mean he's not here?"

"Where the hell is he?"

"Is he on his way?'

"Did he call to say he's running late?"

"We didn't come down here to be jerked around. What's going on?"

"I don't know." The receptionist quivered. "And I don't know why you're all yelling at me. It's not my fault that...that he's..."

The young woman covered her face with trembling hands.

"Stop it, goddammit!" shouted a shrill female voice from the rear of the room. "You all are acting like a lynch mob, for Christ's sake. Leave the poor girl alone. This isn't getting any of us anywhere. Let me talk to her and ask her one question at a time."

The woman who had screamed across the reception area pushed her way forward. It was the red-haired television reporter who had interviewed MacDonald in the courthouse hall after his dismissal.

"Everybody, shut the fuck up!" she yelled. When everyone quieted down, she spoke calmly to the distraught young woman at the reception desk. "My name is Joyce Jones, and I'm sorry to say that I'm a member of this unruly mob. No one is going to yell at you anymore. I'll just ask you a couple of questions without any"—Joyce looked threateningly over her shoulder—"goddamn interruptions. Okay?"

"Yes," the receptionist said, regaining her composure. "Thank you."

"You're welcome," said Joyce. "You don't deserve this kind of treatment. Now, do you know if Mister West is coming to the office?"

The receptionist looked up at the reporter sincerely. "He told me was going to be here by nine o'clock, but he didn't show up. I called his home about fifteen after, but there was no answer. I assumed he was on his way, just running late. But since then, I have called again every ten minutes or so and there still hasn't been any answer. I even called that radio station that gives the traffic reports all the time, and they said there were no problems on the roads, no accidents. I just don't know."

"Thank you," said Joyce. "You've been very helpful. Here's my card. When Mister West comes in, would you please ask him to call me?"

The receptionist smiled. "Yes, I'd be happy to do that."

"When he does," Joyce told her, "if he wants to reschedule, I'll inform the rest of this rabble of the new time. But right now, our respective employers can't afford to have us just hanging around waiting. That should come as good news to you."

Joyce turned to crowded room. "I'm out of here," she announced. "How about the rest of you guys—are you with me?"

Mumbling and grumbling, the press filed out of the offices of West and Associates, going their separate ways to file a story concerning nothing other than that Robert West was rude and inconsiderate of the press.

❊❊❊❊❊

For the next thirty minutes, the office building remained under the hawk-like surveillance of Joyce Jones. When she was sure that the coast was clear of competitors, she reentered the building and went directly to West's offices.

"Hi, it's just me," she said, smiling broadly at the receptionist. "I hate to bother you, but we girls have to stick together. May I ask just one more thing of you?"

250

"Sure," she was told. "You got those jerks out of here. What is it?"

"I'm worried about Robert." Joyce donned her most sincere concerned expression. "I thought it might be a good idea if someone checked on him. I know this is highly irregular, but since he doesn't answer his phone, may I have his address so I can go out there and see if he's all right?"

"I'm getting concerned about him as well," the receptionist admitted. "Let me write it down for you. If you find out anything, you'll call me?"

"Of course I will," Joyce assured her. "Thanks for the address. I'm on my way. Bye-bye."

The reporter had lived in Miami all her life and knew exactly where to go. She was there in fifteen minutes. She recognized West's white sedan parked directly in front of the first-floor entrance and had no trouble finding the apartment in the large complex. She walked to the door and knocked. There was no answer. She knocked again, only harder. When there was still no answer, she went to the manager's office.

She told the elderly woman behind the desk about her concern for the complex's tenant. Then she followed the manager back to the apartment, where the elderly woman banged on the door, getting the same response Jones had. Nothing. The manager opened the door with a master key and they both entered West's apartment.

Joyce reared back in surprise. The place was completely empty; there was absolutely no sign that anyone lived there. The manager looked stunned, as well.

"Would you mind if I used the phone?" Jones asked. "Now, I'm really worried about him."

"Fine with me," said the manager. "I want to know what's going on, too."

Jones dialed the Department of Motor Vehicles and asked to speak to the Miami/Dade supervisor. She was on

251

hold for what seemed like forever before he came on the line.

"Muchen here."

"Eddie, this is Joyce Jones. I'm calling in a marker, and I'm calling it in right goddamned now! I need an address. The name is Robert Wesley West. He lives in Miami. And don't fucking put me on hold—I need it now!"

"Damn, Joyce, cool down. Just a second...please."

Muchen was back on the line in less than a minute with an address—and it was not the same as this one.

"Thanks, Eddie, we're almost even. Bye."

Jones turned to the elderly woman, who looked a bit shocked over the petite reporter's vulgar show of force.

"Thank you for letting me in," Joyce said. "I've got to leave now. I'll be in touch."

Jones left in a hurry. She was on to something; she could smell it. Her instincts were suddenly razor-sharp.

The DMV address was close by and Joyce was there in under five minutes. She parked next to a gray sedan, walked rapidly to the front door, and knocked hard. The door was not closed all the way, so when she knocked, it swung slowly open. Joyce stepped into the darkened living room and let her eyes adjust to the dim light.

Robert West was sitting on the couch. Most of him, anyway. The back of his head was gone. Blood, bone, and brains were splattered across the wall behind him in dark-red chunks. The big toe of his shoeless right foot was lodged in the trigger guard of a twelve-gauge shotgun, the muzzle of the barrel still in his gaping mouth. The place looked like a slaughterhouse.

Jones vomited on her shoes. When the retching subsided, she found a telephone on the kitchen counter. Her first call was to her camera crew, the second to the police. When she hung up, she noticed a note on the counter. She assumed it was a suicide note until she read the

252

scrawl.

boby
sorry bout the mony but got to go home
bubba

Joyce fell to her knees and vomited again until her eyes were filled with salty, burning tears.

"Well, Robert West," she gasped, "thanks to you, it's now a pretty newsworthy day."

The reporter could not stand, so she crawled to the open door, being careful not to touch anything else, and collapsed on the doorstep, her mind fading, wondering who would get here first, cops or cameras.

It was the cops. A patrol car arrived within minutes. And then another, and another. In typical police-overkill fashion, the apartment building's parking lot was soon filled with six squad cars, two unmarked cars, a car from the coroner's office, and two ambulances.

Ten minutes after the arrival of the first police car, Channel One's remote crew was setting up. The white station van had to park some distance from the crime scene, making things more difficult than usual. Still, in just ten minutes, they were ready to broadcast. Five more, and they were on the air.

"Good morning, everyone." The reporter stood steady, professional, and detached from all emotion. She stood in the parking lot of the apartment building, where a uniformed police officer in the background looked toward the scene of the crime. "This is Joyce Jones, reporting live from the Club Biscayne apartment complex in Miami Shores. At approximately eleven o'clock this morning, only thirty minutes ago, I had the shocking experience to be the first person to discover the dead body of attorney Robert West. He apparently died from a self-inflicted shotgun wound to the head."

Jones paused briefly for dramatic impact.

"West recently resigned as assistant district attorney and lead prosecutor for the state in its case against the alleged killer of young Jessica Miller, Bubba Red MacDonald. West had scheduled a press conference at his offices for ten o'clock this morning, but was a no-show. Our Channel One news team was the first to find him."

Joyce struggled to hold her ground as her head spun.

"We will have a full report on our continuing investigation of this tragedy this evening on the six o'clock news. Reporting for Channel One, the first one in news, this is Joyce Jones."

The remote feed to the television station went to black, and so did Joyce Jones. The audio man dropped his mike boom and caught her just before she hit the ground.

"Man," he said, gently lowering her to the grass, "this is one tough broad. Let me rephrase that...one tough lady."

"She sure as hell is," said the cameraman. "And you can bet your last dollar she'll have her full report at six."

Jones was indeed on the air at six o'clock, and the ratings for that evening's newscast were the highest in the station's history. Joyce Jones was the star of the Channel One news team.

Joyce was also a smart, dedicated investigative reporter, who was not going to report on speculations. This story was far from over, and she had knowledge of things pertaining to West's death that only she and the police were privy to. Those things she'd kept to herself.

One was the MacDonald's note to West. The message could only mean that a great deal of money was involved, probably from the prospective lawsuits against the city and its various agencies for their illegal and heavy-handed methods employed in the arrest and prosecution of MacDonald. The second—this one gleaned from the first—

was that West had stashed MacDonald in his apartment, keeping his client from possible harm during the upcoming litigation. And perhaps most importantly: The disappearance of MacDonald.

None of this made any sense. MacDonald obviously trusted West, and after his ordeal in jail, it seemed unlikely he would have left the safety of the apartment for any reason. Besides, she doubted he had brains enough to go anywhere without a guide. As for West, even if MacDonald had fled for home—wherever that was—thus costing him possible fame and fortune, West was not the kind of man to take his life over it.

West had proven himself to be a survivor, and he would have survived this. Joyce was certain of it.

She went to work.

⊟⊟⊟⊟⊟

"Homicide, Detective Higginson speaking. May I help you?"

"Yes, Higgy. This is Joyce Jones. Is Max in? It's important."

"Good to hear your voice, Joyce," said Higginson. "Heard you had a bad time this morning—hope you're feeling better. He just walked in; I'll transfer you."

"Hello, Joyce." Max got on the line. "I thought I might be hearing from you."

"Max, we've got to talk."

"Agreed. But give me your number and I'll call you back."

Joyce did as asked and answered the callback on the first ring.

"I'm sorry for that," said Max. "I wanted to talk from a secure line. I've had a long day too, as you might guess, but I'll be finished up here in thirty minutes. I can meet with you

255

at say, eight o'clock, at Rick's Place. It's a bar in the Grove. Do you know it?"

"I'll be there," said Joyce. "Thanks, Max."

Walking into the dark bar was like stepping back in time. It was a black-and-white re-creation of Rick's Place in the movie *Casablanca*. The chief of detectives waved to Joyce from a booth in the rear of the long, narrow room.

"Please have a seat," he told her. "You're looking pretty good, considering the kind of day you must have had."

"Thanks, Max. I don't feel too hot though. I'm exhausted."

"I can imagine. I heard you beat everybody to the punch this morning at the crime scene and on your evening news as well. Congratulations. I don't know about you, but I'm off duty now and I'm going to have a beer. How about you?"

"A glass of white wine would be perfect."

The waitress arrived and took their drink orders.

"We're both thirsty," added Max, "so the sooner the better. Please put it on my tab; the name's Hurst."

"Sure thing, Mister Hurst. Comin' right up."

"Max," Joyce started in as soon as the waitress was out of earshot, "this West thing stinks. The preliminary investigation is saying suicide, but I don't believe it for a minute. I was in that apartment and saw things that only you guys and I know. In my opinion, suicide is absolute bullshit. What is going on here?"

Max slowly lifted the black cocktail napkin off the white tablecloth and folded it in half. Then he looked up at Joyce.

"Well, lady, that's to the point," he said. "Let me

256

think on this before I answer. Let's wait until the drinks get here, shall we?"

"Okay, Max," said Joyce, "but this better be good, because I smell something very rotten."

The waitress returned and placed two frosted mugs of draft beer and two chilled glasses of Chablis on the table.

"Since we're not busy tonight," she explained, "Rick says it's still happy hour, so y'all get two for one. Enjoy!" She returned happily to her station at the bar.

"All right, Joyce," Max said, "let me begin this way: There are only two news people in this town with any integrity and whom I really respect. One is Sam Miller and the other is you. Sharing what I'm about to with Sam would be out of the question and when I do tell you, you'll understand why. All I ask is that you not interrupt until I finish. Is that fair?"

"Completely fair," Joyce agreed.

"What I'm going to share is very difficult for me," said Max. "I've been a police officer for thirty-two years and proud of it. I still am. But as you said, something stinks about this whole West mess from beginning to end, and it stinks to high heaven. And I'll be damned if I'll allow the police department to be dragged through the shit that's ultimately going to surface.

"You can report this any way you want to, and I'm sure you will and that you'll be fair. I know you're not a cheap, two-bit yellow journalist, which is why I'm telling you this."

Joyce nodded, but remained silent as promised.

"So, here goes. At approximately four o'clock this afternoon, I received a call from the chief saying, basically, that if I had any problems with the findings in the West case, to button up about them and speak only with him and him alone. You know what an ass-kissing bureaucrat the chief is and my first thoughts are proving to be correct: He's

257

covering up. And is he ever."

"What's he—"

"Don't interrupt! I'm coming to that. First of all, West was going to sue the pants off everything that moved. He had inside information and the paperwork to prove that the chief and Bloom were responsible for his client being drugged, beaten, and forced into a confession, fearing for his life. And so—as you have undoubtedly already figured out, if only from the note in the West's kitchen—West stood to make millions and to destroy a couple people in high office in the process—not to mention the fiscal budget of the city of Miami for the next ten years.

"But now, West's death, coupled with the disappearance of MacDonald, means that there is no plaintiff and no attorney holding what I'm sure is highly incriminating evidence. No witnesses to bring charges absolves any guilt from the principal players who had the most to lose, and those are very powerful people, indeed."

Max drained his first beer and then continued.

"The people who *are* going to pay for this are a couple of cowboy cops, Whiting and his crazy partner, Kozloff, along with that quack doctor in the county jail infirmary. And they *should* pay, mind you, but so should the higher-ups who were involved in this up to their butts.

"That judge, Coen, had to release the information concerning the cops' beatings of MacDonald and the doctor who kept him full of dope; that's what blew the case. But that's as far as it went. And that's as far as it will go. Cops won't rat out their own. If West shared anything more with Coen, he was a fool, and that he is not. He was saving the good stuff for himself."

Max paused as the waitress stopped at the table to take his empty beer mug.

"I sat in the D.A.'s office while Sondra Bloom and West planned how to force a confession out of MacDonald.

258

It wasn't exactly on the up and up, I admit, but to be honest about it, we all cut a corner once in a while, and besides, I was certain of MacDonald's guilt. I've always known that Bloom is a ruthless self-serving bitch and I've never liked her, but I never thought that she, or my boss—the chief of police, for Christ's sake—were capable of this kind of crap. We both know they condoned all this shit. They had to for it to have happened. They would have done anything to get a conviction, so they could close this case and get everyone off their backs."

Joyce could see the effects of the stress this was putting on Max; he looked like he hadn't slept in days.

"So where does this leave us?" Joyce asked. Then she answered her own question: "Well, the power base—the ones who hold themselves above the law—I say fuck 'em. They're going to pay too. I'm going to make a career of it. And you're going to help me."

Max paused for a breath and to take a swig of his second beer.

"I'm nearly finished," he told Joyce. "A couple of minutes after you telephoned me, I got a call from a deputy in the coroner's office. He saw your newscast tonight and was smart enough to realize that it's only a matter of time before the shit hits the fan big time, so he decided he didn't want to be hit by any flying dung. I tried to take a statement from him, but right now he would only talk off the record. Seems there was a slight cover-up down in his office also, and West was aware of it. This was his ace in the hole.

"Observation during the autopsy of Jessica Miller was never disclosed," Max explained. "Blood and skin were found under the girl's fingernails, indicating she had resisted her attacker, clawing him with enough force to have left deep scratches. But when MacDonald was in the infirmary being patched up, no scratches on his body were ever recorded. And here's the real kicker: the blood type under Jessica's nails was AB negative. MacDonald's was O positive. There is no possible way that he could have been her killer. No way!"

"Jesus Christ, Max," Joyce finally said. "I'm in such deep shock, I didn't even interrupt. I have a question though: If this deputy won't give a statement, how could West prove these allegations?"

"I couldn't get a statement out of the coroner," said Hurst, "but for a good deal of cash, West did. It's probably somewhere in his office."

Joyce shifted in her seat and leaned forward.

"Max, what the hell are we going to do?"

"I know exactly what *I'm* going to do," said Hurst. "The question is, what are *you* going to do and how are you going to do it?"

"Maxwell, my friend," said Joyce, "I don't have the slightest idea what I'm going to do. Whatever it is requires more thought than I've had time to give it in just the past few minutes. As to the how, I can assure you, your name will never be mentioned. Of course, you already know that, or you wouldn't be here now.

"And if you have any concerns about blanket accusations of the police department or any other agency, forget it," she reassured him. "That will happen, but it won't be coming from me."

Joyce sipped her wine and then looked back at Max. "Perhaps it would be wise for you to inform me when you're going to take action, so that I don't report anything before it happens.

"Oh, and I do have one idea about the what and how: When I was at the West press conference that never happened, I gained the trust of his receptionist. She's already given me information she shouldn't have and before the sun rises, I'll have every damned piece of paper in West's files."

Max's lips spread into a wide smile.

"I knew there was something I liked about you, Joyce," he said. "But in the interest of time—and time could be a factor here—let's cut one of those corners I mentioned earlier. Forget the receptionist; that would take too long. If we know about this, others may as well. If we're lucky, we'll get there first. You've been pretty good at that so far today."

"Maxwell Hurst," Joyce said, raising her eyebrows, "are you thinking what I think you're thinking?"

"Sure am," Max said, inching his way out of the booth. "Let's go. I have a secret mission and now is the right time of night to complete it."

"I can't believe you're suggesting this, Max."

"I can't believe you're suggesting we not do it. You have a better idea?"

"Well...no...but..."

"Oh, don't bat those big, innocent baby blues at me, young lady. It was only this morning that you were guilty of illegal entry. What's one more?"

Joyce's mouth rose in a half-smile. "You're right, Max. We all cut corners every now and then. Well, hell, I guess this is a go. Let's nail the bastards!"

The black unmarked police car slowly left the curb, pointed in the direction of Coconut Grove.

❊❊❊❊❊

It was a few minutes before eight a.m. when the black car parked to begin Phase 2 of Max's mission. Maxwell Hurst got out, wondering why he had chosen the color black. The temperature was already in the low eighties and he knew that before he got to his office, the car would be an oven. He would trade it for a white one tomorrow, he decided, before ringing the doorbell of a modest duplex apartment in Coral Gables.

"Yes?" answered a voice from behind the closed

261

door. "Who is it?"

"Miss Barnes," Hurst said rather forcefully, "I'm a police officer, and I'd like to speak with you for a moment. Would you open the door please?"

"Hold up your ID to the peephole."

Hurst did as asked, smiling at the woman's caution.

The front door opened to reveal Sally Ann Barnes, the newly unemployed receptionist of West and Associates, standing behind the screen door, fully dressed. She looked at Hurst with sleep still in her eyes.

"I don't know what more I can do for you," she said. "I must have spoken with half the Miami police force yesterday afternoon. There just isn't anything more I can possibly tell you guys."

"I understand," Hurst said gently. "I'm sure that you were as cooperative as possible and we appreciate that. However, I'm not here to ask you any questions; I'm here to ask you a favor."

"A favor?" she asked suspiciously. "What kind of favor?"

"I realize this may be an imposition," said Max, "but I was wondering if you would be kind enough to accompany me to West's offices. I know the other detectives have already looked around, but I'm their boss and I just want to make sure they didn't miss anything. I liked Robert West and I want to be absolutely positive that nothing was overlooked." He lowered his voice conspiratorially. "To be honest, I suspect there may have been foul play connected with his death."

"Damn!" Sally's eyes widened. "Nobody mentioned anything like that."

"Well, it's only a suspicion," Max warned. "I just want to be sure everything has been done properly and set my mind at ease. I worry a lot about things until I'm absolutely certain everyone has done their job. I guess that's why I'm the boss."

Max stepped back from the door and pointed toward his car.

"Now, if you're not up for it," he said kindly, "I can obviously get a search warrant, find the building manager, and all that. However, I'd like to save time by simply having you let me in. Will you go with me?"

"Of course I will," Sally answered. "Actually, your timing couldn't be better. I left some things in my desk I need to get anyway. Will you bring me home, too?"

"I'd be happy to," said Max.

"Great. Just let me grab my purse."

⛓⛓⛓⛓

Hurst pulled his car into West's assigned parking space. As he and Sally walked into the building lobby, she began to giggle softly.

"What's funny, Miss Barnes?" Hurst asked.

"Oh, nothing really," she said. "It's just that I've never thought of policemen looking like corporate executives and carrying briefcases."

Hurst smiled sheepishly. "You don't miss much, do you?" he said. "Don't tell anybody, but the only thing in here is my lunch. The reason I'm lugging it around is that it's too hot to leave it in the car."

They got off the elevator on the third floor and walked to the entrance of West's offices. The receptionist unlocked the door and then entered with Hurst right behind her. They had not gone more than two steps when they both froze.

The suite looked like a hurricane had passed through. Drawers sat open with papers strewn all over the office. Law books had been ripped from their shelves, seat cushions were torn open, and framed pictures had been smashed on the floor. Every room in the suite had been ransacked.

It appeared to be a wanton case of vandalism, but Hurst knew better. It was a case of professionalism and very thoroughly done.

"See if your things are still in the desk or wherever they may have been tossed," Hurst commanded. "That looks like a storage room over there...I'll check it out."

Hurst entered the small room to find the filing cabinets emptied and the space as well searched as the rest of the offices. He opened his briefcase and removed a file folder, then he reentered the reception room where the upset girl was gathering up items that had been scattered across the floor.

"Did you find your things in this mess?" Hurst asked in a fatherly tone.

"Yes," she replied, her eyes filling with tears. "It's all here."

"Well, that's one good thing," he said. "When vandals strike like this, it's worse than an invasion of your privacy; it's like a slap in the face. Come on, let's get you out of here and back home where you belong."

"This is just awful," she wept.

"It truly is," said Max. "I'll get my team back out here to get to the bottom of this," he promised. "By the way," he added, "I found something in the storeroom that may be of interest." He held up the file folder. "Would you mind if I took it with me?"

"Hell, no," Sally said. "Take anything you want. I just want to go home now."

Hurst put his arm around her shoulders and took the keys from her trembling fingers. As Max locked the door behind them, he had to keep from laughing out loud. While he was sure no evidence of his and Joyce's previous night's search had been left behind, if it had, this burglary would have totally covered it up. Most importantly, Max had what he came for: An eyewitness who would swear he found this file folder only this morning.

⧉⧉⧉⧉⧉

"Detective Hurst," the secretary announced, "Mayor Blake will see you now. Please go right on in."

Hurst lifted his weary frame from the waiting-room couch and entered the office of the Honorable Augustus R. Blake, an old and valued friend of some thirty years.

"Max, it's been too long. How the hell are you?"

"Not good, A.R." Max got right to the point. "We got big problems."

"We?"

"Yeah, we." Max sighed, concern lining his tired face. "Actually, mostly you, old buddy."

The mayor turned instantly serious.

"Miss Bernstein," he said into the intercom, "hold all my calls, no matter who it is. I don't give a damn if it's the President of the United States!"

"Yes, sir."

"You own me, Max," Black said. "Now, what's our problem?"

Hurst told his old friend the whole story, leaving out nothing. When he had finished, he slumped back in his chair, waiting for a response. It came immediately and without hesitation.

"You're wrong about one thing, Max: We don't have a problem. And I'll promise you this—and you know damn good and well that I always keep my promises—the people you mentioned have the problems and their problems are going to start right goddamn now!"

"Don't you want to review the evidence first, A.R.?"

"Shit, no, Max! Your word is good enough for me;

265

we can get into the details later. Right now, I'm going to start destroying those assholes!"

"Thanks for your confidence in me, A.R."

"No thanks required, old friend. I only wish there were more people like you in civil service. Now...no offense, Max, but get the hell out of here and go home. You look like you could use the rest of the day off."

"I'd rather—"

"I don't care what you would rather!" Blake said, his voice rising. "Go home, and that's an order. I'll call your office and make up some reasonable excuse for your not coming in today because you're doing some damn thing under orders from the mayor. That's me, and I still run this fucking city. So shut up about it and just do as I ask.

"Leave whatever evidence you have with me," A.R. instructed. "I'm sure it's in that silly-looking briefcase you're holding onto for dear life. I will have experts I trust go over all your allegations and hard evidence before I let my actions overload my ass."

Mayor Blake rose from his chair to escort Max to the door.

"Please pardon my shitty attitude, Max," he said. "I'm not angry with you—you know me better than that. I'm just really pissed off and I'm losing my temper. Before this day is over," he promised, "heads are going to be rolling down the steps of city hall, and the place is going to be the better for it. I'll call you later when I know precisely what is going to happen. And then I'll call your partner-in-crime, Joyce Jones, and fill her in. I, and the rest of the city of Miami, owe her that. And then, by God, she can report her pretty little ass off, completing the total destruction of public officials who are guilty as hell of criminal activities on the six o'clock news. Have I left anything out, old buddy?"

"No, Mister Mayor," Max answered. "That ought to do it...sir."

266

"Oh, screw you, Max." Blake laughed. "Now, get out of my office and go home...please. I've got a lot to do today."

❊❊❊❊❊

The *Miami Herald* had granted Sam Miller a leave of absence with full pay after the death of his daughter. The paper's managing editor, William Ross, had insisted on it, not so much as a corporate show of kindness but as an absolute necessity.

Over the past couple of years, Ross and Sam had become more than close associates. The two of them, and their families, had grown to be very dear friends. After Sam's tragic loss, Ross was the first to realize that the man was slipping into a near-comatose state of depression. He was also aware that the last thing his friend needed was to be subjected to violent crime in any form.

Once the sympathies had been given, the shoulders cried on, and the funerals over and done with, he and Sam had talked day and night and gotten roaring drunk together. Getting Sam out of the city room was the only thing left that Ross could do for his star, Pulitzer-Prize-winning crime reporter and, more importantly, his friend.

Since then, no one had heard at all from Sam. And he had been seen only once: Outside the courtroom on the day of the MacDonald hearing, standing alone in the hall. Before anyone could speak to him, he had vanished.

❊❊❊❊❊

Sam Miller was stark naked. There was no need for clothing; he was a man alone in a lonely house, wandering from room to room, searching for nothing. Nothing was all he had left.

267

Sam was barely able to function as a human being, let alone a member of the working press. Ross had been right about that.

So he simply holed up in total withdrawal. He locked the doors, closed the blinds, and pulled the plugs on the phones. When the mail began to pile up, he called the post office and discontinued service. Once a week he called Feldman's, the neighborhood grocery store, and the owner's son left the order on his doorstep in exchange for a check with a note attached, telling him to keep the change. When the boy had gone, the door would open.

The most telling sign of Sam's emotional spiral was his stopping the delivery of his beloved *Miami Herald.* Sam was shut in and the world was shut out.

The single active thing in the darkened house was the television set in the master bedroom. Sam would lie in bed for hours, staring blankly at mindless programming until he finally drifted off into a kind of restless, plastic sleep.

But in spite of Sam's withdrawal, he was still a reporter, and two or three times a week, he would perk up slightly when he caught the Channel One evening newscast at six. He had always respected Joyce Jones and enjoyed her decisive, honest reporting and direct style. Tonight, Jones was at her best.

But when Jones had finished, Sam was at his worst.

MacDonald's reported innocence was Sam's final deathblow. The dull spark for survival that had kept him existing lost its faint glow and died.

▧▧▧▧▧

The next morning, Sam awoke early, his eyes snapping open, glinting new life. For the first time in a long time, Sam had a purpose. He put on his favorite robe and went to the kitchen, where he made a large pot of strong

268

black coffee and a breakfast of three scrambled eggs, a large slice of ham, and buttered toast. Sam cleaned his plate, put his dishes in the sink, and poured another cup of steaming coffee. Then he sat down to do something almost foreign to him now. He pushed away his dark depression and slammed his bright mind into its highest gear: He was thinking.

By noon, Sam knew exactly what he had to do. And how to do it.

A hoarse male voice answered the phone. "Perroni Imports. May I help you?"

"Yes, I'd like to speak with Mister Perroni. My name is Sam Miller."

"I'm sorry, Mister Miller, but he's gone for the day. May I take a message?"

"Gone for the day, huh?" Sam replied sharply. "Please tell Mister Perroni it's imperative that we speak. It's family business."

"Leave your number," the voice snapped back, losing its amiable tone.

"He knows it."

Sam hung up, leaving his hand on the receiver. Less than a minute passed before he picked it up again.

"Hello, Nick."

"Sam, it's been awhile," said the gruff voice on the other end. "Once again, I can't tell you how sorry I am about your loss. But we've been through all the condolences before and that's not what you called to hear, is it?"

"It's all been said," Sam agreed.

"How may I be of service, Sam?" Perroni asked. "Or, to be blunt, what do you want?"

"It's not a want; it's a need," said Sam. "I need to meet with you, Nick."

"I'm guessing privacy is in order," Nick replied. "My table at the Eden Roc in an hour. Does that work for you?"

269

"That works fine, Nick. Thank you."

Sam hung up and dressed. Then he pulled his car out of the garage and drove off for Miami Beach. He returned late that afternoon.

The next day, Sam climbed into his car again and headed for Sarasota. Twelve hours later, he walked in his front door and went straight to bed.

Early the third morning, Sam left his home for the final time. He drove into downtown Miami, parked his car, and walked into the First Precinct of the Miami Police Department. He went directly to the second floor and the corner office of the chief of detectives.

Maxwell Hurst was at his desk, his head buried in paperwork. Sam stepped into the office and quietly closed the door behind him.

"Good morning, Max."

"Goddamn, Sam!" Hurst bellowed. "You scared the hell out of me. I'm getting too old for that kind of shit. What the hell do you mean by bursting in here like this?"

"I'm a bit unsteady," Sam replied. "May I sit down...please?"

"Of course," Hurst replied instantly, his tone conciliatory. "Make yourself comfortable. If you don't mind my saying so, you look awful. What can I do for you?"

"You can take my statement, Max."

Max eyed Sam warily. "A reporter takes statements; he doesn't give them. What's going on here, Sam? What statement?"

"My confession, really," Sam said.

Max combed the fingers of both hands through his stress-grayed locks.

"Give me a break, Sam," he said. "It's too early in the morning to be crashing in here and jerking me around like this. From the looks of you, something's troubling you, but have you been so naughty, it requires a confession to the city's chief of detectives?"

"Yes." Sam nodded. "I killed both West and MacDonald."

That got Hurst's attention. But he looked at Sam like he had gone mad from grief. He'd need convincing.

Sam was trembling and had some difficulty speaking. But as he went on with his story, the detective was forced to take him seriously. Sam knew details of West's death that were never reported in the media. When Sam went on to tell Hurst the location of MacDonald's body, the detective had no choice. Sam was held incommunicado in the Dade County jail, pending further investigation.

⛓⛓⛓⛓⛓

The five men in the Dade County coroner's van traveled west on Highway 84 across the Everglades, with Hurst in the passenger's seat. Following the directions Sam had written, Hurst spotted the aging hand-painted wooden sign with *Gator Junction* crudely spelled out on it and instructed the driver to turn. The van bumped over a rutted washboard road that wound down a thin strip of hard-packed sand, bordered by the deepening swamplands of the Everglades. After about a mile, Hurst saw the wide spot in the road Sam had described and ordered the driver to pull over.

Ten minutes later, two police scuba divers located a heavily weighted sail bag submerged in the shallow brown water and dragged it up to the road.

"Max, I think we got what you're lookin' for," said one of the divers.

"It's not even open yet," said Max. "What makes you so sure?"

"My end here's pretty chewed up," the second diver corroborated, "it just couldn't bite through the chains. But

271

one thing's for sure: Whatever or whoever's in here is gator bait."

"Well, let's see if the forensic boys prove you guys right," Max said.

The coroner and his aid went to work, pulling the zipper down the length of the canvas and opening the sail bag. They carefully unfolded a blanket inside to uncover the contents. The detective looked down at hundreds of scurrying sand crabs and the few shreds of rotting flesh they had left hanging on the bleached bones of Bubba Red MacDonald.

⛓⛓⛓⛓⛓

With Sam's confession, the files on the apparent suicide of Robert Wesley West and the missing person's report on MacDonald were closed and changed to two charges of murder in the first degree. The new double-homicide case was opened and shut by the end of the day.

One month later, Sam Miller was brought to trial and stood before the bench for less than a minute. He was found guilty on both counts of murder one and sentenced to life terms for each, to be served consecutively with no chance for parole at the Florida State Maximum Security Prison at Raiford.

CHAPTER 13
A HIT-STORY HISTORY

January 1953

Be it minimum security or hard labor, time is time. One thing in common is routine. And I had mine. It mainly consisted of studying the books Sam requested from the tiny book room, along with outdated magazines they had available. My "homework" assignments were to write reports on what I'd read.

Sam was a stickler for grammar and detail. He was constantly correcting my speech, and I often became frustrated with his scrutiny.

"Sam, all this studyin' ain't— isn't gonna do a thing for me in here. Why can't you just let me be who I am?"

"It's studyING and it *is* goING to help you outside of here. You're not stupid, kid. That bright mind of yours is part of who you are, so we are going to work together to make it brighter. Got it?"

Sam was a tough but patient tutor. Occasionally, I would mimic his accent by calling him "tyu-tah," which always got a chuckle from my friend and mentor.

Working with me was an opportunity for Sam to redeem himself in some way. I became an adopted son of sorts.

❈❈❈❈❈

Sam's wisdom carried over into areas beyond academia. He was fond of suggesting, in one way or another, that I apply spiritual principles to my life.

"When I worked in Miami," he explained, "I received an assignment to write a piece for the *Miami Herald* magazine about corruption in the church. In the course of interviewing church leaders, I met with a pastor, who, like me, had no regard for organized religion. I didn't get far on the story with him but we've maintained a rewarding friendship."

I was baffled and had to interrupt. "A pastor who doesn't like organized religion? To use one of your words, that sounds like an oxymoron."

"I understand your confusion. He was of the opinion that institutionalized churches had become more focused on attracting people into their fold and paying the bills than on the message of love, repentance, and forgiveness. He felt more inclined to travel and work with small groups, establishing intimate home churches throughout the state as the early apostles did."

"Do you stay in touch with him?"

"As a matter of fact, yes," Sam replied. "He drives up from Miami now and again to see me and also spends time with a number of other inmates here."

"So what about all the injustice people deal with in the world? Is that a fair God?"

I felt like what Sam was sharing had merit, but the image of a father figure who was uncaring one minute and then watching our every move and passing judgment the next didn't sit well with me. "How do you relate to something like that?"

Sam smiled stoically. "On Augie's first visit, he showed me a completely different way of looking at God, which I understood and truly embraced. He explained that if we were created in His image, that design was for divine love to flow through us so that we would share it with one another."

"So it's all about love?"

"Exactly! When I heard those words," Sam told me, "it struck a chord in me."

I was beginning to understand, but... "What about your daughter?"

The painful memory flashed across Sam's eyes. "Pastor Castillo also imparted to me that holding on to anger and resentment was like drinking poison and expecting the other person to die. It took time to let that sink into my heart. When it did, I found myself forgiving those who had hurt me—including God Himself. When I released the bitterness, it was like a ten-ton weight was lifted off me."

I hopped off the upper bunk to sit next to Sam.

"But you know," he went on, "as I've peeled away those painful layers over the years, I've discovered there is one person I need to forgive most of all: Myself. And I admit I'm still working on that bit day by day."

Sam was visibly moved and for once I remained quiet as he collected his thoughts. He reached past his typewriter into the small row of books on the desk and picked out a very old, worn Bible, the margins of its pages filled with notes written in his own impeccable handwriting. He took a deep breath before continuing.

"These are more than just words, kid. This is a manual for living. I've witnessed more than a few men in here with hardened hearts shift into a place of peace because they found a source of love and healing within this book."

I shifted uneasily. "I don't know, Sam...I've never been into religion."

Sam intertwined his fingers together. "Kid, you like oxymorons, so I've got a good one for you: The Bible has absolutely nothing to do with religion."

I raised my eyebrows at him.

"It's about your relationship with God," he explained.

A spark of understanding lit inside me.

"And here's another oxymoron," he said. "My method for living is that I die to myself every day. Now, what do I mean by that?" he asked before I could interject. "It means I release my ego. Kill my pride. After all, look where it got me. And you. So do yourself a favor, and take a moment to listen to that still, small voice before jumping into impulsive, willful action. Let go and let God guide you."

I remained quiet, letting his words sink in.

"Dying to my angry, bitter old self and handing it over to something and Someone greater than me makes my life in prison bearable," Sam told me. "So I have tried, to the best of my ability, to live in a loving, compassionate manner ever since I accepted Christ into my life."

Sam's mood lightened. "Knowing you, kid," he said, "this has raised more questions than it has answered. Take some time to digest it all and we'll talk more later."

⛓⛓⛓⛓⛓

In spite of my occasional frustration at being barred up and walled in, I had a lot to be grateful for. I wasn't stuck in a hole with some hard-timer whose idea of fun was to sodomize his cellmate. No demands were made on me other than reveille and Sam's sometime militant instruction. He gave me the space to explore spirituality on my terms and find my own way into God's word about right living.

The days passed fairly quietly. The food looked and smelled like food, and I felt good about my academic accomplishments and spiritual progress. Sam's and my conversations covered different stories in the Bible and how they applied to the day-to-day world, both in and out of Raiford. We reviewed my not-so-current event reports, which markedly improved now that I had a thesaurus. Sam told stories of his experiences in Italy, New York, and Miami and of the articles he'd written for the newspapers. The beautiful coral-pink Florida sunsets seemed to soften the harshness of the barbed-wire perimeter.

And I noticed a softening on the inside as I cultivated the habit of waking up thirty minutes before the bugle sounded to meditate and pray. Sam said that praying was talking to God; meditating was listening.

For years, I had stuffed rage, hatred, and bitterness deep inside me. But it had come out in acts of violence and rebellion. All that began to melt away as I—to use another of Sam's phrases—"Let go and let God." As personal forgiveness increased, I could look into the eight-by-ten-inch cloudy steel panel that served as our cell's mirror and began to appreciate the potential of who was looking back at me.

⛓⛓⛓⛓⛓

Sam and I left Sunday morning's mess and sprinted for Block A through a driving rain. Sometime during the night, a tropical depression had drifted in from the Gulf of Mexico and settled over North Florida. The storm front had gone stationary and now squatted directly overhead, turning the whitewashed prison compound into a black fortress under siege.

I hung my clothes to dry on our cell's open barred door alongside Sam's, as Sam sat at his desk in his shorts, drying his hair with a towel. I sat down on his lower bunk and did the same.

Sam swiveled in his chair and faced me, a strange, pained expression crossing his face.

"It's a pretty grim day," I observed. "Any Sunday is when we're confined to the block," I added. "But not as grim as you're looking right now. What's wrong, Sam?"

"Ricky Maldonado."

I stopped toweling my hair. "*The* Ricky

277

Maldonado?"

"Yes, the same."

"Sam..." I treaded gently. "This may not be any of my business—and if it isn't, shut me up—but what's so upsetting about Maldonado?"

"The man himself isn't what's bothering me," said Sam. "It's memories that the mere mention of his name resurrects. I spoke with him yesterday."

"You spoke with him?" I blurted. "He's here?" I got up and paced the cell. "How come nobody knows he's in Raiford? And he's got to be segregated until he goes through orientation, so how in the hell did you get in to the New Cock Block? And what—"

"Hold up with all the questions, Clark." Sam raised a hand. "Let me answer them one at a time. Maldonado is here and nobody knows because the administration doesn't want to deal with a horde of yelling media people. That's also why he was convicted and processed in under his given—and quite common—Latin name, Ricardo Maldonado. He was quietly released into the population yesterday.

"Now," said Sam, "this guy has no intention of sharing his identity, or anything else for that matter, with anyone he doesn't know. So, kid, when you meet this man, watch your mouth. Ricky is on his way up here now."

"You're on a first-name basis with this guy?"

Sam nodded. "I am. And it's another long story."

⛓⛓⛓⛓⛓

July 1924

Ricardo Maldonado was a gurgling celebrity. Almost every person of wealth and power in the business community of Havana, Cuba, was looking only at him. His parents could not have been prouder: Ricardo did not cry as the holy water splashed over his glistening head. The child was just three days old when his baptism ended and the festivities began. For Ricardo, the festivities continued nonstop for twenty-two years.

Ricardo was born into one of Cuba's most wealthy and influential families. His mother had inherited thousands of acres of some of the most fertile land on the island, producing the highest quality tobaccos and sugarcane. His father was a shrewd man with a genius for business, and he invested most of the family fortune in real estate, acquiring vast holdings in and around Havana. The Maldonados owned, operated, and profited from the properties, turning a large fortune into a great one. In addition to their tobacco and sugarcane holdings, the Maldonado family became urban land barons.

Young Ricardo's childhood was glorious. He was an only child and the only Maldonado left to perpetuate the family name. He lacked for nothing and could have easily been spoiled rotten, but he was not; he would not allow it. The boy grew into a handsome young man with blue-black hair and black, brooding eyes. He was tall for a Latino, standing a couple of inches over six feet, and weighed in at a hard, muscular two hundred pounds. He attended the finest schools, working harder than any student to excel, and he did so with honors at every level. Ricardo ended his formal education by graduating at the top of his class with a master's degree in Business Administration from the University of Havana before he was twenty-one. Aside from his native language, Ricardo was fluent in English and French and conversational in German. He was well-liked, especially by girls, and was a notorious womanizer.

On the eve of Ricardo's twenty-first birthday, his father gave the young man a reward for being a fine son that would help ease his entry into the world of high-powered business. This token of parental esteem was the Hotel

Havana, a prime piece of real estate located on the Boulevard Reforma, overlooking Havana Harbor. It was an elegant pale-pink stucco building, constructed in the Spanish Colonial style. The elder Maldonado was going to be damned sure that his only son had a decent start.

Ricardo was delighted for two reasons. The first was that hotel management was what he really wanted to do. Being the sole owner of this magnificent turn-of-the-century property made fulfilling his dream even sweeter. The second reason was almost as important: With his own place to live, he would no longer have to sneak women in and out of the family mansion.

The younger Maldonado took up residence in the *Suite El Presidente* atop the ten-story building. After renovating one of the three bedrooms into his command post, he sat down in the plush Gunlocke chair at his new massive mahogany desk and went to work.

When a hotel comes under new ownership, the common practice is to fire the entire property management staff and replace them with your own people. Ricardo did not do that. His simple reasoning was that his managers, for the most part, were very good at what they did. His father was no fool and had chosen well. The general manager had formerly run the Eden Roc Hotel in Miami Beach and the food and beverage manager had been hired away from the Stevens Hotel in Chicago. The rest of the staff was equally qualified; however, all were certain they would be looking for work within the week.

No one had seen any sign of the new owner since his arrival two days prior, beyond the room service deliveries to his suite. On the third day, at exactly nine o'clock Monday morning, Ricardo summoned his staff to meet with him in his suite in five minutes. They were there in three.

The new owner motioned for them to be seated, stood up from behind his desk, and announced his first executive decision: Effective immediately, everyone in the room would receive a ten percent increase in salary. Audible sighs of relief filled the room, and Ricardo knew instinctively that he had just invested a little money in return for a lot of loyalty. Something he would demand.

His second directive was to change the signage, stationery, and everything else that had the hotel name on it. The Hotel Havana was now La Tropical.

Ricardo's next move was not nearly as simple—and it would prove to be rather costly. La Tropical was a ten-story hotel with three hundred and fifty rooms. The first floor was dedicated to reception, the restaurant and bar, offices, and the other functions needed to operate the hotel. Floors two through nine each held forty-two rooms and the tenth floor housed fourteen suites. Ricardo ordered a total renovation of the second floor, ripping out the forty-two rooms and their revenues, leaving virtually the entire floor one large, unbroken space.

The next phase was even more costly. Using all his remaining assets, Ricardo completed the transformation, ensuring that La Tropical, in addition to being one of the finest hotels in Havana, boasted the newest and most exciting nightclub in the Caribbean.

The gamble paid off. Yankee tourists from the Eastern Seaboard flocked to La Tropical in droves like crazed migratory birds. They came to vacation in elegance, bolt down gourmet food and wine, be entertained nightly by the most lavish cabaret shows in the Western Hemisphere, and throw around their U.S. dollars. And throw them they did, directly into the increasingly deep pockets of Señor Ricardo Maldonado.

❄❄❄❄❄

The hot, late-summer sun cast long black shadows

over the city of Havana as it slid slowly down the western sky. Ricardo stood at the window of his tenth-floor office, watching the light over the city change from bright white to pale pink. This was his favorite time of day and he was impatiently waiting for his last appointment of the afternoon. He was thankful it would be a brief meeting—he would give them a few minutes professional courtesy, and that was it.

Ricardo glanced at his watch. He concluded his business day, every day, at precisely six o'clock, so they had better be on time.

At ten minutes to six, the house phone on his desk rang and the front desk announced his guests' arrival.

A few minutes later, his receptionist spoke to him over the intercom. "Señor Maldonado," she announced, "the gentlemen you were expecting are here."

"Thank you, Maria. Please show them in. I won't be needing you anymore today."

The receptionist opened the glass door and two men entered the office. Ricardo was again struck by what a mismatched pair these two were; the only thing they seemed to have in common was age—both in their mid-fifties, he guessed. The handsome one was tall and rapier-thin with pure white hair over an olive complexion. The other was short and overweight with no hair at all. His pallid skin was almost as white as the other man's hair. He looked like an albino pig with a hawk's beak for a nose, Ricardo decided.

"Good afternoon, gentlemen," Ricardo said, smiling as he shook hands. "Please have a seat. I would offer you refreshment, but I am seriously pressed for time. How may I be of service?"

"Well, Mister Maldonado," the tall man said, "as you know from our previous meeting, we're both from New York; so in respect of your limited time, we won't take more than a few New York minutes. If I may reintroduce ourselves, my friend here is Sol Goldberg and I'm Santo

282

Scarcello. In the interest of brevity, allow me to come directly to the point."

"Of course," Ricardo said. "Please continue, Mister Scarcello."

"Thank you. The last time we spoke, you turned us down. This time, perhaps you won't. I sincerely hope that will be the case."

"I doubt it, but go on."

"Frankly," said Scarcello, "when we returned to New York last month without having closed a deal with you, not only were *we* disappointed, but our board members seemed almost angry that you would turn down that kind of money. Still, the board has discussed this at great length, and we are prepared to make you a second and final—"

"Mister Scarcello," Ricardo said, his annoyance building, "I do not need your money and I do not intend to sell this property to you, your organization, or anyone else. Is that clear enough for you?"

"Yes, it is," said Scarcello, unruffled. "And not unexpected. May Mister Goldberg say something?"

Ricardo nodded to the short man. "All right, but make it brief."

"Yes, Mister Maldonado," Goldberg said, his tone a bit nervous. "Our organization needs a five-star hotel in Havana that we can turn into a gambling casino. We have been authorized by our board of directors to purchase La Tropical for twice its value. That amount of money, in U.S. dollars, is in my briefcase. You would be wise to accept it, and if you do, we can conclude this business today. Right now."

Ricardo was angry now, and when angered he became very quiet and stoic. The two men likely thought that he was considering their proposition. And he was. He considered it a deep and personal insult.

"Allow me to make a counteroffer," said Maldondo

softly. The two men had to lean in to hear him. "Get the fuck out of my office, right fucking now!"

Goldberg recoiled as if he had been physically struck. Scarcello did not react at all. His eyes turned stony.

"Do you love your family?" Scarcello hissed.

Ricardo flew over his desk as if he had been shot out of a catapult.

Scarcello was dead before he fell out of his chair, a gold letter opener in his heart. Goldberg moved fast for a fat man, but he had not taken two steps before Ricardo was on him like a big cat, knocking him to the floor, smashing his fists into his fat face on the way down. Ricardo hit him over and over again, until he was a lifeless bleeding red pulp.

Ricardo remained sitting on Goldberg's chest, looking down at what moments ago had been a face. He looked over at Scarcello, who lay facedown, the golden point of the letter opener making a tent in the back of his suit jacket.

Ricardo did not even attempt to get up. He could not believe this had just happened. He also could not believe how he was reacting to it all. Sure, he was a little out of breath from the physical exertion of killing the two men and his hands hurt, but other than that, he felt just fine. He took his own pulse and it was normal.

That's not normal, he thought, realizing he had just made a joke. Then it occurred to him that something else was not normal—far from it. When he had finally stopped beating Goldberg and looked down at the dead Italian, he had been filled with an overwhelming joy. He had loved the act of taking the lives of these men. It had been the ultimate adrenaline rush.

"You know, Ricky old boy," he said aloud, "wealth is power, but taking life is godlike. Fun too."

There was no fear, no panic, no emotion—only cold calculation about how to survive this. Clearly no one had heard anything or they would have been in here by now, so he felt no need to rush anything.

Maldondo's phone rang. He rolled off Goldberg's chest and picked up the receiver on the second ring.

"Yes?"

"Señor Maldonado, this is Hector again. I'm getting ready to leave for the day. If you're going to be working late, is there anything I can have the staff take care of for you?"

"That's very thoughtful of you, Hector," said Ricky. "And there is, as a matter of fact. Would you have Food and Beverage bring me the twelve-ounce filet dinner with all the things I usually have, up to my suite? Not the office, the suite. And have them choose a nice bottle of red wine chilled the way I like it. Ask them to get it up here as soon as they can, too. I'm starving."

"Yes, sir. It's on its way."

"Thanks, Hector. Have a pleasant evening."

Ricardo placed the receiver back in its cradle, locked his office, and went to his adjoining suite. Then he remembered something. He went back to the office, picked up Goldberg's briefcase, and returned to his suite. Then he went to the bathroom, removed his bloody clothes, and quickly showered. His knuckles were beginning to swell, but they had only minor abrasions.

Ricardo put on his robe, went to the refrigerator, and opened an ice-cold Hatuey Cerveza. Then he sat down at the dining room table. He always thought better on a full stomach, and he was looking forward to a gourmet meal with the best beef in Havana.

Other than the problem of two dead bodies, it had been a terrific day. He could not remember being quite this happy since childhood.

<hr>

When a gentle knock announced the arrival of dinner, Ricardo stowed his bruised hands in his robe pockets.

He ate his meal slowly and methodically, consuming only one glass of wine. When he had finished, he corked the bottle and set it aside. He had a lot of thinking to do, and another glass of wine would do nothing to help that process.

When Ricardo put his brilliant mind into high gear, it was awesome. In less than two hours, he had it all well figured out.

The first thing Ricardo did was telephone the Maldonado family's most trusted friend, Abraham Vito Eisenstadt. Ricardo's godfather and the family attorney for three decades, Eisenstadt was half Jewish and half Italian. He seemed to know everyone in the business world, both legitimate and underworld. He was there in less than an hour.

"Come on in, Abe," Ricardo said, opening the door. "Thank you for coming on such short notice and for not asking questions over the phone. I have a lot to tell you, and with your help, we have much to do before morning."

Ricardo told him everything.

Eisenstadt moved with remarkable speed.

The first move was to sell La Tropical to the South Florida Spataro Mafia family who were virtually at war with the New York family (now two members fewer) for control of gambling and prostitution in Havana and the importation of drugs into the United States. With the purchase of La Tropical, the Spataro family stood to make millions. For that, and for having killed off two powerful New York rivals, Ricardo was now, and would forever be, a respected friend of the South Florida mob.

The second step was an automatic. The Cuban government was corrupt from top to bottom, and Eisenstadt had most of the high-ranking officials in his pocket.

286

The next morning, Havana newscasts reported that at first light, Hector Garcia, the captain of a charter fishing boat, had discovered the body of an unidentified dead man floating in Havana Harbor at the foot of the sea wall fronting La Tropical hotel. Late that afternoon, Carlos Ramirez, Havana's chief of detectives, informed the media that the victim had died from a self-inflicted twelve-gauge shotgun blast to the face. Ramirez went on to say that although it had been quite difficult, positive identification had finally been established. The dead man was the owner of La Tropical: Señor Ricardo Maldonado.

Shortly before sunset, as Radio Habana was reporting the Maldonado suicide, the sixty-foot Chris Craft yacht Miss Miami cast off from Abraham Vito Eisenstadt estate's North Shore dock. When the Captain was in international waters, he changed course to north by northeast and entered the Straits of Florida with a direct heading for Key West.

Standing at the port side of the pilothouse, watching a blood-red sun sinking under the swelling horizon, was a smiling dead man.

CHAPTER 14
A JOB FOR LIFE

April 1946

Ricardo Maldonado had turned invisible. The dead Cuban was living a comfortable life in Ybor City, Florida, a city within a city just east of downtown Tampa. Referred to by locals as "Little Havana," the area was filled with the sounds and smells of his homeland. The enclave was noted primarily for manufacturing the finest cigars in the country and for its restaurants serving the best Cuban food outside of Havana. With Ybor City being the largest ethnic Cuban community in America, Ricardo blended in perfectly. Maldonado was a common Latin name, so he kept it, changing only his first name—and even that, not by much. An avid fan of the new television show *I Love Lucy,* he now introduced himself as Ricky Maldonado.

From all outside appearances, Ricky led the modest life of a middle-class Cuban-American. He lived on the top floor of a four-story commercial building in the business section of Ybor City. The first floor accommodated a well-known Cuban restaurant, the second and third floors housed a cigar factory, and the fourth floor loft was his.

In actuality, the entire building was his. The aging stucco structure was somewhat shabby, but inside, the loft was magnificent. The ten-thousand-square-foot living area was private, secure, and only accessible via a private elevator. Decorated and furnished by the senior interior designer of Florence Knoll & Associates in New York, the loft was the finest example of contemporary art and design. Every square

288

foot reflected expensive, tasteful elegance, as quietly understated as its occupant's lifestyle.

Ricky seldom left the loft. He found absolutely no reason to do so when everything he enjoyed or needed was right here, surrounding him with opulent creature comfort. What he occasionally felt he lacked for was delivered, be it gourmet food, drink, or women.

Ricky was a bona fide closet millionaire.

⌬⌬⌬⌬⌬

November 1951

The ringing telephone startled Ricky from a sound sleep. He sat bolt upright in the bed, throwing the arm of the tall blond woman from his chest.

"Yeah, what?"

"Mister Maldonado," a soft male voice asked, "do you recognize my voice?"

"Yes."

"We need to meet."

The woman next to him sat up. "Ricky, what—"

"Shut up," Ricky said quietly but sharply. " Sorry. When and where?"

"Tomorrow at noon," the voice said. "The Napoli restaurant in Sarasota. Can you make it?"

"Yes."

"Good night," the voice said and hung up.

"I'm sorry I snapped at you, Carlotta," Ricky said soothingly. "I just get pissed off when the damned phone wakes me up in the middle of the night for no good reason. Maybe we can get some sleep now."

"Now that I'm wide awake," the blonde said, "maybe we can get some sleep in about thirty minutes."

"Good idea."

⛓⛓⛓⛓⛓

The dark green Hudson Hornet coupe departed Tampa, headed south on Highway 41 at high speed. It was a fast car and Ricky drove it that way whenever possible. He loved speed and was willing to occasionally pay the highway patrol's price for it. His philosophy was that if you could afford it, go for it.

So he did, covering the fifty-some miles to Sarasota in under thirty minutes. He pulled into the filled parking lot of the restaurant and parked in a space in the rear reserved for employees. He entered through a door marked "Employees Only" and walked through the kitchen to the staircase leading to the second-floor manager's office.

A very large middle-aged man was blocking the door.

"Mister Maldonado?"

"Yes."

"May I see some identification, please?"

"Certainly," Ricky said, showing the large man the driver's license already in his hand.

"Thank you," said the guard, opening the door. "Mister Perroni is expecting you. I assume you know the way."

"I do."

The empty office was a small windowless room with another door along the rear wall behind the single desk. Walking through that doorway was like entering another world. The small banquet room it opened to looked like it had been transported from the Vatican. In its center was an Italian Renaissance dining table and nine empty chairs.

Seated at the head of the table, in the tenth chair, was Nick Perroni. Perroni was even larger than the guard at the door and he was not overweight. Ricky knew him well and this was one of the few men in the world he would never screw with. Perroni had made his bones by killing his first victim bare-handed at age eighteen. From there, he had risen in the Spataro family ranks to second in command, assassinating people for over thirty years without ever being charged with a crime of any kind. He was a true professional, making his respect for Ricky also immense.

"Ricky!" Perroni said, grinning ear to ear as he rose from his chair. "It's a real pleasure to see you. It's been a while, hasn't it?"

"Too long, Nick."

The two men embraced in typical Sicilian style, hugging each other with genuine affection.

"Please sit down, Ricky," Nick said, pulling out a chair for him and then vacating his place at the head of the table and taking a seat across from Ricky as a sign of respect.

"I have a special meal planned for us today," said Nick. "I know you have a deep fondness for lamb, so if you approve, I have ordered the chef to prepare a special dish. Not any of that crap with red shit poured all over it that they serve downstairs."

Ricky smiled. "You've never disappointed me, Nick. I don't think you'd start with food, of all things. What is it?"

"*Costolette Di Abbacchio a Scottadito.* Grilled lamb chops, to you."

No restaurant personnel were ever allowed in this room, not even to clean it, so their waiter was the guard who had met Ricky at the door. Surprisingly, the service was as impeccable as the meal. The table was cleared and the pair was served a bottle of fine brandy with two crystal snifters.

"Have a Havana?" Nick asked, laughing.

"A perfect ending to a perfect meal, my friend."

They poured the brandy, lit the cigars, and leaned back in their chairs, enjoying a few moments of silence.

"Now," Nick finally said, the smile leaving his face, "let's get down to business." He slid an envelope across the table. "As usual, everything you need to know is in there.

291

When you have memorized it, please give it back to me. When we finish our brandy, we'll call it a day. I've got to get back to Miami."

Driving back to Tampa, Ricky was careful to observe the speed limit and everything else around him. All his senses were heightened as his mind went into survival mode. From now until this job was complete, he would remain all business. Nothing could disturb that and nothing could stop him from completing his contract. *Nothing.*

He parked the Hudson in its space behind his building and took the elevator to the loft, locking it into position on the fourth floor. Then he disconnected his phone and sat down to think.

Early the next morning, Ricky left the loft with a small overnight bag. He walked over a mile to a pay phone and called a cab that picked him up and took him to the Greyhound bus station in St. Petersburg. There, he took another cab to a hotel in Clearwater. He went to the lobby and used another pay phone to call for a third cab. The third cab delivered him to the Tampa airport, where he used an alternate identity to board a flight to the 36th Street Airport in Miami, which in later days would expand to become Miami International.

Upon arrival, Ricky exited the terminal and walked briskly to the public parking lot. A pale-blue four-year-old Ford station wagon was parked in space number twelve. Its keys sat atop its right rear tire. Ricky unlocked the car, got in, and changed clothes, donning the gray jumpsuit and cap of a Miami electrical contractor along with a leather tool belt, all of which had been left for him under the front seat.

Ricky drove out of the garage in Hialeah and headed directly to Miami, to the apartment complex of Robert

West. He parked his car in a visitor spot some distance from West's apartment and waited.

His timing could not have been better. Within minutes, he saw West walk out his front door and get in his gray car and drive away.

Ricky pulled his own car out of its parking space and backed it into the spot West had just vacated directly in front of the apartment. He put on a pair of latex surgical gloves and got out of the car, leaving the door slightly ajar. With a blanket rolled up under his arm, he walked rapidly to West's front door, making sure no one was in sight. He took the pick from his tool belt and quietly worked the lock, and then gently and silently opened the door.

Bubba was sitting on the couch with his back to Ricky, watching television and eating a huge breakfast spread out on the coffee table before him. Bubba died instantly and soundlessly from a single puncture wound to his heart.

Ricky had been briefed that Bubba was an illiterate half-wit, barely able to write his own name, so no sample of his handwriting would be available to the cops to compare against the good-bye note Ricky had written from Bubba to West. Ricky pressed Bubba's lifeless fingertips onto the paper and placed it on the kitchen counter.

Ricky rolled Bubba's fat body off the couch onto the blanket and wrapped him up. He suppressed a chuckle as he looked down at the "pig in a blanket." He dragged the heavy load to the door and opened it. Seeing no one, he continued dragging the body the few feet to the tailgate of the station wagon. Ricky was a strong man, but it took all he had to load this mass of dead weight into the back of the car. After shutting the tailgate, Ricky reentered the apartment and locked the door behind him. He needed to retrieve Bubba's personal belongings, clean up, and make sure that no evidence of the murder was left behind.

Ricky was finished. As he made his way to the door

with a small armful of Bubba's property, he heard the key turning in the lock. Ricky set the bundle on the floor and was fiddling with a light switch as West entered.

"Who the hell are you?" West was almost yelling.

"Dade County Electric Company. The complex manager reported short-circuiting in this unit and let me in to fix the damn thing so you won't burn to the ground."

"Where's my goddamned roommate?"

"He said he had to take a leak."

"I'll be right back," West said, striding toward the bathroom.

West did not stride far. The ice pick hit him at the base of the neck, plunging into his spinal cord. Ricky caught the dead Robert West in his arms and lowered him gently to the floor, making sure no blood dripped onto the carpet. Although the puncture was almost bloodless, he pressed one of Bubba's shirts into the wound to make sure.

Well, Ricky, old boy, he said calmly to himself, *this could be your first fuck-up—Strike One. Now what?*

He remembered the closet where he had gotten Bubba's clothes. In the corner he had seen a rifle and a shotgun. The shotgun would be perfect. He hoped it was a twelve-gauge; that would make a bigger mess. It was.

Ricky propped West's body up on the smaller, two-cushion couch next to the wall. He took off West's right shoe and sock and jacked a double-ought shell into the receiver of the shotgun. He pried open West's jaw and shoved the barrel of the gun into his mouth. Then, very carefully, he placed West's right big toe into the trigger guard and against the trigger itself and released the safety. Ricky set Bubba's things by the door so that he could get them quickly on the way out.

Ricky was a thrill-seeker—not a chance-taker—but he had no choice. This was a chance he had to take.

"I hate to do this to you," Ricky said aloud. "You

had nothing to do with this; you just had very bad timing, Mister West. Nothing personal, but..."

The roar of the blast was deafening.

Ricky was out the door and into the station wagon slowly driving away before he saw anyone. Or anyone saw him.

⛓⛓⛓

The traffic was light as Ricky drove north on Highway 441. He was going with the flow and would tuck in behind an eighteen-wheeler when he could, being as inconspicuous as possible. When he got to Fort Lauderdale, he turned left on Highway 84 and headed west for about fifteen miles to the Sunrise Motel. He found room number fourteen in the rear and parked. He retrieved his overnight bag from the rear seat and the key to the room from the glove compartment.

When Ricky entered the run-down room, he set his bag on the bed. After drawing the curtains closed, he snapped on the bedside lamp and then knelt down beside it. From under the bed, he pulled out a large, heavy sail bag made of canvas. Everything he needed was in it. He stretched out on the bed and retrieved a paperback book from his overnight bag. It was *Call of the Wild* by Jack London.

⛓⛓⛓

Ricky glanced at his watch, which read 1:15 a.m. He went to the station wagon and dragged the two-hundred-forty-pound blanket into the room. He opened the sail bag and removed the sail, a twenty-foot length of heavy chain, four two-foot lengths of chain with open padlocks, and four concrete blocks. Leaving Bubba's body in the blanket, he stuffed it into the sail bag and tied up the bulky package with the long chain. He carried the blocks with their chains and locks back to the wagon and returned to the room with nothing left to do now but wait.

At precisely three a.m., a soft knock sounded on the door. It was the large man who had been guarding the door in Sarasota.

"Good evening, Mister Maldonado."

"Good evening. I don't believe I know your name."

"No disrespect," the man said, "but you don't need to. What you do need is a weightlifter."

"That's true. Let's go."

Two cars left the motel and drove west on Highway 84. A few miles down the road, they turned onto a dirt road marked "Gator Junction" and continued for about a mile. They stopped at a spot where they could turn around. Bubba was weighted and thrown into a canal that wound through the Everglades.

"Thanks," Ricky said. "This guy was a full load."

"No problem. How was lunch?"

"Excellent, as always."

"I enjoyed being your server, Mister Maldonado. Both then and now."

"Good night."

"Good night."

When the two cars reached Highway 441, they continued in different directions, one heading east toward Fort Lauderdale and Ricky turning south for the terminal.

Ricky arrived at the airport, parked the station wagon as close as he could to the spot where he had found it, and changed clothes. Taking his bag, he put the keys back on the right rear tire and then left, retracing his steps home to the loft.

It was finished.

Almost three weeks had passed since Ricky's trip to Miami. Since his return, he had been giving serious thought to his occasional pursuit of the "ultimate adrenaline rush."

Ricky truly enjoyed the danger and thrill of the hunt, and the killing of prey. It was a sexual thing, too. He was wise enough to accept that, although he considered it nothing more than a character flaw. It was not an issue of morality with him. His thinking was that in each case, except for the last, his victims had deserved what they'd gotten.

Ricky never had felt, nor had it ever been suggested that he had, any indebtedness to the Spataro family. If anything, they were indebted to him. He did not need the money; he by now had more than he would spend in his lifetime. He did what he did for personal reasons. One was that he took great pride in getting away with murder. The other was that it gave him pleasure.

However, he was no longer sure he wanted to continue playing what he thought of as a high-stakes game of life or death. Perhaps his.

As soon as he'd heard Robert West's key in the lock, Ricky had realized that Steinbeck's warning about "the best laid plans..." could ultimately beat him at his own game. The question nagging at him was: Was it worth the risk?

Screw it, he thought, putting the dilemma aside. *I'll figure it out tomorrow.*

Ricky was considering what to order for dinner from the restaurant downstairs when his train of thought was rudely interrupted.

"Mister Maldonado," the voice asked over the phone, "do you recognize my voice?"

"Yes."

"We need to meet."

"Seems like we just did. This is awfully soon, isn't

it?"

"It would be if it were for the usual reasons, but this is different. It has nothing to do with the other, but it is very important. Is tomorrow good for you?"

"Yes," Ricky answered. "I guess so."

"Same as last time?"

"For you, yes."

"Thank you," said the voice. "Good night."

⛓⛓⛓

"What's for lunch?" Ricky asked, smiling up at the familiar large man standing at the door.

"Don't know, Mister Maldonado. But I'm sure Mister Perroni has something tasty in mind for you. By the way, my name is Mike. I'm Nick's little brother."

"Not so little. Thank you, Mike."

"Once again, my pleasure," he said, laughing. "Go on up."

When Ricky entered what he called "The Vatican Room," his blood instantly ran cold.

Nick spoke quickly. "It's okay! Trust me! I told you this was different."

"Sure as hell is! Who the fuck is this?"

"A friend of the family. As good a friend as you," Nick snapped angrily.

Ricky knew Nick was not accustomed to being spoken to like this and he was not a man to tolerate disrespect from anyone. Respect was what kept him alive.

"Now, why don't you just sit the fuck down," said Nick, "and I'll tell you exactly who the fuck this is!"

Ricky felt a rare twinge of fear. He knew he had overstepped his bounds and that Nick would never compromise him for any reason.

"I apologize, Nick. But I'm sure you understand."

298

"I do," Nick said slowly, almost whispering. "But I want you to understand something, too. Please...do not ever speak to me that way again."

"I understand."

"Good," Nick said, standing and walking around the table to embrace his friend. "Now that we've had our little snit, let's put it behind us."

They both laughed, relieved that the tension was broken, each man wondering who could kill whom, and both knowing they never wanted to find out.

The two men remained standing as the man seated at the table rose from his seat. Ricky could see that he was Italian, and if he was a friend of Nick's, Ricky had nothing to fear. He relaxed and waited to be introduced.

"May I use your name?" Nick asked Ricky.

"Of course," said Ricky. "Any friend of the family, as they say."

"Thank you for that," Nick said. "Ricky, this man truly is a friend of the family, as you are. Years ago, he uncovered some things about our business that could have hurt us, but he kept his mouth shut, and from time to time, he has been of service."

Ricky nodded at the man seated beside Nick. The man returned the gesture without breaking eye contact.

"A few weeks back," Nick went on, "he contacted me asking for a service in return—calling in a marker, if you will. And we—you, really—repaid a debt by killing the guy who cruelly wiped out his family: Bubba MacDonald."

Ricky sat motionless so as not to implicate himself until he knew where this was going.

"However," Nick went on, "as it unfortunately turns out, this MacDonald didn't do it."

Mierda, Ricky thought. *Strike Number Two!*

"Now," said Nick, "I'm sure we all feel badly about this, but you and I will get over it. This gentleman will not.

He is a good man and he needs your help."

"Mine?"

"Yes. And when we explain what we are asking of you, the decision will be yours. If you refuse, there will be no hard feelings on my part."

"Fair enough," said Ricky with a nod.

"Mister Maldonado, allow me to introduce Mister Sam Miller."

⛓⛓⛓⛓⛓

For the two assassins, the meal was an unusual one, in that they spoke of business while eating. Sam ate virtually nothing, picking at his plate and doing most of the talking throughout the working lunch.

Sam told Ricky all about the MacDonald case and the cover-up at city hall—the forced confession, the lack of any marks or scratches, and the blood evidence proving beyond doubt that MacDonald was innocent of the crime. He spoke of his devastating guilt at having caused the deaths of two innocent men and his need for punishment, as he searched for even the slightest absolution in order to live what was left of his life in partial peace with God.

When Sam had finished speaking, a long and somewhat awkward silence followed.

It was finally broken by Ricky. "Mister Miller...may I call you Sam?"

"Yes," Sam agreed, through the hint of a smile. "*If* you decide to help."

The side of Ricky's mouth turned upward. "Sam, after killing two innocent men, I suppose the least I can do is tell you what happened, if for no other reason than to make me feel like I've done something bordering on good. I don't mean to be facetious, but your taking the rap for this is in my best interests anyway. So...You help me, I help you."

300

Sam tilted his head in acknowledgment. "Thanks...may I call you Ricky?"

"You sure as hell can."

Ricky told Sam everything he needed to know. When he had finished, Sam smiled for the first time in weeks.

"I'll never betray your trust, Ricky," he said. "And Nick, I'm in your debt. If I had the courage and no spiritual beliefs, I'd just blow my brains out. But I can't and I won't, so now I'll do the next best thing. Or worst thing, depending on your perspective. Oh well, I guess I'll find out if confession really is good for the soul. I hope something is, because mine's about to go down the toilet."

Sam rose from his seat. "Thank you once again, gentlemen. I'll be taking my leave now. I'm tired and just want to go home and get one last night's sleep, if I can, in my own bed."

Ricky shook Sam's hand and then sat back down while Nick and Sam locked in their Sicilian embrace, concluding the meeting. Sam nodded a final farewell and closed the door behind him.

⛓⛓⛓⛓⛓

Ricky turned to Nick, who pointed to a chair.

"Do you have a few minutes, Ricky?" asked Nick.

"I have plenty of time," Ricky replied. "It was a short meeting."

They poured themselves a brandy, lit their cigars, and sat back like two corporate executives relaxing after the close of business.

"Ricky," Nick began, "we've known each other since the family brought you into this country about five years ago—1946, wasn't it?"

Ricky gave a slight nod.

"Anyway, when you walked into this room today and first spoke to me harshly, it pissed me off. However, I should have held my response about it until Sam had left. It was disrespectful of me to speak to you that way in front of anyone. I apologize for that. Any rub we have between us should be kept just that way: between us. And that's also the way I would prefer that this conversation continue."

"Apology accepted," said Ricky. "Please accept mine in return. You're the last guy I want pissed off at me."

"I feel the same."

The two professionals looked at each other and laughed.

"Ricky," Nick continued, "I want to share some things with you, and this is not business as usual; it's personal. And as I said, between us."

"It always is, Nick."

"I know. That's probably one of the reasons we're both still sitting here talking with each other." Nick smiled before continuing. "What I have to say may take a while, so if you like, have another brandy and a Havana. I'm going to."

"Two glasses of brandy?" said Ricky. "That's a first. This must be serious."

"It is," said Nick, as he poured the liquid thoughtfully into the crystal snifters.

Nick folded his hands together in front of him. "I sense that you are, for whatever reasons, giving thought to getting out of this business." He looked Ricky squarely in the eye. "Let me ask you directly: are you?"

Ricky didn't break his gaze. "You're very perceptive, Nick."

"That's the primary reason for my still being alive." Nick rose and began pacing the room. "That aside, here's the story, and forgive me if I begin with some redundancy."

Ricky set down his brandy and motioned for Nick to

proceed.

"You are a trusted and valued friend of the family," Nick said, "and to me personally. You do things for our organization that we will not do for ourselves. It's not that we can't; we just won't. You know our code as much as I do: We never hit an enemy when there is any chance of harming any of their blood family or an innocent person near them. Cops, women, and children are out of the question. And, finally, we never screw around with anyone who is not screwing with us; it is always business."

Ricky didn't comment.

"That's where you come in," said Nick. "You do our dirty work, so to speak, the stuff we won't touch—the Sam Miller thing, for example. I know that one wasn't typical, in that you needed some muscle from us to help you throw that fat-assed MacDonald to the gators."

Nick paused, sniffing his brandy and breaking into a wide smile.

"Changing the subject for a minute," Nick said, "I appreciate your helping out Miller. He's a good guy. Though I think he's nuts for wanting to confess to something he didn't do and go to the joint for the rest of his life because he thinks it's going to cleanse his fucking soul. Who gives a shit about the loss of a moron like MacDonald, and one more attorney, to boot?"

"I agree," Ricky answered. "I'm not going to lose any sleep over it—that's for sure. I'm glad I could make Miller feel better, though. I pity the poor bastard."

"I do too," Nick said. "But that's not our problem. Let me get back to what I was saying.

"I know we have spoken of this before and, you're right: much like Sam, even when the family doesn't do the actual deed, we're the one who had it done. But in the Sicilian mindset, we convince ourselves that by contracting people like you, people outside the family, that the blood is not on our hands. Of course, we both know that ultimately it is, but your services keep the family's conscience clear. That is your true value.

"If you retire," Nick went on, "that's your business. The family will honor that, as they do you. But before we lose your services, I have one final request of you. May I ask that now?"

"Nick," said Ricky, "my time in this profession has been more than enough. I've already pushed my luck past its limits."

Nick nodded.

"However," said Ricky, "I know you wouldn't be asking this of me unless you had a very serious problem. So, just for old time's sake, and perhaps a marker for future family favors, I'm sure I can postpone retiring into the autumn of my years for a little while longer. I'm only twenty-nine. Who's the problem this time?"

"The state's attorney."

⛓⛓⛓⛓⛓

A low-profile job this was not. Ricky's first reaction to putting a hit on the state's highest law enforcement officer was a rush of adrenaline—but not like when he was excited. This was apprehension.

Nonetheless, he felt a sense of obligation to Nick. Nick was against the wall on this one. Word had it that the state's attorney's office had compiled enough evidence to shut down the entire Perroni operation. And if someone talked, that would seal it. The code of *omerta*, the silence that kept families like the Perronis in business, had been broken in New York and Chicago with other families. All it took was one rat turning state's evidence, and the whole thing would end.

Ricky's concerns were also self-motivated: If the right

person came forward, the trail could lead to him.

⛓⛓⛓⛓⛓

It took a year to plan.

All the while, the pressure on the Perroni family and their business-doings was increasing. Nick's impatience escalated into a mild paranoia, muddling his decision-making process. He phoned Ricky at midnight the morning of the hit.

Ricky groggily reassured him and, after hanging up, knew he must distance himself from his increasingly irrational friend. Time to hit the road.

The drive to Tallahassee darkened Ricky's spirits further. The highway was rough, patched in some places with nothing but gravel. The monotonous drone of the tires made it difficult to stay awake. The chilly, moonless night felt like walls closing in. Ricky rolled down the window and stuck out his head, letting the cool wind chase the sleep from his eyes and brain.

Five hours later, the sun was rising on the capital city as Ricky approached the state government building. The state's attorney was holding a press conference today. The subject matter was organized crime and the steps law enforcement was taking to end the reign of corruption and crime. Warrants would be served and thugs would be going to prison.

The deputy to the state's attorney, however, was a reasonable man. He had informed Nick of the impending peril and would be an asset in the Perroni pockets following the untimely death of his superior.

Because of the location, the press, and the inherent danger of a close-range kill, Ricky was opting for a method he had not previously used. The trunk of his car carried a .30-.30 Winchester Bolt Action. There were better rifles to be had, but this was a common gun in Florida for hunters, making a ballistics analysis far more difficult to narrow down. The trunk also held a silencer and a 20x scope; from five hundred yards, Ricky would be capable of drilling a third eye into his target.

Ricky found a diner and ordered a light breakfast of fruit and two poached eggs, waiting for the time his quarry was scheduled to show his soon-to-be-missing face.

A large, grassy park fronted the state building. On the opposite side, a small general store with apartments on a second story above it made the perfect perch. Ricky found his mood lightening a bit. He parked behind the building, got out of the car, and grabbed his gear from the trunk. He surveyed the deserted area before beginning his climb up the fire escape to the roof.

In fifteen minutes, the state's attorney would begin a press conference he would not finish.

❋❋❋❋❋

State's Attorney Martin Landsdowne was not in a good mood this morning. The speech he'd been given was choppy and his perfectionism had kept him up all night, repeatedly redrafting the document. To make matters worse, a judge had recently refused the search warrant Landsdowne wanted that would inevitably take down some of Dade County's biggest organized crime bosses. *Organized crime,* he thought. *Now there's a contradiction in terms.* He'd wanted an arrest to parade in front of the press today, and lacking this put an even bigger damper on his demeanor.

Gruffly, Landsdowne rose from his desk and headed for the elevator. He strode inside and the portal began closing. "Hold it for me, James!" Sergeant Jerry Allensworth called out to the thin, weathered black man serving as the elevator operator.

306

"Couldn't wait for the next one, Sergeant?" Landsdowne huffed. "I'm in a goddamned hurry."

"Sorry, sir," the police officer replied. "In a bit of a hurry myself. I just gave a deposition on an arrest we made last week, and my partner's waiting downstairs. Took a little longer than I thought."

"That's usually how those things go" was Landsdowne's terse response.

The remainder of their descent was spent in silence. The doors opened and the state's attorney filed out to meet the press. Allensworth met his partner at the side exit and they walked down the steps to their patrol car.

"Good morning, gentlemen...and ladies." Landsdowne still had trouble with women journalists. "Before I take your questions, I have a brief statement to make." He glanced down at his notes on the podium. "The scourge of our state has been the infestation of people who have no regard for the welfare of anyone but themselves, for anything but their own interests. In conjunction with state and local law enforcement agencies, we have made it a mission to eradicate these parasites from our midst. Our priority in this endeavor is to..."

❄❄❄❄❄

Ricky Maldonado"s position on the rooftop was optimal. He had a clear line of fire across the park, and the head of the state's attorney lined up perfectly in the scope's crosshairs. Softly he squeezed the hair trigger and heard the dull *phiff* as the rifle recoiled.

❄❄❄❄❄

"...and using all resources available, we will wipe these criminals out of the state of Flor—"

Something struck the wall behind the state's attorney. The eerie whine of a ricochet immediately followed. Landsdowne noticed a small cloud of feathers falling at the far side of the park. An unaware dove had flown into the path of the incoming hollow-point round and was vaporized, altering the bullet's trajectory.

⛓⛓⛓⛓

Sergeant Jerry Allensworth had been sitting in the passenger seat of his patrol car, watching the flight of the doomed dove when it took the bullet. His partner, Jim Cooke, noticed a small puff of smoke rise from the roof of the general store ahead of them a fraction of a second before.

"Did you see that?" they said to each other in unison.

"See what?"

"See what?"

"That smoke on the roof..."

"That bird just— Oh, shit," Allensworth said. "Someone's shooting at Landsdowne!"

Jim Cooke skidded to a stop at the entrance of the store. "I got the back. Go to the northwest corner and keep an eye out."

⛓⛓⛓⛓

Ricky lowered himself down the fire escape, distracted by his anger over the bird's fluke interference and missing such an easy target. This opportunity was lost and the police would be extremely vigilant protecting Landsdowne in the future.

Ricky's rifle got caught between two rungs on the ladder, throwing Ricky off balance. He fell to the ground

308

from nine feet up, landing on his back.

When he caught his breath and opened his eyes, the barrel of a snub-nose .38 revolver was looking back at him.

"Just give me an excuse, spic," the officer said, smiling.

Strike Three, amigo, Ricky thought.

CHAPTER 15
TIME OF THE UNTOUCHABLES

September 1953

The first time I laid eyes on Ricardo Maldonado, I was temporarily blinded. As he appeared in my cell's corridor, his image was black-silhouetted by a brilliant bolt of lightning that flashed in the windows behind him, punctuated by a dramatic clap of thunder. The storm's violent light-and-sound show seemed to be introducing the Devil himself.

The dark figure in the corridor slowly transformed into three dimensions as the man came into focus in the storm's dim light. Maldonado did not look anything like I thought he would.

He stood there, six-foot-two and two hundred muscular pounds under blue-black wavy hair and short sideburns that framed a smooth olive face with bright, deadly black eyes. This stone-cold contract-killing machine was movie-star handsome. He appeared to be not much older than me, maybe in his late twenties. But in spite of his youthful good looks, his eyes were old and ugly-mean.

The hard-looking Cuban rapped his knuckles lightly on the cell's open door. "Knock on steel," he said softly. "May I come in?"

Sam swiveled his chair from his desk and rose with a polite smile. "Of course," he replied rather formally. "Our door is always open to an invited guest."

"Open for the moment, anyhow," Ricardo said wryly. "Good morning, Sam."

Ricardo Maldonado walked into our cell with the easy grace of a panther. He shook hands with Sam and then turned his penetrating black eyes toward me. They seemed to bore into my brain, probing my thoughts. Then they softened.

"And a good morning to you too, Clark," the big cat purred, giving me the slightest hint of a smile. "And please—call me Ricky," he added, offering me his hand. "Lucy always does."

I acknowledged his light humor with a faint smile of my own as I reached for his outstretched hand. "Ricky it is then, Señor Arnez," I said. "Welcome to our humble home."

I was prepared to hold my own in an expected hand-squeezing duel, but that did not happen. The formidable Cuban gripped my hand with a mild firmness that was surprisingly courteous. Intimidation was not on his agenda. I wondered what was.

I wondered about Sam as well. From his reserved welcome, I knew he had not invited this man to join us based simply on old friendship. There was no warmth between these two men...only a cool, mutual respect.

This was going to be an intriguing day. And it dawned on me that I was about to become the middleman—if one can be the middleman of some abstract triangle. *Well,* I thought, *let the games begin.*

"Have a seat, Ricky," I said, seating myself at the head of the bottom bunk and motioning him to the foot.

"Thank you," he said, "I believe I will. But before I do," he added turning for the door, "I need to get something I stashed in that empty cell down the other corridor. I'll be right back."

Sam and I shrugged at each other in an unspoken question and then stared at the doorway, waiting for the answer.

311

It came soon enough. Ricky walked back into our cell carrying a small bundle wrapped in a towel, which he placed in front of Sam, still seated at his desk.

"Here, Sam. It's a modest housewarming gift. It's for all of us really. The least I could do is share it with my new neighbors."

Sam unfolded the towel and glanced up at Ricky with an uncharacteristic, surprised expression. Then he looked over at me like a delighted child and whispered, *"How in the world did—"*

"What the hell is it, Sam?" I interrupted impatiently.

"Sandwiches. Three big, thick ones. Ham and Swiss on rye."

Ricky sat down next to me with a wide, pleased smile on his olive face. "Anyone care to do brunch?"

"Thanks, Ricky," I said, as Sam handed me one of my long-lost favorite things. "You know, there's something about you I'm beginning to like."

"Yeah?" he said. "Well, you're easy. It's Sam I'm worried about. He doesn't seem to want to share with me."

"Sorry," Sam mumbled with his mouth full of contraband sandwich. "I was caught up in the moment. Here, Ricky. And thank you."

No one said a word until we all had washed down Sunday brunch with tin cups of water and were sitting back, contentedly licking our fingers clean of hot brown mustard.

Ricky was the first to speak.

"After being in here as long as you guys have, that must have been a memorable feast indeed. And before either of you says anything, let me say this: No further thanks are needed.

"Also, before you ask how I managed to get that stuff, let alone on just my second day out of that shithole New Cock Block, I didn't really get it. It was given to me. It was given to me for the same reasons Sam Miller got the best

312

house on the block and for the same reasons you, Clark Inger, have Sam for a roommate."

I gazed at Ricky. This guy had some pull and knew more about me than I was comfortable with. So, for a change, I kept quiet and figured I'd save my questions for later.

"From time to time," he continued, "I'll be given things that neither of you will be given for the simplest of all reasons: our mutual benevolent benefactors down in South Florida owe me more—a lot more—than the two of you put together.

"Now, please don't think for a minute that I'm talking down to you," Ricky said. "I never will. But that's just the way it is."

Ricky stood and stretched like a predator waking from its nap, preparing to go on the prowl.

"I will mention just one more thing before this tiresome monologue of mine is concluded," he said. "This prison holds only four of us: Four Untouchables—the three of us and one other. You've never seen the other guy and never will, but I'm sure you've heard of him. His name is Tony "Two Ton" Tomassetti. The poor slob is sitting over there on death row, fresh out of appeals and eating away each day he's got left like a giant hog in an Italian restaurant. I'm told that at the rate my old friend is stuffing himself, he's trying not to fit in the chair. Of course, he will—they'll cram his fat ass into Old Sparky and, on Thursday night, fry two tons of dead meat. Well, fuck Tony. He's not my concern. You two are, and that's the point of all this."

I was indeed still unclear as to the "point of all this," but I bit my tongue as Ricky continued.

"We three are icons—ironic that none of us are made-men. Nonetheless, we're visible symbols of men doing easy time of minimal hardship within the walls of a hard, maximum security prison. We are the living proof that a group of very powerful people is protecting their friends, even in here. Their power is so great they can reach out and grab anyone or anything anywhere and, if warranted, kill or destroy it. Protecting their own is an ancient family code of honor and, more importantly, effective public relations. We are their Untouchables and for as long as I'm around—and I'll be in here the rest of my life—we are going to stay that way.

"Clark, Sam and I discussed most of what I just said yesterday, and he knows exactly what's going on from the old days in Miami. But your old days are not too old, so...any questions?"

"Yeah, one," I said.

"What is it?"

"Before you distracted us with ham sandwiches, you said something about our being new neighbors. The 'new' is obvious, but 'neighbors' is a bit foggy. Just how neighborly do you think we're going to be?"

For the first time Ricky actually laughed. He was still chuckling as he answered: "Good question. I forgot to mention it. The answer is: Pretty damn neighborly. Those two old-timers next door in A-339 just lost their seniority. They're being moved out first thing in the morning, and as soon as the top bunk is out of there, I'm going to be spending the day doing some serious interior decorating." Ricky's bright eyes faded to flat black as he added, "You got a problem with that, kid?"

My body stiffened. "No, I don't 'got a problem with that,'" I said. "However, I do have a problem with you calling me 'kid'; I would prefer that you refer to me as Clark. And no disrespect intended, but I also want to make it perfectly clear right up front that I do not need a fuckin' bodyguard. You got a problem with *that*, Ricardo?"

"Shut up, Clark!" Sam hissed with real anger. "You don't—"

314

The Cuban quickly interrupted. "No, it's okay, Sam," he said calmly. "Everything's cool. I shouldn't have demanded Clark to answer that last question in such a combative tone. I'd get pissed off, too." Maldonado turned to me. "I apologize," he said sincerely. "Are we okay?"

"Yeah, I'll get over it," I replied with a relieved smile as the tension dissolved. "And, Ricky?"

"Yes?"

"If you've got another ham and Swiss, you can call me kid."

"You're a little smartass, aren't you?"

"Better than the alternative."

"You're right about that...and a dumbass you're not. But about the ham and Swiss, I'm fresh out. Can I owe you?"

"With interest?" I asked with a sly smirk.

Ricky slapped me lightly on the back of the head. "Don't push it too far...kid."

Sam sat at his desk, slowing shaking his head and rolling his eyes at the ceiling as Ricky and I broke into gales of laughter.

Prison has a way of forcing caged men to make instant decisions concerning survival, including instinctively choosing who will be enemy or friend. Ham sandwich or not, from now on, Ricky could call me kid anytime he wanted to.

⊟⊟⊟⊟⊟

The next twenty-six months went by one hell of lot faster than the previous eighteen. Grubbin' hoes, yo-yos, and brick ovens were a lifetime away. Compared to the torturous days in the road gang, this was a cake-walk. Sam worked with me constantly on spelling and grammar, sharing with me his passion for language. Ricky made life easier with his culinary escapades; I was actually gaining weight. Although it was considered contraband, Ricky managed to supply me with brushes, watercolors, and paper. At last, I was free to explore my first love: Painting. The warden liked my work and even had one of my renditions of the prison hung up in the administration building.

Two years of my young life were spent in the company of a hired killer and a brilliant journalist. Both taught me valuable lessons. Ricky's arcane sense of humor brightened even the darkest days. But Sam gave me a gift that would carry me through the rest of my life: he inspired compassion in me.

"Don't ever look down on someone because of what they do for a living," he advised. "All work is sacred—and you might find yourself having to do that same job someday. Treat everyone with respect, even if you think they don't deserve it. You'll find you get more of the same. And most importantly, remember this: The true measure of a man's maturity is in his ability to care for other people."

❉❉❉❉❉

Sam and I were outside, enjoying a lazy Sunday morning in our territorial patch of yard, when Ricky ambled over rather awkwardly to join this week's gathering of the Sunday Morning Movie Review Board—my very last.

"Ricky," I asked, "is that bulging wet spot in your crotch a sign that you're excited to see us?"

"I'm always excited to see you guys," he said with a smirk. "Especially you, young stuff."

"So I noticed."

"Yeah, well notice this, kid!" With a sly grin, Ricky unbuttoned his fly, pulled out something wrapped in a grease-stained rag and tossed it into my lap.

"Ricky, I'm not touching anything that came out of

your pants," I said, flipping the greasy bundle over to Sam.

Sam caught it with one hand and quickly hid it behind his back. He looked up at the grinning Cuban who was casually re-buttoning his fly. "Ricky, is this trouble?" he asked. "What am I hiding here?"

"It's not trouble," Ricky reassured Sam. "Not for long, anyway. I don't throw trouble into the laps of my friends. Not even unappreciative friends who are looking a gift pig in the chops—that's a metaphoric hint."

Sam squeezed the giftwrap behind his back and broke into a pleased smile. "Well, I'll be. Pork chops."

"Three of 'em?" I asked.

"Of course, three of them," said Ricky. "But since they came out of my pants, I suppose you'll be passing on brunch this morning?"

"I've changed my mind," I said quickly, bowing in mock worship. "I love your greasy pants."

"I thought you might." Ricky smiled that perfect smile and sat down and facing us with his back to the yard, his body concealing three happy cons wolfing down the only prison food that men had been known to fight and die over.

We ate in silence until the bones were picked clean and buried in the dirt.

Sam was the first to speak. "Ricky, the cooking crew hasn't even finished cleaning up breakfast. How did you manage to get those chops—cooked, no less—this far ahead of the lunch hour?"

Ricky shrugged. "Just like anybody gets anything in this joint—negotiating the barter-and-trade system. Those kitchen guys eat better than the warden. They all have Sunday lunch chops with real eggs for breakfast. One of the cooks who owed me fried up a few extra and wrapped them up for me. The grits server owes the cook and slipped them on my tray. The egg server owes the grits server and covered up the chops with a pile of those shitty powdered scrambled

317

eggs. Now, I figure you two fine gentlemen owe me at least a big burp and a kind smile."

I could not bring up even a small burp, but I flashed Ricky a sincere smile.

"That's all well and good," I said. "We all know that those kitchen guards look the other way and let the culinary crew eat like pigs just so they won't get served with human shit. *But* I do know they count what the crew pigs out on *and* they inventory every single damn pork chop allocated for the general prison population. They add 'em all up like a headcount. What happens when their addition comes up three short?"

"Great question!" said Ricky. "You're getting wise beyond your years. That was the critical part of the pork-chop caper."

I looked at Sam, who just shrugged.

"So what's the answer?" I asked Ricky.

"It's simple enough. Just add three more people to the equation: One for each pork chop. Then it all adds up."

I was losing patience with this cat-and-mouse Q and A.

"Damn it, Ricky. What's the answer?"

"Calm down. You can figure it out for yourself if you'll allow me to answer your question with a question. Okay?"

"Fine," I said. "I'll play this game. Now it's 'What's the Question?'"

Sam continued to sit silently smiling into space as Ricky further enlightened me as to the workings of his cunning criminal mind and his manipulation of what now added up to at least half a dozen people. All in order to smuggle three illegal pork chops.

Ricky stood, as if delivering his summation to a jury. "Who would willingly give up the single most coveted foodstuff in here for next to nothing—maybe, say, a Hershey bar?"

I contemplated. "A vegetarian?"

Ricky snorted. "As far as I know, there are none of them in this place. Try again."

I continued thinking until a light went on. "A Jew?" I guessed. "Better yet, three Jews?"

Ricky beamed. "Exactly. Orthodox Jews. They won't eat pork—not big chunks of it, anyway. They *have* to overlook the little chunks of fatback floating around in the beans or greens we get every day, of course; otherwise they would starve to death."

I nodded in acknowledgment, once again fascinated at the geometric thinking of Ricardo Maldonado.

"Ricky," I asked, "did Sam happen to remind you that today is the Sunday Morning Movie Review Board?"

"As a matter of fact," said Ricky, "that's one of the reasons he invited me over. Mind if I sit in?"

"Did you see it?" I asked.

"I sure did. Anything to get out of my cell. The new inmate next door is a hillbilly who only speaks some kind of unintelligible redneck gibberish and continually sucks his tooth."

"In other words, he sucks," I interjected.

Ricky nodded and then remarked, "So did the movie."

I agreed. "I saw it when I was young and it stank then, too. Sam?"

"The ending was the most disappointing part for me. Fading to the credits with that passionless kiss was the final idiocy. It would have been more meaningful if Roy Rogers had shot Dale Evans in the final scene. The arse-end first and then one in her head for poor acting. What are your thoughts, Ricky?"

"Your criticism is absolutely correct and surprisingly perceptive as well," said Ricky. "Your cinematic insight

319

amazes me. You couldn't possibly have known that the original ending ended up on the director's cutting-room floor after the studio determined that it was not quite right for perpetuating Roy's image to the youth of America."

Sam leaned forward with interest. "Is that so?" he asked.

"Yup. And I saw the movie in Havana, in its original, uncut form," Ricky told us. "It was much better then."

"How did it end when *you* saw it?" I asked the smiling Cuban.

Ricky looked at me conspiratorially. "Since you're a convict and not a shining representative of American youth, I'll tell you. But only if you promise not to let it cloud your image of Roy."

I nodded in mock-seriousness. "Go ahead on. My youthful mind is cloud-free."

Ricky shook his head. "Okay, you asked for it. Sam was on the right track. Here's what really happened: Dale reached out to Roy. But just as she was about to embrace him with cowgirl love, Roy shot her between the eyes, splattering her brains all over his next victim, a gasping, gut-shot Gabby Hayes. Then Roy turned his smoking six-guns on the Sons of the Pioneers, firing countless rounds without reloading and blasting every last one of those whining bastards all to hell. When they quit twitching, Roy holstered his guns, turned on his boot heels, and broke into a nasal rendition of 'Riders of the Purple Sage' as he walked off into the sunset.

"And that's how it really ended."

Sam and I both cracked wide grins.

"Wait." I held up a hand. "He walked? Roy Rogers *walked* into the sunset?"

Ricky shrugged. "He had to. We just had his horse, Trigger, for brunch."

As I snorted with laughter, I marveled at how Ricky

had once again defied his reputation as a stone-cold killer.

⛓⛓⛓⛓⛓

The late-morning Sunday sunshine felt glorious as the three of us continued basking. At times like this, simply hanging around with two friends, I sometimes forgot where we were. I felt peaceful within myself and the world.

But that was to last only a moment.

One of the trustees, a wrinkled old raisin of a man who worked in the warden's office, walked over to our outdoor sanctuary looking more than apprehensive.

Sam's mood darkened dramatically. "You know not to disturb me when I'm in my office, Pops," he said. "I trust you have a valid reason for—"

"Sam, I'm clear on yer rules," the trustee interrupted, "but I jus' heard somethin' I think yer gonna want to know 'bout right away. Can we talk...in private?"

Ricky and I looked at each other, then to Sam. He gave us an *It's okay, give us a minute* look. Ricky obviously did not appreciate being dismissed and I could tell he was about to give the old fellow a scolding.

"C'mon, Ricky," I said before he could start in. "Let's give 'em a few. I want to ask you about something anyway." This was too nice of a day to ruin it over a bruised ego.

The old man was let off with only a small dose of Ricky Maldonado's evil eye, but it served its purpose. The trustee visually recoiled.

We walked out of earshot without turning around. In prison, privacy is an extremely valuable commodity; Ricky and I respected Sam's space when he wanted it, as he did with us.

"So what did you want to ask me?" inquired Ricky.

"I...well..."

321

"BLOODY CHRIST!" Sam's bellow echoed throughout the prison yard. Ricky and I spun around to see Sam consumed in fury. We rushed back to him and the trustee, who stood stock-still, following Sam's agitated pacing with only his eyes.

I was ready to slap Pops silly. "What the fuck did you say to him, old man?" I asked.

"I think he oughta be the one to tell ya" was all he replied before walking away.

"Sam, what the hell's going on?" I asked.

"Don't get the wrong idea, kid," Sam said sternly, "but this doesn't concern you. I need to talk with Ricky. Alone."

"But Sam..."

The tortured look in his eyes said it. Whatever the news, it had raised up some kind of demon in him. I nodded slowly and walked away. It was my turn to harbor a bruised ego. Ignoring prison etiquette, I glanced back and saw Sam talking to Ricky as though seeking counsel from a priest.

As I turned back toward the yard, I caught sight of the trustee, still making his way toward the administration building. I caught up to him just before he passed through the gate.

"Listen, old-timer," I said. "You know well enough that Sam and I are good friends. He's real torn up about whatever you said, and if there is any way for me help him, I gotta know what this is all about. Now, either you tell me, or I'll make damn sure—"

"Don'tcha go tryin' to threaten me, ya little shit," he said. "I've seen hundreds just like ya come and go in this place. One stroke with my pen'll change yer life, got it?"

I was immediately contrite. "No, look, I'm sorry," I said, meaning it. "It's just that Sam's been...what I mean is..."

"Ya ain't got to say nothin', kid. That's what he calls

ya, right? Kid? He's told me about him helpin' ya out with yer letters and such. I know he means a lot to ya. And loyalty is somethin' I admire in a body. Now *if'n* I tell ya, ya better make damn sure to keep it to yerself or I'll be the one makin' *promises*, not threats—ya got it?"

"Got it, Pops."

He inhaled deeply. "Some of the fellas 'round here that I gots respect for," he began, "have had run-ins with folks outside of here. It might do a body good to know if they gots an enemy comin' their way. Sam's told me enough about his past so's I know who to look out fer."

I nodded.

"Now then," he said, glancing nervously toward Sam and Ricky, then all around to make sure nobody was in earshot, "I just found out about a new inmate we got comin' in, bein' transferred from down South. Gonna do a twenty-year stretch for armed robbery on a liquor store in Coconut Grove. Shot the cashier in the leg and they had to amputate it. Anyway, the fella's also got hisself a record from up north, New York way. His name rang a bell so I made a call to a trustee who works da Miami/Dade admin. Well, the trustee told me 'bout how this big mouth's been braggin' to his cellmate 'bout how he got away with settlin' an old score with some newspaper man. He went on to say that the guy *killed* another man, thinkin' he was the one that done him wrong. Now, he didn't mention nothin' 'bout no little girl, but I reckon he knew enough not to—ya know what happens to rapists and child molesters 'round here. But then he started laughin', saying as how the dead man's attorney got it in the head as well, jokin' 'bout how the bes' lawyers is the dead ones. That's when the trustee down there put two 'n ' two together."

I also put two and two together and stared at the trustee, awaiting more information.

"Yup," he said, reading my look. "Looks like we got

323

the fella who *really* raped and killed Sam's daughter. Goes by the name of Peter Burkey."

⛓⛓⛓⛓⛓

Ricky looked as shocked and upset as Sam felt. The two just stood there a while, each thinking their own thoughts. Sam was about to go back to his cell when Ricky stopped him.

"Sam," said Ricky, "you and I both know it's too late to find enough proof to indict Burkey. Even if his cellmate told a judge what he knew, the D.A. would argue something about another con trying to get a reduction in sentence, preferential treatment, or some other bullshit. But—" Ricky caught and held Sam's gaze. "I got another solution. See, when you went to Nick Perroni and hired me to take care of the prick who—"

"Don't even say it," Sam interrupted. "This is like reliving the worst nightmare of my life. This *is* the worst nightmare of my life!" Sam paused as he tried to rummage through the rage, grief, and despair that were coming faster than he could process.

"Ricky," he finally said, "before you do anything, give me some time to sort this out."

Maldonado shrugged. "If you say so. Let me know if I can help."

⛓⛓⛓⛓⛓

Sam retired to his cell. I chose to remain outside, in respect for his obvious need to be alone.

I observed Ricky making his way to the far end of the yard. Although the general population of the prison was not officially segregated, the inmates had their own divisions. Ricky approached a group of black men who were holding

324

their own version of Sunday socializing.

The apparent leader of this association was a six-foot, nine-inch rippling mass of sweating, grunting coffee-and-cream covered muscle. He stopped his set of bench-presses and sat up to address Ricky.

I was too far away to hear the conversation, but he and his cohorts were clearly taunting Ricky as they slowly surrounded him. Maldonado may have been a ruthless killer, but it wouldn't be right for things go down this way. Frankly, I was surprised that Ricky would walk into a trap like this; getting shanked by a gang of bull queers on their own turf was a bad call.

As I took my first steps toward what would surely land us both in the clinic and probably solitary afterward, Ricky smiled at the gang and patted his front pocket. The tension ebbed immediately as the face of the towering hulk bearing down on him broke into an enormous grin. Ricky turned and drifted my way.

I was about to ask him what the hell he was thinking, but he simply shook his head at me, and with a sly grin and a wink, strolled past me toward A Block.

⊟⊟⊟⊟⊟

Sam, You hired me to take care of the guy who did this thing, Ricky thought. *The least I can do is get* you *close enough to Burkey to wrap things up...along with a Plan B— for insurance.*

Ricky's next stop was the gate leading to the administration building. He asked through the gate if he could speak with Pops. The guard responded with a power-tripping "I'll see," before going inside. A few minutes passed before the trustee emerged.

"What do ya need, Ricky?"

"I want to know if you can get Peter Burkey released

325

into the general population after he's let inside."

Pops' brow furrowed. "I don' know..." he replied. "I could get in a lot of trouble if'n somethin' was to..."

Ricky slipped the old man a fifty-dollar bill, entirely changing the tone of the conversation.

"...paperwork gettin' fouled up all the time in here," Pops murmured. "People endin' up where they're not supposed to be—you know how it is. Burkey'll prolly end up workin' laundry a day or two after he gets here."

Ricky nodded.

Step two complete.

⛓⛓⛓⛓⛓

I was leaving soon. I wanted to spend as much quality time as I could with my friend, but in the days that had passed, Sam's funk deepened. And he still wouldn't talk.

Although I knew what it was about, I'd promised old Pops I'd keep quiet. I almost went back on that promise a couple of times, but in the end, I had to respect Sam's desire to keep it to himself. Him and Ricky, that is. I could only imagine the torture Sam was going through and what he might be planning in terms of revenge.

CHAPTER 16
THE LAST LAUGH IS FREE

November 1955

The start of the new day, like all the other days, was harshly announced by the grating of two hundred forty steel barred doors sliding open in the cellblock. However, the early-morning routine was altered by one simple but profound act. As Sam was making up his bunk, I was stripping mine. I rolled my sheets and coarse gray blanket into my mattress and placed it on the floor at the foot of the bunk.

Peter Burkey had arrived before dawn and was ushered into Raiford's solitary confinement ward for breakfast. But then, as with any bureaucracy, a clerical error occurred and Burkey found himself assigned to the laundry detail.

Sam took a detour after the cellblocks rolled open and skipped breakfast. I knew what he had to do.

But while I knew it was important, this was to be my last meal with my friend, so I was more than disappointed.

<hr>

Burkey was relieved that he moved through solitary so quickly but was confused in that not a single guard or trustee gave him any orientation. He was only told his cell number and led straight to the laundry room.

No time to unpack or even settle in with the neighbors, Peter joked to himself.

327

The heat from the dryers and irons, coupled with an autumn high-pressure system that Burkey knew was not unusual for Florida, made the laundry a virtual sauna. The men working around him all wore a sweaty sheen.

Burkey was assigned a washing machine, a massive piece of equipment that could hold up to fifty pounds of laundry. Six of these behemoths stood in a row, each with its own dripping attendant nearby. Above the roar of the washers, dryers, and pressing irons, an inmate yelled instructions to Burkey on how to operate the machine.

"First, you get a coffee can full of soap from that bin over there. Throw it inside and then fill 'er up with clothes. When all the cycles're done, take the clothes, put 'em in this cart, and carry 'em over to the dry-boys. They'll take it from there. When you finish with the clothes, we got plenty of sheets and blankets to be done."

The inmate ambled away and Burkey reached for the coffee can in the soap bin. Out of the corner of his eye, he caught movement from behind. He whirled around.

It took a moment for the recognition to sink in. *Sam Miller. Well, I'll be...* Burkey fell into a boxer's stance. He had no intention of going down without a fight.

"This shit will blind ya but good, Miller," Burkey sneered in his Cockney accent, jumping on the balls of his feet and waving the can of powdered soap between him and his nemesis.

"I'm sure it will," Sam replied, eerily calm. "But you mistake why I am here. Frankly, it's out of my hands. You and I have cast our lot in life and this is where we both ended up."

What is this bozo on about? Burkey laughed, softly at first then rolling into a maniacal howl.

Sam continued to stand motionless, giving Burkey the creeps. His raucous laughter subsided.

Burkey's eyes darted left and right, making sure he

wasn't outflanked. The entire laundry room had ground to a halt, observing the tense scene.

"Peter," Sam said for all to hear, "I want you to know I forgive you for what you did."

Burkey started. Was this bloke for real? He was about to laugh again when he saw the threatening looks on the other prisoners' faces. For whatever reason, Sam commanded real respect here.

"Thank you for hearing me out," Sam continued. "For although I'll spend the rest of my life between these walls, now I am truly a free man."

And with that, Sam Miller turned and walked away.

When Sam returned to our cell, he remained mum about what had happened. I could only imagine.

We spent the rest of the morning lost in our own thoughts.

But twelve o'clock was looming. For the first time in a very long time, Sam and I would be heading out of A Block in different directions: He to the mess hall for lunch and me to the main gate for release.

"I hope you get a good roommate, Sam," I finally said.

"I'll see to it. I managed to get you, didn't I?"

"That's true. You lucked out there."

"Luck had nothing to do with it. And I've still got enough stroke left in this place not to get stuck with some double-digit-IQ psychopath sleeping over me for the rest of my life."

"Sam," I said, "I'm going to miss you a great deal. Most of all, I think I'll miss your counsel."

Sam's lip lifted in a smile. "I don't think you'll be missing my counsel all that much, kid. When we first met, you were a smart-mouthed scared street punk who didn't know much of anything worthwhile. You're leaving here a better person than when you got here. By the way, here's a bon voyage present for you. Sorry I couldn't get it gift-wrapped."

He handed me a book the size of a New York City telephone directory. It was a brand new Webster's Dictionary with his favorite leather bookmark sticking out of the top.

"Sam, I don't know what to say." I cracked open the heavy book and landed on the word *gratitude*. "Wait...allow me to rephrase that: Thank you very much. And, as you have always instructed me, if you don't know, ask. Where in the hell did you get this?"

"Well, I'm not going to start lying to you at this late date. I ordered it months ago for the library. Actually, I stole it."

For Sam to steal anything was totally out of character. "Why you two-faced old thief, you've preached over and over that—"

"I know, I know," he interrupted, "but this is a special occasion."

I stopped myself. I certainly wasn't going to make an issue of this now.

"Thank you," I said.

"You're welcome. Use it. And for God's sake, learn to spell."

"I'll try."

"That's all I've ever asked. Now, I'm going to ask one last thing of you." His voice constricted with rare emotion, and it was difficult for him to continue. But of course, he did.

"Once you're out of here," he told me, "you're out of my life, as well. You have your own life ahead of you and, in my opinion, you're rather well-qualified to make it a good one. This is my final request of you. I love you, kid, but I never want to see or hear from you again."

I gazed back at Sam, filled with emotion and loss.

As the silence dragged on, Cell Block A's public address system hissed to life and crackled its recorded announcement that Sunday's lunch was now being served.

"In the long run you will understand," Sam consoled me. "Now get the hell out of here."

Sam was right. It was time to go.

I picked up the heavy dictionary from my sagging bunk springs and put it in the cardboard box with the rest of my few personal items. I kept my back to Sam as I folded the top of the box shut; I was close to tears and crying is something you try very hard not to do in prison, no matter what the reason. Three and a half years in the joint had taught that lesson well, and by the time I tied the twine around my going-away box, crying was out of the question.

There was only one thing left for me to say.

"I love you, too, Sam. I always will."

We embraced and Sam hugged me so hard I thought he was going to break my ribs.

I tucked the rolled-up mattress under my arm, Sam handed me the cardboard box and we looked at each other for the final time. A single tear ran down his cheek.

Sam wiped the tear from the edge of a soft smile. "When you're out there in the free world, it's okay to cry," he told me. "Sometimes it's the manly thing to do. Try to remember that; it's important. Now, as I said before, get the hell out of here. And...make me proud of you."

"Sam, for once, I'm not going to try. I just will."

"That's the best reward you could ever give me," he said. "Now, for the third time, get the hell out of here."

⛓⛓⛓⛓⛓

With the bedroll and cardboard box in my arms, I walked to the guard station at the end of the corridor looking for Walcott. A guard I had not seen before was standing at his station.

"Where's Mister Walcott?" I asked.

"He's on other duty today," he replied. "You Inger?"

"Yes, sir."

"Go ahead on. Good luck."

I left Block A and walked unescorted to the prison laundry room where I was greeted by Pops, standing behind a long counter.

"Ya 55109?" he asked formally.

"Yes. That number is plainly marked on my shirt, isn't it?"

"So it is," he answered. "Stupid question, but I gotta ask it. Rules are rules, ya know."

"Yes, I know. I've grown to understand that."

"Well, short-timer," he said, passing a brown paper-wrapped bundle over the counter, "Here's yer new wardrobe. It's fresh from Paris, France, and don't have no number on it nowhere. No labels neither. The free-world clothes ya had when ya got here're under the state-issued stuff on top. Ya can change in here and when yer done, I'll walk over to the administration building wid ya. Be back in a few minutes."

He turned and disappeared through a green steel door framed in the wall behind the counter.

When he had gone, I realized that I was absolutely alone and no one was watching me for the first time in years.

I placed the bundle on a steel bench that was under a series of coat hooks on one wall and opened it. Inside was a neatly stacked pile of the standard state-manufactured clothing issued to all inmates when they were released: An ill-fitting dark-blue suit, a stiff white shirt, a black necktie, a plastic belt, socks, and a pair of fake leather shoes that appeared to have cardboard soles. Under this pile were the street clothes I'd been wearing when I got off the prison bus from the county jail over three years ago. I was surprised to find that everything had been cleaned and pressed, looking as new as they were then.

The only thing I was taking out of this place was a lot of memories, most of them bad, and I sure as hell wasn't going to be taking any of their cheap clothing.

I had to relent on one small point, though. I could not fit into my old Levis. The blue suit pants fit well enough when I cinched up the belt. Coupled with my tan Brooks Brothers sport coat, light-blue oxford button-down shirt and brown Gucci shoes and belt, I probably could pass as a citizen. I wished I had a mirror but had not seen a real one larger than my hand in a long time.

The green door swung open and Pops entered. "Hey man, yer lookin' pretty sharp there," he said. "If ya ain't gonna to be takin' any of the other stuff, I'm sure I can find it a good home."

"I'm sure you can, and you're welcome to it. You ready to go?"

"Yep, and I know damn well y'all are too. Go out the door ya came in and I'll meet ya outside," he instructed, once again disappearing behind the steel door.

All the inmates were in the mess hall eating lunch as we walked across the strangely empty and silent yard to the gate leading to the visitors' compound and administration building. The guard in the watchtower nodded at the trustee, opened the gate, and we continued down a white, stone bordered path leading to the administration building.

"So what you think 'bout Sam's meetin' with Burkey?" Pops asked.

I was stunned. I stopped walking.

"He didn't say a word, Pops," I stammered.

"You look as taken 'back as them boys who seen it,

333

from what I heard."

"What the hell happened?"

"Bes' I can tell, Sam goes into the laundry room and tells dat crazy fuck all is forgiven."

I was speechless. And it hit me right then and there: I understood clearly why Sam had not elaborated on his meeting with Burkey. My respect and admiration for the man went through the roof. He was truly walking the walk, modeling the lessons he had poured into me. In a non-verbal display of humility and spiritual maturity, Sam once again raised the bar on living my life outside these walls.

Pops and I arrived at the admin entrance.

"This is as far as I can go," said Pops. Thanks fer not running on me." He grinned broadly. "And thanks fer the clothes, too. I really can use 'em.

"Now here's what ya do: Go through those doors and go down the hall to the second desk on yer left. They'll take it from there. Wish I was goin' with ya. Good luck on the streets."

"Thanks."

I entered the building and followed his directions to the second desk on the left, where I was met by a second trustee, a thin, frail-looking elderly man who motioned for me to sit.

I sat.

"Here are your release papers," he wheezed, handing me a ballpoint pen. "Sign at the second line from the bottom."

I signed.

"Here, open it," he said, sliding an envelope across the desk.

I opened it and found the second prison item I would take with me: The standard state ten-dollar bill guaranteeing financial security on the road to a fresh new life. Clipped to it was a receipt.

334

"Sign it."

I signed it and when I did, he reached into a bottom desk drawer, pulled out a large manila envelope and handed it to me along with another receipt.

"Open it."

When I did, I discovered my old personal effects that had not been allowed on the inside: My wallet containing a lot of stuff I did not remember and the small fortune of twenty-three dollars. A smaller envelope held a ring of keys to things long gone and my Gruen Curvex wristwatch that had stopped three and a half years ago.

"Is it all there?"

"Yes."

"Sign the receipt."

When I did, the old con jerked his gray head in the direction of the main business entrance to the building.

"Go out those doors and follow the path to the front visitor's gate. Somebody there'll take you to the bus station. It's against the law to hitchhike, you know."

"Is that it? I don't have to see any state authorities?"

The old man's lips pulled back over rotting teeth as he replied, "Hell, no. They don't have time for any of this shit. The inmates really do run the asylum. You ought to know that by now. Sam tells me you're one o' the good ones, and for that, I wish you well. Hit the streets with your feet runnin', kid."

"Thanks. They're already moving, old-timer."

I put my things in the cardboard box, got up from the desk, and went out the doors, following the path to the visitors' gate. The guard there asked for my release papers, inspected them, and nodded to the tower guard to open the gate.

"Go on through. Your ride is waiting for you in the driveway."

For the last time in my life, I followed a prison

directive, and this time I was happy to do so. As the gate slammed shut behind me, it finally hit me that this was all really happening. It was over. It was finally over. I was a free man!

ⓉⓉⓉⓉⓉ

A white unmarked state pickup truck was parked in the circular driveway. The driver's door opened and out emerged a familiar face. I almost did not recognize him in street clothes.

"Hi ya, kid!" he said cheerfully. "It's real good to see you on the outside. Thought I'd work it out so I could take you into town. I didn't know if that was you at first. You look like a new man."

"I am now, Mister Walcott. I guess I can call you Wally now. I always did anyway—just behind your back."

"Hell, yeah, you can me Wally now. Better that than what some cons call me. I ought to call you Clark, huh?"

"You were always a good guy, Wally, and thanks for taking the trouble to do this. It's a nice way to leave. And, to answer your question, you may now address me as Mister Inger."

Walcott laughed harder.

"Come on then, Mister Inger, hop on in here. I'd be pleased to drive you into town."

He leaned across the seat, opened the passenger door, and motioned for me to get in. When I shut the door, he put the truck into gear and we headed down the drive, the grim prison buildings growing smaller in the dust behind us. Just as we were turning onto the two-lane blacktop highway, a prison siren began to wail, softly at first and then joined by others, the sound escalating into a screeching howl. The sirens rarely sounded but when they did, it was for something serious, calling for a total lockdown.

Good-bye to you too, Raiford, I thought.

"Now I'm really pleased to take you into town. Better here than in there, now. I wonder what the hell's goin' on. Nothing good, that's for damn sure."

The truck gathered speed and as we made our way on the twelve-mile trip to the little town of Starke, the sirens of Raiford gradually faded away.

My excitement was overwhelming. Outside of those hellish walls, the colors were brighter and the smells sweeter. Walcott had the courtesy to remain silent while I sat wide-eyed, looking in every direction except behind me. I was absorbing everything. Even the sound of the tires humming along the asphalt was beautiful music. The taste of freedom was truly a wondrous thing.

"Well, here we are," Walcott said, grinning, as we pulled into the bus depot. "The local hound pound. I know the schedule by heart, and your silver dog to Orlando leaves in about thirty minutes."

"Thanks, Wally."

"You're welcome, and good luck to you. Besides the pleasure of seeing you out of that shithole, I wanted to tell you something in confidence and I couldn't do so inside. I know how close you and Sam have been and I wanted to tell you that I'll be watching out for Sam as best I can. He's one of the few good guys in there."

"Thanks, Wally, and thanks for Sam. You're one of the few good guards in there. Take care."

"You too," Walcott said, pulling the truck away from the curb.

He made a U-turn, and as he headed back toward Raiford, I suddenly felt totally alone. Not lonely, just alone.

It was wonderful.

I pushed open the creaking screen door of the Greyhound depot and entered the single small room. The only things in it were a single worn wooden bench, a ticket

337

counter, and two restrooms: One for men and one for women. Underneath their respective labels, the sign read *NO COLOREDS*. I walked over to the ticket counter and gave the clerk my state going-away present of ten dollars for a one-way ticket out of town and change. Walcott had been right. My bus would be boarding in about thirty minutes. The clerk was the only person in sight and I did not want to look at him or this musty old room for the next half hour. I went outside.

Across the street was an aging gray-boarded general store. Its sign on the door read "We open at 6 a.m." and that was exactly where I needed to go. Inside, it was a grand old place filled with great stuff. The proprietor was a very old man fiddling with the dial of an ancient Philco floor console radio. Country music suddenly filled the room and he seemed satisfied. It was only then that he looked up.

"You open early," I said.

"Close early, too. Can I hep ya?" he asked.

"Yes, sir, you sure can. I'd like to buy a pair of those Levis. Seems I've put on a few pounds and I'm not sure of my waist size. Do you have someplace where I can try them on?"

"Sure do," The old man said, his face cracking into a toothless grin. "See them curtains over there in the corner? Try 'em on in there. Bye the bye, Sonny, I been doin' bidness here for a whole lotta years. Seen a bunch of folks goin' in and out of that old depot across the street for a lotta years too. I don't mean ya no offense, but when ya go, if ya ain't gonna take them state pants with ya, can I have 'em?"

I had to laugh. Being old did not mean being stupid.

"No offense taken, sir. I'll give them to you on the way out."

I closed the curtains of the tiny space, listening to the music coming out of the old Philco and started trying on jeans. The second pair fit perfectly and as I was buttoning

338

the fly, someone was singing about rain, trains, and prisons. It was at that moment that I swore an oath to myself: No one, ever again, would have a clue to my years of crime and punishment.

I gave the old man the state-issue blue pants, paid for the Levis, and walked out into the warm Florida day without one single piece of state anything. My prison break was complete.

⛓⛓⛓⛓⛓

The southbound bus rolled slowly down the street and with a hiss of its air brakes, stopped in front of the depot. The door swung open and a few passengers stepped out to stretch their legs. I was halfway across the street when I heard the old man holler, "Hey, Sonny!"

I turned and he motioned for me to come back. The people who had gotten off the bus were milling around and did not seem to be in any hurry to reboard, so I walked back, curious as to what he wanted. He beckoned me closer.

"There's somethin' on the radio ya might want to hear. Don't worry about the bus none; this is a rest stop. It don't leave for a few minutes." His voice lowered to a whisper and he went on. "It's somethin' about...you know...where ya just come from."

I remembered the sirens.

"Thanks anyway," I said, "but I don't care about any of that anymore."

I recrossed the narrow street and boarded the bus, gave the driver my ticket, and looked around for a window seat. They were all taken in the front, so I continued walking to the segregated colored section in the rear where I found an empty seat next to a window and settled in. The window was important. I wanted to see everything and that was impossible from a seat on the aisle.

339

I had been out for only a little more than an hour and I was already breaking the law by sitting with the black passengers.

I felt a hand on my shoulder. It was the driver and he looked upset.

"You can't sit there," he ordered. "Move forward."

I started to get out of my seat and do as I was told but then something clicked. Never again would I be ordered around by anybody and certainly not by a racist bus driver. I had a new set of tools with which to handle this and future situations: *Words.*

I gave him my best baleful stare and spoke very softly in a voice only he could hear.

"Kindly take your hand off my shoulder. I am quite happy with the seating arrangements, thank you. I suggest you adhere to your schedule and continue with your duties. You may go."

For a moment he did not know what to do. Then he shrugged and shook his head as he returned to his seat behind the wheel. The bus started and we left the depot with the sound of the diesel engine drowning out suppressed giggling throughout the colored section.

Sam once said, "If it's a bad law, break it." I had just taken my first step toward making him proud of me. And somewhere, Leroy Washington Tanner was smiling down with his golden smile.

The rear of the bus was a fun place to be. Besides having a window seat on the shady side, I was offered halves of sandwiches, cold fried chicken, potato salad, and a paper cup of home brew. A woman, whose two small children were occupying all of her attention, smiled kindly and loaned me her portable radio. I was listening to music, my mouth full of delicious fried chicken, and washing it down with the first liquor I had tasted in a very long time. My head was tilted back in the seat, happily watching a fresh and beautiful new world roll by. This was great.

The music I was listening to on the small radio began to fade as we continued south, so I turned the dial searching for a station with clear reception. I could find only one coming in without static.

A voice that sounded exactly like all other radio voices was droning on about yesterday's news in a monotone so boring that whatever he was saying was even more boring. I was about to resume my music search when the voice stopped me mid-sentence:

"...We now have an update on our continuing coverage of the earlier breaking news story coming out of the Florida State Maximum Security Prison at Raiford..."

So here it was. I was destined to find out what had happened.

Burkey and the others all stood silently, watching as Sam Miller disappeared. For the first time in his criminal career, Peter Burkey felt ashamed, as the impact of Sam's words washed over him. Every eye on the laundry staff was turned on him. There was nothing Burkey could do but put his head down and go back to work. He was already dripping from the heat in the barely ventilated room.

"As we had previously reported, early this afternoon, at approximately twelve-thirty, an inmate was found in the prison laundry after not appearing for lunch."

Although the din from the washers and dryers was deafening, men held conversations that amounted to shouting matches. A few hours after Sam left, as the lunch announcement was being issued, a lack of loud voices caught Burkey's attention. He stood up from his stooped-over position and found himself surrounded by four very dark, very grim faces.

"The man was discovered inside a drum of detergent," the reporter went on, "apparently the victim of an assault by another prisoner."

He never had a chance. One of the bull queers slammed Burkey's head into the door of the washer. He was stunned but far from being out. A series of punches, followed by kicks when he hit the floor rained from all around. The subhuman gang stood him up, turned him toward an open washer, and stuffed his head inside.

"Warden J. Thompson Rosco has just issued a brief statement, saying that the victim's condition is guarded and at this time, his assailant remains unknown."

The real pain started right after Burkey heard "Someone say you like little girls so we gonna treat you like one."
Four angry animals proceeded to gang-rape Peter Burkey. The first brutal penetration felt like a hot poker had been shoved up his anus. It continued, unabated, for fifteen eternal minutes. He was numb when they jerked his head out of the machine.

"Prison authorities assure us that...excuse me...thank you. We have received information from the prison infirmary that just a few moments ago, the assault victim was officially pronounced dead."

By the time Burkey saw the shiv, it had already done its work. He tried to scream, but he could not; he was too busy choking on his own severed penis.

"His name was Peter Burkey, convicted of armed robbery in Dade County."

So, there it was.
I clicked off the radio.

My heart was in anguish, knowing that, after everything, my friend must be tormented to have things turn out this way. Tears filled my eyes.

But then I then smiled. That bastard deserved whatever he had gotten. I sure wasn't gonna lose any sleep over it. And indirectly, Sam had provided me with a final lesson. Revenge may be sweet, but at the end of the day it does *not* provide the last laugh.

In the end, the last laugh was what *I* had. I was free.

EPILOGUE

Endings always open doors to new beginnings. God blessed me with the freedom to walk out of the Florida prison system as one of the few with a solid decision to make something of my life. When it came to values and principles, Sam gave me everything I could ask for in a mentor. That foundation gave me belief in myself and my abilities. He added an element that I never had in my formative years: Love. It was a recipe that led me into a marriage with a good Christian woman, two healthy, intelligent children, and a rewarding life as a professional artist. I honored Sam's request that we never meet again, but his words and his heart remained with me always.

Before embarking on my corporate career path, I spent one year traveling solo throughout Western Europe in a VW bus, picking up freelance work as an artist for a number of projects. It was a year of creative growth and, more importantly, healing a life of abuse, lies, theft, and violence. The ornate cathedrals of Europe quietly spoke to me, insisting I needed to find a deeper relationship with God. Returning to the U.S. via New York, I got a sense of what Sam must have felt when he first arrived on those shores to start an exciting, new life. A new chapter was ahead for me too.

I had the good fortune to enjoy a lengthy career as an Art Director with some top advertising agencies, creating major ad campaigns and developing everything from artwork to ad copy to jingles.

After retiring from the mad ad world, life got

simpler. Although our marriage didn't work out, my former wife and I put our hurts behind and remained on friendly terms. My lovely daughter had two children. I was now a granddad.

When the cancer diagnosis came, I was not prepared for the impact it would have on me. Time was running out. I was dying and still had much to do.

I got rid of the house and all the extras, bought another VW camper bus, and toured the southeast art festival circuit with my paintings, mostly Santa Fe-themed.

My next—and as it turns out, last—order of business was working with my son to get this story outlined. He was living in Los Angeles; I no longer had the strength to travel, so I had holed up in a cabin in the woods north of Central Florida with a husky and golden retriever. As this story came together, my son and I spent hours on the telephone discussing all the things he never knew about me.

If there is a legacy I can be satisfied leaving behind, it is this: A young man impulsively ruled by anger, crime, and violence is blessed by the Grace of God to find a mentor and role model in the most unlikely of places, who helps him turn a dead-end life around and make the best of what he's been given.

Looking back on it now, I'm thankful to have one more last laugh.

POST SCRIPT

I have a confession to make: I had help writing this story. Clark's Dedication and Clark's Notes were penned by my biological father, the man who lived through this experience.

Family assumes many guises in this day and age. I didn't meet the man who sired me until I was in my late-twenties. I was put up for adoption and brought home to a loving family when I was five days old... and I am certain it saved my ass.

When Clark and I did meet, it answered a lot of questions about who and sometimes *how* I am. We are / were both creatively driven. The parallels of rebelling against conformity, the adolescent attraction to danger and adventure are uncanny. No doubt you can sense the rage and frustration of an un-nurtured young man whose poor choices led to dire consequences. My life could have easily followed the course of Clark's save the wonderful people who adopted me that I call Mom & Dad. My parental model was as close to Ozzie & Harriett Nelson as a guy could get. I was loved and supported at every step. When my teenage behavior mirrored Clark's juvenile delinquency (to a far lesser degree), it was met with patience and firm guidance. Incidentally, my fathers eventually met at my biological sister's wedding & got along well. This isn't the time or place to compose a dissertation on the influence of genetics vs. environment but where does it start? Or, more importantly, end?

When Clark discovered his illness was terminal, he asked me to write this story. We talked for hours on the phone and in his hospital room. I was given his notes, some fragmented chapters then he promptly left this plane of existence on New Year's Eve of 1999-2000. I sat on the project for a year before I could begin. When I did, I discovered even more about the man I lovingly refer to as Bio-Dad. The day I agreed to do this, Clark smiled through the haze of the morphine, which kept the pain demons at bay. He knew this task was an opportunity for us to get to know each other more deeply than most fathers and sons do.

Because of that, I will say this: I am a man of two fathers. These parts of me conflicted with each other for years. My burden has been to merge these men and the best of who they were into the person I am, a hybrid of wildly contrasting characteristics. But aren't we all...

-Gordon Noice

ACKNOWLEDGMENTS

First and foremost, I give all the glory to God for the ability to live, love, laugh... and write.

My loving, patient wife, Iwalani, always holding me accountable with a smile.

Jennifer Thomas at Beyond Words Editing, for holding her ground when it was appropriate and giving in to my creative flow when it served the story.

Jacklyn Attaway and the staff at the State Library and Archives of Florida, for helping me locate the perfect cover image for this book.

Cal Sharp at Caligraphics, for creating a cover that gives me chills.

Danyale Reed, for her formatting and design prowess. Mahalo for polishing this gem.

Mark Hardcastle, who through inspiration and a friendly verbal shove gave this book a fighting chance to be completed.

The multi-faceted string of human pearls I call family: Your insanity, neuroses, faith, and love are my guides and guardrails.

Clark, my biological father- I am grateful you were not there in the beginning so we could be together at the end.

- G.N.

ABOUT THE AUTHOR

Gordon Noice is a Florida native, an author of books, and has an extensive background in theatre and the film & television industry, with a current focus on faith-based projects. He is an ordained minister with a degree in Theology. His unique style of speaking & coaching and message of encouragement & empowerment are well received wherever he travels.

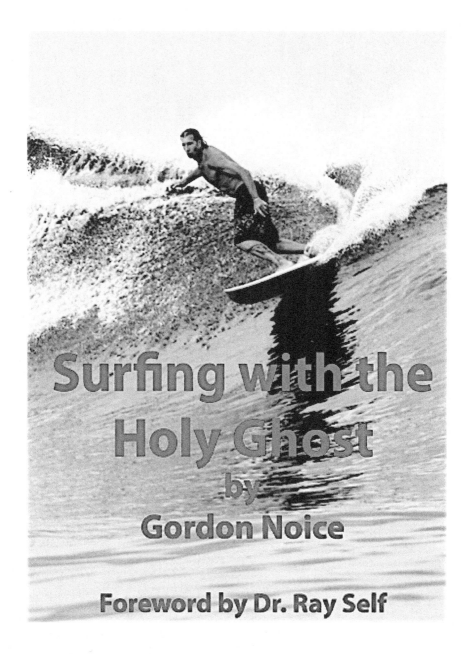

Surfing with the
Holy Ghost
by
Gordon Noice

Foreword by Dr. Ray Self

Made in the USA
Middletown, DE
03 June 2024

55168638R00195